Raven's Tears
Revised & Expanded
The Raven & The Iris

by Alesia & Michael Matson
©1999—2014 Metaphor Publications

ISBN 978-0-9754107-6-9

Prologue

When war came to Menelon, it stayed for one hundred years. It ground up millions of lives in its gaping, insatiable jaws; those who avoided death in battle were in turn ravaged by disease and famine, war's boon companions of old. Humankind faced genocide by orcs and dark elves, let on by wretched men and women who looked like humans, but who had sold their souls for money and power, and thus could hardly be said to be "human" anymore at all.

When war came to the continent of Sylantia, it divided the great kingdoms of that land and tore them asunder. The remnants of humankind were refugees in their own lands, hunted, killed, enslaved, and eaten by the tens of thousands. Though an enclave of elves gave shelter on the borders of their wood, and the Knights of the Guardian Paladin protected the holy Plains of Isen from defilement, the kingdoms of Vin-Nôrë, Vin-Llamáz, and Surmeidän burned.

Püran-Khir, once the jewel of Vin-Nôrë, the great City of Kings, Diadem of the Northern Peaks, the City of Fountains, had for 60 years been raped, pillaged, scavenged, and defiled. In the grim aftermath, it was little more than a ruin, its populace consisting of deserters, criminals, refugees, and the few natives who had learned to do whatever was necessary for survival. Thus, they could hardly be said to be "human" anymore, either.

In point of fact, the flickering remnants of humanity sometimes flared to life in the least expected hearts. Even amidst such savagery and anarchy, a man who had lied, thieved, raped, beaten, intimidated, deserted, and murdered on two continents could find himself pausing as he passed a blasted doorway into a desecrated church, somewhere in what had once been Püran-Khir. What he saw there—a child, barefoot, filthy, emaciated—should have arrested him, for a moment at least, had he any shred of humanity left in him.

Whatever it was that prompted him to pause, Ralphy didn't bother to debate it. He spent perhaps thirty seconds speculating, then crouched down and fished a crust of bread from his pocket. When she spotted him and began to sidle away, he held the bit of food out to her, urging her to come closer instead.

"'Ello, cricket..."

Chapter 1

Looking back on it years later, she could see how the most important truth she'd ever needed to learn had been exemplified by the nesting dolls she'd played with as a child. The outermost portrayed the Lady of Paladins, armed and armored, resplendent in Her glory. Parts of the ungainly outer shell detached from one another to reveal a second doll, the Shield Maiden, portrayed in Her strength and innocence, and ripe with the promise of fertility. Within the second doll was a third, the Defender of the Hearth, the fierce, yet nurturing mother who would willingly fight to the death to protect Her own. Just beneath Her, the Matriarch was revealed, robed and crowned, wise, compassionate, and just. The last secret, the tiny mystery at the heart of the toy was a delicate porcelain figurine, not of the Lady in any of Her guises, but that of the Lord of Paladins, portrayed as the crowned and sceptered King in Glory.

It had seemed so simple then, but like so many other girls, she'd missed the point completely.

Baron Bonsall's summer townhouse, the City of Angels, Greater Fernwall
15 Amerian 580, 1500 hours

    Lady Angelique Blakesly paced restlessly.

    Sunlight filtered through the lacy curtains at the open windows, fragrant with blooming roses, fresh mown grass, and spicy notes of *m'banda*, the tiny northern flower the elves had named 'love's prison.' Wisteria dripped seductively from blossom-laden boughs, caressed by budding tips of foxglove, and delicate azaleas blushed all the pinkened shades of a maiden's confusion, serviced by the bees that probed at them them to draw forth their sweet nectar. Summer was a rioting orgy out there, just meters away, and though she had been pacing inside for the past quarter-hour, she knew there was no escape. In Angels, the refined northern enclave of the city of Fernwall where the Guardian Paladins dwelt, lace could be every bit as confining as iron bars, and as difficult to escape.

    It occurred to her then, as she turned away from the windows, toward where fine Angström porcelain clinked delicate grace notes over muted and

1

banal conversations, that she'd been spending too much time lately pacing the confines of an over-upholstered cage.

"My dear Carlisle, do please sit down. Your pacing could make a soul frantic." The voice was that of her friend and patron, the elderly Lady Emilia Nielsen, the Countess of Remington. As Guardian Paladins sometimes did, she had addressed Angelique by the name of her baronial holding. It was their way of reminding one another that they held responsibilities that went far beyond personal gratification, Angel had learned. It was one of those little cultural affectations that was easy for outsiders to learn, though they'd never grasp the subtle nuances of its significance the way those raised within it instinctively did.

Conversations ceased, and the eyes of the half-dozen or so other ladies in the room turned in Angelique's direction as one. She drew an even, steady breath, and rejoined Emilia and the other noble ladies in the room's interior, where it was much cooler. She sat beside Emilia, whose gnarled old hands idly fondled a strand of prayer beads. The older woman had lost her vision decades ago after a series of strokes, though her sightlessness never seemed an impediment. It was said that their God, the Guardian Paladin, had granted her a special kind of inner sight in compensation, an exchange that had served her well in her declining years.

"I have no wish to make anyone frantic," Angelique murmured apologetically, schooling herself once again to the role she was expected to play. *And Vin-Nôrëan-born baroness is better than most*, she reminded herself, taking up her accent along with the cup and saucer she'd abandoned, earlier. "The gardens here are lovely, Mercía. Such beauty has always caused me to feel restless, though I can hardly think why."

Mercía Devon, Bonsall's portly baroness, nodded her thanks for the compliment. "Our groundskeeper has been with the Devon family since my late mother-in-law was a child. Claims he's lost more blood to the roses here than he lost in the War!"

The baronesses Anne Carter of Lansdowne, Patrice Vickery of Willston, and Georgiana Dawes of Grafton tittered obligingly at the old jest. They were near enough in age to Angelique, but as near as she could tell, had been reared in an unbelievably sheltered world. Many of the nobility were proud that they were raising children who had not had to taste of war's privations. Carlisle's brand new baroness had kept her opinions on the matter carefully to herself.

"Ladies, let us turn our minds back towards our discussions today," Lady Beatrice Wilkinson-Foster, Countess of Liberaune, interrupted, thereby saving Angel the tedium of thinking up a clever reply. "We've just this last hour together before the exhibit opens to ensure our duties have been completed. Remington, have you been able to convince Fernwall's police commissioner to release some of his blue-jackets, as additional security for Bishop-Florian Hall?"

"He has done what he can, Beatrice," Emilia replied quietly, but firmly. "It is a little late to be concerned about such matters, now. You'd have been better served to listen to the advice you sought, and moved the Santí exhibit to a venue more easily secured. You can't expect the commissioner to leave Merchants' and Docktown completely unpatrolled to oblige you, now."

Liberaune's countess frowned disapprovingly, but though their titles matched, Emilia's leadership in matter of both church and state meant she outranked almost everyone. "It's as well, Emilia. The magical wards are supposed to be fool-proof. A thief could break in to look at the display, but I doubt he or she could successfully remove any of it."

Not without magical help, anyway. Which isn't hard to find, if one knows where to look. Did her imagination vanish with the assumption of her title? Angel didn't snort aloud, and was rather proud of it. She sipped her tea, and listened closely.

"If you will forgive me, my lady Countess, perhaps Lady Angelique could speak to Sir Vincent about the matter." The suggestion was offered by Lady Georgiana, Grafton's heir. It prompted another round of nervous tittering, which was shushed abruptly by Lady Beatrice.

"Pray tell," she drawled, in that acerbic way that made her juniors flush furiously, "what wisdom a convicted criminal who is serving his sentence in bond to the State could possibly have to offer, which highly paid experts in the field could not?"

Georgiana, still flushing, lifted her chin and answered. "My father has said that the best way to catch a thief is to use another," she offered pertly. "Since Lady Angelique takes pains to be on speaking terms with him—"

"So that's why she raised his name," Angel thought wryly, handing her cup and saucer to her young attendant, her face a mask of pleasant neutrality. "She's snooping around for another gossipy tidbit which she can tear to bits later with the rest of that coterie of savages she calls 'friends.'" But Lady Emilia had cut off what Georgiana was about to add.

"In strictest terms, Sir Vincent Sultaire was convicted on counts of extortion and blackmail, not thievery," she told them, conveniently omitting that the charges of burglary and "unlawful entry of a domicile" had been dropped, Angel noted. "Whatever his crimes have been, he is atoning for them, and shall for the next seven years of his life. Justice has been done."

"*Urilian* justice," Lady Beatrice snorted, the words plainly leaving a sour taste behind.

"Ours is not to judge," Emilia reminded her calmly, black opal beads clicking softly in her hands. "Neither legally, nor morally. Lady Angelique's association—and friendship—with Sir Vincent no more than models the Lady's teachings in this matter."

"I still think a good horsewhipping would have served him better." Lady Beatrice was from very old and honored Cascadian nobility, none of whom had taken kindly to having given up their hereditary rights of justice under the new constitution. Her words snapped, as whip-like as in tone as in subject.

Angelique shuddered. Unlike everyone present save perhaps Lady Beatrice herself, she well knew what such punishments looked like. "If that is a

3

sample of the Paladin's justice in your desmesnes, my dear lady countess, then I must be relieved that Urilia's justice here in greater Fernwall is more forgiving. Such brutality is better left to the Confederation orcs, surely."

Liberaune turned her unsparing gaze upon Carlisle's young baroness. "Some of us know that such things may appear 'brutal' to less experienced eyes, but are in fact more compassionate when looked at in context of what is best for all," she stated flatly, holding the younger woman's gaze.

Afraid she'd been caught out, Angelique flushed hotly, and looked away. Was it yet another obscure nugget of Paladin cultural knowledge that she was supposed to know? Georgiana, Mercía, and Anne had gazes that bounced between Beatrice and Angelique so avidly that all three jumped when Lady Emilia's voice broke into what had become an awkward silence.

"Be that as it may, Beatrice, even your father would not have applied the whip without first examining whether a whipping would appropriately address the crime," she said pointedly. "Nor would you, and we both know it."

Liberaune's countess snorted once, but allowed herself to be mollified.

"But, not all of our peers have been so graced with wisdom, or compassion, and so the people revolted, and we have Urilian justice now," Remington went on to remind her. "In the instance of Sir Vincent, I am of Angelique's mind where the dispensation of justice is concerned. If she errs on the side of gentleness, well, we all know the reasons for it. And perhaps, in this post-war land of ours, she will have the right of it, after all. Now, shall we continue our *serious* discussions about the last of the preparations for tonight?" Her question was rhetorical, and her blind old eyes had not even once flicked in the direction of the younger ladies, but all three knew they'd been censured for unwarranted frivolity, and held their silence.

The rest of the hour passed rather quickly, and with the "last hour" discussions laid aside, Angel judged it appropriate to rise and return to the sunlit windows, and her contemplation of Bonsall's gardens. Her companions of the afternoon would decide she needed time to calm herself, after her confrontation with Lady Beatrice, and they were right, as far as they knew.

It was not long before Georgiana and Mercía joined her at the window. The former was carrying a fresh cup of tea, which she offered to Carlisle's baroness with the air of one who was offering an apology.

"I think you were very brave, earlier," Georgiana said, as Angel smiled and accepted the tea. "And very eloquent in Sir Vincent's defense."

"It was quite remarkable," Mercía rushed to add. Angelique found the baroness of Bonsall to be a silly creature, but doubted there was any real malice in her. "But then, you must live the Lady's words every day, and recite them as your prayers every night! How do you abide the company of that young rakehell, Vincent Sultaire? Your virtue is at risk with each moment you spend in his company! Are you not ... afraid ... ?"

Angelique's response was automatic by this time, and sounded very natural even to her. "Afraid of what, my lady? Sir Vincent claims he desires my company, and is willing to abide by my terms for it. As such, he dares not insult me in any way, or I shall reject his company. He knows this."

Mercía glanced nervously at where the two older countesses were speaking quietly together with Lady Anne. "I have never heard that the young lord forebore effrontery for any reason. Your virtue is at risk with each moment you spend in his company. My lord husband has forbidden his presence here, and anywhere near my younger sisters while they're with us. I've also heard," she whispered, with another nervous glance toward the corner, "that he's considering apostasy—to the Urilian church!"

Angelique did not roll her eyes, but it was an effort for her. This was yet another familiar embellishment in the rigidly structured social lexicon they used. "Apostasy to the Urilian church" translated to "damned to everlasting torment." Proper ladies of the Guardian Paladin were not supposed to judge such things, of course, but it didn't seem to stop them from gossiping about it. She maintained her customary reserve as she sipped her tea, and thought about how best to answer.

Toss the bitches a bone; they'll leave you alone, she reminded herself, and pursed her lips briefly in preamble ot her reply.

"He has entertained the notion," she admitted, taking covert pleasure in the horrified expressions her words evoked. "And discarded it, after he brought it to me for examination. It isn't Urilia he wants, my ladies. It is forgiveness."

Whether it was *that* which shut them up, or the quiet approach of Lady Emilia on the arm of her maid, Angel would never know.

"Mercy. Compassion. Forgiveness." Her dry, husky chortle went on quietly for a moment, while the other ladies attended respectfully.

"Angelique, you are either very brave, or a fool. In truth I know not which. But if young Vincent Sultaire can be redeemed by anyone, it will be by someone with fortitude enough to forgive him all that he does, and yet remain somewhat detached from his charms in the doing of it. Lady bless you and help you, child. You will need it."

*　　*　　*

"'...virtue is at risk with each moment you spend in his company,'" Angelique repeated, mimicking the horrified gestures of the Baroness of Bonsall. "'I've heard that he's considering apostasy–to the Urilian church!' I swear, Raven," she went on in her own voice, using her companion's more notorious street name like an endearment. "She tossed that into the room like she'd toss a bone to a pack of wild dogs."

The muted sounds of the horse's steel shod hooves clopping on the cobblestone street, and the squeaking of the rented carriage kept the young couple company. Vincent Sultaire watched his lovely Angelique raptly, his steel blue eyes glittering with suppressed mirth.

She placed her hands demurely in her lap, and resumed her own, overly-correct Vin-Nôrëan accent. "'He has entertained the notion,'" she continued, playing her own part to the hilt, "'And discarded it, after he brought it to me for examination. It isn't Urilia he wants, my ladies all.'" After an appropriately dramatic pause she delivered the conclusion with the finesse of a seasoned story-teller.

"'It is forgiveness.'"

The young lord stared at her for several heartbeats, then collapsed in gales of helpless laughter. "Forgiveness?" he gasped, howling with glee. "Oh, by all the gods and goddesses! Forgiveness?" It was hard to say which was more amusing, the ignorant self-righteousness of the ladies at tea, or the sight of the infamous Raven, incapacitated by the idiocy of it all.

Finally, he got himself back under control.

"Oh, burning bright, that was rich. Forgiveness indeed," he sputtered. "That was very good." *If all too true*, he thought quietly to himself.

She bowed slightly from the waist, no mean feat considering the restrictive nature of noble ladies' fashions. The pendant she wore about her neck, an etched silver replica of a long sword's sheath, thumped softly against the fabric of her blouse as she settled back. It glittered with peridot and amethyst, stones appropriate to her rank as a baronial land-holder. Its companion sword would have been around the neck of the husband she'd buried several years previous, in Vin-Nôrë.

With a rueful grimace, she removed the necklace and stuffed it into a skirt pocket. Vin-Nôrë was the last place she wanted to think about.

"Why, thank you, darling. Those teas would be tedious indeed, if I had no way at all to amuse myself, during. And," she went on, delighting in the play of sunlight in his dark hair, "if I didn't know you would be there to rescue me, afterward."

He moved across the carriage to sit beside her, nimble fingers at the tiny buttons of her neckline, and then scalding the flesh of her throat. "Ah," he breathed, his hands caressing the pale, supple skin between her breasts. "For you, the moons, burning bright," he breathed into her lips. His hands caressed their way to her cheeks. "Or Commissioner Roland. But I don't think you'd want him." He wrinkled his nose.

"And what," she kissed him, trusting the anonymity of the carriage for the moment, "does your parole officer have to do with this?" The City State neither imprisoned nor jailed offenders. It sold them into slavery for the term of their sentence. Technically, Vincent was a slave, bound in service to the State by Police Commissioner Hal Roland, who had purchased his bond. For the remainder of it, the young lord would serve his term under Roland's thumb, an outcome many, like Beatrice Wilkinson-Foster, regarded as outrageous privilege.

Angelique didn't want to think about that, either. Just then, Raven's sensitive hands were on her bared skin, and he was clearly enjoying the "impertinence" as much as she. "More than the moons," he grinned impishly. "It's usually *his* carcass that has to be moved for me to rescue you." He kissed her again. "This isn't the kind of investigation that he finds stimulating."

Her answering chuckle was soft. "No doubt he finds supervising the infamous Raven stimulation enough, these days. No one envies our police commissioner that, so far as I have heard."

"Ever the black sheep," he sighed tragically. Unfortunately, there was more truth in the statement than anyone wished to face—including Sultaire himself. Instead, he turned his attention to the lovely female before him. She was an interesting study, a pleasant facade which gave no hint of the intricate depths beneath. Thick, ashen-blonde hair piled loosely into a proper and stylish coiffure atop her head, framing deep-set hazel eyes, high, delicate cheekbones, and mobile, expressive lips. Angelique's build was slender, willowy, markedly patrician even if it did not bespeak a typical Sylantian heritage. It seemed he never tired of looking at her—and he had been looking at her for nearly two years.

Yet within... *within* that prim, socially-correct exterior beat the heart of a woman of tremendous wit, passion, and sparkling-dry humor. It had taken him nearly six months to get underneath the mask she so expertly wore, and another few to earn enough of her confidence to tease out the hints of the real woman that lived just beneath. Her mind was quick, facile, and grasped new ideas with ease. She kept him thinking, guessing, laughing, always wondering; a glittering, changeable jewel wrapped in soft, fragrant velvet. Once she'd decided to trust him with her secret heart, she'd begun to confide in him, and he'd never since ceased to delight in her double-life: Baroness Angelique Blakesly of Carlisle for the public; for him, his Angel-fire, burning bright, tender, inexhaustible lover, wanton slut...

The thought caught him unaware. 'Wanton slut'? The term was loaded with imprecations, laid upon it by both his church and, more influentially and forcefully, by his father. Farmers were stupid peasants; craftsmen illiterate tradesmen; Urilian judges arrogant whores; and of course, any woman with a healthy sex drive was a wanton slut. It was the undercurrent that ran through him, and caught him unawares: his father's diatribes about a world he couldn't control any better than his trouble-making youngest son. Rebellion against it had ignited Vincent's burning desire for freedom— freedom from his father's abusive tirades, from the manor, and from the religion of his caste. It wasn't *his* church, he'd never felt comfortable or accepted there. It was the church of his hated family, and of the social mores they promulgated. It took what few wanted to give, commanded what few wished to obey, and denied what many passionately desired. Many women, he knew, refused to be stigmatized, and wore the label like a badge of honor. Were it not for her responsibilities to her barony and within that church, Angel could have been one: a proud Wanton Slut...

He looked deeply into her eyes, hazel eyes that seemed to turn sea-green, even as he watched. Almost idly, he reached up and loosed her hair, ignoring her mild protestation. It tumbled about her shoulders in a silken mass to frame her lovely face.

"It is always the black sheep, I am told, who make the very best lovers," she murmured in response, lips twitching at the corners. One thumb stroked his clean jawline softly even while her other fingers wound their way into the soft, dark hair at his collar.

7

"A myth," he whispered, occupied with fluffing out her hair. He firmly believed that the only reason in the world for women to do themselves up with such complexity, to invoke such passion with their beauty, was so that they and their lovers could have the joy of *un*doing them. "The best lovers are the ones who have a true passion for the fine arts of sex and seduction. And in *that* august world, you, burning bright, hold no seconds."

He saw his words soar deeply into her, and hit the center of her heart with uncanny accuracy. In the next moment, she was writhing like living flame in his arms, lips pressed to his, mouth open and sweet. It was like that with her, almost every time. Her natural reserve and quiet, demure countenance became ignited by one word, or perhaps a look, into a bonfire. From the very center of the conflagration emerged the wanton, alive and seething against him, setting his own barely-banked fires aflame.

He met her there, heart to heart, passion to passion, his lust blossoming with hers. Twining her long hair around his hands, he drank her in, losing himself in the kiss, in the smell of her hours-old perfume, now perfectly blended with her natural scent. It took only moments for him to be completely intoxicated.

Before either of them sank too deeply into the other, the carriage slowed, then negotiated the hard-angled turn onto Queen's Street, where the Raven kept his tiny flat. Angelique stiffened, straightened, and pushed herself free of his arms even while her lips refused to relinquish his.

"I may indeed," she began between kisses, "*be* the woman taken in adultery... but it would not do... to *be seen* like that... in public." Pulling free of him with a breathless laugh, she retreated to the other seat and began twisting up her hair, eyes shining with excitement.

Vincent watched her hungrily as she hurriedly made herself 'presentable.' She beat the coach's roll to a stop by scant seconds, smiling triumphantly. He chuckled at her, then opened the door and handed her out. The red brick building looked much like those on either side of it, three stories of apartments, complete with window boxes and a wrought iron railing at the steps. Not a typical domicile for a baron's younger son, but all that the Raven, convicted criminal and indentured police officer, was permitted during his servitude.

"Unimposing pile, isn't it, Baroness?" he drawled, flipping a coin to the coachman.

She smiling fondly at him as he ushered her to the front door. Raven always kept the truth of his thoughts masked by a witty remark, his passion checked—or perhaps merely deflected—by clever repartee. He had his masks, and many layers of being, most of which he never bothered to recognize. He was a rakehell playboy and a reformed criminal, a con man and—lately—a "cop" who figured every angle; but also within him lurked a tender, gallant lover whom she named aloud only in private. It he who incited her passions with ease, and then fanned them into explosion over and over again. He was the one to whom she'd clung afterward, when they cradled each other through the aftershocks of lust and orgasm.

Angelique loved him with an intensity that sometimes frightened her. She was almost certain he knew. "What is it the sailors say? 'Any port in a storm?'"

"They say other things, too," he chuckled over the sounds of the retreating coach. "Like how dangerous most ports are to enter in a storm."

With a shrug at her quick laughter, he swung open the door and let her through, then bounded ahead of her up the stairs to unlock the door to his flat. She ascended at a much more dignified pace. Once again, he ushered her through before him.

"Ah, perfect!" he exclaimed, pointing at the bottle of wine already set to chill. He kicked the door shut, threw his jacket over the back of a leather-upholstered chair and headed for the cooling wine. "I told the old biddy to have one set out for me about noon. She actually remembered. I think I'm in shock."

Angelique snickered, touched his arm fondly, then moved through the small, quaintly furnished room to lay her purse on the low table. The fabric at the back of the divan had faded from exposure to sun, the rug beneath her booted feet was old and somewhat worn from use. An air of carefully aged, fragile gentility pervaded the room. She thought it actually had a great deal of charm, and knew that her fondness for its inhabitant had colored her perceptions a bit.

The cork came out with a pop. He handed her a long-stemmed glass. "I hope you don't mind a bit of ceremony. I have neither seen you nor bedded you in thirty six hours—almost," he amended, noting the time on his small mantel clock.

"Raven! I'm touched," she drawled, accepting the glass with one of those graciously lofty nods—the same one she'd once used to distance herself from him when they'd first met. This time, however, she relented almost at once, expression relaxing into one of relief and gratitude. "Ah, but I've missed you."

The roguishness melted off his features like rain, and he was next to her before the storm that took them had passed. "Oh, burning bright, I've missed you, too. Your flame burns away the darkness, and for a while I almost believe I can see." *Myself,* he wanted to add, but didn't.

The dark cloud had arisen unbidden, and was as quickly dismissed. His lover, however, was unconscionably perceptive.

"'See...?' See what, *Mar'leven?*" It was the word for 'raven' in D'wanese, her native tongue, and she reserved its use for the intimate moments between them. It demarked the third side of Raven's personality, the one he so rarely showed, and then only in private.

He shook his head slightly. "Dark thoughts," he murmured, dipping a finger into his wine and caressing her lips with it, mesmerized as they parted, sucking his finger tantalizingly. He withdrew it slowly, then licked the wine from her lips. "Not for afternoons stolen for moments of pleasure."

Angel wanted to ask, but instead accepted his words without demur. Raven had his secrets, and a deep-running instinct told her that she probably

9

didn't need, or want, to know them. She was quite certain he didn't need to know hers, not while he was indentured to Fernwall's law enforcement department, anyway. It was enough, more than enough, to take what hours they could together.

"Had you plans for dinner this evening?" she asked instead.

"Yes," he murmured, his lips still brushing hers. He led them to the divan, where they could sit comfortably together. "You. Or are you otherwise engaged?"

Her delighted laughter answered him, soft and low. "Not until nineteen, or so. The Arts Exchange Conference wraps up its exhibit tonight. There is a dinner party afterward. Given that I am on that committee, I must attend. Until then, my love... I am all yours."

"Promises," he murmured accusingly, again releasing her wondrous hair from its pins. "You've been telling me you were mine since last winter." He kissed her again, expertly parting her lips with his tongue, kissing her in that way which promised much more than an afternoon's delights could fulfill.

But she laughed in spite of herself, pulling away from him just enough catch his gaze. Hers, he noted, was as green and restless as the sea.

"And like the woman scorned," Angel finally managed, around burbling mirth, "here I yet sit, unmarried despite all my shameless offers."

He chuckled mockingly. "Ah, but my lady, you are of the greater station. It would be improper for me to presume."

After a moment's shocked disbelief, Angelique laughed out loud, a light, ironic laugh that went on for some time. "Presume, Raven? You presume as easily as other men draw breath!"

He looked at her, his face a perfect mask of boyish innocence. "You injure me, my lady!" he said with a perfectly straight face.

"No," she corrected, the lights in her eyes dancing. "I *know* you."

He looked positively crestfallen, like the boy whose wagon was hopelessly, tragically, broken. "Ah, well," he sighed, hands almost idly unbuttoning her blouse again. "I guess all that leaves is sex."

"I was beginning to believe you'd forgotten how," she murmured, tugging at the knot on his impeccably tied cravat. How rich, the irony of it: Raven wouldn't ask her to marry him because of her rank. It was completely true, yet it was not all of the truth. As an excuse, it would do, and they both knew it.

What they both did *not* know was that she could not have married him, either.

His long, deft fingers slowly released each and every tiny pearl button on her blouse, until her corset and chemise were revealed. "Ah," he breathed at last, standing with facile grace to assist her to her feet, all traces of his feigned tragedy gone. High fashion for the ruling class did a competent job of disguising most of a woman's charms. Layers and layers of fabric interceded between the eyes without and the skin underneath. But, for all the intricacy

10

of fabric, ribbon, lace, buttons, and bows, he found they held not a candle to the loveliness of the treasure hidden within.

A flush of pleasure coursed through him when, the corset gone, Angel drew her first free breath; a sleeping princess, freed from her torpid tomb. A bird spreading her wings in first flight. Passion released. The sudden, aching lift of her ribcage, nipples crinkled, creamy skin coloring from forehead to shoulders, and the sinuous, sybaritic stretch signified liberty, a kind of freedom from the constraints of a society she lived in, but was not *of*. Lady Blakesly, he had been delighted to note, had already adopted a gartered arrangement to hold up her stockings. Pantaloons were now for virgin maids and older women, of which Angel was neither. He stepped back to admire her, then coaxed her back down onto the cushions of the sofa, and began massaging muscles held motionless for hours by clothing, and the somewhat sedentary demands of her station.

Rivers of knotted tension flowed from her freely under his sensitive, clever hands. Angel, he'd noticed on several occasions, suffered from a single disadvantage where the corset was concerned. She was an active woman and toned muscles complained when forced into motionlessness for protracted periods; thus, his ministrations to her abdomen and chest were both therapeutic and arousing.

As he finished kneading the tight muscles of her back and assisted her to roll over, her small, pink nipples were taut with building desire. He answered their mute pleas with his lips, licking each pert nipple even as she arched her back to meet him. Then he claimed her mouth again, slowly, passionately, fully in the grip of his desires. "Beautiful, as always," he murmured into her half-open mouth.

"*Mar'leven*," she whispered, the name tingling on her lips. "Thirty-six hours—almost—is too long. By far." It was her turn to unfasten, unbutton, and tug at the clothing she could reach, hands trembling; but men's fashions were as restrictive as their feminine counterparts', and from where she lay she could not quite reach them all. Waist-coat, vest, suspenders, double-starched shirt, undershirt... At last, his smooth chest stood exposed to fingers that traced across his skin, trailing arousal in their wake.

His eyes closed, and he shivered slightly. *Thirty-six hours. Too long indeed.* Wordlessly, he lay across her, the bared skin of their upper bodies touching, her small, firm breasts pressing delightfully against him.

The kiss that followed, cuddled closely there on his divan, was long and languorous. Despite the urgency, there was no real hurry, no rush to satiation. Each knew the other's body well, understood what fed the fires, and what sustained them. What had passed before was as tinder and kindling to the ultimate blazing glory to come.

Once again Raven took control of her, and put at risk all the things she hadn't had the courage to tell him. His hands and mouth drew forth more than the honeyed fluids of her body, and excited her to more than mere orgasm. In a surfeit of passion, Angel ached to hurl the truth of her heart at his feet, to release herself from deception and guilt as easily as he released

11

her from the sweet agony of desire. In quieter moments, she often wondered if he knew just how close he was to baring her completely, or if he would care. Or, if he would hate her, afterwards. . .

Fortunately, the ache passed, as did the need for thought. He was a running river of erotic energy, one that drew ever more from its source; as she poured herself forth to meet him, she became blissfully lost in the torrent. Again and again, he pressed her to that quivering edge, her body shimmering expectantly around his shaft as she danced at the lip of the abyss, only to back away in the heartbeat before the plunge. Breath by breath, he reveled with her in exchanged ecstasy, until every other thing in the world disappeared, and all that was left was their shared passion, and its spectacular release.

They clung together in the aftermath, he whispering her name, and finding the taste of it sweet in his mouth; she, hearing that name, was suffused in a kind of joy she'd never known before.

"Mar'leven," she whispered finally. turning in his arms to kiss her own fragrance from his face. It was something to focus upon, like his hand at her cheek, or his lips touching hers. He kissed her again, and the world once more narrowed to shut out everything but what was in the sphere of their shared heartbeat. Angel felt herself alive again, vibrantly alive after thirty-six hours of living death.

"How you set my heart afire," Raven was saying—when had he broken that kiss? "The passion burning beneath that proper exterior. . . I can hardly believe. . . "

Words seemed to fail him. For but a moment, they did for her, too. There was too much, it seemed, she might say to that. Things like, *I'm not really who you think I am*, or *There are things I haven't told you*, things that, once said, could never be unsaid. Things that were much, much too late to say.

Instead, she summoned up a helplessly tender smile. Just barely in time, she summoned up the accent that should accompany the words. "Then it would seem, darling man, that I am not the one to redeem you, after all."

His look became puzzled, and his caresses paused. "Angel?" he said softly, questioningly.

"It was what Lady Emilia told us all earlier, just before she removed you as a topic of conversation at tea today." Her fingers traced the outline of his lips, fighting down her own flickering smile. "She said that if you could be redeemed by anyone, it would be someone with the capacity to forgive you anything, and yet remain free of your 'charms'," she chortled, indicating the euphemism in the inflection, "in the doing of it. Though I'm sure I could meet the first condition, it's regrettably obvious that I'm completely lacking in character for the latter."

He chuckled softly. "Ah, but burning bright, are you familiar with the Urilian form of baptism?"

She feigned Lady Mercía's actively horrified expression from earlier that afternoon. "Certainly not! I mean, *really!*" Expressions changing like quicksilver, she grinned and asked, "Are you?"

He waggled an eyebrow. "So how, my Angel, do you know you have not just *become* my salvation?"

"Your Urilian salvation?" She stifled a moment of laughter. "An unlikely position for a proper lady of the Guardian Paladin to find herself, wouldn't you say?"

"About as unlikely as finding a proper lady of the Guardian Paladin here in bed with me," he agreed, his naughty grin fading into a kind of wistfulness that made him seem much more vulnerable. "Ah, burning bright. Thirty six hours is too long." He pulled her to him again, and cradled her close.

"By far," she agreed, kissing him with all her heart.

He shuddered from the tips of his toes to the ends of his hair. Many were the women the Raven had wined, and dined, and then bedded. Many more were the women he had simply seduced for the sheer animalistic pleasure it brought. None had ever regretted it—though admittedly there a good many fathers who didn't share their daughters' views of the matter. But this woman... to be inside her, to move with her, to feel her whole being shudder in pleasure... the sense of merging he felt when with her was so far outside his experience that it bore little resemblance to anything he thought he knew.

For an immeasurable time he held her there, eyes closed, breathing softly, her delicate hand lightly caressing the hairs on his chest. Unbidden tears welled in his eyes. Something far down in the hidden depths of his immortal soul shifted ever so slightly. The irrepressible rakehell of Fernwall gave in to what he already knew, but couldn't admit. He'd fallen in love.

Silently those unbidden tears wound their way down his cheeks.

Baptism complete.

Chapter 2

The Auguste Santí Exhibit,
Bishop-Florian Memorial Hall, Angels
15 Amerian 580, 2145 hours

"Bishop-Florian security is tight for this exhibit," Louis had told her, stretching out the floor plans for the venerable old building over his desk. *"They'll have attack dogs, of course, and extra guards besides. That's nothing new,"* he'd smiled; a mirthless expression, but Angel had already become engrossed in the drawings in front of her.

She had always been a quick study. It had been one of the qualities that had originally endeared her to him. The woman who greater Fernwall knew as Lady Angelique Blakesly, in fact, possessed a suite of talents that had once made her a desirable apprentice in the slippery, chaotic world of post-war Püran-Khir: keen intelligence, fast reflexes, good instincts, decent strength, and cold-blooded fearlessness when faced with a challenge.

Happily, these were also traits that made her an even more valuable "associate," lacking a better term for it, in the confines of peaceful, civilized Fernwall. Louis had watched her avidly, almost greedily, as she pored over the drawings, delighted with what he saw. Angel's mind was taking in the information before her at a phenomenal rate, memorizing and collating data with an ease that surprised anyone who might have mistaken such loveliness for shallowness.

This job was much more challenging than any she had previously attempted. Still, he had few doubts she'd succeed. Any woman who could successfully deceive the entire noble class of Fernwall and keep that web of lies intact for years could certainly figure out how to infiltrate a museum and take whatever she wished. In this case it was a mere bauble, a necklace crafted by dwarven smiths so far back in history, humans had no clear record of it. The necklace, '*Mâgun-Zak*,' had been a gift to the royal family of Vin-Nôrë from their dwarven neighbors, and was quite literally priceless. The metal wasn't silver, but *niobïtan*. The centerpiece was molded and etched to resemble a raven's head and wings, bejeweled and shining iridescently. Each stone, tear-drop cuts scintillating like the source of light itself, were "flawless" by human standards. When one looked closely, one saw that each delicate link in the interlocking chains had been etched with countless dwarven rune-letters, reputedly a prayer to Eldar their ancient God, to bless the wearer with health, protection, good fortune and long life.

Louis didn't believe any of it. But then, Louis had lost his faith in a lot of things long before The Great War was over, and had resigned himself to the reality that most people stubbornly insisted on clinging to theirs. What he believed in today was power—and money, because money was the fuel every engine of power required. To that end, he'd once recruited a very young girl in a very bad place, raising her up into what had become a very interesting and lucrative partnership.

"Angelique Blakesly" was a fiction, of course. A cover, suitable for hiding her true purpose in the city: gathering information, from the inside, for the high-stakes thefts he selected, and directed. *A quite lovely fiction,* he mused, watching her complete her first study of the floor plans. Louis understood young Vincent Sultaire's fancy for her. He didn't quite understand what she saw in Sultaire; but then again, a woman's mind was always a mystery. He'd resigned himself to that, too.

"You've studied The Spider's methods," he'd then said, puzzled at her extended silence. *"Do you know how you'll do it, yet?"*

Only then did she lift her gaze to his, a small flickering smile playing about her lips. Louis was arrogant beyond the bounds of belief when on his own ground, but these were her strengths, learned even before she became known as "the Iris," there in the shifting, shadowy wasteland of post-war Püran-Khir. After she'd come under Louis' protection, he'd helped her hone those skills, first by making a child's game of them, a way to amuse her, or keep her quiet. As she grew, they changed into contests, and became more difficult. Her technical skills in thievery and disguise had surpassed his by the time she'd turned sixteen; by the age of twenty she was better known as "Iris" than as Louis' little play-toy, "Angela," and knew quite a bit more about his life and pursuits than she'd bothered to share with her erstwhile mentor.

"In reverse, of course," she'd replied. Now, peering at the imposing edifice of Bishop-Florian from the seclusion of the cedar grove in the park just beyond, she felt a little giddy recalling her own supreme arrogance at the remark. *In reverse. Sure, Angel. Only it's not as easy as you made it seem.*

She checked her watch, a piece much more costly than was apparent from its carefully antiqued look. It had to be. For work like this, seconds sometimes meant the difference between success and failure—life and death.

Two more minutes. Like the clockwork gears within her watch, Angelique's mind worked its way through tonight's preparations, piecing them all together with facile precision. Time pulsed through her with every beat of her heart, every indrawn breath. Every cell, every fine hair on her body was achingly *alert*, aware of each breath and heartbeat in a way she'd only ever duplicated in Raven's company.

Raven's tears. He'd wept earlier, silently, even as they both approached the pinnacle together, then lied about it, preferring to turn away from his own feelings rather than share them with her. She knew he'd lied about it; she'd felt it in the way only another deceiver can sense deception. The woman in her longed to know why he wept, yearned to comfort him, to promise him anything to honor the tears he cried, but he smiled, and lied, and danced away from the precipice of truth, leading her away from it, too.

"*Mâgun-Zak*," a dwarven gift in honor of a human king. Named for both the clan that crafted it, and for the heraldic device of the king who had accepted it. *Mâgun-Zak* meant "raven's tears," and the irony of it was damned distracting.

She shifted the wide leather belt over her shoulder, welcoming its bite into her flesh, and the pain that brought her back into her task. It was a piece of jewelry, no more. An exquisite artifact which would this night be stolen by one who could take it, sent on to another who would pay handsomely to own it, or so she assumed. No one else in this city may ever know the truth of its theft besides Louis and herself, but that was all right. Secrets like *this* one were best kept as closely as possible.

The low, metallic *'bong'* of the Clock Tower echoed to her from the harbor below. It was time. She again shifted the weight of her pack, and worked her way around to one of the side entrances to the old building. It had originally been constructed to honor performance arts, and later expanded to showcase every art form imaginable. Those late expansions added architectural peculiarities that made it a security nightmare. The committee of the Ladies' Auxiliary that was responsible for this exhibit had been prevailed upon mightily to change the venue by the police force and the security agency they'd hired to bolster the Hall's normal precautions. But Bishop-Florian Memorial Hall was so immersed in custom and tradition that the noblewomen of the Ladies' Auxiliary of the Guardian Paladin Church had believed no other venue would do. Lady Angelique Blakesly of Carlisle had carefully kept her opinions to herself during those discussions.

Tonight, that stubborn, righteous, arrogant blindness of her so-called 'peers' would be turned to her advantage. Raven would have loved the idea, if he'd known of it. Not that she could ever tell him.

Late afternoon sunlight, angling through the bedroom window, glinting mockingly in the shining rivulets on her lover's face....

Firmly, she pushed down her heart's memories and wrenched her concentration back to the matter at hand.

The guards on the grounds changed shifts at twenty-two. At 2201, Angel was letting herself into a well-used side door to the building, one that permitted staff and maintenance personnel entrance and exit, out of sight of visiting patrons. Since Angelique Blakesly was a junior member of that committee of the Ladies' Auxiliary, she had been given responsibility for the many tedious details to which the senior members didn't wish to attend. Such duties had made it necessary for the Lady Blakesly to keep a partial set of keys to the building.

This key hadn't been on the ring when the baroness had accepted it, but it was a rather convenient addition. She slipped into the interior without so much as a breath of air to mark her passing. The halls and offices were quiet. Even with the bolstered number of guards on duty, they hadn't found it necessary to patrol these areas, since nothing critical was kept in the office wing.

She checked her watch again. *It takes a few minutes for the guard shifts to resettle themselves,* Louis had discovered, and shared with her during their supper together three nights previous. *But no longer than twenty-two ten, Angel darling. If you're late, your neck is as good as collared.*

Quickly and silently, she flew through the narrow corridors of the ground floor, then up a maintenance stairwell. *Collared.... and unlike Raven, my father wouldn't save me from my fate. He'd probably be the first to throw me into chains, if he knew what I've become. Raven's luckier than he knows.*

With the keys in her gloved hands easing her way, Angel was on the proper floor by 2208, their use having nullified several magical alarms designed to defeat unwanted intruders. She ducked into a pre-selected janitorial closet, her pulse pounding in her ears, but she'd pushed herself beyond fear to ride the swelling crest of nervous energy and exhilaration. Her motions smoothed and tightened to the barest economies, but her heart, suffering on her lover's behalf, continued to stray.

He'd rolled us over, locked together... his tears falling like rain, as clear as truth... steeped in lies....

With great care, she pulled a blowgun from her pack: silent, deadly with the right darts, but subject to random drafts. These darts had been tipped with a potent drug that would cause temporary paralysis and unconsciousness for several hours, if it could only find purchase in the skin—

Heavy, booted footsteps turned the far corner of the hall, grinding away distraction with each thudding crunch. Angel froze, deliberately pulling air into her lungs to force her blood to move. The point of no return was almost upon her. She could hear the man's breathing now, guessed him to be overweight by 20 kilos, irreverently glad that the drug itself could have knocked out a dwarf with a single dose.

Come on... come on...

Silence. A window latch rattled, tested secure, and the man clomped towards her again. Her heart kept time with his slow march even as her nerves screamed out for him to hurry it along.

Close, closer, closest...

Pah-whunk! The tiny dart streaked through the air, almost invisible in the dim light. The guard turned, slapped at his neck, then caught sight of his assailant in the shadowy recesses of the closet. Angel caught her breath, sure in that expanding moment that the drug had failed. The guard opened his mouth as if to shout, even as she primed herself to move, *move now!*

The shout froze on his lips. Panic took him, silently. His eyes widened, then they rolled back. Knees crumpling, he crashed to the floor.

Already propelled forward by her own moment of panic, Angel dashed out, grabbed the inert lump by the belt and collar, and exerted all her strength to drag his unconscious form back with her. With two lengths of fine silken cord (amazingly tough for its slenderness), she bound fast the man's hands and feet, then rolled him over so his snoring wouldn't alert anyone else.

One down.

She'd no sooner risen, sweating, than the footsteps of the next guard turned the same corner. Concealed in the darkness, Angelique felt no fear this time, only anticipation.

Again, she waited. Again, the window rattled, the footsteps approached. Once again, the dart flew true.

The female guard fell as easily as her male counterpart had and, within moments, she too was bound and sleeping comfortably at his side.

Two down, outer hall secured. First objective complete.

Freed now of her distractions, yet still mindful of the press of time, Angel turned her thoughts to the next set of challenges. She had spent several long nights combining what she knew of the exhibit layout with the details Louis had discovered about the security involved. She thought there might be a way to get to the item without killing anyone. Only close observation of the situation within the hall itself would allow her to know, either way.

Four guards patrolled the exhibit hall where the *Mâgun-Zak* was displayed, along with many other works of art from the collection of the renowned Vin-Nôrëan art dealer Auguste Santí. Ordered to patrol with some precision, they could see at least one other of their number within seconds of losing sight of the last, and were to sound the alarms if there was any lapse, any at all, in the rhythm of those sightings. The bells would ring loudly, alerting the guards several floors down. One of them would run to the closest police precinct. If Angel failed in muscle, nerve, or timing, she'd have just that margin of time to get what she came for, and get clear. Or simply get clear, if things went horribly wrong.

She watched for a quarter of an hour, learning the rhythms of each guard, checking them against her watch; seeing which guards looked in which directions, and at what things first, and which they ignored. It was easy to mark where they might rely on the sightings of the others, from the layout of the exhibit during the baroness's duties here, earlier that day.

Yes. Just so. There. Start with the tall, bald one, then the husky female. The blond woman always pauses there... and then hurry to take down the last. Timing: One minute, fifty three seconds to disable all four guards, consecutively, moving against their clockwise pattern. She'd have to move faster than she'd ever moved in her life.

Angel crouched, never so alive as in that moment, caught in the interval between the plan conceived and its execution. Her pack slipped silently to the floor. There she crouched, waiting for him to come within her ambit, waiting through the diminishing seconds...

Do it. She moved toward her first position, spinning the ring on the middle finger over as she went. The exhilaration of the challenge rose within her as the first guard approached.

She let him pass, then jumped him from behind. A quick blow to the neck put him down. She flipped the cap on her ring, and pricked him with the needle.

Thirty-five seconds.

Silently, she raced to her next position, ducking behind an ornate suit of armor and shaking out her garotte. Between two more heartbeats the next guard was down, the slender cord twisted sinuously about the woman's slender neck.

The needle kissed its victim. Angel hurried on.

Sixty seconds.

Time. Time. Time. It froze around her, and she moved through it like a wraith. From behind an arras, she pricked the third guard, who collapsed where she stood.

Minute twenty-three...

They met eye to eye, his expression rife with disbelief. The flashing heel of Angel's hand removed that thought. Stiffening, he toppled backwards. The last dose of the drug entered his skin.

One minute, fifty-one seconds.

It was done. Triumph thundered through her, as heady as orgasm.

Four of them! She wanted to shout, laugh, scream, dance! For an absurd moment, she wanted Raven there to share this victory with her, wanted to hurl herself into his arms and laugh out loud, chasing away the tears he'd cried... but those thoughts sobered her abruptly. Tonight, Sir Vincent Sultaire would not have been her lover. Police Inspector Sultaire would have been yet another in the ranks of the opposition.

Sobering indeed. Shaking it off (and grieving just a little for what her lover would never know), Angel returned to where she'd left her pack, retrieving an odd-looking pair of spectacles, and then unwrapping the most preciously enchanted things she'd ever seen. The double set of paired crystal wands thrummed in her hands; apparently, one needn't have been mage-born to sense the magical power held in those clear depths, for she couldn't cast a spell to save her life. But, placed properly, they would nullify the magical protections placed around her objective. Placed improperly...

She glanced at her watch again. Twenty-two twenty-two. She had forty minutes to steal the necklace and get clear of the premises. After that, she would leave it and the crystals at the pre-arranged drop point, then rush back to the gardening shed where she'd left her gown and jewels, change, and return to the party just five kilometers away.

The most time consuming part, she thought irreverently, as she approached the clear crystal case where the *Mâgun-Zak* was displayed, *is going to be getting back into that damned gown.*

When the artifact itself was before her, Angel found herself staring at it through the glass in abject fascination. It really was a breathtaking piece of artistry, and she paused a moment to appreciate it. A warrior might wear it across an armored breastplate; even with the seeming delicacy of the feathered "wings," it had a very martial appearance. The jewels, fashioned into tiny teardrops, seemed to attract all the light in the room, throwing off scintillating flashes of fire. The minute etchings were indistinct from where she stood, but discernible. They gave the entire piece a 'feathered' look, muting the glimmering metal, and somehow accentuating the brilliance of the gems. They danced before her eyes as if they were alive, and she found herself almost mesmerized by the effect.

Pay attention, Angel! Shaking her head, she placed the pair of specially-crafted spectacles over her eyes. Abruptly the necklace and the rest of the room disappeared. All she could see were scintillating lines of arcane energy, wherever magic had been used to secure the items on display. There were quite a few, and now she knew with certainty where each and every one of them were.

Within the crystal dome that covered the display, four of those brightly sparkling lines interlaced, touching the edge of the covering in eight places, equidistant around the circumference. Two lines were red. Two more were blue. The key to blocking the spell was *not* to place the crystal wands where any of the lines of force touched the clear crystal dome, but alongside where the red and blue lines met in brilliant violet stars.

Had a thief placed the wands in four of the places where lines touched the circumference of the dome, it would dispel them completely, thereby triggering a more subtle alarm in the guard headquarters below. Part of the genius of this crime was that the magical protections were left in place. The item itself? Vanished.

Focus.

Angel readied the first two crystal wands, forcing her sweating hands, tense arms, and shoulders to relax, lest that tension cause the kind of trembling that made unfortunate accidents likely. She'd never used the real things in her practice sessions, of course, just simple glass substitutes of the right size and weight; handling the truly enchanted versions, she would have taken an oath that the two devices seemed to interact with each other as she handled them, though it was impossible to describe the effect.

She dismissed imminent concerns of failure from her mind. *The crystals are enchanted to work in pairs, that's all it is. Like lodestones, maybe. You don't have to be a mage to know what that's like. This is going to work.*

Drawing her focus down once more to the task at hand, Angel lifted the first set of crystals and alighted them with their appointed positions. With exacting precision, she lowered them down into their appointed places outside the dome. Sweat ran from her brow, threatening to blind her. Time lost all meaning. It was neither frozen in place, nor hurtling onward. There were four glowing violet stars in her universe and two crystal rods. No more.

Millimeter by millimeter, each hand sought and adjusted minutely during the descent of the rare, precious things. For a moment, she thought she felt a very faint "shimmering" from the wands when she had them positioned correctly. It was so very subtle, she wasn't entirely sure she felt it at all, but she found that when she relaxed to it, the descent flowed very naturally.

Angel knew nothing about spell-work, but her muscles and nerves under-stood what her mind could not. The crystal wands touched the base of the display simultaneously; the two sparkling violet points pulsed once, then resumed their steadily glittering glow.

She wiped the perspiration from her hands and brow, then picked up the second set of crystals. This time it was somewhat easier. Not only did her body know what to expect, the effect was consciously noticeable; she suspected that was due to the first pair already being in place. When their companions were properly aligned, all four points began pulsing in steady rhythm—and their component lines withdrew perhaps one centimeter away from the circumference of the crystal dome.

Using the same care, Angel lifted the dome and set it aside. The jewels in the necklace were irridescent in the room's bright light, much like a raven's wings, glittering in quick, unpredictable flashes of light.

Mâgun-Zak... Raven's tears hadn't glinted so colorfully in afternoon sunlight... but they were no less precious...

Wait. Where did that come from?

Irritated with herself, she stuffed the precious thing into the velvet pouch she'd brought, then carefully replaced the quartz crystal dome on the bare pedestal.

The crystal wands were easier to retrieve than to set; the arcane energies resumed their caress of the inside of the dome. For all reasonable purposes, the guards below would not know what happened until it was much too late. It left her... twenty minutes, she thought, then checked her time-piece to confirm it. Plenty of time to put the final artistic stamp on the job.

From the floor-plans she'd studied, and from her own explorations of this end of the building, Angel knew her egress would be at the other end of this particular addition to Bishop-Florian. It was ridiculously easy to avoid the sole guard still conscious, and still very clueless as to the fate of his co-workers this night. There were three locked doors, and though she had the keys for all of them, she picked the one nearest the guards' patrol route, and into the keyholes of two other doors she poured an acidic solution *after* opening them. The smell was horrible, so acrid it burned her nostrils. Angel was careful not to touch any of it. She had no idea where Louis had gotten the stuff, and in truth had not wanted to know.

A deep bay window had been selected for her exit, complete with soft pillows where patrons might rest themselves from their artistic pursuits. She unlocked the window, and pushed it open. The last piece to this amusing game of misdirection was at hand. From her pack, she removed her miniature crossbow, able to be held and fired with one hand; and then the specially constructed bolt which, when fired, carried a long length of silken cord upward, burying its head obligingly into a wooden support beam near the roof. With a casual flair that belied the intense triumph she felt, Angel fired off her bolt, safed her tools, and then secured herself to the line. Pausing only to push the window closed, she shimmied up the fine, spider-like twine to the roof above.

Guards and their trained attack dogs, blissfully unaware of what had just occurred, continued their patrol routes below.

A fine caper by anyone's standards, she thought, gazing down on slumbering mass of towns and villages that had become Fernwall, during The Great War. It spread out before her, the lights on the masts of the ships in the harbor sparkling just beyond. For a moment, Angel ignored the press of time and took in all of the vista before her. Fog filled the Thieves' Quarter and the lowest levels of Docktown, twining insubstantial tendrils into the winding streets of Merchants' and the gentle hills and well-manicured lawns of lower Angels. Even from this distance, she heard the faint cloppings of horses' hooves, pulling the innumerable hired traps and hacks carrying people to and from their engagements. A low warning note from the lighthouse on the other side of the harbor flashed light through the thick mists, warning ships at sea of hazards near.

The entire city pulsed. *Life... life... life...* It was in the breath, the movement, the very air—the whole city *lived* and loved and hated by full measures, stinting nothing to those who were willing to throw themselves in its flow. Standing atop the roof of Bishop-Florian Memorial Hall, having taken down six security guards to pull off one of the most spectacular jewel heists ever, Angel felt herself vibrantly alive, *tingling* in every pore for the first time in almost a year. Only her irregular sexual escapades with Raven had come close, but even they could not make her mind and body sizzle like she'd just missed getting struck by lightning.

A remarkable thing, by anyone's measure, she thought again, turning her mind reluctantly to the remaining loose ends of this caper. Her alibi must be firmly established. That meant returning to the party at the summer home of the Earl and Countess of Liberaune, the noble family who had been the Patrons of Name for the exhibit.

It also meant returning to a way of life that forced her to live as if she were half-dead. After all of this flushed, pulsing, vitality of being, it was as if a tomb door yawned open below her and began to suck the life-pulse from her, pulling her back into the lonely, gray nothingness. The dead never willingly released their grasp on their own.

For a brief moment, Angel angrily resisted that pull. It was entirely possible to throw over Angelique Blakesly completely. The baroness could disappear, and she could become Iris permanently, and live very well here in greater Fernwall by her wits and talents, much as she'd done in Püran-Khir, only this time in a city where one might enjoy being rich...

And always one breath away from death, or maiming, or a collar, she reminded herself, sighing quietly. She'd made her choices, back when all her choices had included the fiction of Angelique Blakesly, by default.

Time to return to the coffin.

*   *   *

The grounds and residence of the Earl and Countess of Liberaune lit up most of the hillside upon which it sat, liberally dotted with the magitech crystals in a display of wealth that few in the City-State could afford. The estate had been newly refurbished and redecorated since the war's end, and the extensive gardens landscaped to provide a more appropriate setting for the nobly-born of the old kingdom to gather. In the Crimson & Ivory Hall, where the night's gathering was centered, intricately structured melodies wound in and around the sounds of celebration. Tile floors shined, oaken banisters gleamed. Bright laughter punctuated animated conversations, and was graced by the tinkling of crystal glasses, and wisps of fragrant smoke. Everywhere one looked, beautifully garbed women flitted like exotic birds around their male counterparts, who were dressed more conservatively in black formal attire.

The exhibit had been a resounding success, yet another sterling achievement to top the list for the noble Wilkinson-Foster family. So pervasive was the air of satisfaction, so persistent the triumph, that not even the inexplicable hysterics of the Countess's little lap dog could diminish it.

The poor beast tore through the assembled in the Hall, the great library, and the garden, yapping and snapping ribbons and lace and anyone unwise enough to approach. It drew a great deal of shrieking, and curses, as the quicker among them were dispatched to capture and calm the poor thing.

Angel made sure to dispose of the tiny dart that had fallen from the little dog's coat as it ran. It had been difficult to find a drug that would give the creature a fright without permanently harming it, but essential. Even as Iris, Angel had never stooped to poisoning a dog, and hoped she never would. She slipped through a door and into the darkened interior. A woman reclined upon the divan, a blonde who was wearing a dress that was the exact copy of her own. Angel touched her on the shoulder, then assisted her out of door with a purse full of coin.

Near the door but not quite out of sight, Doctor Alfred Martin leaned out of the door of one of the smaller sitting rooms, curious over the outburst, wondering if his gifts would be needed yet again this evening, and if perhaps he oughtn't leave his resting charge for but a moment to check...

A gentle, deferent touch at his elbow interrupted his thoughts. He turned to meet the clear, hazel-eyed gaze of the Baroness of Carlisle.

"I am most appreciative of your concern for me this evening, good doctor," Angelique began, smiling bravely for his benefit, her accent making the Cascir language seem like a song. "But, I am much recovered, and no little embarrassed at having kept you from the party for so long."

"Milady, are you sure, then?" He took her hand and looked at her meaningfully. Though retired from active practice, Dr. Martin was a profoundly gifted healer as well as a highly decorated combat surgeon. "Yes, I can see that you are," he smiled. "Then allow me to escort you to our host's refreshment table. A bit more nourishment and a few more kilos here and there would only serve to enhance your beauty, and your health."

She graciously accepted his proffered arm, calculating just how much she might allow herself to lean upon it as they walked. "I feel quite the fool, doctor. I should have found a way to eat something before the ceremonies, but Lady Beatrice was relying on me, and I did not wish to be late."

"Your devotion to duty becomes you, my lady. But it might be worth your while to consider sustainability versus tardiness." He stopped her and looked at her meaningfully. "I am a married man, my lady, but even I must confess to being taken by your elfin-like beauty. Unfortunately, as with all things in this world, there is the other side: You have few reserves to draw on at need."

Angelique returned his look, suppressing any of several truths in favor of a reply more fitting her station, and his kindness. "I shall surely keep your advice close to my heart, doctor, and remember your kindness in my prayers this night."

With a proper bow over her hand, he left her there at the refreshment table.

"Another admirer," Sir Eric Wilkinson-Foster, younger son of the Earl and Countess of Liberaune smiled as he approached. He was tall, muscular, fair haired, and a handsome young man by all accounts. Many thought they made an attractive couple. Eric thought so, too, and had made his intentions to pursue the matter clear by courting her with remarkable patience and persistence.

Eric. She sighed internally, wondering at the man's dogged devotion to her presence, while simultaneously understanding it. He was a product of his culture, after all, and had never imagined there might be a freedom from it. To him, she was a baroness in need of a baron, and for many Guardian Paladins, she knew it was just as simple as that. Oh, she was beautiful, surely, a potential bride with whom he could not be embarrassed in public, and one who would prove a valuable connection for his family. Her intelligence and wit would be considered an accomplishment for him, and none of them would know or care that she lived the rest of her life in quiet desperation, half-dead. . .

Angel shook herself, internally. Eric had bowed over her hand, and then set about filling a plate for her with items of her choosing. "I'm glad to see you've recovered," he murmured. "The Lady knows the evening will be far more enjoyable with your companionship."

Make the best of it, Angel, she urged herself. Eric's tender deference was flattering, even if it completely lacked Raven's suave, outrageous style. She smiled at him with some fondness—truly, he was a very *gentle* man, and a kind one.

"And here I had thought you would have found one of yon maids more to your liking in my absence." She nodded over to where a group of girls congregated near the doors to the garden, pale gowns seeming to glow with youth and innocence. They were new to this year's social circuit, introduced

25

to Paladin society at the parties during SpringFest, some months past. As Angelique Blakesly, she'd learned that all young nobles went through an introductory season in the big city, one carefully directed and supervised by the older adults. The tradition served several functions. Most of those outside the culture thought it was to show off "the marriageable young," as she'd heard Louis say, and with his usual snide disrespect for what he didn't understand. She'd since discovered that there was more to it than that, and that the ties these young persons made in this season could well determine their positions of leadership, in the church, community, and country, for decades to come.

"Once," he admitted, smiling at the remembrance, "and to be candid, my lady, some have set their eye on me." He handed her a plate—artfully arranged, he really did have a flare for it—and caught her eyes. "I have, however, made my choice, and I do not regret it."

Angelique had often wondered how any man his age could have retained a gaze with such clarity of soul. Eric wasn't precisely an 'innocent,' but his life and heart were uncomplicated in ways which the lady before him envied, in her quieter moments.

"Your patience in this matter has been remarkable," she conceded, leading them over to a pair of chairs near the open double doors, "and remarked upon, on more than one occasion."

"Then I do us both honor." His smile was as easy and graceful as his carriage. He handed her into a chair almost unconsciously, a striking contrast to Raven's palpable attentiveness. Eric Foster was a gentleman of proper breeding and training, through and through. "I would not have it said that I have courted you improperly, or treated you with any less virtue and respect than is your due. I believe you yourself have said that a widow needs time to grieve, more time than society often allows her. I respect that, Lady Angelique, and honor it."

She fought down the laughter at that, as she'd thrust away thoughts of Raven, earlier. *Rich, the irony of it.* "You have certainly been above reproach in that, my lord. When the time comes that I might entertain such marital thoughts—"

"You'll break every heart in the city," Lady Anne Carter, the young and pretty Baroness of Lansdowne, broke in to shower them both with the words. She'd nearly overset Angelique's plate in her enthusiasm. "Oh, you're looking ever so much better, dear lady! Are you *quite* recovered?"

"Yes, thank you, Lady Anne," Angelique smiled, carefully hiding her amusement at Eric's expression. His dismay at the interruption was momentarily palpable, though he covered it with yet another display of consummate good breeding.

"Well, good. Good!" Anne gushed. "And you, young man. You just keep after this lovely lady you've set your heart upon. You're a striking couple. Indeed! A much better use of your time than that Sultaire fellow, if you don't mind my saying so."

Angelique could almost hear Eric's silent agreement to the Baroness' views. She swallowed carefully (truly hungry, dissembling aside), and phrased her reply with precision, quoting from the Precepts of the Abbeé of Trumont.

"'But for the good lord / who must keep the fields of wheat and the fields of rye, / who must render up to his liege of all the things in his domain, / Shall he not also look to the stray sheep of his flocks, / and count them among his own, also?'"

She didn't even bother to smile politely; the truth of the words did not need such adornment. A woman who had truly been raised in a cloister of the Sisterhood of the Guardian Paladin would allow them to so stand on their own, after all. "My lord Eric. Lady Anne. I am not so free of sin myself that I can feel comfort passing judgment on Vincent Sultaire, or any other. So do I treat him."

"Well said, Carlisle." It was the venerable Countess of Remington come to support Angelique again—to the dismay of young Sir Eric. "I must say, I am truly chagrined at the predilections of some of our Auxiliary members for judgment and gossip."

Anne's cheeks flushed as though she had been slapped, but she was still young enough not to know what to do about it. She remained nearby as the aged Countess took a seat near Angelique, resting her cane across her lap. "I trust the Lady has seen fit to return you to us in good health?"

"Yes, my lady," Angelique replied, unconsciously straightening her spine in Lady Emilia's company. "Thanks to She Who Wards Our Prayers, and through the kind offices of Dr. Martin, who recommends a tonic for my memory, lest I again forget the need to eat like other mortals," she chuckled, taking a conscientious bite as if she were a biddable young girl.

"The Paladin does work through us all," the elderly matron agreed. "And it is not for us to judge how He chooses to do so." She turned to the still-flushing Baroness of Lansdowne. "Do be a dear and fetch an old lady a cup of tea?"

Angelique hid a smile. Was the woman supposed to say no? Apparently, Anne had reached the same conclusion, for she curtsied politely and glided off, her cheeks bright pink, but her head held high.

"And now, my child," Lady Emilia turned back to Angelique, a more serious look crossing her wrinkled face. "I must ask you to perform a small favor. And of you, my young Sir, I must ask patience and indulgence. The members of the press are insistent that one of our number, at least, give them an interview. I'm far too old for such nonsense, my dear. The Lady has blessed you with a wisdom beyond your years, however. Will you do so?"

Frustration threatened to win the battle against patience, but Eric fell back on duty. Hers, in this case. If he truly wished to marry this woman, he was going to have to get used to her social competence, and the demands it placed upon her.

Angelique blanched, and it was not entirely feigned. "Ah, my lady Emilia...it is not my place. Should not the Patroness of Name speak for the endeavor? It was that noble lady whose vision brought such beauty to us, after all."

"So it was, and so she has," the Countess replied. "As has her husband. But, it was the committee who did the work, you more than most of us. You deserve the credit, child. Modesty becomes us all; false modesty is as pretentious as arrogance. Never shy away from what is your right and due."

"Yes, my lady," Angelique agreed meekly, mind whirling. "But—I've never spoken publicly in my life! What does one say?"

"One answers their questions," the crone replied. "Never fear, child. This isn't politics, so the usual double-speak and taciturn tactics will not be required." The aged Countess, herself a rather large political wheel who'd been in the center of politics of the City State for decades, seemed almost regretful. "I have already insisted that one of their number only do the questioning. She is a girl of noble birth whom I have known since infancy. The others will simply take notes for their papers."

Well-caught now, the young baroness could only nod obediently to her elder's whims, and submit as gracefully as she might. Angelique had an unreasoning fear of speaking in public. Eric and the Countess would likely regard it as virtuous modesty, perhaps even shyness on her part, and count it among her better traits. Angelique herself, however, knew terror for what it was, and could not name it as a virtue.

Suddenly, the food on her plate was quite unappetizing. Still pale, she unthinkingly handed it to Anne, who was returning with the requested cup of tea; Angel barely remembered her manners in time. "You are no servant of mine, Lady Anne, but have warded my virtue as a sister might. Would you do a sister's further office, and lay this aside for me? I... have no further appetite for it."

Anne flushed slightly, but seeing Angelique's sudden paleness, she smiled in sudden understanding, and took the plate.

Angelique turned to the Countess of Remington with the look of one who was to be led to the gallows. "Where is it to be done, my lady?"

The aged crone "looked" at the paling Baroness of Carlisle for several heartbeats before replying. "I can have them called over here, if you like. I shall be right here to intervene should things get out of hand." The Countess of Remington was a favorite with the city's more disciplined reporters, but was shunned by the gossip rags. Annoying "the old battle-axe" was something most reporters would not chance more than once.

"I... I shall be grateful for your presence, Lady," Angelique admitted, striving with some success to keep the desperation out of her voice. Clutching the tatters of her dignity about her, she remembered who she was in this place, and turned to the handsome blond knight at her other side. "Sir Eric, you too, if you would extend me that kindness."

"You have ever but to ask, and I shall be at your side," the young man said, bobbing his head.

"Spoken like a true gentleman," Lady Emilia murmured.

"Who is to do the interview?" Lady Anne asked the Countess. "I'll fetch her for you, my lady."

Angelique smiled her gratitude. A lesser woman might have resented the dressing down she'd gotten earlier.

"The young Lady Katherine, of the *Paladin's Herald*." Anne nodded and moved off, wondering just when she'd decided that such duties were no longer beneath her station. Her counterpart was striving to get a real breath from within the whalebone of the corset she wore. It wasn't even laced that tightly, and yet was still so restrictive she almost felt faint. Panic tried to take her, but, conscious that Lady Emilia watched her measuringly, the younger woman backed it down with the same will she'd used to complete the yet-undiscovered theft.

It might have been hours, but was more likely only minutes later that a dark-haired, petite young woman in simple evening attire approached. She had the bearing of one raised in a noble household, though she wore neither badge nor pin that might have distinguished her family. She was followed by a gaggle of a half-dozen men and women, each with pad and pencil in hand. "My Lady Emilia, I thank you for giving us this opportunity," the young reporter said.

"Not at all, Lady Katherine. This city needs more journalists with noble bearing, even if they are not of noble birth. Now, as you all know," she went on, her tone changing noticeably, "it was the committee of the whole that organized this exhibit. However, rarely does the entire committee involve itself in the actual work necessary to see that such a production comes to fruition. For the success of this stunning display of artistic talent, we have to thank the young Lady Angelique Blakesly, Baroness of Carlisle." The matronly Countess patted Angelique's hand reassuringly. "It was she who did the bulk of the foot work, and the organizing required to see to its success."

Returning Lady Emilia's touch, Angelique accepted Eric's assistance to her feet, and faced down a personal dragon. It came to her, as she fielded the first of the polite questions put to her, that this was a task anyone of the Ladies' Auxiliary could have handled—a 'color interview,' the press often called them. Throughout, she felt the old dowager's sightless eyes studying her bearing, and evaluating her replies with relentless intensity. In truth, toward the end, Lady Emilia's regard was making her more nervous than the reporters, or their questions.

As Lady Katherine thanked her graciously and led her colleagues away, Angelique turned back to her mentor there in Fernwall, mouth flickering in suppressed mirth. "You set that up," she said, tone missing accusation only by inference.

Eric's eyebrows lifted at Angelique's uncharacteristic bluntness.

"Obviously." The old woman replied calmly, not at all ruffled. "And you did well."

Angelique laughed ruefully, and took the Countess' hand in hers. "Will you never cease pushing me, my lady? What have I done to deserve this?"

Lady Emilia's answering smile spoke volumes. "Often the loss of one thing leads to the gain of another. It has been so with me. Blindness has given me sight, child. A gift from the Lady, no doubt. But one day, after I am shut of this world, you may send a prayer of thanks for my having done so." She squeezed the younger woman's hands.

"For having left us bereft of your guidance and good sense?" she parried, glad for once of the socially-expected reply to that. "May our Lord cut out my faithless tongue with Isenbrand, first." On impulse, she bent to kiss her elderly friend's cheek. "May you be with us for many years to come, lady. Fernwall would not be the same without you."

"Lady bless you child, but I hope not!" The Countess snorted, but Angel lost the rest of what Emilia said, as a commotion arose at the door.

"I'm sorry, my lord!" The insistent voice of Liberaune's butler carried in from the adjoining room, interrupting all conversations. "But this is a *private* party. No one without an invitation is permitted."

"Will this do?" came a familiar voice in reply, rich with amusement.

Raven. Angelique felt as if her entire being leapt into joyous life at his voice. *Raven!* How had she so quickly become so accustomed to this living death without him? Like everyone else in the room, she turned her head toward the row, smiling faintly.

"It seems as if our scapegrace young lord is here," she murmured to no one in particular.

"Your salvation," Lady Emilia murmured, so quietly only Angelique could hear her, "and your damnation."

The younger woman's eyes flashed to her suddenly, wondering if Emilia had guessed something that Angel had held closely for months. But, would even wise old Lady Emilia understand?

"I see," the butler's voice eventually responded, though he sounded as if he were choking on the words. "Welcome then, young... lord."

There was quite a tittering from the corner where the Spring Maids had gathered as Sir Vincent Sultaire breezed into the room, his face alight and his eyes sparkling. He was dressed in an immaculate, pearl white tuxedo. A blood red, fluted rose graced his left lapel, and it looked like both banner and challenge. He paused to take in the assembled, hiding his thoughts behind that knife's-edge smile.

Angelique felt that metaphorical knife *thud* into her would-be suitor's heart. The evening was not going well for Eric. She couldn't pity him, though, for he would not have accepted it. Instead, she squeezed his arm gently and smiled. "I haven't thanked you for your support earlier, my lord. It was well done of you."

"It was my honor," he said thickly. "Would the lady honor me by joining me in the garden?"

All eyes watched Raven's charm and skill with prestidigitation cut a broad swath through the assembled nobility. For the Countess of Liberaune, he produced a lovely purple rose out of thin air (or rather, his sleeve), and thanked her outrageously for the invitation—which she had not sent, of course. His bold grace blunted most of the annoyance the lady's husband evinced at the rogue's presence.

Angelique gazed up at Eric's face. He clearly knew he'd lost this battle before it could be waged, and wondered if she had transgressed upon some unwritten societal rule about courtship, and what, if anything, she owed a man who clearly regarded her with more affection than she felt for him.

"It would not spare you, if I did," Angelique murmured, entirely distracted by Raven's progress across the room, charming lords and ladies alike, producing roses from hair, bustline, and air by the score in a virtuoso display of sleight-of-hand. The honor and courtesy he bestowed upon the ladies worked a bit of magic on mistrusting fathers and husbands, but because he was still Raven, it left most of the virgins present blushing furiously.

It took him nearly a quarter of an hour to make his way to where Angelique sat with her unfortunate suitor, the elderly countess, and the hovering Lady Anne. His eyes had locked with Angelique's halfway across the room, and the smile he'd borne since entering broadened on his face. And then he was there right before them, bedazzling Anne with a lovely pink rose. The baroness' cheeks matched its color perfectly as she looked at the flower that had magically appeared in her hand.

"Ah, wisdom also graces your presence this night, burning bright," he breathed, glancing at his lover, but turning to the countess. His countenance turned reverent, and he actually knelt before the elderly woman, taking her knotted old hands in his. Angelique wasn't sure whether she should laugh or be astonished at his antics. Fortunately for her, no one seemed to expect her to do either.

"The Lord and Lady have blessed you, my son," the old woman said, squeezing his hands, "But blessings, like molten metal in the forge, must be worked by skilled hands to be fashioned into a thing of beauty."

Raven looked at the aged Countess for several heartbeats, his face unreadable. Then he kissed her hands and, before them all, a perfectly white "Lady's Rose" blossomed there.

"For you milady," he murmured softly. "From the rakehell of Fernwall."

"A holy gift," she replied. "From one not so unholy as he thinks."

"Thank you," Raven replied simply, rising. Only then was Angelique sure of him; for all his irreverent ways, her secret lover bore a great respect for the elderly woman who was her benefactor here. This was yet another side to this very complex man. It was all she could do not to fling herself into his arms.

"If you will excuse me, milady," Eric murmured, also rising, and admitting defeat.

"As you will, dear friend," Angelique murmured, not quite knowing what to do. She'd never promised Eric anything, and yet she had known of his feelings for her. Even as he kissed her hand in parting, she wondered if that knowledge obligated her in some way of which she was not aware.

But, here was Raven, at a party where he'd no right to be other than what his boldness had earned him. That boldness had swept her heart away and breathed life into it; how she had ever managed to hide what she felt for him? How was it that only blind, old Lady Emilia could see? She sat

31

beside them quietly now, hands folded over her cane. Serenity illuminated her otherwise calm expression.

"Ah, burning bright," Raven breathed, barely keeping his own countenance within propriety's bounds. He took her hands and, in similar fashion to what he'd just done for Lady Emilia, grew a delicate corsage of deep red roses, right there before her eyes. "For you, milady." Behind that simple sentence was the truth of his heart, one he hardly cared to hide from the world.

Stunned speechless, Angelique tore her eyes away from the fragrant bouquet to gaze at him. Every fiber of her being felt as if it surged up through her eyes. As if from somewhere nearby, she heard that distant drumbeat again, and this time she felt it in the very depths of her bones.

Life... life... life. That pulse, headier than any wine, more seductive than sin, was louder in her ears than the breathless, tittering gossip swirling through the room in Raven's wake. He'd come to her again, calling her forth from this wretched tomb, from the living death she'd chosen for herself here.

Life... life... life.

From her nearby chair, Lady Emilia cackled softly.

"It would seem," Angelique whispered, clearing her throat to try again. "It would seem I owe you a word of thanks, Vincent. These are... lovely."

"Ah, burning bright, my simple legerdemain pales when compared to you," he replied softly, his heart in his eyes.

Unseen behind them, Anne Carter flushed and silently excused herself.

By the Lady's girdle, we are going to cause a scene, if we keep this up. Yanking herself back under control, Angelique voiced another soft "thank you" and pinned his gift to her bodice. The fragrance of summer roses swam in her head.

"But why are you here?" she asked, smiling in spite of herself. "I did not know you were to attend," she added, phrasing it carefully.

"You," he replied simply, melting her heart all over again. In her presence or out of it, he had the way of causing her concentration and good intentions to fly away. Putting her on his arm, Vincent headed them out to circulate. The single admonition which followed them from Lady Emilia's direction caused Angelique to stiffen.

"Patience, children. Patience."

She glanced back. The old woman still sat, smiling serenely. With a precognitive shiver, Angelique resumed her sedate pace at Raven's side.

"I believe the only hearts you haven't slain are yet in the garden," she mused, for his ears alone.

He chuckled roguishly and steered them in that direction, trailing a giant wake of speculation and gossip behind them. They descended the steps onto Liberaune's well-lit garden patio, drawing looks both covert and quite open as they did.

"Ah, yes, the *unsoiled* virgins, rather than last year's crop." His eyes danced in merriment.

Gods, but he is an unrepentant scoundrel!

"So, my love," he breathed softly. Now, that was a first. *My love*. He'd never called her *that* before. The pulse-beat she hadn't been able to shake rose into something like thunder inside her. "I hope you didn't mind my intervention too much."

"When have I ever?" she asked, the rhetorical question torn from her before thought could censor it. Too much was at work inside her, on too many levels of being to keep separate and distinct. *My love?* "I have not been able to stop thinking about you all evening."

"I like the sound of that," he murmured. "Ah, isn't this a lovely rose!" He'd trapped the eye of a white-gowned girl who was having an extraordinarily hard time keeping her eyes off of "the rakehell of Fernwall." Angelique got the distinct impression that the youth would rather have been in her own shoes, and wanted it so badly that it hurt to breathe.

With Angelique still on his arm and anything but forgotten, he paused to caress the younger girl's cheek, sending a shudder through the youth that started somewhere near her toes. When he pulled his hand away it bore a blushing, tender rose of palest coral. "May you blossom as beautifully," he murmured to the girl, handing her the flower.

They walked on, Angelique barely able to retain an expression of dignified impassivity. "If you don't stop that, I'll hit you," she swore, almost choking on her laughter.

The grin he flashed her was anything but repentant. "It's one way to get a bit of privacy," he murmured, his eyes following the trail the youth had made back to the clouds of white-gowned girls. They descended like a storm upon the maiden for whom he'd produced the flower, chattering excitedly. "And yet, we're still. . . 'chaperoned.'" He drawled the last word with heavy irony.

"That's my Raven," she whispered, voice trembling despite the irony in her own words. "Always one step ahead of everyone in the room."

"We can hope," he chuckled. In the privacy of the garden, he dared to caress her cheek. "My Angel. . ." and then, rather abruptly, he felt awkward, or perhaps embarrassed, by the sudden surge of emotions that threatened to spill out into the garden. There was so much he wanted to say; so much he wanted to allow himself the liberty to feel. Instead, he found himself speechless and numb, paralyzed by the emotional habits of a past still too close to the present. In his father's world, an unguarded word, the unexamined emotional outburst, the secret look caught brought whippings, enforced labor, weeks of mind numbing toil—or, most recently, a collar. For all of his carefully crafted, outrageous behavior for the public, Vincent just couldn't allow himself to express his heart to her freely, not here. Not now. *This* was different, and in a way he didn't yet understand.

Angel paced in silence at his side, aware of his turmoil, but unable to discern its causes. She had her own to manage, and it was growing more difficult by the second. As if drawn, she turned to Vincent, risking that much of her social standing for one heady moment in his arms, there under the summer stars. "Tell me you're taking me home soon."

His reply was barely whispered into her half-opened mouth, and was followed by the first of many stolen kisses. It was a simple affirmative that promised anything but simple pleasures, or consequences. They stood there in the garden amidst the symbols of their personal dichotomy: The tender, innocent dreams of youth juxtaposed against the hard, uncompromising duties of Guardian Paladin society, and of life.

"Yes."

Chapter 3

Despite their best efforts it took another hour to get away from Wilkinson-Foster's party. The tiny Lady Katherine, who wrote for the *Paladin's Herald*, insisted on "just another question or two," most of which were directed at the infamous Sir Vincent Sultaire, whose indenture, ironically enough, *could* be said to be Lady Emilia's doing. The changes to the law that subjected the nobility to the same terms of indenture as the common-born were just a few of the radical notions that Lady Emilia, with the backing of the people, had built in to their constitution. Sir Vincent was the first noble to have been sentenced to indenture under those laws, so the press was understandably curious. Vincent's urbane manner charmed them with the same easy faculty it had everyone else that evening. To Angelique's private amazement, it appeared his quick wit and ready tongue could dazzle most of the columnists there that evening almost as well as the powerful presence of the inestimable Countess of Remington.

His talent also saved Angelique immortal embarrassment over some of the more pointed questions: "Baroness, isn't there more to your relationship with Sir Vincent than meets the public eye?"

The gentleman who asked the question was a society columnist from a rather gossipy, weekly publication. Raven didn't turn so much as a hair in response. "*That,* goodman, bordered on rudeness. My Lord Earl," he called across the room to their host, as affably as ever. "I believe this man from the *Evening Star Gazette* has worn out his welcome this evening. I, for one, will not tolerate his impertinences to Lady Angelique."

And that was that, save for Eric looking like he'd just as soon stick a dagger in Raven's back for having saved Lady Blakesly's honor. Angelique managed not to look blatantly relieved, but then more than a bit satisfied as Lord Foster's footmen escorted the columnist to the door.

"I suppose I'll have to learn to do that," she murmured afterwards, fanning herself in relief. Eyes as green as the restless sea angled up to him. "Would you care to give me lessons, my lord?"

"Hold that thought," he recommended dryly. Capitalizing on the recent unpleasantness, he sought out Lady Beatrice and mentioned that, considering her recent illness, Lady Angelique might be a bit over-wrought by such rudeness, and was promptly matched by those who spoke of her dizzy spell, earlier. The Lord Earl himself suggested Sir Vincent escort "our dear Baroness" home—again, to his own son's bitter disappointment.

The young lord of Valemont didn't waste any time, however. In another half hour, Clarice had been sent back to Blakesly House by taxi, and the two lovers were at last in an enclosed carriage, clopping toward his Queen's Street flat.

"Finally," he breathed. "My darling, I was beginning to believe I was *never* going to be able to extract you from the grips of that crowd."

Her soft laughter filled the air around them, and heedless of her lovely gown, she threw herself into his arms—an unusual gesture for her, even in private. "The dead don't like to release their grip on anything, let alone other corpses. Lady's girdle, lover-mine! There are times they come so close... too close."

"Not while I'm around, my love," he murmured, enfolding her in his arms. There it was again. *My love.* That was the second time tonight.

Angelique shivered, there in the privacy of their carriage, grateful she no longer had to hide it. "No," she agreed. "Never, while you are around. You are the very breath of life, Raven. My love. The world is so very gray when you are not with me."

It was his turn to shudder, to close his eyes and drink in the full meaning, the total import of those words. "You know," he murmured finally, eyes still closed, "I have never been so, not to anyone in my life." Vincent looked at her again, catching glimpses of her face as the dimness around them shifted. A hand caressed her pale cheek, even paler now in the dim, flickering light cast from street lamps as the carriage passed through the well-lit streets of Angels.

"A love?" She shook her head, but her eyes never once left their rapt study of his face. "You don't let yourself be loved, Raven. Not easily. You're too well-defended against it. A woman has to be patient to see that inmost heart of you... and love you for it." Her hands, seeming small and frail there on his chest, smoothed up his pearly white waistcoat. What she felt at that moment was too large, and too true, to be contained any longer. It was a risk, on emotional ground—and she was more terrified, at that moment, than she'd been in years.

"To love you... as I do, *Mar'leven.* I love you."

Once free of her lips, the words quivered there, and Angelique fought the urge to flinch away from the scathing sarcasm that once would have been his reply. But... he'd wept, earlier. He had shared his tears with her, even if he had withheld their meaning. Instinct told her that it must have meant something...

His dark eyes, shadowed in the low light of the carriage, remained a mystery. He searched her eyes for a long moment for some sign of jest or trickery, some indication of what his doubts told him: that she could not be sincere. The clopping of the horse's hooves and the grinding of the carriage wheels over cobblestones were all that reminded her that time was, indeed, passing, for it felt as if her heart had stopped.

"I never thought I'd hear those words," he finally whispered, eyes still drinking her in. "Least of all from you."

"Why is that, Raven?" she whispered. "Did you think me immune to it? Incapable?" Angelique paused to swallow, only managing it with difficulty. Louis had often assured her that she could never fall in love, and for a very long time, she had believed it. "I could not be sure, myself," she confessed softly. "I've never felt this way before. Never been in love with anyone. Not like this."

"You were married once. Didn't you love your husband?" He felt her flinch. *Bad move Vince,* he thought, and immediately apologized. "I'm sorry. I have no right to ask that, I know." He sighed, and turned to watch the shops and parks of Angels pass, while the woman in his arms bit her tongue to keep silent while he thought.

"It's not you I question, Angel," he finally continued, speaking slowly, as if every word pained him. "It's me. The 'rakehell of Fernwall,' remember? The irrepressible playboy, second only to Captain Terrell himself. Much to fancy, perhaps, but not much to fall in love with, I would say."

Her hand on his chin pulled his gaze back down to hers. "Modesty is accounted a virtue, but you simply undervalue yourself, my darling." In the closeness and intimacy of the moment, Angel dared to say what she never would have in any other circumstances. "What you have shown me, and *given* to me, is all the more precious because I know you do not share it easily." A small smile flickered at the edges of her lips once again. "Your scapegrace ways are a defense, every bit as formidable as a suit of armor. Do you think I don't know this?"

The effect of her words hit him like a blow. She was almost sure she saw his head snap back, and tears filled his eyes, almost black in the gloom. "You are a remarkable woman," he said thickly. "I have no idea what I have done to deserve such as you. And, I love you, too."

He kissed her then, unhurriedly, a kiss full of his heart, a kiss in which Angel felt as if every particle of her being rose up within her, clamoring to be accepted and loved by him. For all the intensity of the feeling between them, the force of her own gave her a moment of panic, for there were still too many secrets to be kept, and too many lies between them.

In the face of the stark truth of her heart, and his, however, she would not let herself falter. Angel loved him with a passion that rocked her to the very foundation of her being. What she found even more remarkable was that he actually loved her, too. Joy flooded her eyes and spilled down her cheeks in shining rivulets. For once there was no witty repartee, no turning away on a moment's notice from emotions that were too delicate to touch, no shading the truth behind the power of lust. They clung together and wept, intimately, unabashedly, as the carriage traveled for well over an hour, halfway across the city to the building that contained his tiny flat, in the middle of the Merchants' Quarter.

Angelique's hands were still trembling when the carriage slowed to negotiate the acute angle onto Queen's Street. She pulled up the deep cowl of her summer cloak, knowing there would be few awake to notice their arrival. Raven climbed out, flipped the driver several shillings, then quickly led her inside.

"No wine," he murmured apologetically, closing the door behind her. "I'm sorry, beloved. I wasn't sure..."

Beloved. Another first. It was like a dam breaking.

"Ah, well." He'd lit the small candle by the door, then turned to face her, momentarily captivated at how her elegance and loveliness made his dingy flat seem like a lord's palace. "I guess we'll have to make do with each other."

"We always have," she whispered. Unable to bear being apart from him, Angelique threw off her cloak and moved into his arms again, pulling his face down to hers for a kiss to make him forget about wine, or the lack of it, or anything else other than *her*.

He picked her up, startling her again with his strength, and carried her into his bedroom. There he laid her out on the bed, then sprawled atop her, hardly able to bear it for the milliseconds his lips had parted from hers. Sudden tears stung in her eyes one more, spilling out from beneath the closed lids. Her lips pressed into his so hard it hurt, and yet he still wasn't close enough.

"Easy, my burning bright," he murmured into her panting mouth. "Let's rid ourselves of these vestments of aristocratic society so we can immerse ourselves in each other."

She nodded, shaking so hard she could barely stand whenever his hands left her. Angelique forced herself to her feet, turning her arms over backward to reach the hooks at her back, because not even Raven could know that this dress was constructed to open from the front, too.

More lies. She hated the cursed dress with sudden, irrational fury. *Lady's Love, let it burn to cinders, and take the damned lies away with the flames!*

"Oh, burning bright!" Raven, laughing gently, moved to unfasten the back of her dress. "First love has not robbed me of my manners. At least not all of them, I hope."

His words made her cry even harder. *First love. He's killing me.* "Just get it off me, Raven. Please." *And don't ask me to explain, because I can't...*

He chuckled, but complied. It was mere seconds before her lovely gown rustled to the floor, leaving her in little but her underthings. For perhaps the first time in his life, Raven wished the women of his caste were allowed to dress more simply. He just wanted to touch her, to hold her close, and have nothing between them; to crawl inside this new, precious thing they shared, and stay there, immersed in the sound of their hearts and bodies mingling in the total silence.

Angelique seemed to echo his thought, and amplify it—she stepped free of her discarded gown, then kicked it into the corner of his bedroom fiercely, and wiped the tears from her cheeks. "There are just times... when I loathe that, Raven. All of it."

He blinked, wondering if he'd understood her reference. "I'm not sure I got all that," he murmured, pulling her back to him to unlace her corset.

"*That*," she gestured imperiously, pointing to the shapeless pile of fabric and lace in the corner, "and all that goes with it." Angelique shook her head then, knowing she sounded irrational, and knowing that she couldn't really explain. As ever, it was easier to opt for the lie, and the bitter taste of it made her want to cry even harder. "It represents nothing so much as living death sometimes. I don't want to be dead, Raven. Not when you make me feel so very alive."

Then he thought he understood her. The rules, the strictures, the formalities, the enforced pecking order, the codes of proper dress, the interminable treadmill of "morally correct conduct" expected of the ruling class, and lovingly codified in Byron's *Manual of Proper Form* to which the ruling class were expected to pay lip service, at least, or face censure. They were the very rules, traditions, and customs his father and early tutors had tried to pound into his head—or his backside—for as long as he could remember. He'd been running from it, and from them, ever since.

How ironic. She's running away from all that by coming to me, and I've run right back into Lord Byron's stuffy societal regime by falling in love with her. "Then perhaps," he said huskily, fingers upon the last laces of her corset, "in each other we have found respite from the same interminable disease. The chains of Paladin society are something I've been trying to escape for as long as I can remember."

Angelique pushed herself free of her corset so quickly it might have torn, were it of any finer material, then hurled it with all her strength toward the crumpled dress, breathing hard and free for the first time in hours… since just after she ducked into a garden shack outside Liberaune Hall, hurrying back into the gown she'd just violently rejected. She stared at the heap of fabric on the floor, half-afraid it would stand on its own to confront her with every lie, every deception, every half-truth she'd ever uttered in this man's presence.

"*If love is your new truth, how dare you let him love a lie?*" it seemed to demand, the thought coated in Louis' slimy, condescending tones. "*You're nothing* but *lies, Angela Rose Corwin.*"

The fierce, new-born devotion she felt for Raven rushed through her like a cleansing fire, and she burned in shame. When she turned to face him, it was with a haunted look she knew he'd misinterpret—yet another lie of omission to add to her sins. "If you ever find a way to outrun it completely, beloved, come back for me. Help me win free, too? Please?"

"On that, you can count," he replied fiercely, peeling her underthings from her. Again, he had to step back and admire the lithe beauty that she was. The perfection of her small breasts, complemented by her slender waist, and the gentle curve of her hips. She still wore her heeled dancing slippers, and her strong, shapely thighs were yet covered by stockings and garters. Those simply added to the overall sensual appeal.

Vincent shook himself free of the trance her naked body always seemed to invoke. "Later, beloved. Dark thoughts later. Questions later. Social lies later. Tonight, let's just be together, and let that be enough."

"More than enough." Angelique said it with the force of a vow. She stepped up to him, helping him hurry out of his own formal wear. As handsome as he was in it, she wanted him free of it. She needed to hold him against her, skin to skin. Only when he was as naked as she was (more naked, as he wasn't wearing stockings) did she begin to relax, breathing deeply at the sight of him.

Raven was a lean, wiry man of unexpected physical strength, but at that moment, the muscles were quiescent under smooth, fair skin. A dark forest of lust and desire tangled at his groin, thinning to a shadow over long, powerful legs. Broad shoulders narrowed down to waist and hips. Again and again, he struck her with his fierce masculine beauty, which contained elements of the sleek virility of a jungle cat, and the power of a running wolf; his entire bearing radiated danger and excitement. For Angelique, it had always been a nearly irresistible combination.

He took her hands reverently, then led her back to the bed, stretched her out on the soft down comforter, and spread her wide before him. Her sex shone luminously in the low light of the room, silent testimony to her aroused state. He kissed her there, as deeply and reverently as he'd kissed her mouth only moments before, then slid atop her, his manhood sliding easily into her body. Their commingled moans were thick with passion, and with love acknowledged at last. It was like finally, *finally* coming home.

Angel burst into tears yet again, crying hard and holding him to her with all the strength in her arms and legs. The cushion of air between them grew, dense with heat and sourceless wellspring of new love, tinged around the edges with a nameless sorrow that seemed merely to accentuate the joy.

Home, yes... The thought suffused him. He was home at last, and home was within her... and she was within his heart, and never wanted to leave. *Home.* It was enough simply to be there together, coupled so tenderly. What urgency they felt was for their union, not for release and satiation.

As Angelique acknowledged these things, her body began to move in time with her heart, and with his. Words from the *Cantons of Joy* came unbidden, and swirled in the spaces that had somehow opened in her mind:

> *And know ye this also. From this day forward should any two or more of you join in communion in My name, there in your midst shall I also be.*

Blasphemous though it seemed under the circumstances, the purity and simplicity of the text pierced her as surely as her new love, thundering inside her like the coming of dawn. For a moment, she thought she must surely be mad, but there had been no judgment in the Paladin's words, no preconditions, nor any stipulations. In fact, it seemed to be saying that her confession of love to Raven, and his to her, made their joining a consummation, a holy communion, of sorts; an act of honor and commitment, at the very least, that needed no priest, church, or parish for legitimacy. As the *Cantons* stated it, the two of them had but to name it so, and in the eyes of their God, it would be so.

"Oh... my... God..." she gasped, body shaking with the immensity of a truth it couldn't hold, not on its own. "Oh, God... oh, Raven... *Mar'leven...*"

He rolled them over, putting her on top of him and caressed the supple skin of her back. "I... love you... Angelique," he whispered into her ear, his voice choked, his strong arms trying to pull her within his breast. "I love you. I love you. I love you." Each refrain brought new tears and new waves of joy; Angelique joined him in that chorus, her husky, tear-drenched voice whispering both harmony and counterpoint.

"Don't let me go," she sobbed, still gasping, wrapping her fingers in his soft, dark hair, kissing him around his words, and her own. "Hold me... I love you... don't ever, *ever* let me go!"

In one remote corner of her mind, she suddenly understood the tales of the mystics she'd heard, over the years; how, during prayer hour, they would flay their own flesh, tear it away in frenzied passion that looked, from the outside, like willful self-destruction. But oh, no... the passion, she knew now, was for a kind of dissolution in love. She knew it because, were it in her power, she'd do much the same: Tear away the flesh of her own body if it would help her be closer to him.

... join in communion in My name...

Something greater, something joyous and wondrous that was created in that moment by the essence of their very souls, born of each of them, greater than the two of them. It germinated in the joining of their two bodies, was watered by their mingled tears, and nurtured by their words of confession. The air around them became charged with the power of minds, words, bodies, and hearts so devoutly joined.

... join in communion in My name...

Deep within, both knew orgasm was coming; the first sacrament to a new birth, the last sacrifice to pretense and denial. It might even be an acquiescence to a new calling, a new life, a new future.

Say the Name.

It moved within her, as certainly as she moved atop him, and as surely as the climax that built between them. *Say the Name?* A name so holy and sacred most would have condemned her to the burning death for blasphemy for invoking it in the midst of an act of adultery? The questions caromed among the new, unmapped angles in her mind, fracturing and rejoining to compel her anew.

41

"... by the Paladin Himself," she cried out, rearing back to capture her beloved's eyes with her own, "and by the Lady Who embodies Him do I love you! In that name, I swear it, *Mar'leven*. Raven. Vincent! I swear it! *I love you!*"

The release from tension was spectacular, and it tumbled them, body and soul, into climax. Deep inside Angelique, Vincent's manhood exploded within her, the sacrifice of his seed flooding her sacred womb in a ritual as old as mankind. It coursed through them like a storm in spring, cleansing and purifying. When at last the chaos subsided, everything in them and around them stilled. They remained tightly wrapped in each others arms, but by then drenched in sweat; he still held deeply within her. As if to confirm the God's acceptance of their oath, the Clocktower bonged in the distance, and was echoed in church towers throughout the city.

Another quote intruded itself on Angelique's awareness:

And shall they, the young among you, leave the habitation of their mothers and fathers, and so join with one another. In their joining shall the sacrament be made; and having been made, they shall then become as one flesh in My sight.

Raven was stunned. All oaths were sacred to Guardian Paladins, but this one... She had locked their eyes, and hearts, their minds and their bodies, and she'd sworn a holy oath before the Paladin. In the throes of passionate adultery, stolen together from a life of lies, she had sworn her love before the Lord and the Lady—and the force of it had cascaded him into the most powerful sexual experience he'd ever shared. His mind refused to compass it. The import made him dizzy. He clutched at her even harder, closing his eyes to steady the room that was swirling around him.

"Ah, burning bright, what have you wrought?" he asked, nuzzling into her neck.

"I am not sure," she whispered, body finally at rest, so replete even her trembling had ceased. "I have never... there has never been anything like that... I just needed for you to hear me, *Mar'leven*. Beloved. Perhaps that is all it was."

He was silent a moment, drinking in the feel of her, wet and fragile in his arms, intoxicated on the scent of her perfume. "Perhaps..." he said finally. "But..."

Vincent hesitated, then pushed on. It wasn't as if this was going to be news to her, though it was the first time the topic had come up between them. "Beloved, I have had more lovers—or maybe 'had sex with' would be more accurate—more women than I can easily remember, and... well, I've never experienced anything like that."

It was her turn for silence, a quietude of thought that went on just long enough to make him doubt the wisdom of his confession to her.

Then she said, "I... had been told about them. Knowing your passion as I do, it was only reasonable to assume you had found outlets for it. I have... envied you that freedom, betimes." She let the silence fall again, as she tried to sort her way through jealousy, envy, and the fledgling love to which she'd just pledged herself.

"Is it love that transforms the experience, Vincent?" Angelique had never used his given name in private at all, but it felt appropriate, somehow, as if it were a name for a *beloved,* as contrasted with a *lover.* She had avoided discussing his former sexual liaisons, and could feel his relief at that. It ran off him like a river for several seconds.

Then he burrowed closer, kissing her forehead gratefully. "I don't know," he admitted. "It... it doesn't bother you?"

Pale blond hair shifted against his chest when Angelique shook her head and sighed. *How could I possibly hold your past against you, beloved, when my own is pitch-slimed?*

"I suppose it should. It's supposed to." She was silent another moment, then said, "I don't know. I rather think I pity those women in your past. They knew your body, and perhaps your mind. But they never got to share your heart. Or your soul." Ardent love flickered at the edges of her sensitive, beautiful mouth. "You've gifted me richly with both, *Mar'leven.* How should I be jealous of what you once shared with anyone else?"

Again, relief made him feel weak. "I don't understand everything that happened, but I'm very lucky," he murmured, caressing her tousled hair. "Maybe we both are."

Angel left a soft, wistful kiss upon his mouth, then lowered her head back to the safety of his chest. "Oaths are powerful things, so we are taught from earliest childhood. I kept hearing verses... from Holy Writ. The *Cantons of Ecstasy.* In my mind."

She squirmed uneasily, but as he held his peace, she tried to tell him what she'd felt, and experienced. "A most inappropriate time, and place, I thought, in bed with my lover, engaged in what most priests would consider to be an adulterous tryst. But they kept coming back to me, over and over. '*Chains of Light,*' chapter three, verse twenty-three. Familiar with it?"

He chuckled ruefully. "I must confess, Angel, I was never a very attentive student at catechism."

Angelique squeezed him tightly. "It's good I didn't expect you to be. '*And know ye this also. From this day forward should any two or more of you join in communion in My name, there in your midst shall I also be,*'" she quoted for him. "No judgments in that. No conditions. Just a simple statement: Any communion offered under His name is surely holy in His sight." Another, tighter sigh. "I am aware it isn't commonly interpreted that way, but it is what I... felt, for lack of a better term. Blasphemous, I suppose."

Her lover had grown thoughtful; he took the opportunity to shift their position so that he lie beside her, still coupled, sliding his renewed erection in and out of her lazily. "I would have to say what we experienced tonight runs counter to your average Paladin Church dogma," he said carefully.

"Whether that makes it blasphemous or not. . ." He shrugged lightly. "I'm afraid I'm probably not the one to discuss such things with, my love. The Paladin and I came to an understanding when I was sixteen. I live my life according to what seems right to me, and if the Lord and Lady aren't happy with that, then it's up to them to show me plainly how I've fucked up. It's amazing how often They just seem indifferent."

His lover stared at him blankly for a moment, then filled the room with rich, appreciative laughter that somehow wasn't loud at all. "Oh, Raven," she finally said, around her mirth, "it is indeed. It surely is, indeed. I cannot even begin to fathom why the Guardian Paladin would send words into my head, of all his wayward, disobedient children. Perhaps it was nothing at all, and it was love, and love alone, that created the experience we shared."

"And your oath?" he reminded her gently.

Silence. "I don't know, beloved. All I do know is that I *meant* it. Every word of it."

"Maybe that's the important part. Maybe that's the real power behind any oath." He shrugged, his interest returning to her body. "Right now," he murmured, his pace quickening. "I know I want more of you."

He pulled her across him until she straddled him again, their lips locked in a scorching kiss, love flaming anew through their union and their simple joy in each other, in being together, coupled so intimately; a carnal, and perhaps even holy, celebration.

Lady Emilia, Countess of Remington, shot bolt upright in her bed, a strangled gasp all that remained of her scream. In her dream, a tiny silver long sword, nuptial token of a Guardian Paladin bridegroom, had driven itself into the bride's bejeweled sheath, breaking both asunder. Before her sightless eyes, the horrid vision of the shattered marriage tokens remained crystal clear, undisturbed by her waking. The sword was now blackened iron; the jeweled sheath had turned to wood and leather, set with cut glass baubles.

"Bright Lady, have mercy," the old woman whispered. "The young have no patience."

Chapter 4

Blakesly House, Angels
16 Amerian 580, 0400 hrs.

The boulevard paving stones gleamed wetly in thick fog, shining almost like ice in the intermittent light. The streetlights themselves, all adorned with halos, illuminated the streets in the way saints were said to shed their blessed holiness. Fernwall was so quiet this time of night. Given her first moments of privacy to mull over the astonishing array of events in the last twenty-four hours, Angelique found herself sinking into deep, thoughtful silence. It was an unusual experience for her; though quick to comprehend most things, as a rule she did not enjoy the effort it took to manipulate information at any more than surface levels. Nor did she often care for the conclusions which inevitably came, when she did.

"Ah, burning bright, what have you wrought?" He'd asked, holding her so tightly it had been difficult to draw breath.

What indeed? There in his arms, so much was right, obvious, even. When she was with him, Angelique knew what she desired, and that with a depth of passion that continued to astonish her. She wanted a life with him under whatever circumstances permissible, a life full of excitement, passion, and this vivacity of being she knew nowhere else. She wanted to grow old with him, make him laugh, keep him thinking, guessing; always "burning bright" for him. . .

The trouble began when she found herself apart from him, and other truths, equally persuasive in their own ways, asserted themselves. For Lady Emilia and the other members of the Ladies' Auxiliary, Angel was the Baroness of Carlisle, a product of a cloistered upbringing, the widowed lady of Sir Enri Fin-Amôn of the Drak-Soeurpat estates, in what was left of the kingdom of Vin-Nôrë. And, as hard as she strained against the strictures of that society in Raven's presence, she could admit to herself that there was comfort and security in the civility she enjoyed as a noble lady of the City-State of Fernwall. After the childhood terrors of surviving (she couldn't think of that time as "living") in the sewers of the ruined capital, Püran-Khir, there was a great deal of charm to be found in good food well-prepared, in clean, beautiful clothing, and in a warm, well-lit home where she was safe from nightly beatings, robberies, and rape. Angel could admit to herself that, comparatively speaking, living a polite lie here among the Paladins of Angels in exchange for these things, and more, was a bargain any female who had once been trapped in that existence would have made, without a moment's hesitation.

And Ah would make it again, and again, with no regrets, she mused. Without the need for the discipline of the disguise, Angel found her mental voice slipping back to its more natural state, that of the young girl who'd learned Cascir as a milk language, though in a dialect from a land far south of Fernwall's paved streets. *Ah was not in Püran-Khir by my choice, but by any God and every One of them, when I had the chance t' get out, Ah took it, and brushed the dust from my boots as Ah boarded that ship.*

Boarded it, with Louis. Willingly. Happily, even. No matter which guise she wore, Louis always seemed to be there, hovering in the background with his under-bred manners and over-ripe opinion of himself. He'd changed, too, since they'd returned to this country, and seeing him here, contrasted against good men of real breeding, civility, and honor, Angel realized for the first time just how thinly the veneer of civilization laid over her old savior, protector, and mentor. He probably came the closest to knowing the whole truth of her, and in some ways, required the least amount of pretension from her. In other ways, he demanded more of her than she felt comfortable giving. *No sense in going there now, Angel. You made your choices. Louis is one of them.* She sighed aloud, turning her attention beyond the carriage window, out to where the fog rolled along the banks of one of the winding strands of the Caspian as it found its way to the bay.

But not even Louis c'n change how Ah feel, not where Raven is concerned. The steel-rimmed wheels took on a hollow echo as they rolled over the last bridge before the turning to the street where she lived. Home was nearby, somewhere out there in the fog. She recalled, with almost painful clarity, how small and frail her hands had looked, there in the dark, as they'd smoothed up the lapels of Raven's waistcoat. How she'd finally confessed her heart to him, and had held her breath until she was sure he had not rejected her for it.

If Raven had any way t' see the inmost truth of me, would he still love what he'd find there? Who am Ah, really? Is Lady Angelique Blakesly any more or less real than Iris? Am Ah just Raven's "burning bright?" Or Louis's pretty little fuck-toy? Lackey? Or worse, his pawn?

Or maybe you're really still just Angela Rose Corwin, daughter to the ex-mistress of the old Duke of Asbury's brother. You're nothing but an inveterate liar and confidence artist, pulling off the sham of the century, living in the center of a web of lies and deceiving everyone, even a man you just this night professed to love.

The trap rolled to a halt at the address Angel had specified. She exited quickly, paid her fare, and then hurried through the back-garden entrance to her home. She let herself in quietly, knowing her housekeeper slept soundly,

46

but even so, she had no wish to advertise her "shameless" state to the old woman, who disapproved of everything by nature. Even though the house had been open for a year, Angel had yet to staff the place appropriately—a time-consuming, painstaking process—and for the moment, she was glad of it.

"Ah, burning bright, what have you wrought?" Dawn had just begun to leech the inkiness from the waters of the harbor by the time she'd eased her way out of the gown she'd worn to the party. Tears fell unnoticed upon her hands, which shook as they undid the hidden clasps.

Clasps in the *front* of the gown, so that it would be possible for Angelique to get in and out of it without assistance. Necessary for her alibi earlier, hateful to her now; but, rather than kick away the dress and the detestable lies it represented, she refastened the clasps and laid it upon the end of the bed. It was Clarice's duty to care for it, though Angel herself had been taught how, once, and could have done it.

Such a thing would not have been proper for one of her elevated station, of course.

Angel sighed, shrugged into her robe, and sat in the rose-upholstered chair by her window. She brushed out her hair and watched the world pale into grayness with the advent of the sun, still lingering sleepily below the eastern mountains. For all the splendor of the morning to come, Angel's eyes were turned inward, remembering. She'd professed her love—more than that, she'd gone beyond that simple declaration, and had plunged headlong into either salvation or blasphemy, depending upon how one wished to view it. Oaths carried much significance for those who followed the tenets of the Guardian Paladin. In a surfeit of passion had Angelique called on Him, and the Lady Who Embodies Him, to witness her declaration of love for Vincent Sultaire.

Foolishness. Perhaps. But the climaxes that had resulted immediately afterward had left them both stunned, reeling, and uncertain of what had happened.

"Ah, burning bright, what have you wrought?" He'd whispered the question, as stunned as she had been by what had happened. Angel had no satisfactory answer for either of them.

How can Ah swear t' love him when Ah can't even tell him who Ah really am?

The sky had resolved itself into pale azure blue, reflected in waters of the harbor below and in her memories of Raven's eyes. Clarice moved about in the sitting room just beyond her bedroom door; sails bellied out on ships making their way out of the harbor on the morning tide, bound for ports all over the world. This day had a will to begin before she'd even put to rest what had happened in the one before.

How could she profess to love him when she did not even know who she really was? *Perhaps it is finally time for me to discover that. It might even be that Raven would help. One thing is certain: Louis certainly won't.*

Disarranging the covers on her bed to simulate the sleep she hadn't gotten, Angelique Blakesly stepped into her private sitting room. As was always the case, her morning tray rested on the low table before the divan, with the new day's correspondence just beside it. She retrieved the strong coffee Clarice had brought, sweetening it liberally before riffling through the modest stack. She knew she'd need its energizing effects before this day was done.

She hadn't gotten to the bottom before the summons arrived

*   *   *

Bishop-Florian Memorial Hall
16 Amerian 580, 0700 hrs

The hired carriage bearing the Lady Angelique Blakesly jerked to a stop before the massive edifice of Bishop-Florian. The horses hadn't fully come to rest before the blue-jacketed men and women of Fernwall's law enforcement division had seized their heads and demanded the driver halt. *More than time Carlisle had a carriage of its own. A coat of arms on the door would have saved all of us some trouble this morning.*

Angelique exited the carriage holding the letter of summons before her like a shield. The officer in charge accepted it, read it gravely, then called off his squad.

"Begging your pardon, my lady, but we're under orders. If you please, one of my squad will escort you up to the crime scene."

"I would please, indeed. Thank you, Constable," For his benefit, she tried to muster a brave smile, but failed. The man, an older fellow, seemed understanding. "What... what has happened here? The summons isn't very specific. Only that the Santí exhibit was under investigation."

He sketched a regretful bow. "I'm sorry, Baroness, but I'm not permitted to say. Belike you'll find out when you get up there."

Angelique nodded, and followed by a rather square-looking person in another blue jacket, she ascended the steps to the grand entrance at the front of the hall. Her escort seemed sufficient to get her past most layers of interference, and what he could not, her summons did. Openly curious now, and looking no little intimidated by the number of personnel the police could bring to bear on this matter, she entered the old section's third floor and was immediately accosted by Lady Beatrice Wilkinson Foster. The old noblewoman looked as if she were ready to spit nails, Angel mused quite privately. Her sharp eyes were raking the assembled as if she'd expose the guilty by the force of her will alone.

"Baroness," the countess snapped. "You've heard, I trust?"

"Why, no, my lady. I had not," Angelique began, but was interrupted by a weepy Mercía Devon.

"Oh, it's *just* horrid." The portly Baroness of Bonsall should never have been caught crying in public if she could have prevented it, Angel mused. "That lovely necklace! Vanished! As if it took flight all on its own..."

"Hush, Mercía," the countess replied, snapping orders like the cavalry officer she'd once been. "My Lady Angelique, the *Mâgun-Zak* has been stolen. Sometime during our party last night, if the local constables are correct. Their chief investigator will wish to speak with you presently, I'm sure."

She gestured imperiously over to where stood a man who met the stereotypes so vividly he could have been nothing else but a "cop."

Gaust, as though summoned, noticed the new arrival and headed in Angelique's direction. "Good morning, my lady," he greeted her, bowing to her perfunctorily. Gaust was a thick man with above average determination and minimal education. Grit and literacy had won him a warrant during the war, and he doggedly parlayed that rank into an inspector's badge after mustering out; but nobody had ever accused Gaust of being overly bright. "Stubborn as a mule and dumb as an orc," was Roland's favorite private description.

"I'm Inspector Philip Gaust, my lady. I'll be leading the investigation. I hope you don't mind if I ask you a few routine questions." He turned without awaiting her answer, and motioned for a police clerk to take notes.

"This lady is Angelique Blakesly, the Baroness of Carlisle." Lady Beatrice instructed the man sternly. It was plain that the countess would brook no foolishness where the observance of proper forms and customs was concerned.

"It's quite all right, my lady Countess," Angelique murmured, unconsciously smoothing the front of her fine linen skirt. "Of course I shall answer the inspector, as best I may."

"Thank you, my lady," Gaust murmured. "Now then: At what time did you leave the exhibit last night?"

"At about twenty-thirty, I believe. With the rest of the Ladies' Auxiliary committee." The countess nodded her agreement with that.

"And you went where?"

"*'My lady,'*" the Countess prompted him, eyes flashing dangerously.

Gaust flushed, though it appeared to be more in irritation than embarrassment. "Forgive me, Countess. Investigative habits are sometimes a bit abrupt. Where did you go after leaving here last night, *my lady?*"

"Into a carriage, Inspector Gaust." The corners of Angelique's mouth flickered almost imperceptibly.

The clerk snickered—until Inspector Gaust glared at him.

Oh, Lady's Garters, this is not the time for irreverence! "With the Baron and Baroness of Lansdowne," Angel added, almost at once, "for the ride over to Liberaune Hall."

"I see," he murmured. "And you spent the evening at the party with the other ladies of the Auxiliary, is that correct?" He was watching her intently. Too intently, as it turned out. He was making it almost impossible for her to remain serious about any of this.

"I did."

He shuffled through the notes on his tiny pad. "The baroness, uh, hm, Lady Anne here, says that you had a fainting spell at twenty-one fifteen, and were then taken into a nearby sitting room to recover, supervised by a Doctor Martin."

At his second lapse in as many questions, the countess again put her foot down. "*Inspector* Gaust, you will either address the ladies here by their titles, or with the proper honorific, *or* I will see you removed from this investigation for unprofessional conduct!"

Before he could draw breath to answer, Raven was there. He strode onto the scene of the crime, the hem of his great-coat flying behind him. Angelique's face froze into the mask of mild irreverence she'd worn, even as her heart stopped inside her chest. *Raven is here...? Why in the world...?*

The answer hit her with the equivalent force of a blow. *Of course he's here, don't be a idiot. His indenture, remember? Likely he's here to help Gaust, so take a breath, and try not to act like a damned fool.*

Gaust spotted Raven, and lumbered over to him. "I need you to get your butt up to the roof, Sultaire," he began. Several of the ladies winced at his blunt language.

"Report," Raven ordered, looking the larger man dead in the eyes. Angelique started, then concealed it by pretending to twitch her skirt away from a display rack. Her surprise was genuine, for the level of command authority he invoked with that one word was absolute. She'd heard ship captains who couldn't have managed it.

"I don't think you understand the situation here, kid," Gaust replied, as though he *were* talking to a child. He had been waiting *years* for his promotion to chief inspector. This was his big chance to prove to Roland he was worthy of that authority, and he'd be damned if he was going to let an upstart nobleman's wayward brat stand in his way. "You're a convict who escaped the auction block because of a rich daddy and a noble birth. And now, you've received your obligatory noble promotion to chief inspector. You think anybody on this team's going to take you seriously? Shit! We've got a girl fresh out of the academy with more experience than you. So why don't you just do what you're told, stay out of the way, and let the *real* cops do their jobs."

What happened next was a blur. One moment Philip Gaust was standing there. The next he was sprawled on the floor, blood running from a torn lip. Raven hadn't changed expression, and his rapier was at the man's throat before his eyes could clear.

The room was deadly quiet. The rest of the team members migrated to the scene to watch, filing in behind Angelique and the other noblewomen silently. Normally, a challenge to a duel was issued with a cursory slap. That the new arrival had seen fit to deck the man who'd said he was in charge told them all they needed to know about Vincent Sultaire's intentions.

"Your badge," Raven growled, his voice deadly quiet. "Show me your badge or draw your sword."

Oh, Lady's Mercy... Raven, don't do this...

"You wouldn't dare," Gaust replied, his eyes challenging. He wiped the blood from his lip, apparently unconcerned about the sword pointed at his

50

throat. "A fucking bond-slave, holding a cop at sword-point. Get serious. Arrest this bondsman!" he shouted. Angel caught her breath.

Raven's other hand dipped into his pocket and emerged, holding up his badge, mounted underneath his family's coat of arms. Across the badge, enameled blue letters blazoned the word CHIEF. "Anybody who obeys that particular order will not only lose their badge, but will find themselves on trial for assaulting a knight of the state."

Those who had dared begin to obey Gaust froze in their tracks. It was all Angelique could do to restrain herself from going to stand proudly at his side. This was yet a fourth side to her irreverent, rakehell lover. He was going to burst her heart, if he kept this up.

"You see," he told the man on the floor and all who were listening, "not only have I been promoted chief inspector, I am still under arms, a sworn knight of the Duke of Trobiere and of the City-State of Fernwall." It was an odd twist to the law, but the statement was quite accurate. Technically, he was a slave; but the court had quite carefully refrained from stripping him of his knighthood, an important distinction in his status that left him disgraced, but not removed, from the ruling class. Slowly, he lowered his sword to Gaust's waist, hooked the bell guard of his sword and pulled the weapon out of its scabbard.

"You've been issued a challenge, Inspector Gaust," Sir Vincent went on, his voice still icy calm, "and you've been given an order to show me your badge."

Raven, Raven, are you out of your mind? Angel's mind was screaming. *He outweighs you by thirty kilos...!*

Philip Gaust slowly got back to his feet, and equally slowly took his sword from Sir Vincent. Then he glumly showed the young lord his badge, which was pure silver, the word INSPECTOR undifferentiated from the field.

Putting it away, he took in the rest of the room. The other officers on the team were around, as were the bulk of the Ladies' Auxiliary, knights, baronesses, and countesses, most of them. He had over-reached himself, and underestimated his opponent—badly. Even if he won the sword fight, he would still face a reprimand, and possible dismissal.

All eyes in the room were now on him. The decision was his, and his alone. There was only one choice, and it apparently was a painful one. Everyone in the department knew Philip Gaust had wanted only one thing in his adult life: A badge like the one Sir Vincent now carried, and the title, prestige, and power that came with it. As if holding firmly to that thought, he reversed his sword and knelt before the knight.

"I will serve under you, Sir Vincent," he mumbled, holding the hilt up to Raven. Unheard by anyone, Angel slowly released the breath she hadn't been aware she'd been holding.

Vincent sheathed his sword, and took the one proffered. "Thank you," he told Gaust. Placing the blade on the larger man's shoulder formally, he added, "and I accept." Then he reversed the blade, and offered it back to its owner.

51

The release of tension in the room was as palpable as the shift of command. Angelique experienced a sudden, inexplicable attack of nerves. She fought her way back to self-control if only to be worthy of him, and of the authority he'd just assumed. Most assuredly, she ignored how carefully she was refusing to think of the consequences of what this meant.

"Now then," Vincent went on affably, as though nothing had happened. "Where are my inspectors? I want to know what's gone on while I was being briefed by Grumpy."

Titters of laughter wafted through the room, releasing more tension. Gaust was joined by a young woman in her early twenties. "Barbara Cole," he gruffly introduced her. "Just over a year out of the academy. This is her second case, first burglary. She just finished the Boweman murder case. We may lose some time from her to the trial, but..."

By then, Vincent knew that was routine. "Chief Clerk!" Sir Vincent called across the room, turning his attention to another matter. "Get over here! Inspector," he then greeted Cole, and turned back to Gaust, and said, "I'll be with you in a moment."

The two inspectors retreated respectfully as an elderly-looking, uniformed officer approached. "I want a summary of all preliminary reports in my hands in fifteen minutes."

He clapped the old officer on the shoulder, sending him on his way, then turned his attention to the assembled members of the Ladies' Auxiliary. "My lady Countess, and ladies all, " he bowed before them gallantly. "I beg your forgiveness for that bit of unpleasantness. Inspector Gaust is a bit of a bulldog at times." Angelique, who knew him well, caught the irreverence just beneath the proper, dignified exterior.

"Am I to assume from that uncouth, vulgar display that *you* are to be the inspector in charge of this investigation?" Lady Beatrice asked—rhetorically in light of what had just happened, but it still required an answer.

"Those are my orders from the commissioner, my lady," Vincent smiled. "And I can assure you that the next time such discipline is needed on this investigation, the perpetrator of this crime won't be lonely on the auction block. Now, I expect the members of the Auxiliary will be available at need for interviews, and so on?"

"Some few of us have already been questioned," the countess admitted, not quite mollified but obviously unwilling to engage in yet another vulgar display. "Inspector Gaust was interviewing Lady Angelique when you arrived."

His gaze flicked to her. In contrast to his behavior the night previous, he confined his greeting to a mere nod. Still astonished by his behavior, and uncertain what to think, Angel merely returned it, discreetly.

"Then I'll review those reports before subjecting any of you to the deadly excitement of further police procedure," he drawled. "Now, ladies, if you please, events this morning have been handled poorly enough, already. You could help matters considerably by either confining your movements to specified areas of the building, or retiring to more comfortable quarters."

"Then I believe we shall retire," Lady Beatrice announced, gathering her subordinates to her with the simple act of arising from her chair. "We'll be in the restaurant on the top floor of the new section, young lord. Having tea, or what have you, until we are released."

"My Lady Beatrice, I doubt they shall be prepared for custom this early," Mercía said dubiously.

"Then they shall either *become* prepared, or lose their positions," the countess stated flatly. "Ah, there's Director Gregory. Such things are the stuff of *his* position, after all."

"You're the chief inspector on this case?" boomed an older, rotund man from across the room. The fellow waddled hurriedly in Vincent's direction, the sea of bodies between them parting like a bow wave.

"Sir Vincent Sultaire," one of the other uniformed officers supplied.

"Well, my young fellow," the fellow wheezed. "My name's Gregory, Executive Director of Bishop-Florian Hall." He bobbed a perfunctory bow. "And you just need to do something about all this straight away, young man. I can't have this entire— "

"Has all good form simply evaporated today?" the countess of Liberaune demanded, working her way up to full voice in those seven words. "Chief Inspector Sultaire was introduced to you as 'Sir,' Director Gregory. A man of your position should not so presume!"

After a startled look at one of the main patrons of the hall (therefore directly responsible for his livelihood, of course), the huge man's entire bearing changed. "My Lady Beatrice, I crave forgiveness for my over-boldness," he cringed, nearly falling over himself to take the countess' hand, "but, they've closed down the hall, my lady Countess! Bishop-Florian Memorial Hall simply canNOT be closed down over the whims of the constabulary!"

After staring down Gregory to the point of insignificance, she wrenched her hand away from him, and turned one sharply raised eyebrow to the knight who'd said he was in charge. "Sir Vincent?"

"Goodman Gregory," Raven drawled in his best nobleman's voice. "*I* put that order in place. I did so under the authority vested in me as chief investigator of this case by the parliament of the City-State of Fernwall. Not even Commissioner Roland would dare countermand that order and, under the circumstances, I most certainly *will not* change it. An irreplaceable item of incalculable worth, on loan from a distinguished collector who is also a scion of a powerful Vin-Nôrëan family, has been stolen. I'm sure you can begin to fathom the political ramifications."

"But… but—"

"Under the circumstances, Director Gregory, you've been outranked," the countess of Liberaune stated, cutting him off neatly. "Since your agenda for the day just got cleared, you can make sure Diva is ready to receive those of us who await the pleasure of the police to give our statements and be dismissed."

"But—" Gregory sputtered again, vocabulary momentarily reduced to that single syllable. Then he recovered himself. "That's precisely the problem, Countess! They won't let in *any* of the staff! There's no one in the restaurant right now. They can't get in!"

Again, Lady Beatrice flashed that eyebrow at the younger nobleman like a blade.

"Countess," Vincent sighed. "As I'm sure you're aware, and I believe I've mentioned, thus far this case has been handled deplorably. Cases such as these are resolved through collecting and collating details, my lady. Every extra body tramping through the building reduces our chances of discovering those details and so reassembling what actually happened. So I would appreciate it if you would use a suitable facility *off* these premises."

With a lofty nod, she assented. "I merely meant to keep us all within your convenience, my young lord, but if that is not necessary, then we all certainly have better things to do with our mornings." She looked over the scene again, and shook her head. "We were warned. We should have listened." Then the formidable countess turned her attentions to her subordinates again. "My ladies, you are welcome to join me at Liberaune Hall this morning, if you wish."

With that, she swept out, the lower ranking women trailing behind her. Angelique was one of the last to leave. She caught Raven's eye, and smiled unconsciously.

He winked at her, and blew her a surreptitious kiss, then turned his attention to the case before him—and his new command. A wave of his arm motioned his two inspectors back over. Raven almost absently took in the approaching figure of Inspector Cole. She was a small woman with dark brown hair, and big brown eyes that sparkled with intelligence. Well-endowed, and curvy to the point of being voluptuous, she was actually quite attractive. She was also eying him rather closely.

"It was Spider's job," Gaust began, as he too stepped forward. His new boss hadn't requested a report, but Gaust knew the routine as well as any of them. "To the letter. The alarms weren't triggered, several locks were melted open, others picked. The guards were lured into traps. A couple of them report seeing a black-garbed figure before they were drugged—another Spider trademark. They were secured with silk cord, and the the ingress and egress route was from the roof, via silken line. Quite a list."

"But nobody's been up top yet to check things out?" Raven asked.

"Not yet," Cole replied. Even her voice was attractive, low-pitched and husky. "We've been kept pretty busy dealing with guards, and trying to keep the public from tramping all over the scene before the blue jackets got the building cordoned off."

"I've sent several officers to pick up the Spider," Gaust continued. "We've had his residence under surveillance for several months now, just waiting for him to try something like this. All goes well, this could be the shortest case in history."

"I don't think the Spider's going to be that stupid," Cole supplied. Gaust gave her a dirty look, but the woman refused to be intimidated. "He's reputedly pulled off six burglaries, all without getting caught, or even leaving enough incriminating evidence for a conviction. It doesn't make sense that he's just going to be at home sleeping after doing something like this."

Raven smiled. The girl was a quick learner.

"Sir Vincent," boomed a deep baritone. The owner was a huge man, whose police uniform marked him as a full-fledged constable. Vincent signaled, and the man marched up. "Inspector Gaust ordered us to arrest David Cooper, the man known as the Spider. He was at his residence, asleep in bed, Sir. He's in chains, headed downtown right now."

"Good call, Cole," Raven chuckled. Then he turned to Philip. "Gaust, since this was your idea, why don't you trot over the headquarters and interview the man. Cole can finish up with the Ladies' Auxiliary. We'll meet for dinner there, in the cafeteria, at seventeen."

Gaust nodded. "If you'll come with me then, Inspector," the constable said. Raven watched them head out, then turned back to Barbara Cole.

"Alone at last," he grinned at her roguishly.

She glanced at the horde of inspectors and blue jackets the room. "We're obviously using a definition of the term with which I'm not familiar," she noted wryly, turning back to him. "What is it you want me to disinter from the noble ladies of the Paladin's Auxiliary, Sir?"

He chuckled again, remembering how Angel had spoken of them similarly, just the night before. "Every minute detail there is to know about them, the meetings they held, and the work that was done to put this show on. Rumors, gossip, how good the tea was. *Everything!*"

This time, she turned to look about the room in earnest. "You don't think it was the Spider, either." It wasn't really a question.

"Would *you* use every classic trick in your arsenal to steal something like the *Mâgun-Zak*, and then go home to bed?" The question was rhetorical, and they both knew it. "Somebody went to a great deal of trouble to frame the man, precisely so that an inspector like Gaust would come along and follow that trail—probably long enough for the necklace to be smuggled out of the country, but that's just a guess. Our job, Inspector, is to find the trail underneath the trail."

Cole nodded thoughtfully. "Minute details. The meetings. Rumors, gossip." She flicked a dark glance up at him. "The tea. This is going to take me a while, you know. There are probably a dozen members of that committee."

He nodded. "I know. And it's probably a waste of time, but it has to be done on the off-chance that it's not."

He watched as Cole debated with herself internally for several moments, not interfering until she'd reached her decision.

"I've already heard a rumor, if you're interested, Sir."

Raven looked pained. That was the second "Sir" in as many minutes. "Inspector, when we're more or less alone call me Vincent, or Raven—my nickname—*not* Sir. I've been running from my patronage all my life. I don't intend to wallow in it just because Roland was stupid enough to make me a chief inspector.

"Now, what's your rumor?"

Cole gave him a minute shake of her head, a minimal gesture, then stepped away from the bustling work going on around them, putting a layer of discretion, and hopefully privacy, about them. "The rumor I heard was that *you* were pretty high on the list of suspects," she murmured, meeting his gaze unflinchingly. "Nobody on the force is blind—except for Gaust, maybe—or deaf. Everybody knows you've been seen with one of those ladies, yourself. She was here, in fact. The Baroness of Carlisle. If anyone could pull a job like this, and needed inside information to do it, it would have been you. Or so the rumor mill says."

She hadn't quite called him "sir" again, but it hung on the end of that remarkable statement nonetheless. Vincent stared at her hard for several heartbeats.

So that's what the old fox was up to. "I'll be damned. Old Grumpy's more adept than I gave him credit for," he murmured, more to himself than to her, it seemed.

"But no finesse," she rebutted, shaking her head. "If he'd been smart, he'd have let you come in here uncontested and given you enough rope to hang yourself with, if you were guilty." Raven noticed that she was still watching him quite closely.

He chuckled again. "That's not exactly what I meant," he said ruefully. "No offense, Inspector Cole, but if my jailor had really suspected me, I'm sure he would have put someone better than Gaust and more experienced than you on the team to ferret out the truth. What he said about Philip Gaust to me in private this morning does not bear repeating in polite company. And from what I know of the man's history, it's pretty accurate."

Cole shrugged. The side-motions were disguised by the dark blouse she wore, to Raven's private disappointment. "I didn't credit the commissioner with the rumor, Sultaire." The name was a compromise. She didn't have enough experience to conceal that completely. "It's pretty widespread in the ranks below that, though. Do with the information as you see fit. I just thought you ought to know."

"Thank you," he smiled. "In a way, the rumor's quite correct. I could have done it, and I think that's why Roland gave me the case. Now, unless there's something else, you should probably get started."

"Right. See you at seventeen then, at headquarters."

He watched her go, enjoying the view, then turned to the miasma of confusion around him. The supreme irony of her rumor was that he was a bit envious of the thief—not so much that he'd pulled it off. Raven had gotten away with his fair share of "impossible" crimes. No, it was for the money involved. The *Mâgun-Zak* itself was probably unmarketable, but that didn't mean some rich crime boss might not have wanted it. So, assuming that he didn't get caught, and was smart enough to bargain for a good commission, that fellow was now one rich son-of-a-bitch who could afford to live out the rest of his life as he damned-well pleased.

Why hadn't *he* thought of this?

Never mind, Vince. You're on the other side now, remember? Or so everyone thinks, anyway.

It took several hours to get the chaos turned into some semblance of order, so it was nearly lunch time before he had a chance to look at the evidence on the scene first-hand. There wasn't much, and again he felt envy for the thief. A consummate professional, who'd left no trail with an obvious double for disguise.

Or perhaps, the double trail is the real one?

Interesting thought. He'd done that a time or two, too. Which would mean the rope to the roof was real, and not a sham as he'd first thought. Only one way to find out: Climb it.

He stripped off his overcoat and jacket, then unfastened his cuffs and rolled up his sleeves in preparation. *Whoever did this was athletic,* he mused as he shimmied to the roof. *Okay, now we're up far enough. Over we go, and... there.* Doing a handstand on the rope, he lay himself face down on the roof, unknowingly repeating the exact same motions Angel had gone through the night before.

At this location, the roof of Bishop-Florian Hall was nearly flat, pitching sharply less than a meter back from the edge. He stood up with a grunt, and looked around. The roof here, like roofs all over the city, had piles of ash built up in windrows between the various peaks of the complexly-constructed building. Not two meters from where he stood, he spotted four distinct footprints in the ash, headed towards the nearest western pitch. The trouble was, they were all wrong!

*   *   *

While her lover eased himself somewhat successfully into his first command, Angelique returned to her townhouse at the far western end of Angels. She ate a light brunch, then canceled all but one of her remaining appointments for the day. There was some thought, or realization, just outside the scope of her ability to reason at that moment, some understanding or revelation that was going to give her a great deal of trouble, until she had resolved it. With some deep instinct for self-preservation, however, she understood that teasing it out at that moment might well have been disastrous. What she needed, and intended to get before the next crisis descended upon her, was sleep.

She collapsed into bed for what turned out to be a blessed six hours of uninterrupted, almost dreamless slumber. It was Clarice who awakened her even then, bringing in a tray with afternoon tea and tiny sandwiches, along with a stack of calling cards, and the paper the baroness had not had the time to read that morning.

"Oh, no, dear, put it on the table," Angelique insisted, pulling a light robe over her shoulders and swinging her legs out of the bed. "I'm not an invalid, after all. Just tired. The last few weeks have been..."

"Too much work, if milady will forgive my saying so," the girl insisted, obediently placing the tray and then arranging the table attractively. "You put so much of yourself into that exhibit, and now it's been ruint by a common thief!"

Or an uncommon one, perhaps. The girl's indignation bore all the earmarks of the adolescent, Angelique noted, seating herself in her chair by the open window. The sun felt warm upon her skin, even in the fresh breeze, and the waters dancing in the harbor were brilliantly blue. The day had remained bright, after all. *Ah'd half-expected t' find a storm brewin', but Ah can't think why.*

Something tried to intrude itself upon her awareness just then, but her maid's fussing proved a welcome distraction.

"No, thank you, Clarice. I shall manage the rest of this on my own. Thank you." With a sigh, she turned her mind toward the cards on her tray. "If you'll return in an hour or so, you can help me dress for my day."

Clarice bobbed a curtsy and withdrew. Her ladyship looked so much better after her nap, long though it was. The cook and the housekeeper would be glad to know it.

Angelique sat back and sipped her tea, alone with her thoughts again. The events of the day past, and earlier that morning, were somehow blurred together, indistinct, some as fuzzy as if they'd happened long ago, and others—the lovemaking with Raven, and the memory of *Mâgun-Zak* itself—seemed as vivid as if they'd happened in the last hour. Try as she might, she could not seem to fit together their significance. They had to have had one, she was certain of that.

But what could it be?

Bemused at herself for her momentary vagueness, she shook her head, and retrieved those cards which had been left by callers while she slept. At the bottom of the stack, she discovered a police investigator's card. An Inspector Barbara Cole had called to finish the baroness's interview.

Barbara Cole. The name was oddly familiar; she'd heard it before. Typical of her disjointed thoughts, though, she couldn't place it.

Then suddenly, she did.

Nervous laughter around her, as the tensions generated by confrontation evaporated. A large man, one who had tried to question her, Gaust was his name, lumbered to his feet, lip still bleeding from the blow Raven had struck him. A woman joined the tableau, small, dark-haired, voluptuous. "Barbara Cole," Gaust introduced her. "Just over a year out of the academy…"

One of Raven's investigators, here to finish their interview, only to be turned away, as the Lady Angelique Blakesly was fast asleep.

One of Raven's investigators. He was their chief, newly promoted, and in charge of finding the thief who had stolen the *Mâgun-Zak*.

Oh, for the love of the Lord. He's in charge of findin' me.

The day did darken, then. In fact, the entire room swam for a dizzying moment or three. *Raven is goin' t' find me, he's goin' t' find me out. Like that awful Dawes woman said, you set a thief t' catch a thief! He could do it if anyone could... and then I'll have to answer for the pain of his betrayal, endure his scorn, and then the clank of irons on the auction block...*

Stop it, Angel! Stop it at once! She jumped out of her chair at this, then paused to draw a deep, steadying breath, and began to pace. As she'd once done, in another life, a world away, she braced herself against the onslaught of fear with a dash of cold-eyed pragmatism, phrased in an inner voice that sounded as if it might have come from any bar in Docktown. *The only thing for Raven and his investigators to find is the trail you conveniently left them. It does not point to you at all. There is no evidence linking you to that theft in any fashion, and your alibi is air-tight. That's how you and Louis arranged it. Remember that. Remember it.*

In fact... and this caused her to smile softly, *in point of fact, Chief Inspector Sir Vincent Sultaire is going to have his first big success as a bonded servant of the state. He'll be responsible for the arrest and conviction of the infamous Spider for the theft of the* Mâgun-Zak!

Chapter 5

2313 Compton Place, Upper Merchants
20 Amerian 580, 2130 hours

"So your boyfriend has been made chief inspector of the case," Louis smiled, jabbing a finger at the evening paper he had folded neatly beside his dinner plate. They were at his luxurious townhouse on the north side of Merchants, a part of town preferred by many of the city's upper-middle class Urilians—business executives, bankers, attorneys, speculators, flush with cash in the war's aftermath. Louis's "new money" townhouse missed being on the south side of Angels only by definition, and was actually a much better appointed place than hers. "And, he's already taken your bait, Angel darling. Spider was arrested before the clock struck eight that next morning."

The champagne in her glass sparkled. She sipped it carefully. Louis liked dry vintages, such as were imported from their ostensible homeland. However, the sweeter, more robust wines from Asbury had been part of the blood in her veins since before she'd been born, and she much preferred them.

"Ah would not call him a 'boyfriend,' Louis. The term doesn't really fit." The Vin-Nôrëan accent was missing from her soft speech. In private, with Louis, she didn't really need the deception it represented.

"As you prefer," he shrugged. "It does represent a relationship a bit more platonic than yours, I suppose." He seemed smugly proud of his detailed knowledge of her private life. "But here's to success. A wonderful job, darling."

"Thank you." She quirked him a momentary grin. "Ah could wish you spent less time under my bed, though."

"Occupational necessity," he smiled unapologetically. "Prevention costs less than repair, as you know. Your choice of lovers leaves a bit to be desired, my love."

'My love.' Louis had often used this with her as a casual endearment, but now she found it sounded vulgar in his mouth. "Do you count yourself among them, Louis?" she asked, uncharacteristically acerbic with him.

"That depends," he smiled, wiping the corner of his mouth with a crisp linen napkin. "Do you like your new life? At least my loyalties are plain. Your young lord has none, as you may discover, should he get lucky." He pointed at the paper again, for emphasis, a touch of the lash, coated in silk.

Internally, Angel found herself backing away in response, retreating into momentary silence before diverting the subject. "Is the item clear of the city yet? Or do you know?"

"I do," he said calmly, in that irritatingly superior tone. "And you need not know that information, darling, though you might surmise the answer from your bank balance."

"Ah hadn't checked it," she murmured, eyes still fixed upon her plate, her mind in turmoil. "That's what a widowed baroness relies on her solicitor for, after all, is it not?"

"Or her banker," Louis drawled, and she could hear the smug smile he offered her, as he condescended to explain. It was an old habit with him, and for the first time, she saw it for what it was: A way for him to reinforce his control, lest her recent successes make her bold. "Very well. As of close of business today, a total of twenty five thousand pounds has been deposited into Carlisle's accounts, as per our agreement," he said in his best "lawyer" voice. That was enough to run her household for a year. "Should your contract hold—and I'm sure it will—you should be seeing regular payments of that amount for the next several months."

"It is difficult for me to think in numbers that big, you know," she murmured, mostly making conversation, playing for time while her back-brain went into emergency-scramble mode. "Carlisle becomes more a liability than an asset, just from the the totals at the bottom of the balance sheet."

Louis ate quietly for several moments, keeping his thoughts to himself. Then they were interrupted by his household slaves, who brought in the after-dinner sherry, and set out scrumptious looking puff-pastries, drizzled with cherry sauce.

"That need not be so, my love," he offered at last, after the slave had left. "One of my apprentices was reviewing the Carlisle file last week, and discovered some... ah, 'irregularities,' shall we call them? In the handling of routine administrative matters, you understand." In point of fact, they were "irregularities" that, along with its remoteness, had made the barony the perfect choice for her, and thus for his purposes. "To put it simply for you, I believe the earl is helping himself to more than his share of Carlisle's revenue."

Angelique stared blankly at him, then burst out into the light, dry laughter more characteristic of the woman he'd known. "You cain't be serious, Louis. Camrose? Corrupt? The man isn't that subtle!"

Louis sat back in his chair, twirling a long-stemmed champagne glass in his perfumed fingers. Rufus Ashford-Black, Earl of Camrose, had a reputation for being a gruff, vulgar, grasping man, and that had been another compelling reason to place Angel at Carlisle.

She sat quietly while he thought, wondering at his silence, because it almost never boded well for anyone else when Louis was thinking.

"Not corrupt," he finally replied, quietly. "Competent. What he's doing isn't illegal, darling. It's unethical, and then only when done to a vassal. What's going on smacks more of habits bred from Carlisle's long stewardship, than from corruption. That's how it's done among the well-bred, you know."

"Oh," she said, placing her knife and fork properly on her plate. "Do you think it's in my best interests t' point this out t' him? Or should Ah let it ride?" she asked, folding her hands neatly in her lap. On the surface, Angel deferred to him as she'd always done, and played for time.

Louis reached for his little silver bell, and rang it. Several of his house slaves appeared promptly to remove the plates and glasses, replacing them with a dessert wine.

"I think it in your best interests to consider getting control of your estates," Louis smirked as their glasses were being filled with a sweet, aromatic vintage.

"It's not as if Ah need the money," she insisted, after his property left the room. "Ah may need his good will a bit more. Difficult, if Ah've alienated him by accusing him of screwin' over the barony."

"So don't accuse," he advised expansively. "Darling, *you're* the Baroness of Carlisle. Who is under your employ is entirely up to you. If the Earl of Camrose's people do not obey your commands, then you dismiss them. No accusation is necessary. You simply stop any money over and above the taxes due from being siphoned off your land by the earl's well-meaning servants."

She stared at him for several moments, fighting a losing battle with a rising tide of rage. He enjoyed this kind of thing too much. While the child she had once been was cowering, somewhere down in the dark recesses of her consciousness, Angel found a new voice in her anger. "You go too far, Louis," she breathed, clenching her fists in her lap, where he would not see. "I'm *not* the baroness, I wasn't raised to be a noblewoman, I don't know *any* of the things about stewardship that those fucking Paladins seem to have soaked up with their mothers' milk—I learned how to *look* like a Paladin noblewoman, and act *like* one, not *be* one, and you bloody well know it!"

Louis, however, remained unruffled. If he heard the changes in her voice, it was not reflected in his manner. "You *are* the Baroness of Carlisle," he replied, cutting a bite-sized piece of pastry. "And, if you need proof, we can visit the Office of Heraldry, wherein they will prove it to you with sufficient force to stand up in any court of law you care to name." He let her ponder that for several heartbeats. "So it is not a question of whether you are or are not. Legally, you are. The question is, when are you going to start acting the role you've been assigned?"

Acting the role. Acting the role. The words seared into her, highlighting every filthy lie and detestable deception she'd lived since returning to these shores. The lies had stuck in her throat, in the face of Raven's ardent declarations of love, and the tears that had accompanied them.

"Acting the role?" she repeated, soft voice shaking, hardly aware that she'd said anything. "Louis, what in all the hells do you think I've *been* doing? Can you believe all this," and she gestured to her lady-like appearance, somewhat vaguely, "doesn't require 'acting a role?' Try dozens of them!"

He took another bite of dessert. "Roles not yet perfected, I see."

That was too much. "You can go to right to any hell you choose," she hissed. Even wearing one of the baroness's fashionable evening gowns couldn't stop her from rising in fury, and sailing toward the door.

"You will find him at police headquarters, discussing your case with his, ah—'staff.'" Unperturbed, Louis reached for his glass.

It stopped her in mid-step, and held her motionless while the implications settled in. Of course he would monitor the investigation. Most especially the head of it. Her lover. *Of course.*

Even Louis didn't, *couldn't* know everything, and she wasn't about to give away to him how accurately the blow had landed. She turned, face pale in the soft light, feeling the muscles and skin of her face settle into a neutral mask. "My case?" she repeated, numbly. Somewhere within, a voice was screaming for her to run.

"Forgive me, darling," he said expansively. "But you *were* the one who broke into Bishop-Florian Hall last night, were you not?"

It would be no effort for Louis's people to tip off informants, and plant evidence that would lead right back to me, in much the same way I planted the trail that led to the Spider. Angel summoned the strength and clarity she'd felt in her anger and turned to face him, deliberately replying in the way she knew he expected.

"No. It was the Spider. Or so the evidence suggests."

"Then—perhaps you can explain why your young lord spent the last three days combing Bishop-Florian Hall from basement to chimney top?" He took another bite of the dessert pastry. "You should really try this, darling. It's very good."

Is he truly trying to frighten me? Or simply bring me back under his control? "I'm sure it is. Whatever Raven is doing doesn't matter. They'll find what they expect to see, and no more. I can at least do *that* much competently."

"I don't question your competence," Louis lied, smiling. "Nor do I question the competence of the police. Your boyfriend, however, is not a cop. Most certainly *not* a cop. Do you know who the experts in our most august police department consider the prime suspect to be? I think you'll find it enlightening."

She held her ground, though it was hard for her. All her instincts were screaming at her loudly, leaving her with with the very clear feeling that she'd better start playing her cards more carefully. This was Louis, the man who had befriended her when she was abandoned and alone in Püran-Khir, who had sheltered her in his own home while chaos raged in the streets. He'd been the mastermind behind her pose as the Baroness of Carlisle.

Yes, and he was the man who cold-bloodedly instructed me in how he expected me to repay him for his kindnesses, too. Saying "no" had never, ever been an acceptable answer. One simply did not refuse Louis Arnot.

When she had not supplied the expected response in an appropriately short amount of time, he cast her a glance, then gave her the answer.

"Vincent Sultaire."

"Why?"

Louis laughed. "Oh, come now, darling. Think! How many other burglars in this city could have done what you did last night? I can think of four, one of whom is said to be dead, another was arrested this morning, the third is still at large, and the fourth is doing time—as a chief inspector."

Another lashing stroke. Again, Angel dissembled rather than allow him to know how deeply he'd scored her. "And you think," she answered him, "that they will think I helped him."

"That is the rumor, yes," he replied. "Though I doubt that it reaches as high in the department as the commissioner's office. If it did, Sultaire would not have one inept inspector and a new graduate on his investigative team. The commissioner, I think, has more sense. He rammed a promotion down the committee's throat to give Sultaire free rein on this case, an expert thief to catch an expert thief."

He toasted her with his glass, then looked thoughtful, staring at the amber liquid with narrowed eyes. "I hadn't counted on that counter-move by Commissioner Roland, I do confess, but he can be a slippery one sometimes. Roland was a damned good cop."

Still standing at the door to the dining room, Angel stared at him as if he'd sprouted horns. "Is this all really just one vast game to you, Louis? And I, another pawn on the board?"

"Of course it's a game," he laughed. "So is war, politics, business, *life* is a game, darling. Those who are good at playing get rich. Those who aren't are poor—or dead." He let that sink in, then caught her eyes with his own. "So far, you've played well, love. Don't start making bad moves now."

Such as leaving this room before I'm through with you. Angel heard the unspoken threat in that as clearly as if he'd said it. He'd never threatened her before, not even indirectly. *He never really had to—the threat was all around us, back then. But now?*

They barely saw each other, and lived in a civilized place, one that had not been touched directly by the gruesome realities of decades of fighting, and its aftermath. *And I've outgrown the body of the barely-pubescent girls he prefers to bed, though he still enjoys using this one occasionally. And, I've found a lover who doesn't make me feel slimy and defiled, afterwards.*

In other words, I've become the threat.

She returned to the table slowly, letting that radically new world view settle in place of her old one. Angel had never before considered that she might be a threat to Louis, in any capacity. It was entirely bracing to discover that he had already begun to think of her as one.

She resumed her seat across from him, though whatever appetite she'd brought with her was completely gone. In a voice that sounded numb, even to her own ears, she asked, "What do you want me to do?"

"Enjoy your dessert," he replied, toasting her, and then draining his glass.

Time to dissemble. We've lived this lie for years now; we can live it right here with Louis, for a while longer. "I... My apologies, Louis" she began, allowing her voice to regain strength and color slowly, naturally, "but, if you wanted me to eat dessert, you shouldn't have fed me so well. Current fashions for well-bred ladies don't permit them to overeat, you know. Not comfortably."

He sat back, looking at her openly, admiring her fair form as he had done on many occasions. She suppressed the repulsed shudder that threatened to give her away. The gown she'd chosen for the evening, lavender satin worn off the shoulder, emphasized the creaminess of her skin, even accentuating her small decolletáge fetchingly. It was her best color, and no doubt he thought she had selected it especially for him this evening.

"Oh, come now. You can't pass on dessert. I had it made just for you! However, if you'll permit me the pleasure of mixing two parts of our evening, I've always enjoyed looking at you. May I have something more comfortable fetched for you to wear?"

Now that he was sure he had her cooperation, it was all phrased so politely. Louis was offering to have her prepared for his use, as he had done before, and she could no more refuse him that than she could have refused the offer of comfortable clothing, or to eat the damned pastry. Aware of the threat, Angel dissembled, mind working in high gear, knowing she faced a man who knew her well, and who had become her enemy.

Capitulate. Play for time. Watch for an opportunity.

"It would help," she replied, smiling a little for his benefit. "I've been pushing hard these last few weeks. It's worn on my temper, I'm afraid. I'm sorry for my outburst earlier, Louis. Please forgive me."

"Of course." He reached for the bell.

It was only a few moments until an entourage of young house slaves were holding up a dizzying array of revealing negligees for his inspection. All of them, she noted grimly, would leave her more exposed than covered. Louis walked back and forth up the perfectly straight line of presented garments like an army general at inspection, musing over each.

"Either of these would look lovely on you this evening, my love," he said finally, pushing two of the slaves forward to show her the ones selected. "Which do you prefer, darling? I cannot decide." He threw up his hands and sank back into his chair.

The first was barely more than a silken, lacy, frilly bit of girl's night-wear, made and sized for a woman's body. The other was a be-ribboned, satiny white brassiere and panties, with a gauzy, translucent robe. Even as she pretended to consider them, Angel found it amusing, in a hideous sort of way, that she was then playing her own role for Louis, consciously imitating the woman he expected her to be, right down to the accent.

"Well," Angel mused at last. She'd known which he preferred as soon as she saw the selection. "Ah'm flattered, Louis. They're both so lovely, and Ah am fond of satin... but white is for innocence, and an innocent Ah'm not.

As you have reason to know," she said, smiling primly, and utterly falsely, ostensibly for his amusement. "So the pink one, Ah think, if it still pleases you."

"Wonderful, darling," he beamed, gesturing to his property. They filed out dutifully, leaving the one slave holding the selected item, and two other girls, naked save for their collars, who stepped forward. Gently assisting an impassive Angel out of her chair, they expertly—and slowly—disrobed her, right in front of Louis, who sat back with his wineglass, obviously enjoying the exhibition.

The girls had been trained to please their master in their work, and apparently had been afforded many opportunities to practice, if their expertise was an indication. If there was an erotic way to pose her body, they found it and exploited it, and all her resistance might have done would have been to alert him that something with her was amiss. She well-remembered how Angela, Louis's passive, slutty little fuck-baby would have suffered the slaves' attentions to give Louis his voyeuristic pleasure; she could not allow him to know that the woman with him at that moment merely temporized by doing the same.

By the time the slaves had dressed her in the pink peignoir, her face felt flushed, but if Louis noticed it, he would not have guessed the true reason for it. She pushed a stray wisp of her hair back into the sleek up-do in which it belonged, and returned his gaze as if she were a woman merely awaiting his pleasure. It had already been pointed out to her quite plainly that he was the one person in this city she could *not* afford to cross. Beyond that she must not allow herself to think, to speculate, lest any hint of it surface in her face or bearing. Somehow she had become aware that Louis was her enemy. It would take everything she'd ever learned, not to let him become aware of it, too.

"You look ravishing, darling," he smiled, indicating she should retake her seat, which of course gave him a wonderful view of her breasts. "I have no particular agenda in mind for our evening, you know, but I am *starved* to hear the details of your adventure. I would be delighted if you'd recount the experience while you finish your dessert. There is no hurry," he assured her suddenly.

Angel allowed a mildly bemused look to steal over her face. "Was there some reason there should be?" she asked. "Are you late-datin' me, Louis?"

He laughed, his icy gray eyes dancing. "Ah, no, my love. Despite your unfaithfulness, you have still quite stolen my calloused heart."

"Or whatever you're using in place of one this week," she drawled, taking a dainty bite of her dessert. She barely tasted it.

He lifted his glass in toast. "How true. They are more trouble than they are worth, are they not? In your case, I recommend remedial procedures immediately!" His tone had once again resumed that tone of smug expansiveness that now irritated her like a rash. "But, in this, darling, we are at *least* equally disingenuous with each other. You cheat on me, and I cheat on you." His eyes were roaming openly over her artfully-cupped breasts and bared shoulders, as if she were there simply for him to enjoy, another piece of finely rendered art in his vast collection.

Angel squelched the internal comparison to Raven's devoted adoration of her body, fought back the shuddering revulsion, clung to the facade she held up to Louis as if it were a lifeline... and muffled a rather unlady-like snort into her napkin.

"It's only cheatin' if there's a contract that prohibits the behavior t' begin with," she pointed out, grin flickering at the corners of her mouth. "If my recall in the matter is correct, a monogamous relationship between us, romantic or sexual, was never mentioned."

"True," he agreed, waving his hand dismissively, "but it's still an amusing conceit. So, tell me about your adventure."

Her nod was as expansive as his tone had been, earlier. With a bit of distance from her danger, the role she played became somewhat easier. "It went as planned. No unexpected hitches or obstacles. Your informants are as good as they've ever been." She took another delicate bite. "Correct, as always, Louis. This is quite good."

His eyes had yet to stray from her body. "Your favorite, if memory serves. If not, I'll have to see my physician, then revise my statement to the chef. He takes your pleasure in his cooking quite personally."

"Really? Ah'm touched," she murmured, voice schooled to the dry, pseudo-sincerity he seemed to appreciate most. "The sauce is both tart and sweet. If he cooked for me all the time, Ah believe Ah'd be fatter than Mercía Devon. Imagine me hauling a behind like *that* up a rope t' the roof..."

Louis laughed, something he actually did rather easily, and placed his empty glass upon the table. "Somehow, darling, such a prodigious fundament would not be fitting upon your slender frame." He sat back, regarding her both speculatively and possessively. "But you have dissembled, my love. I am still awaiting the details."

"Well, you've distracted me with puff pastry, Louis," she replied, as if that explanation were so obvious it hardly bore mentioning.

"Which raised thoughts of Mercía Devon's rather large behind," he drawled drily refilling her glass. "And so, now that we've entertained the distraction of refitting your pert posterior into the likeness of hers, pray answer my query."

Angela's light, ironic laughter rang out momentarily, disguising the renewed disquiet he'd aroused with that innocuous-seeming statement. As if in assent, she pushed her plate back, with perhaps the last third of the pastry still uneaten.

"Prevention," she drawled, eyes sparkling in a kind of malice he would mistake for mere cattiness. Before he could get irrational about the delay, however, she relented, and considered how to begin. The soft drawl that characterized the speech of those from the duchy of Asbury faded, and what emerged was not Lady Angelique's refined D'waanese accent, but rather that of any professional working woman there in greater Fernwall.

"The ingress went without incident. The keys you furnished me to augment the set I was given allowed me access through the office suites, right up to the third floor of the old building. There were no guards, as I'd overheard and you'd confirmed. Not until I got up to the floor on which the exhibit was held."

Louis nodded, refilling his own glass as she sipped from hers. Again, if he noted the new cadence in her voice, he didn't indicate it—but when Louis considered himself unbeatable, he could be strangely inured to such clues. Rather than give in to paranoia, she inhaled deliberately, and continued.

"The first two guards patrolled the halls, and both went down without raising any outcry," Angel went on, relieved to see his characteristic spike of pleasure when she mentioned violence. "I dragged them into the janitorial closet and bound them with some of Spider's silk cord. They were snoring contentedly when I left.

"The four within the exhibit itself were the biggest dilemma." Despite her earlier reticence, Angel felt herself warming to her recounting of the heist. She hadn't realized how badly she'd needed to tell *someone*. "As we'd discussed. It did finally just come down to a pattern analysis. I watched their routes for perhaps a quarter-hour. That suggested pretty plainly where I needed to start, and in which order they had to be taken. They were patrolling the route clockwise. I ran them anti-clockwise."

Her emerging smile was a particularly dangerous expression, even in reminiscence. "One. Two. Three. Four," she recited, extending the appropriate number of fingers as she did so. "All of them down in one minute, fifty-one seconds, Louis."

He smiled at her, his eyes alight with appreciation. "Of course," he replied quietly. He was watching her the way a cat watches a captured mouse and, like the cat, he was enjoying every moment of his captive's torment. It raised the fine hairs at the back of her neck again, reminding her that there was much more to all this than a simple after-dinner conversation between friends. Louis intended to fuck her, she knew. She also knew she'd just reminded him of one of the reasons why he still enjoyed it.

Steady, Angel. "After that, retrieving the item itself was exceedingly simple," she said, pushing on in an attempt to forestall the inevitable. "The crystals worked as designed, when put in the proper places. I—"

Louis leaned forward abruptly, interrupting her. "What do you mean, 'they worked as designed'?" At her puzzled frown, he relaxed back into his chair, turning one palm up to indicate an inquiry. "I've never worked with reflecting crystals personally, Angel darling. What's it like?"

She frowned again, and shook her head. "I can't really explain it, Louis. It was odd, though. I could tell they were designed to work in pairs. They reacted with each other kind of like lodestones do, you know? Not exactly like that, but close."

"Really? I see." Louis nodded, but his eyes had narrowed again in speculation. By the time he lifted his glass to her again, however, the expression had cleared. "Do go on, darling."

Angel doubted that Louis really did see, but had no time to wonder it. "I secured the item, replaced the dome, removed the wands, tucked away my gear, then placed the clues which would lead to the Spider. That I was successful can be measured by his arrest, I think."

He nodded slowly, and his heated gaze seemed to burn her skin. "Well done," he murmured. "Very well done. You should be rewarded properly. I'll attend to that whenever you're ready."

She could almost feel his hot breath on her lips. Her reactive shiver caught her unawares, but not so much that she couldn't append a small, secretive smile. "The reward is in my bank account, Louis," she replied softly, clearly. Her heart was sinking rapidly, however. The chance to escape what was to come was almost completely gone.

"*That* was your payment," Louis drawled, his voice thick with arousal. She was such a wanton slut, he knew, and he doubted young Sultaire had any idea what lurked in the deepest crevices of her depraved, tormented soul. Even now, as she composed what he knew would be a demurral, the nipples of her small breasts crinkled tight in expectation. "The reward, my delectable Angela, shall be delivered personally unto every delicate, quivering part of your beautiful body."

He didn't miss the sudden catch in her breath. It made the growing ache just that much more poignant. She couldn't refuse him, and he knew it.

"Ah." Angel fought down the urge to edge away from him. The last chance to escape was gone. She was, once again, going to have to find a way to endure what was to come. Louis had known all of Angela's nasty pleasures, and would expose them all, one by one, until she'd beg to give him whatever he asked of her. To her horror, she felt the onset of arousal, the sickening desire burning within her, and part of her was melting right down at the heat—and depravity—in Louis's voice.

The rest of her ran shrieking for Raven.

"Silly of me to misunderstand, I suppose," she went on, annoyed at the sudden breathiness in the words. Unable to tear her eyes from his, she choked, "When have I ever not been ready for you, Louis, darling?"

"And when have I ever failed to satiate your considerable desires, darling," he purred. Now openly devouring her with his eyes, he reached for the bell and rang it, then rose to hand her out of her chair. One of the young slaves appeared before the tinkling had left the air. The slave girl obediently followed as her master led the way through the house and up the stairs, their glasses and half empty bottle in hand. She closed the bedroom door behind them, quietly placed the bottle and glasses within easy reach, then unobtrusively waited at one side of the enormous bed.

Louis' hands found Angel's hair before the slave had finished her minuscule duties. His lips parted hers, his hands twined through her hair and held her face to his while he sampled extensively the cup of her open mouth. Abruptly, Angel felt as if she were being smothered, suffocated under the press of lust, and of circumstances too far gone to control. He was asserting himself, controlling her as he used her; and her body, in yet another betrayal, was already shuddering in response.

Interpreting her revulsion as lust, Louis drove on. Breaking the kiss, he slid the pink silk from her shoulders, baring her breasts. His lips found her nipples, and he sucked at them, arching her backward over his arm. Angel shivered again, hating herself for the tiny little moan that threaded its way out of her throat. In point of fact, her only protest came when his teeth bit down on her nipple tauntingly, and that simply encouraged him. The silk parted under the pull of his hands, snarling like an enraged cat. He bit and sucked at her breasts and nipples, a ravening animal, like the vicious two-legged animals who'd roamed the ruined streets of Püran-Khir, preying upon the weak.

Abruptly, it was too much. Something inside her awareness twisted, separating some part of itself from that which reveled in the body that encased it. Most of what had been Angel fled, abandoning Angela's treacherous flesh to Louis' attentions, but watching in bitter self-loathing as she enticed him with every trembling response.

Restraining her arms behind her with what was left of the expensive silk, Louis laid her out on the bed. Fingers that had just ripped fabric now tenderly massaged her feet and calves, as if to soothe her, but without warning leaned in to bite her tender instep. He merely laughed when she jumped and protested, his hands smoothing up her slender legs to where they met, fingers poised above the dark blond hair at her cleft.

"You want it, don't you, baby," he purred, taunting. His fingers brushed back and forth across her clitoris. "Tell me how badly you want it, Angela. Tell me."

The part of her that loved being Angelique Blakesly screamed so violently that she couldn't have heard what Angela said in response. The slave girl watching from her position beside the bed heard it, though. So did Louis.

"Please, Louis," the panting slut begged. "Don't do this to me... don't torment me... please..."

He laughed softly, his fingers still brushing across her clitoris in agonizing, feather-light strokes. "Such a lovely slut," he purred. His tongue darted into her sex. Angela jumped, tilting her cleft up to him obligingly. "Hmm... " he sighed, tasting its musky dampness. Her throaty moan answered his, catching in a breathless sob when his ministrations stopped.

"So what would you like, darling?" he continued, his voice deceptively soft. "What unearthly delights are sufficient reward for such unparalleled success?"

Name your poison...

"Your mouth," the slut replied, spreading her thighs for him. "It felt so good, Louis... please...?"

The most intimate kiss, and the slowest poison of all, you stupid whore.

"Such a slut," Louis repeated, delighted. Again his tongue dipped into her sex, then slid up her cleft to dance over her clitoris with the expertise of a master sexual technician. He touched her nowhere else just then, gauging her lustful responses, dispassionately taking her to a purely physical peak of desire, only to pull back, getting his satisfaction only when she began to beg him for release. Every touch, exhaled breath, licking stroke, or tickling tease was offered with the same remote solicitousness he might have used in opening a door for her, or handing her out of a carriage.

Angel, from her safety in the remotest aerie of her mind, shook her head sadly. *That's how it starts. He gives it t' you in a way you cain't refuse, because it feels so good. But then the poison's in you, an' it just keeps spreadin', until you're so numb you can't feel anythin' anymore.*

The wanton, needy animal under Louis' ministrations couldn't answer that, couldn't do anything except hurl herself and her lust repeatedly towards the climax that she wouldn't reach until he allowed it, and Louis, turned on by the thrill, wasn't about to allow it. He expertly brought her up onto the knife's edge again and again, holding her there until she'd been cut deeply by her own desire, only to let her slide slowly away, unfulfilled. Desire burned in her body like acid, until she lay before him a writhing, tortured mass of flesh, and tears were the only thing left her.

Fool. You're not dead yet. You'll just wish you were. You'll walk around, an ambulatory corpse, interacting with the living, and it will take a man like Raven to resurrect you from your self-inflicted hell...

The howl that emerged from her at this could have been torn from the damned. Louis merely lifted his head. "Yes? What is it, baby girl?" he asked solicitously.

"Aaaah, damn you!" she shrieked, sobbing. Her flesh writhed uncontrollably still, hungering for what he could never give her. "Louis... Louis, please... What... What have I done... to deserve this?"

"Am I not pleasing you, my sweet darling?" he asked, his concern a sick, self-satisfying pretense. "Perhaps... perhaps you would like me to fuck you? Yes, that must be it."

"No." Her tear-streaked face glimmered in the soft light, half-childlike, half-insane, wholly Angela. "No," she repeated, wrenching her arms free of the remnants of the fabric. "I can't stand this anymore! You're killing me!"

Don't you wish! Safely distanced from the tableau, Angel laughed sadly. *Do you really think he's goin' t' let you go? Just because you're cryin'? He'll just think his prowess has overwhelmed you. Watch.*

With a lust-filled chuckle, Louis motioned to the slave, and pushed Angel's legs back, ignoring her half-hearted struggles. The slave girl climbed upon the bed, and knelt on Angela's arms so she could pin her knees down, beside her ears, baring her utterly to Louis intentions. He'd stood quickly to doff his clothes, but paused to massage his raging erection as he regarded her appreciatively.

"Louis... Louis! Please! Gods, please! This has to stop...!" She was still sobbing, body and nerves drawn out to such extremes that she had no reserves of control left.

Oh, you duplicitous little whore. He's goin' t' give you what you really *want. He's goin' t' fuck you now, and for some time t' come. He'll fuck you until you're screamin' for it, until you cain't remember what your body was*

72

like without him inside it. He'd actually be a superb lover, if his heart were somethin' other than stone.

"What a lovely little slut!" Louis exclaimed. "You've missed my attentions, clearly. You're so happy, you're weeping, and all for the attentions of someone who knows these sinful pleasures of yours so intimately—and who'll indulge 'em."

Stepping up to the edge of the bed, he smoothly inserted himself into her swollen, hot sex with a long satisfying sigh. Her reaction was more ambiguous, a groan of child-like despair that Louis naturally interpreted as agreement, and arousal.

"Oh yes," he hissed hotly, through his lust-filled haze. "Much better than your scape-grace boyfriend, wouldn't you say? You couldn't beg a Paladin to fuck you like this... and you need it, don't you, baby... I had almost forgotten how good it feels to be inside your body, just how good a *fuck* you really are."

The slave girl held her down, doubled over, totally exposed and completely vulnerable. She watched avidly as Louis drove his thick cock into the body she held, mesmerized by the sight. His slow, driving rhythm sent waves of pleasure pounding through Angela like a drum. *Now* he would give her the release she craved, on his terms, his shaft working deep inside her, grinding against her clitoris, then pulling almost free of her only to thrust again. Angel watched with an obscure sort of pain as her other self fought against the inevitability of Louis, a child building sand-castle moats against an encroaching tide. There was no tenderness to this, no love despite the lies in his mouth. He took her body with all the lack of regard he'd give one of his slaves. With each shred of resistance, each nuance of anything less than surrender, he drove himself into her more fiercely, invoking an inhuman degree of control to slam-fuck her into submission.

Resistance shredded, sand-castle moats collapsed. Her own body undermined her, driven into a fever pitch by his pounding pace. Even as she tried to fight it, orgasm took her and hurtled her over the unseen edge, into an inky abyss of poison, lies, and treachery. Convulsing rhythmically, Angel's toned legs flexed in the strength of her passion, throwing off the slave who'd restrained her. Louis growled, grabbed her, held her, *rode* her thrashing, spasming body through the very last of its contortions even as the slave struggled frantically to regain control of her charge. Only when she lie limp beneath him did he abate his pace. Seeing her cue, the slave hopped off the bed and hurriedly fetched a towel to mop her master's sweat-beaded brow, then returned to her post.

"Wonderful, darling," Louis complimented her, rolling her back over so that the slave girl could again pin her down in a submissive position. "Absolutely wonderful. How many more would you like, tonight?" he grunted, slipping himself back into her body. "This *is* your night, after all. It seems only fitting to be thoroughly fucked, and in all the ways you crave, don't you think?" He was idly sliding in and out of her as he waited for an answer.

She gave him the only answer she had for him: She wept.

Stupid, stupid fool.

Chapter 6

It was a "cop shop," and there was a part of Raven that still couldn't believe he had become as much a regular here as the other constables and inspectors of Fernwall's Police Department. The Blue Jacket had taken its name in honor of the distinctive uniform of those who served the city, and was as much an institution as the department itself. Promotion and retirement parties were usually held here, and the mellowed old hardwood floors had borne the tread of Fernwall's finest through the terms of the last ten commissioners, including Hal Roland.

By long standing tradition, when socializing at the Blue Jacket, "the rank came off." This morning's breakfast meeting, however, wasn't a social affair. Chief Inspector Sultaire was reviewing the information he and his inspectors had collected over the past seven days on what what had been reported in the daily papers as "The Theft of the Decade."

"The usual?" the server asked him.

"Certainly," he replied with a grin, and a wink for Inspector Cole. "We Paladins just *adore* tradition, after all."

"And for you too, eh, Philip?"

"Yeah," Gaust yawned his answer.

"And for the shining new face on the force?" she asked Barbara, who smiled slightly.

"I don't eat in the mornings, thanks. Just coffee—black," Cole said.

"All the late night meals after hours, no doubt," Vincent grinned at her.

"I'm on a meatless diet, Sultaire."

The server laughed, and headed off to fill their orders.

"Pity," Vincent drawled, watching the oblivious Inspector Gaust yawn hugely. "A bit of meat always adds such a glow to a woman's complexion."

"Your concern for my continued good health is very gallant, I'm sure," she murmured, flashing him a dark-eyed glance.

Their server breezed by, depositing three cups of coffee as she passed.

"Is there some reason we're discussing diets, rather than business?" Gaust groused over his steaming cup.

It was all Vincent could do to keep a straight face. "It's better than staring at our hands while we wait for you to wake up." His eyes flashed to Cole, and they both laughed outrageously.

The older man winced at the volume. "I never claimed to be an early riser," he grumped. "Are you two ready to cave on the Spider yet? Or do I get to spend another day chasing down dead-end leads?"

It was Cole who eventually replied. "No, I'm not ready to cave on anything yet, but it's not looking very good." She turned to Raven, the mirth draining from her expression. "I've got just the one interview left to do in the Ladies' Auxiliary angle. Did you get anywhere with the alchemists on either the drug used, or the acid?"

Vincent sat back in his chair, staring deeply into his own cup. "Nothing definitive," he admitted, taking a sip. Then he sighed. "The problem here is that we're dealing with—well, to be candid, we're essentially dealing with me, and that's part of the trouble. We're finding almost exactly what I'm expecting us to find at every turn. Hints, suggestions, inferences, but never a hard clue. I used to consider it a game. How many inferences could I leave without dropping a trail, or screwing up the trail I wanted the cops to find?"

"Well, you could always confess right now," Gaust offered. "Save us all a lot of trouble, and the Spider goes free."

Cole scowled at him. "We're arresting the wrong crook, either way." Then the irony in what she said struck her. "Sorry, Sultaire. I didn't mean that the way it sounded."

Vincent smiled at her. "You may get your way anyway, Philip. Roland told me last night that *somebody* is going to the block for this, innocent or not. The politicians have to have a gull." He let them absorb that for a few heartbeats, then continued. "So let's go over this again from the top. Literally, on top of Bishop-Florian Hall were four distinct footprints. Size six women's. Boots most likely, though there were no cobbler's markings left in the print. From the stride we can deduce our thief to be about a hundred and sixty five centimeters tall. Considerably shorter than Spider's one-seven-five. Next?"

"The one guard who got a good look at the assailant claims he was Spider's height, easy," Gaust pointed out.

"I had a thought about that, if you're interested," Cole said, looking at Raven.

"I'm always interested," *in you,* his eyes finished extravagantly.

"Everyone knows that," she parried. Gaust snorted, this time picking up on the subtext. "Anyway, the guard's statement says he was struck with the heel of the perp's hand, and he specifically says that blow drove *up* into his chin. That was confirmed by the medics on the scene. A man that guard's height, or taller, wouldn't strike with the *heel* of his hand, from below. That's a smaller person's move," she concluded. "I ought to know. It's how I was trained to fight."

"That doesn't prove anything, either," Gaust snorted.

Vincent's eyebrow had shot up, however. "I'll have to remember that. And no," he said to Gaust, "it doesn't. It's a trifle. But as I told the countess last week, it's the trifles that are going to make or break this case. Time's on your side, Philip, not mine. Next?"

"Well, next would be the rope," Cole offered. "It was definitely the means of egress, may have been the means of ingress, but there were no corresponding footprints that would confirm the latter."

"Silk braid, the same weight and diameter the Spider uses," Gaust supplied. "As was the specialized crossbow bolt that embedded it into the timber."

"As was the acid," Vincent added. "So let me ask you this: If the Spider came and went the same way, then why take out two guards in the office wing? That's off the route."

"And why go all the way to the top of the building just to go back down again if you don't have to?" Cole asked, ignoring Gaust's shrug. "It's a pretty robust theory, to me, that this perp came in the way the rest of us mortals do—through a door, or maybe a ground-floor window."

"That actually may go further to prove Spider did it, if you two are even close to right," the big man pointed out. "Something to throw the trail off himself, after all."

"I'm not sure I followed that," Vincent admitted.

"You're the one who claims Spider isn't stupid enough to pull a caper like this and leave such an obvious trail. Maybe he came in via the ground floor to throw off suspicion."

"He's also got a Seer to swear he denied committing the crime while under the influence of the truth serum," Cole shot back. "Think you could keep a string of lies straight with that stuff in your bloodstream, and a Seer noting every discrepancy?"

"Let's say the perp did come in through the ground floor," Vincent moved on before yet another argument between the two got started. "How? Several locks were picked *inside* the building, but none of the outer doors were tampered with. The one Cooper classic missing from this case, by the way," he said, more for Gaust's benefit than Cole's.

"I didn't know that," Gaust grumbled. "How in hells did you?"

"I know him," Raven stated simply. Cooper hadn't been a close friend, exactly, but the two had exchanged professional courtesies on more than one occasion, before the Raven's wings had been clipped by the penal system.

That silenced them both. "Then, I guess he would have to have gotten hold of a key to one of the outside doors," Gaust begrudged, not entirely stupid, despite appearances. "Which we did not find in his flat, by the way."

"There were a good many things wrong with his flat," Vincent remarked. "But stealing keys is *not* a Spider habit. He always comes and goes via traceable means: picked locks, jimmied windows, cut glass. You'll find a lot of variance in his overall methods, but that one?" He shook his head.

"But keys. I think you're right in that, Philip. There's a key involved, which tends to lead right back to the noble Ladies of the Paladin's Auxiliary."

"As well as a dozen staffers," Gaust supplied. "I asked Director Gregory about that. He had all the keys of the hall's employees inventoried that afternoon, and had collected the sets loaned out to the Ladies' Auxiliary. None were missing, though that would have been too easy."

"The members I've interviewed so far have all contributed to the confusion," Cole added. "Though they were quite responsible about returning their sets to the E.D., they all admit that the keys were out of their sight for protracted periods of time." She winced. "The Countess Liberaune got quite sharp with me about that."

"Toughen your spine, girl. And if you need help, call me," Vincent drawled, leaving the offer open-ended. "Nobles are habitually impressed with their authority—and themselves."

Their server showed up then with Gaust's and Raven's breakfasts, filled their coffee cups, then quietly retreated. "Sure you wouldn't like to add a bit of meat to your diet?" Vincent asked Cole again, surveying his plate.

"Are you thinking of hiring out as my chef?"

"Look, do we have to go into that again?" Gaust snapped, looking thoroughly disgusted. He dug into his own large platter with gusto, however. "Cole, you said you had one more interview to do?"

"Yeah," she said, watching Sultaire struggle for composure in private amusement.

"Which one?"

"Lady Angelique Blakesly of Carlisle," she supplied, covering whatever expression she might have had by sipping from her freshened coffee. "I've had a hell of a time catching up with her. Or actually, just catching her awake."

Vincent's amusement level dropped sharply and his eyebrow arched. "Oh?"

Cole nodded. "I tried to interview her the day after the theft, and again four days later, and then again, yesterday. Her housekeeper claimed that the lady was fast asleep. Exhausted. Each time. Apparently, she's not been sleeping well since the night the *Mâgun-Zak* was stolen."

Was she taking this personally? She had been in perfect, erotic health that night, though she probably hadn't gotten any sleep. But yesterday? Vincent didn't like the sound of that, but "Interesting," was all he said.

Gaust and Cole were both watching him. Cole said, "There was a card on my desk late yesterday afternoon, Sultaire. The baroness asked my forgiveness for being unavailable, and further asked for an appointment with me later this morning to conclude her interview. I'm meeting her at ten-thirty."

"Wasn't she the one who had the fainting spell at the party that night?" Gaust rumbled, the workings of his brain obviously lubricated by the food and the pot of coffee he'd drunk. "Do you suppose it's related somehow? Vince? The lady in delicate health?"

"Perhaps," Vincent mused. "Though she's always been fairly robust and gregarious when we've been together. This isn't normal," he concluded finally. "You might look into that a bit during your interview today, Barbara. For my sake. I haven't spoken to Lady Blakesly privately since the party. Now I'm concerned."

"I'll let you know," she promised, tossing off the last of her coffee as she stood. "And since it's probably more than an hour over there by cab, I'd better get started."

"See you tonight."

"I've heard tomcats can see in the dark," she mused, winking at the clearly mystified Gaust. "But you'll need more than night vision to see me, Sultaire. 'Bye!"

Both men watched her leave in thoughtful frames of mind, though the thinking was on quite different tracks.

*   *   *

The minute hand of the clock on the mantel slipped down towards the appointed hour. Lady Angelique Blakesly of Carlisle sat in her bedchamber, outwardly calm and composed, gazing out through her window at the cobbled lane that led to her front door. Large, fluffy clouds were already building in the sky, darkening behind their mountainous parapet to the west. When they finally tumbled over it, the sharp peaks would rip their darkened under-bellies open, spilling rain and wind and lightning into the valley beyond.

Angelique had always liked lightning, even though the loud claps of thunder that accompanied it rattled her nerves long after the storm itself had passed. She didn't like the thunder. It was too predictable. The jagged spikes of energy that shot down out of the sky never were, and something in her found them exhilarating. Raven had made love to her in a storm once. The memory of that heady afternoon had livened her entire being for weeks afterward.

Perhaps the storm alone would be wild enough to wake her corpse-like body from its waking death. She could barely remember returning to Blakesly House that awful night, but she vividly remembered emptying the contents of her stomach, violently, into a basin, while Clarice had held her hair, and clucked over her in sleepy concern. Before it could drive her mad, Angelique had sent the girl back to her room, and had finished heaving, unproductively, in private.

It had been a purging, one that had continued through three long days and two nights since. That morning, as she considered the darkening skies, she was little more than a well-dressed void occupying a chair; a pretty shell empty of life, feeling, or anything at all that might have made her human.

She'd seen nothing from Raven at all since the day he'd gotten his promotion, nor heard aught from him in the long days and nights since. It

79

hurt to remember the purity of their lovemaking that last night, and the memory of the vows she'd sworn to him had seared her, repeatedly, in punishment for her sins. He had since taken the lead on an investigation that had already seen a man arrested, and yet he labored, investigating leads, weighing evidence, examining minutiae. She'd read his statement in the papers yesterday, that he meant to be sure they'd collared the right thief.

He meant to be sure. Collaring the right thief will break his heart. And somehow, even *that* thought didn't invoke the usual shimmering pain, nor could it summon her forth from this cold, numb place, the aerie into which she'd retreated when Louis had come for her.

He wanted Angela, his little girl, to dress up and pain-fuck, and shame-fuck, just like old times. I couldn't fight him, I just... couldn't. So I left him Angela. What choice did I have?

None. Louis had taken everything else, but he couldn't take that.

Finally, a hired trap pulled by a single horse trotted smartly up the gentle hill. Its lone occupant stepped out and turned to pay the cabbie. Angelique arose, waiting through the passing bout of vertigo, and stepped through her private sitting room, startling Clarice from her needlework.

"Inspector Cole has arrived." She paused, and drew a deeper breath. "See that Mrs. Reynolds escorts her to the gardens. Hannah will serve us coffee there."

"Yes, my lady," Clarice nodded. Angelique could feel the girl's concerned gaze upon her back as she arose to follow her mistress from the room.

"Inspector Cole," the baroness nodded in answer to the young woman's greeting. "Thank you for coming. My apologies again for having turned you away thrice. It was not my intention."

Angelique remembered her then, and against her will remembered the way Raven had looked at her when she'd approached him that morning at Bishop-Florian. Something inside did stir a little at that, feather-light and too far away to reach this quiet no-place. She heard her own voice in her ears, and knew it sounded too quiet, too weak to handle the implications of meeting her lover's latest chosen lover. If Barbara Cole were that...

Although Louis had known that she and Raven were intimate, she doubted Inspector Cole did. That thought restored what meager strength she'd managed to bring to the interview. She couldn't imagine it would last for long.

"I thank you for receiving me," Cole replied. The young woman watched her intently. Not with the stupid intensity of Gaust, but with that calm reserve that missed little, and gave away nothing. "I hope you're feeling better, Baroness. I read in Inspector Gaust's report that you had a fainting spell at the Countess Liberaune's party."

Angelique nodded. "I did, and have had trouble sleeping ever since. My physician assures me it's simple nervous exhaustion, however. I should recover fully, in time."

"That's what caused your fainting spell at the party?" Cole asked politely, following Angelique to a small table that had been set for them in the garden. The lady paused at a rose bush beside their table, profligate with golden blooms. She cupped one in her hand and inhaled its heady fragrance, then took a small pair of pruning shears from her pocket and trimmed it neatly away.

Without quite smiling, she handed it to her guest. "In combination with not having eaten that afternoon, I should imagine," she answered.

Barbara Cole beamed as she accepted the rose, for it had been a gracious gesture, one that savored of an older, more elegant world. She hadn't missed Carlisle's near-complete lack of emotion in the delivery, however, nor was she quite experienced enough to hide it.

"Why, thank you, Baroness. A girl who chooses law enforcement as a career rarely gets flowers."

"That is most unfortunate," Angelique murmured, the words more form than substance. She gestured for Cole to be seated. "Perhaps I'll start a new custom for your department, then." She folded herself gingerly into her own chair, and waved Hannah in with her coffee service.

Cole smiled, and sniffed her flower. "According to Inspector Gaust's report, you rode from Bishop-Florian Hall to the Liberaune villa with several of the other ladies and stayed there until Sultaire—umm... Sir Vincent—drove you home at about midnight. Is that accurate, my lady?"

The servant poured coffee for them both, and had withdrawn respectfully before Angelique answered. She noted with a distant sort of relief that the young inspector hadn't specified *whose* home. "Yes."

Cole's face was still partially hidden behind the rose. She nodded slightly. "Do you remember when you had your fainting spell?"

"Not directly, but the inspector said it had been at about twenty-one fifteen." Angelique briefly wished she could summon more strength into her voice for this, or even a shadow of the irreverence she'd used with Gaust; *anything* not to feel so very exposed before this woman, irrational though it was. "That is as well as I can place it, I'm afraid."

"I see. Well then, do you know when it was you felt strong enough to return to the party, my lady?"

Angelique sighed lightly, as if even drawing such a breath took more effort than she had to spare. "As closely as I can place it, Inspector, it was about twenty-three. I may be off by as much as a half-hour, either way. Doctor Martin might remember better than I, though. He tended me."

"I see," Cole replied, finally placing her rose on the table in exchange for her coffee. It gave Angelique a momentary pause, enough to wonder mildly if something had been wrong with the answers, but the question faded easily away under her interviewer's next words.

"My lady," Cole continued. "I would like to move on to another subject. Several informal meetings took place between the most influential members of the Ladies' Auxiliary *prior* to the formal committee meeting in which it voted to make the presentation. What was the substance of the discussions at those informal teas?"

"Oh, my. That was some time ago. Let me think. . . Well, the proper venue, of course," Angelique mused dully, sipping her sweetened coffee carefully, "as well as which agencies to employ in order to bolster security in the hall that was chosen. Ah, I believe we discussed scheduling, among those of us who volunteered to be present during the hours the exhibit was open to the public, and managing the details of the social events which took place during and around it. Preparations were quite extensive, as you may imagine."

"Of course. So the question of whether the committee would actually act as presenters for the *Mâgun-Zak* was never entertained prior to the actual vote?"

Angelique blinked. This particular line of questioning had stirred mild astonishment. "Of course not. The *Mâgun-Zak*, and all the other pieces in *F'ral* Santí's collection were part of a whole exhibit, Inspector Cole. Surely you must have been aware of this already? It was discussed thoroughly in the dailies."

"Precisely my question, my lady," Cole smiled. "The vote at the meeting held by the full committee accepting responsibility for putting on the Santí exhibit was no more than rote. The question was put. The vote was taken. The motion passed. But there were three informal teas attended by the senior members—and yourself. What, my lady, was discussed?"

The shadow of a frown flickered over the lady's pale features. "I hardly recall, Inspector Cole. We discuss many things during those afternoons, most of it hardly worth recording anywhere. I might be able to answer you more clearly if you asked me something more specific."

Inspector Barbara Cole, Angelique then learned, had an excellent memory, and no point was too small to warrant her detailed attention. The young cop took her through each of those three meetings, one by one, using her memory of who was present, what they were wearing, what they ate, and most unnervingly, Carlisle's baroness found herself recalling with uncanny clarity the details of conversations she had long since thought she had forgotten, but it was all trivia: the little, social talk women will engage in without men or children about to distract them. *Dull as ditch water. What could the inspector possibly find so intriguing about that?*

It was perhaps halfway through her dogged recounting of the second meeting that it dawned on Angelique that Barbara Cole simply did not know how things were done at the highest levels of Guardian Paladin society. The information for which she was fishing simply did not exist.

"Hold, Inspector," the baroness interrupted gently, after the sixteenth or sixtieth tedious question in a row. "We might dispense with most of this tiresome discussion if I knew whether you knew how such events are arranged in this city?"

Cole shook her head mutely. Angelique nodded, sinking back into resignation. "My dear, when the dowager Duchess of Winchester decides that she wishes a thing to be done, she does not ask *permission* of her social inferiors," she explained dully. "That simply is not done. The same is true with any of the duchies, or the greater earldoms. And when Countess Liberaune conceived a desire to bring *F'ral* Auguste Santí's exhibit to this country, she did not need any of the rest of us to put our stamp of approval on it."

The noblewoman passed a tired hand over her brow. "She informed us of her desire. As was our duty, we worked to bring it to fruition, under her guidance. As such, the teas held before the committee vote were just that—afternoon socials. The plans for the exhibit were discussed, certainly, but there was never a doubt that the exhibit itself would be held."

The girl closed her eyes, whether in embarrassment, consternation, or mental concentration, Angelique could not tell. Cole seemed to possess the maddening patience of a saint and the poker face of a hustler. It took several minutes, so long that the forerunning storm clouds had begun to obscure the sun, so long that Angel mulled the advantages of questioning her interviewer. Finally, Cole opened her eyes again, and sighed.

"Then perhaps, my lady, I will waste less of your time by moving on to what would appear to be more pertinent matters. Such as these details you mention."

"Of course, Inspector," she replied, settling back into her chair.

Cole took a sip of her coffee. "Let's turn our attention to the meetings, official and unofficial, where discussions about the exhibit were held."

Angelique nodded, sighing quietly. Despite her attempts to shorten the interview, she spent the next half-hour answering even more tedious questions. The morning's breeze had freshened into a constant, but gentle wind, tossing the flowers in the garden restlessly. Angel watched the beautiful bearded irises nodding and bowing to the nearby roses in a fair imitation of what the Paladins considered to be polite behavior, even while urging herself to pay at least *minimal* attention to the rote answers she was supplying.

It's no wonder why Raven is so irreverent about how he's serving his bond, she thought, quite privately. *Cops seem to have a passion for collecting minutiae.*

In the end, she was sure Inspector Barbara Cole had learned nothing new. The Baroness of Carlisle's votes in the meetings had been a matter of record, after all, and in the discussions beforehand, a mere baroness was rarely expected to voice her own opinions. Angelique's quiet answers were all truths, on the surface, and those truths were hardly incriminating.

Cole had absently picked up her rose again and gone quiet. "Thank you, my lady," she said finally. "A few more questions, and then I'll be finished." She looked at her again. "You had a key to the Foley Street entrance?"

The Foley Street entrance. . . ? For once, Angelique was grateful for the cocoon of numbness that had so safely insulated her from the rest of the world, even from her own heart, else Cole's question would have rocked her world, and exposed a single loose end that might have unraveled far enough to collar her. That had been her true entrance that night—it seemed a lifetime ago—and one of the extra keys that Louis had obtained for the job. But no one else could have known that!

"No, I don't believe so," was all she said, however, lifting a disinterested gaze back to her interviewer's face. "The sole street-level door I used was the one on Delancy Avenue." And even though she wished to know *why* Cole had asked, Angelique, for the first time in days, had to restrain herself from showing enough interest to ask.

Cole seemed to bore in. "Then just what keys were on your ring?"

Angelique allowed another tired, flickering frown to wrinkle her brow. It had been bait, no more. Cole was fishing. "Ah, let me think... The keys to the exhibit room, of course. The one to the entrance on Delancy. One to a storage room for the printed materials on the exhibit, though we ended up storing table linens and such there, for the afternoon socials that were held. One to the pantry on that floor where foods could be prepared. I believe that was it."

Thunder rumbled in the distance. "I see. And did you keep those keys under your charge at all times?"

"They were not on my person at all times, no," she admitted.

Cole smiled, and Angelique thought she detected a hint of smugness in the expression. "Can you recall when they were not?"

She allowed herself a tired, fretted expression. It wasn't completely an act. The woman's obsession with trivia was irritating. "Perhaps with your memory, you could recall them, Inspector. I cannot."

"Forgive me, my lady," Cole begged genuinely. "But as your friend, Sir Vincent, is so fond of saying, it is often the trifles that are most important. So let me take you through this one step at a time, just like we did before..."

"No, Inspector," Angelique said, voice and hands trembling openly. She'd mentioned Raven again, and Raven was too close to her personal despair. "I cannot go on like this today. It has been more fatiguing than I imagined. If you have further questions, you may return again tomorrow, but for now, I must go lie down."

Cole looked at her closely again, seeing more there than Angelique felt comfortable revealing—a woman pushed back to the edges of exhaustion. The girl nodded at last, and stood. "I understand," she said quietly. "If you'll excuse me, my lady, I'll trouble you no further today."

"Of course. If you would, ask Hannah or Mrs. Reynolds to send Clarice to me, on your way out." She would have felt better had she been able to summon tears, but it just wasn't in her. "Thank you, Inspector Cole. Good day."

Barbara Cole looked at her again somberly, concern clearly visible in her liquid brown eyes. Then, as the sun disappeared for the last time that afternoon, she nodded, picked up her rose, and left.

*   *   *

Vincent's hard-soled boots clicked loudly on the polished stone floor of the city jail. He had stopped by the commissioner's office on his way. The hearing was in three days. It would take at least a day to collate all the information he and his inspectors had collected into a form that would allow him to present a clear picture of the case to the magistrate.

Not that it mattered. Roland had reinforced that point, too. The Foreign Office was dancing feverishly for the Royal Government of Vin-Nôrë, trying to paint a pretty face over something that was damned ugly; so ugly, in fact, that the aged patricians of the Ladies' Auxiliary had been hauled before the full House of Lords to explain just exactly *why* they saw fit to ignore the opinions of the security experts they'd hired.

My, how the arrogant have fallen. "Cell one-oh-eight," he told the cell block guard, holding up his badge.

The guard yawned. "You want him brought to an interrogation room?"

The dumbest cops were always assigned to jail duty, and for obvious reasons. "No," Raven explained patiently. "I would have sent an intern, had I wanted that. I'll talk to him *in* his cell. Now let's go."

The guard shrugged. Keys rattled in the lock, and soon they were walking down the long corridor of cells.

Cell 108 looked like every other cell in the block, mere holding pens where the accused remained until their trials were completed. Each contained two simple cots, a shelf on which a bowl could be placed for washing and shaving, and a hole in the floor with a grille over it for bodily wastes. What poor lighting existed was provided by either torches or oil lamps, recessed deeply into the walls. They weren't meant to be appealing accommodations, merely clean and temporary. The thief known as the Spider had an advantage over some of his neighbors in that at least he was alone in his tiny cage.

Cooper, seated desultorily on his bunk, looked up at the approaching footsteps. He wasn't a handsome man by any measure, though he was fairly intelligent and competent at his chosen profession.

"Raven," the prisoner grunted, leaning back against the cell wall. "Think your pa can bust me out of this one?"

Sultaire motioned Cooper to wait. "Let me in, then return to your post," he told the guard. "I'll call when I need you. This might take a few minutes."

He waited patiently, and silently, while the thick-witted guard complied, then lumbered off. "Dave, right now a duke couldn't get you out of this, and that's why I'm here."

"No shit," he said, resignedly. "I thought you were a cop, now."

Raven's eyes warned Spider to caution. He reached into his pocket, pulled out his badge, and showed it to Cooper. "You've been framed, Dave," he murmured, putting his badge away. "I know it, the commissioner knows it, everybody on the case brighter than that guard knows it. And, under normal circumstances, when I got through presenting the evidence to the

Magistrate, they'd figure it out, too. There's enough there. The problem is that Parliament needs a gull. Since you're handy..."

"I'm going down," he nodded. "I already made that when I didn't get sprung after spilling my guts in front of the Seer. What I don't make is who did do it, or why they wanted me to wear the collar for it."

"That sums it up pretty nicely, yes. It was a she, about a hundred sixty-five centimeters tall, with access to inside information and resources. She's damned fast, and a pretty good mimic. That ring any bells?"

He sighed. "Coulda' been Spectre, but I don't want to make it like that, Raven. She's always played by the rules. No way she'd leave fingers pointing at me like that."

"True. And she has her own methods," Raven reminded him, "none of which entail tussling with armed guards."

"Then there's Camille," Dave shrugged. "But that ain't her track. And no convenient corpses littering the floor to say otherwise."

Raven shook his head. "I don't think so. This woman took out six guards without permanently hurting anyone. Camille would have left six corpses— never mind that, like you say, robbery's not her gig. And all the gods know, she certainly doesn't need the money. How about vendettas, Dave? Got any old fucks after your ass?"

"Not to sell me off to the Man," he grinned quickly. But this was too big, and too serious. The humor didn't last. "Not that I know of, Vince. I been making it over and over, lately. Nothing else to do." He waved a hand at his cell. "I can't think of nobody wants me out of the way *that* bad."

Raven visibly slumped on the bed. He was almost totally out of leads, and time was running out. He'd been told that being a cop was supposed to mean doing good, protecting society, especially the innocent; but here was an innocent man, a man someone went a long way out of their way to frame, and his badge wasn't helping one bit. In fact, it was a hindrance.

"You're sure?" he said, his tongue feeling thick in his mouth.

"Hey, man, I'll fuckin' let you know if that changes, believe it." Spider shook his head. "I think we got a new player, to tell the truth. And this one's connected to the big players. Has to be. Small-timers don't get access to the kind of magic muscle it woulda' taken to get around those wards without tripping 'em."

Raven's head snapped around. "What did you say?" he demanded.

"I said," he repeated, looking Raven in the eye, "it ain't just anybody's got access. Those reflecting crystals are the like ballista against most magical security. You got to be connected in the right places, and those places like nice, big chunks of change to convince them your heart's in the right place. Unless the new player's a spell-slinger, he needs that access. And got it, somewhere."

Raven's eyebrow arched, then he looked at the ceiling. "A mage, or big connections," he mused out loud. "And my money's on the connections. Hiding behind a famous burglar would be just their cup of tea." He shook his head. "It isn't much, and it's probably a tangled trail," he told Spider, "but I'll follow it. Can you give me a list?"

The man looked at him oddly, intently, and then regretfully shook his head. "You're a cop, Raven," he reminded Sultaire softly. "If I go down for this, at least I'll still be alive. I start spilling shit like that to you, and I'm as good as dead." He sighed heavily, and rubbed his face briskly with both hands. "But hey. You were a pretty good con, once. And you still know where enough bodies are buried."

Raven winked at him. "Suit yourself," he said, standing up. "Guard! I'll do what I can, Dave. See you at the hearing."

"I ain't going nowhere else," Spider shrugged. "But Raven? Thanks, man."

* * *

Blue Jacket Tavern, Merchants
23 Amerian 580, 1730 hours

"... but anyway, that's the last of it," Gaust was saying, droning through the last of his report. "The last restricted areas of Bishop-Florian will be re-opened for visitors tomorrow, much to the delight of Executive Fucking Director Gregory." The big cop looked as if he wanted to spit, but settled instead for a swallow of the good brown ale he'd ordered. "The findings will be on your desk in the morning, Chief."

Raven nodded and turned to Cole. "Inspector?"

She waved at an acquaintance across the rapidly filling room, then addressed herself to her boss's inquiry. "The Baroness Carlisle gave me nothing new to go on. Just like the other ladies, she couldn't recall any details of any of the conversations that had occurred before the Auxiliary voted to sponsor the exhibit, and just like the rest of them, she was pretty careless about safeguarding the set of keys she had. I've got all the testimony recorded, though."

Raven sighed, and ran his hand over his eyes. "Time to start to wrap things up then, I guess. The hearing's on the twenty-sixth. I've got one more lead that I'm chasing down—mostly because I've got the contacts to do it. Not just anybody can get the magical muscle needed to thwart the wards that protected that necklace. So what I need you two to do is digest what we know—objectively," he pointed right at Gaust. "What says he did it. What says he didn't. Unless we make another arrest, what I get up and tell the Magistrate is really beside the point, but I at least want the court record to show all the evidence on both sides."

They both nodded, and looked at Raven speculatively. Neither said what was on their minds about the nature of those "connections," though.

"I think you're wasting your time," Gaust finally said, "but it's your time to waste, and I can follow an order. Anything else?"

Vincent smiled at him ruefully. "You're probably right. And even if you're not, I'd just be dumb lucky to dig my way to the bottom of that little corner

87

of the underground in seventy-two hours. So no, I think that's it. Time to go off duty."

Gaust rose, and clapped him on the shoulder. "You might make a good cop yet. Run you home, Cole?" he asked.

"Not yet." She looked directly at Raven. "Got a minute, Sultaire?"

Gaust shrugged in some disappointment, but finished his ale, and lumbered out.

"More than that, if you're interested," he smiled tiredly at her.

She quirked him a grin. "My interest in more than a minute might increase, once this case is docked and you're not my case leader, anymore," she admitted, "but that's not what I wanted to talk to you about."

"That sounds promising," he chuckled. "Even potential friendships seem to be running a bit thin. Intimate ones even more so." He gave her a sidelong look. "I hope you don't mind if I tease you outrageously between now and then. I've kind of been enjoying that. So, what's up?"

"I noticed," she drawled, hiding most of her expression behind the liter of Danvers she'd ordered. "I have some information for you that isn't going into my record of the interview with your friend, Lady Blakesly." Again she paused, sipping at her beer and watching him.

"Oh?" He arched an eyebrow and absently flagged a server. "Stay for dinner?"

"Sure," she nodded. "Though being on this case with you is running up my tab here hellishly. I don't know how you can afford it."

"I've got a rich daddy," he drawled sarcastically. "So I'll buy. You could even consider it our first date."

Cole snorted. "No, I could not," she asserted firmly, "and it will be separate tabs," she further ordered the waiter who'd just approached.

"I'm crushed! But far be it from me to gainsay a lady," he waved at the waiter. "Menus, if you please."

The waiter nodded and returned with them. Cole waited until they'd ordered and the waiter had left before returning to the subject.

"I'm no lady, Sultaire, but I'm concerned for one you seem to care about." Barbara Cole was a determined young woman, and obviously had no intentions of allowing the knight across from her to pursue any further romantic intentions at that moment. "Lady Blakesly did not look, or act, well. She was pale. Listless. Like it was an effort for her to get up the energy to speak to me at all. That's not how the papers described her the night of the Liberaune dinner party."

Raven felt the room turn momentarily at Cole's description of Angel. Not wanting to give away too much to the rookie cop who, it seemed, had yet to completely figure out how to put away her badge, he drank from his mug of ale. Something was niggling at the back of his mind, a thing that seemed important, but the harder he tried to trace the thought down, the faster it ran from him. One thing was certain, however. This wasn't the Angel he knew. Not at all.

"I see," he said finally. "And what's her explanation?"

"She said her physician called it 'nervous exhaustion,'" Cole replied as quietly as the room would let her.

Damn. What was it? It was right there... "I see," he repeated. "It sounds as though it's time for me to make some time to see Lady Blakesly."

She nodded, and again Raven watched her pause to wrestle with something internally, before refocusing her gaze on him. "You might as well hear it from me, then. The baroness dismissed me before our interview could be concluded. I... I think I pushed her for too long in questioning her, Sultaire. She was pretty close to the edge when I left."

Angel? Exhausted by an interview? Once again the room attempted to invert itself. He was definitely going to have to see her—alone!

He nodded to his companion, unwilling to discuss the matter with her further. "Thank you," he said simply. "Any more juicy tidbits, or is it time to talk about the weather, and other such fascinating things?"

That eased up her intense regard of him, and made her laugh. "We can talk about the weather, if you want. Some storm today, huh?"

It was nearly dark by the time Raven and Barbara Cole left the Blue Jacket. She was headed home to her small flat; he, across town to drop in on Angelique.

Dinner, he decided as his trap clopped across the city, had gone well. Cole had collapsed several times in gales of laughter, and had opened up to him considerably. She was the eldest daughter of a prosperous family in Merchants', right in the heart of Fernwall. Her father managed a retail store, and her mother worked as a secretary in a law office, which allowed the family the luxury of a full time cook, housekeeper, and even a third general servant.

He looked up as his trap drove past one of the hundreds of huge brownstones that dotted the city's skyline. Barbara had grown up in one just like it. So had half of the city's population, probably. And, like some lucky children did, she had attended an expensive, private school for her education. She got good marks, and knew by the time she was thirteen that she wanted to be a cop. She was witty, smart, and pretty, in a wholesome sort of way. She seemed to get the point of Raven's dropped hints, that he desired a more intimate friendship with her.

In point of fact, it would be nice to have a few friends like her. Most of the friends he had before his trial either didn't trust him now, or had abandoned him altogether after his conviction; and while he hardly considered himself a cop, it was a simple statement of fact that he spent more hours with them than anybody else. It was also true that Gaust's attitude toward him was actually friendly, compared to most of the force who, as Barbara had indicated, gave even odds to him for being the culprit in his own case. He was neither cop nor thief, slave nor freeman. He truly was "the black sheep" that fit in nowhere. *And, you know you've got nobody to blame but yourself!*

The sound of the horse's hooves on the pavement turned hollow as the trap rumbled over a bridge, not far from Angelique's city home. City workmen were uncovering the magical crystals in the street lamps that illuminated the bridge during the night. As he looked down river, he could see the mist rolling up out of the bay already. It would be another foggy summer night in Fernwall. *All the better.*

With a sigh, he pushed his ruminations aside and started changing into tight, coal black clothing covered with an equally dark cloak. The use of his grandfather's Raven Wing had originally earned him his "Raven" nickname, but Roland had taken it, and the magitech gear that went with it, for the term of his indenture. Though it didn't provide him the limited kind of flight the wartime artifact did, equally important was that it masked his body shape in shadows, and against the night skyline. An indistinct, dark blob was harder to discern in low light than a human form. Also like the Raven Wing, it doubled as a serviceable shield when needed; though, unlike the nearly indestructible artifact, such punishment was hard on the cloak.

With a couple of sharp stomps, he tugged back on his boots and waited. He intended to spend the better part of the night with Angelique, if he could. That meant knocking on her front door would be a very bad idea. It would not afford them the privacy he was almost sure they needed. Fortunately, there was a trellis right beside her bedroom window on the second floor. He'd used it several times before, and he intended to use it tonight, leaving her maidservant, and the rest of the staff, blissfully ignorant of his presence.

The driver dropped him at an intersection near Angelique's townhouse. From there, he walked. Other than the illumination from below-stairs, where her servants still worked, the only light visible came from Angel's bedroom window—a single lamp, or set of candles perhaps—and one toward the back of the house from the room he knew to be Clarice's.

He made his way back to a small opening in the hedgerow, checking for unwanted eyes, then ducked beneath it and made his way to the trellis. Angel had always kept it in good repair—for his use, she'd often jested. It was wound about with ivy, honeysuckle, and climbing roses, and placed so that the breeze that blew off the bay carried in with it the fragrance of the flowers, during spring and summer. This evening the window was open, and the storm-cleansed breeze riffled the lacy white curtains.

He paused near the top, peering cautiously through the open window. Her bedchamber was simply appointed: a four-postered double bed, chest of drawers, mirrored dressing table, and a small table flanked by two richly upholstered chairs, placed just before the large bay window. The wallpaper design featured roses, irises, and lilies, and they were echoed in the design of the comforter on the bed, the rugs on the floor, and the fabric in the chairs and drapes.

Angelique sat in one of the chairs, lamp burning on the table beside her. She was wearing a nightgown and robe in pale green, her ash-blond hair loose about her shoulders. There was an open book in her lap, but she wasn't looking at it. She was, in fact, staring with calm resignation at the figure in black, who peered at her through her bedroom window.

Raven deftly climbed on through, crossed to her, and knelt before her, to take her hand in his. It was frighteningly cold. Abruptly, he found himself without words and could do no more than search her eyes for some clue as to the nature of her state. They were more brown than green, and sunk in dark hollows beneath her pale brows. She looked like a walking corpse. His own heart sank in what he could admit, privately, was fear.

"Angel?" he whispered, surprised at the wavering catch in his voice.

Something, some response flickered in her without quite making it to the surface. She murmured his name, and it fell from her lips like ash.

He found himself fighting back tears and a fear that made him want to shake. "Darling, what is it? Are you unwell? What's happened?"

Her eyes moved over him, in some resemblance of her old affection. Her chest lifted, pulling air into lungs that seemed to resist and resent the intrusion. "You came," she murmured. The words were merely the mildest of tremors in flat, D'wanese inflections. "I had not... expected to see you. Your Inspector Cole again, perhaps. But not you." It seemed to mystify her, albeit mildly. Whatever had initially stirred within her, at his appearance, began to subside again.

"I... I've been trying to find out who ruined your exhibit." His eyes searched her face imploringly, and again he saw something move within her, impossibly deep, too far away to touch. "But, I was told, privately—earlier, this evening—how... I had to come. I would have come sooner but..." Frustration complicated the emotional chaos that threatened to drown out clear thought.

"Someone was arrested for that, days ago." Still her eyes were fastened upon him, as if her life depended upon it, in fact. The thought chilled him again, and he shook his head.

"Wrong man," he said softly. "It was obvious within thirty minutes that Cooper had been cleverly set up. But you! Burning bright, tell me what's wrong. What more can I do?" He had to fight to keep it from sounding like a sob, and even then he wasn't sure he succeeded.

"Raven." This time it was stronger, and it was a plea. But then, she shook her head, as if negating something he'd said. Her eyes closed, in resignation perhaps, or defeat.

"Dr. Lagrange says it is exhaustion. Nerves. Nothing more." Even as she said the words, he could hear how little they mattered to her. "I... can't seem to sleep..."

The incongruities fought a three-way battle with known facts, and with fear, for his attention. He'd seen her go though mild episodes like this a few times, but never to the point of insomnia. In the past, a day of rest and solitude had set her to rights, brought back the fires, burning bright—like she had been that night, at the party, like she had been in the bed they'd shared afterwards. Now, whatever was wrong with her only seemed to become worse with her enforced isolation. The stress of what happened to her exhibit, perhaps? And why the unspoken plea, hidden in her voice? What did she want? Why couldn't she say?

He mentally shook himself to clear his head. *Think, Vince. Clear your head and think. You can't help her if you're an emotional basket case, too.*

He did visibly shake his head, partly for his own benefit, partly in answer to her. "That may be some of it, darling," he said gently. "But just a few days ago, you lit up whole rooms, tired or not. What's happened? Please tell me?"

Again it moved within her, like form within smoke; a vast rolling so deep in the interior of her psyche that all an observer could discern was a subtle *lifting* on the surface, which then receded quickly. Her shoulders sagged.

"I cannot seem..." Angel began slowly, presence slowly returning as she concentrated, as if she were drawing on his strength for it. The fingers of her other hand drifted out to touch his clean-shaven cheek. "I... the oath I swore, that night... I can't seem to stop thinking about it, hearing it, echoing in my mind."

Were those tears gathering? He caught his breath. "Remembering what happened..." she went on, the last words barely exhaled. "Raven, it's changed everything..."

"Yes," he whispered, holding her frigid hand against his cheek. Tears did well up in his eyes then, and there was nothing he could do to stop them. Fear, frustration, and love all roiled within him like a disjointed symphony. Wordlessly, he stretched up to kiss her, trying mightily to express through that kiss what simply wouldn't come out in any other way. She flinched back instinctively, and then her lips trembled, and moved under his woodenly, as if she were forcing them to respond. Angel started to shake. She inhaled sharply, unevenly, and then her mouth opened under his, and her entire body shivered so violently that the book she'd been ignoring slid, unheeded, to the floor.

Raven silently exulted as he felt the barrier between them fall, and somehow, as her sweet mouth opened to his, he knew things would be all right. With that knowledge, a dam opened, and his love for her burst through him like a raging torrent, bathing her in it, baptizing her in it, as she pulled her heart free from its tomb.

Finally, almost reluctantly, he pulled back from her, just a little, the better to regard her once more. Tears rolled silently down her cheeks, washing out the deadened brown in her eyes, and bringing back the green that matched the robe she wore. When she spoke to him again, her voice was still husky from days of disuse, but it trembled from the emotional onslaught he'd just unlocked.

"Oh, you would bring me back, wouldn't you?" she breathed, hands still on his face. Her voice was shaking as hard as the rest of her. "Of all souls in this sorry world, you would be the one to break through my despair, and drag me back to life, to live again..."

"As you have me," he whispered, his own tears still falling. "And yes, I will, again and again." Relief was making him light-headed, but at least his internal, emotional chaos had begun to resolve itself into order. She was alive. It was buried, but the flame still burned, and he could still call it forth.

He picked her up and carried her to the bed, then quickly doffed his cloak and hung his sword over the bedpost before lying down beside her. "You've brightened the darkness of my exile, and I draw you forth from the tomb of noble indenture," he whispered to her, caressing her cheek.

"To live again," she sighed, still weeping. "To face love, and pain. Desire, and heartache. Oh, *Mar'leven,*" and now her voice seemed to be strangling in its own sorrow. "Where were you? You didn't come, and I thought..."

He pressed a finger to her lips, stilling her. It was his rakehell, playboy reputation again. The Guardian Paladin church had turned him into an icon of sin, the "ignoble man," an example to young boys of how not to act, a caution to young girls of whom not to love, for he stole their hearts, and then broke them. Even Angel, it seemed, had fallen prey to the propaganda.

"You thought I'd stolen your heart, only to leave you," he voiced her unspoken accusation. "Yes. I realize that now," he said sadly, looking away. "I'm... I'm sorry. I didn't realize you... I guess I should have," he finished lamely, wiping the tears from his cheeks.

"No." That denial, at that moment, had more force than all the other words put together. "That's not what I meant... You bear no fault..."

It was her turn to shake her head, as if to clear it. Even as Raven watched, Angel seemed to reach some decision, or point of no return. Will and agency flooded back into her, almost by the heartbeat. "By all the Gods, I have been a fool, beloved. A silly, weak-minded fool. Too much at the mercy of my own weakness, and of a mind that sometimes cannot escape itself. I have not been worthy of you, *Mar'leven,* of your strength, or of your courage. I can do better, I think. If you'll forgive me."

"Forgive you?" He snorted ironically. "You're asking *me* to forgive you?" He looked at her, his eyes dancing with love and suppressed mirth. "It's you who are supposed to be *my* salvation, remember?"

He laughed at this, but stopped as soon as he saw the despair bleach the color from her eyes once more. He gathered her in his arms and held her tightly. "Oh, burning bright. If you need it, you have it in full measure. For simple love of you, you have it."

Angelique quietly nestled against his chest for several long moments until the sounds of the night without intruded themselves, time measured by the ticking of the small clock at her bedside. He could sense that she was deep in thought.

"You are my salvation, Raven. Never doubt it. I suppose we'll be that for each other, and more. Until you release me from that oath I swore. Until you can tell me you don't love me anymore, and make me believe it."

Relief raced through him like a torrent, again making him light-headed. On the one hand he expected no less of himself. She was lying in his arms, head on his chest, and had just affirmed to him—to herself!—the oath she'd sworn the last night they'd spent together, the night of the Liberaune party. But, there was another side of him, a side that ran under the surface like an ocean current, always in motion, never still, always seething in his father's gravelly voice. She was too smart, too pretty, too devout, too well-connected, and of too high a station to be interested in a dolt like him, because *he* was too stupid, too inattentive, too slow, and far too slothful to be of interest to a woman of her quality. He'd heard that, and every variation, on a daily basis, before he'd finally run away; but running hadn't quieted the voice. It had simply turned it into a ghost.

"Then..." the words came thickly, "then perhaps we should consider— marriage." A large part of him sat gawking at the fact that those words had actually come out of his mouth. He held her there, squirming inside for a moment that likely seemed longer to him than it truly was, while Angel, who had gone quiet, considered her response.

"Likely we should," she eventually replied, and he could hear the gentle smile in her words, "but I was not aware that one in your... ah, *unique* position could marry."

"I can't," he agreed quietly. "Yet. But I can be betrothed, and between good behavior, and the intentions of an upstanding citizen and noble of name, there's a decent chance that my sentence could be reduced." *Yeah, and you could find the real thief of the* Mâgun-Zak, *too.*

Angelique pushed herself back, just far enough to allow her to watch his face intently. "I can hardly believe I'm hearing this," she whispered, eyes searching his carefully. "You would actually want to marry me, Vincent?"

He didn't need to think about the reply. He already knew it, and had known it for several days. He couldn't have given less of a damn that she was a baroness. Socially, marrying her meant he would be vaulted to equal peerage with his father. Although there was some ego-satisfying irony in that, he had to admit that Angel could have been a pauper's daughter, and his answer would have been the same.

"In a cold minute," he whispered, meeting her gaze, a bit surprised at the lump rising in his throat.

"Heart of the Lady," she swore softly, eyes refilling with tears. "What have I done to deserve this of y—"

Something, some thought or memory darkened her eyes momentarily, and she closed them tightly, visibly willing it away. When Angelique looked at him again, the newborn clarity and determination in her gaze shone with all the promise of the dawn.

"Then I would be your wife, *Mar'leven*. While my oath stands intact, I could be no other."

Had he been standing, his knees would have buckled. As it was his breath came in a ragged gasps, and for all the world he could not keep her face and the entire room around it from spinning.

"Oh, burning bright... what have you wrought?" He was shaking. A part of him refused to believe what he'd just done. Another part of him was exulting joyously. It felt for all the world like he'd just begun a new life, with a new purpose. One that could carry him through the intervening years between this night and the seven years into the future when his bond expired, when the privileges of citizenship and nobility were again restored.

"I don't know," Angelique repeated, recalling how similar the circum- stances were to the last time he'd asked her that. "But, I suspect that we will need some help with this, my love." He could almost have sworn she shivered, but he was shaking so hard himself it was difficult to tell. "Perhaps more than either of us knows. I think, however, I know where to get it."

He nodded, and slowly got his body back under his control. "I'm glad someone does, because I'm fresh out of help." It was half-jest, half-serious. "Right now," he pushed on, "I want you." He slipped the knot on her robe, revealing more of her thin nightgown, and the barely concealed breasts just under it. "Unless, of course, you're going to refuse me."

The shudder that took her passed visibly through her entire body. "I could as easily refuse my own breath." She let him help her free of her robe, leaving only a thin layer of fine linen between her body and the heat of his hands. His kisses started at her lips, then traveled hungrily over her, heedless of her nightgown, but tenderly, reverently, so unlike Louis's savage ferocity. The life energy Raven had kindled within her flared under his passionate ministrations, and Angelique felt herself shake free of the last, cloying vestiges of the wooden numbness into which she'd retreated, the last time her body had been thus touched—by Louis, who still held the mortgage on her future...

Angel had no idea what she was going to do about Louis, and about the sea of lies and deceptions between her heart and that of the man she'd just promised to marry, but here with Raven, in his arms, all things seemed possible.

The pressure he'd brought to bear in trying to penetrate linen with his hands and mouth had become painful, but it was a welcome kind of pain, one that stirred her inert flesh to life. Even as his sharp teeth nipped her, and she cried out in response, Angel thrust away the disgusting memories of Angela's responses, and tried to pull Raven closer. But, he stopped suddenly, and lifted his head to look at her, or perhaps *through* her. He was breathing hard, and his eyes burned with a kind of desire she'd never seen in him before.

It was a kind of desire he'd never felt before.

Slowly, almost reverently, he peeled back the last layer between them, removing her filmy nightgown, now damp from his attentions. He rose then, and doffed his own clothing, pausing only to gaze upon her as though he were seeing her for the first time. A lithe form, her body seemingly illuminated by the shining halo of her hair spread out beneath her head. Emotions raged within him: This beautiful, intelligent, willful woman had agreed to become his life's-partner, his heart's mate, had given herself to him despite his past, and very public shame. Even in spite of the teachings of her own church, Angelique Blakesly wished to be his wife! What kind of creature was she, who could cast aside such faults and desire to possess him for her own?

Reverent indeed, he ran his hands over the length of her, a feather light touch that sent shivers coursing through her like tiny bolts of lightning. His hands caressed her calves, then the inside of her thighs, spreading her legs gently. He touched her bush, then the lips of her labia, then bent over to kiss her there, the most intimate of kisses, before looking at her wonderingly.

95

"Is this real?" he asked, his voice full of wonder.

Matching his every breath, his Angel answered him. "It is. It is the most 'real' thing in my life, *Mar'leven*." Her voice broke in a sob. "It feels like the *only* thing left that is real."

"And... and you really want me?" He asked, his voice a barely audible whisper. "You really want *me*, of all men living, to be your husband?"

"Gods!" Angel hissed, all the ferocity of the shout she couldn't release impregnating that single, breathy syllable. "*You* are real. *You* are truth. You are *life!*" In one single, fluid move she'd sat up, clasping his shirt in her hands to pull herself up to him. "Love! Strength! Passion! All the things I most want to be, and all that I am not, when we're apart... Raven, I would gladly do whatever it takes to hold onto that, in you, forever!"

His eyes widened, and then he kissed her wildly, his tongue seeking hers in a fury of passion. His arms crushed her to him so tightly she could barely breathe. Within, his doubts clamored at him, denying what he'd heard, mocking him for what he'd done. In another heartbeat, he'd dismissed all that, coalescing and galvanizing his intentions into the only part of this that he could really understand and accept: He loved her. More than that, he was *in love with* her, and the separation of being in two different bodies was more unbearable by the second. He wanted to be inside her, to live there within her tangible grace, to forget what it had ever been like *not* to be there.

"I want you," he said fiercely. "I want *all* of you. Now."

All of me. He wants all *of me?* By the gods, she did desire to give him all of herself. She ached to spill every wretched lie, every hateful deception she'd ever perpetrated, and beg for absolution, and forgiveness.

Do it! Just tell him! This is Raven, he'll understand!

They trembled there upon her lips, the first tentative cascade of confessions, beyond which there would be no going back. Tears stung her eyes once more, and she kissed him again, forcefully, stopping the words before they could come, knowing herself for a coward. She couldn't tell him. Not then. The unspoken words seared with blinding intensity, and she wept as, their bodies joined at last, the truths she needed to tell him remained unspoken.

Oh, dear Lord and Lady, he is all I really want in this life...

The world disappeared entirely, and all that was left was the feel of their hearts and bodies, moving as one. Everything they had shared, and had not shared; everything they had promised, and promises already broken; everything they could be, and now could never be, swirled around them and between them, coalescing into a moment that stretched into forever, and yet ended all too quickly. For all that was to come, in that interlude, they at last became aware of what they really were: They were one.

Chapter 7

The trap creaked to a stop. Raven jumped out into the damp, early-morning fog, paid his fare, and headed down the street, boots clicking loudly on the cobblestone walk. The previous night's events were still tumbling through his mind. As had so often happened in the past, when he bothered to reflect upon his life, his thoughts were laced with bitter irony and self-deprecation.

He and Angel had given themselves to each other. They were now privately betrothed. The improbability of it made him want to collapse in helpless gales of laughter. *You've done it now, Vince. Not only do you wear the collar of the state, you're about to shackle yourself with a wife.* He chuckled aloud, and shook his head in spite of himself.

Have I gone that insane? Have I fallen so much in love with her that I actually want to marry?

"Relationship" had never been a word that fit easily in Vincent Sultaire's mouth. Sex had always been something in which he'd engaged for reasons no more profound than arrant lust; or, more often, it was part of the game, an infinitely pleasurable tool for gaining information. In truth, when it involved a willing female, it was the one he tended to rely upon the most.

"Uncle Bill's Emporium," the sign seemed to swim out of the surrounding fog. Raven paused and seemed to gaze up at it, though he barely saw it.

And then there's Angelique.

The one woman in Fernwall capable of conning the entire upper social class and Church of the Guardian Paladin with such facile grace that her assumption of Lady Emilia's place in the Church upon the old matron's death was an article of faith. *And you're dumb enough to want to marry her. Vincent, you're an idiot. If you're going to be that stupid, why not marry Roland? At least he only wears one face: Grumpy!*

Yeah, except Roland wouldn't be any good in bed. That concept set him to chuckling silently again.

Angel was a woman whose religious trappings came off with her clothes, whose easy acceptance of her own sexuality made her as much a whore in his bed as paragon in her church, and who knew as many of the earthy names used for sexual expression as she knew scriptures from the *Oracles of the Interregnum*.

Is that why you want to marry her?

Physically, he supposed Angel was no prettier than any number of women he slept with on a regular basis, and she wasn't nearly as gorgeous as some few that he bedded from time to time. *Be honest, Vince. They're all prostitutes, call girls, or thieves. Their importance is measured solely by the rules of the game: We fuck, and during that lust-filled hour or two, buy or sell a tidbit of worthwhile information.*

With Angel, it had been different. Her double life had quickly become a cornerstone of their relationship. It provided both of them with hours of amusement, and at times fueled the fires of their passion. *And what's new there, chum?*

With a deep breath, he shrugged and entered the shop. The place reeked of old leather, mildew, and stale smoke. It was filled, wall-to-wall, with furniture, art, knick-knacks, jewelry, and hundreds of other used items, all available for sale—a pawn shop, by any other name.

A con, Spider had called him. *It's probably apt.* Sometimes even he had trouble figuring out where the game began and ended. At first glance, he could only think of one person in his life that he *wasn't* conning: Angelique.

That gave him pause.

His feelings for Angel went so deep he was afraid to look at them, betrothed or not.

What if that's it, he mused. *Maybe I'm not conning her, I'm conning myself.*

"May I help you?" a portly woman asked.

As if on cue Vincent spun around, a winning smile on his face, his great coat flying. "Certainly," he beamed. "Tell Uncle Bill that Raven wants to make a sale."

The woman's eyebrows shot up, but she merely nodded, and then ducked behind the faded curtain that served as a door into the back room. A moment later, a man who was easily as fat as his female counterpart emerged, wiping his spectacles on the cloth of his shirt.

"Raven?" The man known as "Uncle Bill" peered around suspiciously. "Ain't you out of business, son? Or did you come to pawn your badge?" He replaced the spectacles on his face, but the suspicious stare remained.

"I already did that," Raven drawled, "but they keep giving me new ones. They're useful at times. Got a minute for me in the back?"

"Uncle Bill" didn't drop his suspicions. "What ya' lookin' for, son?"

"Things best not bandied about right out here in the open," Raven said pointedly, voice low. "So either tell me to leave, or let's go visit your back room."

Raven watched in private amusement for another moment, while Bill's curiosity wrestled with his good sense. Curiosity won out, as Raven knew it would. The portly man stepped back, holding open the curtain for his guest to pass.

Wordlessly, Raven passed through the office into a small, nearly-empty room which contained only two bare, wooden chairs and a small table. A single candle provided the only illumination. Sounds here died quickly, and even footsteps sounded dull, thanks to the layer of cork which lined the floor. Once inside, he paused, and waited for Bill to follow.

After a murmured exchange with the woman (his mistress, Raven had cause to know), he appeared, stepping with business-like precision to his customary chair. "You're giving me grief, boy," he said, gesturing curtly for Raven to sit. "This had better be worth it."

"Have I ever let you down?" Raven grinned enigmatically, ignoring the rotund man to take his accustomed place—sitting on the corner of the table. "This badge they nailed on me has proved interesting. As it turns out, when things in the underground change, I get to see it first. Specifically: Somebody went a long way out of their way to set up the Spider. Coop didn't steal the *Mâgun-Zak*."

"Yeah? What's that got to do with me?"

"Think, Bill. You don't take out competition in this business unless you want to start a turf war. And turf battles are usually about more than thieves." He let that sink in for a few heart beats, then baited the hook. "Whoever stole that necklace was good. Damned good. I've got one chance left to spring Cooper, and it's through the back door. I've got to find out who provided the jinx that bypassed the security on the necklace itself. That's Spectre's domain. I need to know where to find her."

"And you think she's gonna tell you how she's connected? Get serious, boy. You can come in here and talk the talk, but everybody knows you're walkin' at the end of Roland's leash, now."

And the fish takes the bait. Now to set the hook. "Yeah and everybody knows you're an upstanding store owner in the second-hand business, too," Raven chuckled. "You want me to rattle off the names of people you've ratted out to save your fat ass when things got too hot? The Raven's still alive and well, old man. Give me an hour on the streets, and we'll just see who believes what."

It hung there for one tense moment. Raven saw the first beads of sweat that broke out on Bill's brow. The older man swallowed once, uneasily.

Time to reel in the catch. "Now, do you want to play nice, or do you want to play dirty?" Raven murmured, in low tones. "If you'll remember, 'dirty' costs more."

"I know who would know," he said.

*   *   *

Blakesly House, Lower Angels
20 Amerian 580, 0900 hours

"I was a fool, beloved. A silly, weak-minded fool."

She'd sent him off before the dawn, and he'd covered her face with kisses, promising his return even as he balanced himself halfway out of her window. And then he was gone, but he had left her with an effervescence boiling inside her, as if all the will and energy she'd repressed in the past three days had come back to her, demanding all at once that it be put to some use. Angelique paced the floor of her bedchamber, replaying their lovemaking in her mind again and again, holding it within her heart as if it were a talisman that could protect her from her own fears.

There was a web of lies that had to be unwoven, somehow, without unraveling the life she'd built around them. It needn't be impossible; with her return to the world of living at Raven's behest, no problem seemed beyond her reach to resolve.

It'll be difficult, and risky. Angel found herself nodding along at this thought, eyes narrowed. *It involves Louis, and he's had time to plan, but I swear by all I hold holy, he will* never *touch my body with his repulsive "unlove" again.*

Louis' hold over her, she saw then, had been born in fear, and nurtured by years of hunger, cruelty, and neglect. The man had used words like he had used his knives, cutting and nicking away at her attempts to be independent, stabbing and then twisting when he wanted to remind her of her place, or to keep her under his control. She'd been a child then, lost and abandoned in a nightmare world not of her choosing.

But I'm not a child anymore, and only a weak-minded fool, indeed, would continue to act like one now.

She cast her mind back to the events of the night previous once more, how it had felt something like being reborn, when she emerged from that gray, numb place and had fallen, weeping, into Raven's waiting arms.

Angel paused in her pacing to open all the windows to the breeze that had come up with the sun, breathing in *life,* determined never to allow herself to retreat back into that place of numbing, unrelenting nothingness again.

Louis' place. That's weakness, too.

More than anything, she wanted to be worthy of the courage her lover (*betrothed!*) had shown, worthy of his love for her. "Weakness" had no place in that scheme, and so the fears Louis used to control and manipulate her must become hers to master and defeat. She was a highly intelligent woman. Louis himself had admitted this, from time to time.

Time to use that intelligence to your benefit, rather than his.

She stood with her hands on the open casement in her sitting room, looking out over the tall battleships carefully maneuvering around the Merchant Marine wharves in the busy morning light, pondering just what, exactly, one actually did to implement this kind of thing. Clarice had been in with her morning coffee and left again, and still, Angel had no answers.

It's all well and good to make pretty speeches in your head, Angel. Again, that cool, confident inner voice interposed itself, and she found herself leaning into it. *But, if you want to have any chance at all of making this work, you're going to have to have a plan.*

She considered this, realizing in a moment of cold-eyed clarity that making such a plan couldn't be that different, or more difficult, than creating the plan to steal the *Mâgun-Zak*. Even as the implications of this settled within her, her heart once again cast itself back into its memories of the hours just past.

"*I . . . have not been worthy of you,* Mar'leven." she'd murmured, nearly strangling on her grief. "*Of your strength. I can do better, I think. If you'll forgive me.*"

It still amazed her that he *had*. He'd forgiven her with facile self-deprecation because he had no idea just how badly she actually needed his forgiveness.

It wasn't his absence during the last few days and nights that over-set you.

Was it because he didn't come to save me?

No. It was because you didn't act to save yourself.

The thought burned inside her like acid, but its truth was as pure and clear as crystal, in her mind.

"*I can do better. . .*"

She'd been a weak-minded fool, all right. Too much at the mercy of her own fears. Too willing to place her own power and authority in the hands of others It had left her in that place of powerlessness, manipulated and controlled, at the mercy of events instead of their mistress, but not this time. This time, there was a very obvious step that she could take.

It was, of course, a risky one. If she had misjudged, the entire weave of the web would unravel faster than she could attempt to repair it. That thought—no, that fear—caused her to quail for a moment.

"*I can do better. . .*"

There was no way forward that didn't involve risk. If she were ever going to get herself out of this predicament, she was going to have to risk something, if she were not to lose everything. *Choose your risks wisely,* Louis had once told her, back when she was learning the burglar's arts in the streets of Püran-Khir. *Some things, you can control. Others, you can't. You get success when you minimize what you can't control, but ride what you can far as it'll take you.*

I am a dullard, indeed. Why have I never understood that this applies across the board, not just to stealing!

It was time, and beyond time, that Angela Rose Corwin became Lady Angelique Blakesly, Baroness of Carlisle in earnest. Ironically, this was precisely what Louis himself had urged her to do. It made her laugh aloud. Given what she knew, this was a reasonable risk. *Best undertaken today, in fact, before you lose your nerve.*

Angel chuckled softly again, and picked up her cooling coffee to sip at it in satisfaction.

Your turn to be careful what you wish for, Louis. Lest you get it. In trumps!

* * *

Remington Hall, Angels
20 Amerian 580, 1030 hours

Remington's butler showed Lady Blakesly to the antechamber of the Countess's formal drawing room just as her previous appointment was leaving. An older man sailed through the double doors, garbed in the flowing red and white robes of the priesthood of the Guardian Paladin, and trailed by no fewer than three similarly-robed subordinates. Though they'd only ever been introduced once, the ranking cleric of Fernwall's Guardian Paladin church was a distinguished-looking man, one who wore his rank and power as naturally as he wore the white hair atop his head.

"Your Eminence!" Angelique exclaimed, dropping a startled curtsy to cover her confusion. The man outranked her, even had he not been the *Yl-Sarjan*—the spiritual head of the Cascadian church—and one of the most powerful men on the planet. "It is an unexpected honor to see you today."

One of his white eyebrows shot up at this, and the tails of his gold-braided stole swished dramatically around the hem of his surcote as he came to a stop. "Well, good morning, my child," he rumbled, laying a hand on her bowed head in benediction. "Baroness Carlisle, is it not? Our Lord's blessings be upon you this fine day."

"Indeed. Thank you, *Yl-Sarjan*," Angelique murmured, feeling the old, familiar awe come over her in the man's presence. She found herself rather naturally kissing the signet ring on his other hand, and then stood there, dumbfounded, in his wake after he departed.

"Milady?" It was Rebecca, Lady Emilia's lady's maid, who called her out of her bemused reverie. She stood in the door to the countess' sitting room, her hands clasped before her over a fine gown of sober color, and conservatively trimmed. Rebecca was a baron's daughter, and bore a title in her own right; such was her love and devotion to Remington's lady that she'd remained in her service, and at her side, for decades.

As Angelique's attention refocused, Rebecca smiled gently, and gestured for her to enter. Lady Emilia sat in her accustomed chair, facing a large hearth that burned and crackled merrily, even though they were in the midst of a glorious summer morning.

"Come in, dear, and do sit down," Emilia smiled. Not for the first time, Angelique became acutely aware that this dimly lit, overly warm room represented one of the few seats of real power in the City State. As a peer—a member of the House of Lords—and lay leader of the *Yl-Sarjänat* of Cascadia, it was from this room that aged Remington's influence over matters political, civil, and religious extended.

"Thank you, my lady." If *Yl-Sarjan* Augustus never failed to generate confusion and awe within Angelique, then it was also true that Lady Emilia tended to cause the opposite. Peace and serenity radiated from the woman in gentle waves, and her young visitor felt herself absorbing that the way flowers absorbed sunlight. "I see you have been hard at work today. Did His Eminence benefit from your wise counsel as much as the rest of us do?"

"Only time will reveal that," Lady Emilia chuckled. "It is much much harder to hear wisdom and put it into practice than it is to merely listen."

The words echoed Angel's own thoughts from earlier that morning, and she took this as a good sign. Emilia dropped her prayer beads into her lap, and picked up a cooling cup of tea as she went on. "But you did not request an urgent appointment to discuss the internal policies of the Office of the *Imprimae.*"

Angelique smiled fondly, and took up the cup that Rebecca had handed to her. "Affairs of such high state are beyond my little sphere, my dearest lady." She hesitated, sipping her tea quietly, feeling it as the smile faded from her face. "In fact, I must confess that even my little sphere seems quite beyond my control of late. It's that for which I've come to ask your guidance, today."

"At times, that's true of all of us, dear," Emilia replied dryly, "but how can I help you?"

The question was put so bluntly Angelique found herself floundering. "I... I hardly know where to begin," she confessed, figuring it was a better place to start than most. "It seems as if everything I touch lately has gone awry, despite my most sincere efforts. The only thing I feel I've done right may be viewed as my biggest mistake of all, and I do not know what to do to change any of it."

The aged matron took one last sip of her tea in a silence broken only by the faint ticking of her mantle clock, then set the cup down. "Perhaps it would be best to start with this thing you call your 'biggest mistake of all,'" she replied quietly, her beads once more clicking softly between her fingers.

Sudden, paralyzing fear again gripped Angelique for a single moment, choking off her supply of air. Here it was, and she was faced with telling truths to this gentle, powerful, perceptive lady, the one who'd heard the first lies from her mouth when she entered society two years previous. After a few frenzied moments, she quelled her panic. It was only right that she begin the unraveling of that web *here,* where, in a real sense, it had begun.

So telling herself, she forced a deep, steadying breath into her lungs, then exhaled slowly. "You have probably already discerned it, my lady. I've fallen in love with Vincent," she confessed softly, "and he with me."

"Yes," Lady Emilia replied simply.

"I cannot consider it a mistake," Angel rushed on, "for I've never been happier in my life. But... I am aware, possibly more than most, of just how outcast he has become."

Again, there was silence before Lady Emilia replied. "Vincent's social estrangement is part of what's troubling you," she eventually said, "but it is not all."

"That is correct, it isn't, but it is illustrative of the dilemmas I'm facing. I feel so powerless to control my own life, my lady!"

Frustration drove Angel to her feet, and caused her to pace as restlessly as she had in her own room, earlier. "There are matters at Carlisle that I don't understand. My solicitor brought them to my attention."

Some deep instinct made her avoid mentioning Louis by name, but she had no time to consider it. "Those who serve there do so at the command of my liege lord, the Earl of Camrose," she plowed on, though Emilia did not show any urgency to interrupt. "They still owe their loyalty to him even though they've sworn oaths to me. They're stealing, my lady, at Carlisle's expense, while the barony itself teeters on the brink of ruin. I do not have the faintest idea how one changes that, especially without angering the man who placed them there!"

"Go on," Emilia encouraged her, unruffled by any of it. "Let's get it all out where we can sort through it. It's hard to sort through one's jewelry box when it's crammed full. It's best to toss the contents onto the table so you can see the tangles clearly."

Angelique sighed. "Lady's tears, that would be enough, on its own, and then there is Vincent, too. He's asked me to marry him, my lady, to wait for him, for the duration of his bond. And I've consented. More than that, I've sworn it." The memories of those powerful, passionate oaths seethed through her again, and she wrapped her arms around her chest as if to keep them contained there.

"I see," Lady Emilia said. Her hands fell to her lap, and her blind eyes rolled up toward the ceiling. "So, you and Vincent have been lovers, of course, and you now are betrothed, oaths sworn to each other, no doubt. Hence your concern for his social estrangement. And, having not been raised a baroness, you have no idea how to manage a baronial holding. That seems to have given the Earl of Camrose's bailiff license to do as he sees fit. Is that it, child?"

Startled and dismayed by the lady's accurate summation, Angelique felt her legs buckle beneath her. She sat heavily in a nearby chair. "How... how did you know...? We've been so discreet..."

"Of course you have." Unconcerned, Lady Emilia waved that off. "But, the Lady blessed me with blindness so that I might see more clearly, child," the old crone explained calmly.

Oh, the church deals so harshly with adultery... "And you are not... distressed by this?"

Had the lady eyes, they would have burned straight into Angelique's heart; even so, the intensity of regard the aged matron turned upon her was almost unbearable.

"You will find no judgments here, Angelique," she stated, though with enough compassion to gentle the reminder. "Not for this, nor for anything else with which you would reproach yourself.

"Now, as you have raised your relationship with Sir Vincent, let's start there." She returned her outward attention back to her beads, and Angel remembered to breathe. "Your young lord has acquitted himself rather honorably where the theft of the *Mâgun-Zak* is concerned, wouldn't you say?"

she mused thoughtfully. "He was promoted chief inspector, and made an arrest within hours of assuming the case—the outcome of the hearing is fairly certain, I understand. It is all political, of course, but these things usually are."

Emilia paused, whether in thought or in invitation, Angel couldn't tell. She waited quietly for several moments, trying to discern some subtle point in the older woman's statement of the obvious.

"In fact, he has acted honorably, as a true knight should, to restore the honor of the Ladies' Auxiliary, has he not?"

Angel's swiftly indrawn breath forestalled whatever Emilia had been about to add. "He has, hasn't he. Lady's tears, it is exceedingly simple. Why did I not see it?"

She laughed, suddenly giddy with it. "And, according to those same ancient chivalric codes by which they so abuse him, he is owed a sign of our favor in return, is he not?"

Emilia nodded silently, a small smile playing quietly at the corners of her mouth.

"Oh, my dear lady, that is brilliant. Does love make us all fools?" The question was largely rhetorical, of course. Poets, sages, and philosophers had been saying as much for centuries.

"Would a dinner party, given in his honor, suffice, do you suppose?" Angel laughed again, this time with much more irony. "As an expression of gratitude for his prompt and professional actions on our behalf?"

"Very good, dear. I expect most of the influential members will be happy to attend."

"With your good example publicly scourging them," Angelique drawled, already on fire with yet another thing she'd never considered before this moment. "They'll attend. We need not pretend that any of them will be happy about it."

"Oh, I think they will be," Emilia chuckled. "Had not your betrothed made an arrest so quickly, the hearings in the House of Lords would undoubtedly *still* be going on. His prompt and professional action has not only proven him a worthy knight of the State, but has also saved the honor and reputation of several members of the Ladies' Auxiliary from their own foolishness."

And as long as I don't let myself consider who truly did commit that theft, it all makes the kind of gallant sense that only Paladins can understand.

"My betrothed," Angel repeated with a happy sigh to accompany the term. She was pacing the room once more, but this time not from frustration. "Oh, my dearest Lady Emilia, you have done it. I have never seen any of this more clearly than when I look at it through your eyes."

"Not a bad trick, for a blind woman," Emilia cackled, "but perhaps it is now you who should now enlighten me, child. One is never too old to learn from one's actions, after all."

"I am thought to be quick-witted, but at times I am as dull as a village idiot," Angelique exulted. "I should have seen it before. My lady, when you explained how Vincent's actions must appear to 'socially correct' eyes, you put an entirely different slant on his indenture to the State, and made it into a valuable and worthy thing. You, in essence, have turned Vincent's disadvantage into an advantage."

"In truth, it is your betrothed who has turned the disgrace of his station into a potent weapon," the older woman demurred. "It is not surprising, having watched young Vincent Sultaire from childhood."

Angel laughed and nodded. "Yes, of course he has, but it's you who have seen it. Are we not exhorted, again and again, as Paladins, to turn weakness into strength, stricture into liberty? Even our Holy Lady urges us to it in *The Charge of the Castellan*. Ah, lady." The younger woman knelt by Emilia's knees, capturing the old woman's gnarled hands in hers. "I've been looking at it all backwards, haven't I?"

"That, perhaps, is the truth for which you have been searching, Angelique." Emilia sounded happy for her young friend, if a bit mystified at her rapid change of mood. "Soldiers call it 'strategy' or 'tactics.' It is no more than the ability to look at each situation in which you find yourself, and see clearly the strengths and weaknesses inherent in them. Every situation has them. It's up to you to put them to good use, because if you don't, your enemies—and we all have them—most certainly will."

Enemies... Louis. "I must either take advantage of a strength, or use a weakness," Angel breathed, reclaiming chair and tea. "Perhaps it is time to take that and use it to regain control of matters at Carlisle, too."

"You *are* the baroness," the countess pointed out, unaware that she echoed Louis' own words a few night's previous. "So long as you violate no laws of the State, or of your liege, on your land your word is law. To violate your law is a crime punishable in State Court. You have *enormous* power, dear. Use it discreetly, and fairly, to call these administrators to account. Set your own policies, and leave it at that. Stewards and bailiffs are not fools. They know when the winds have started to blow in a different direction."

"Hmmm. . ." It occurred to Angel then that Louis had used those words to disempower her, but Emilia's use had had the opposite effect. *Likely because he knew that once I learned how to wield power, I'd know how to wield it against him, too.*

Miraculously, she began to believe there must be a way to contain Louis, as well. If not through her own strength, then perhaps through using a weakness.

"All right, I will, and I'll ask for Vincent's advice on the specifics," she added, "since he was born to these matters, and I was not."

"You could do worse," Emilia chuckled. "The man you have promised to marry will make a strong, compassionate baron, and more. Since you are new to this, it would not hurt to have him present when you meet with your administrators. Sir Vincent knows our laws and customs. The administrators may be able to fool you with their rhetoric, but with him present, I doubt they would even try. Sir Vincent's father rules with an iron hand, and his children were educated accordingly."

Angel didn't want to think about the odious Baron James Sultaire of

Valemont, not just then. Those matters were so distant that they bore little weight with her. Two of her immediate dilemmas had almost resolved themselves already today. The third, that of Louis himself, would quickly follow, of that she was certain.

The clock on Emilia's mantel chimed the half-hour. Angelique looked up and smiled. "Ah, it would appear my time with you today is almost over. Only thirty minutes, and you have worked a miracle, my dearest lady. In my eyes, you are a living saint. Never doubt it."

The old woman smiled. "Thank you, child, but now I must ready myself for my last meeting of the morning, before traveling to Parliament this afternoon."

"Yes," she nodded, leaning forward once again to clasp Emilia's gnarled hands, and to kiss that wrinkled, yet oddly soft-skinned cheek. "But it is I who thank you, of course. For all that you've done for Vincent and for me."

"It is as nothing, Angelique," she replied fondly. "Go with the Lady's blessings, and be certain that She, too, wishes you to be happy."

*   *   *

The trail had led to a very uptown apartment building, in what had become a very trendy neighborhood. The city's newly rich had gravitated toward these generally run-down blocks in the south end of Merchants' to throw their new wealth into restoring the once-grand old buildings with almost frantic glee. What resulted were pockets of beauty and prosperity in what was otherwise becoming an extension of original Fernwall, or "Thieves'" as it was now more commonly known.

Raven's information had led him to the very top floor of this four-story building, and to an artist's flat for a very reclusive artist. The only way up into her studio was via a trap door in the ceiling, from where the stairs ended on the third floor landing.

Chuckling to himself, he knocked on the door with the butt of his sword, then stuck the rose he'd collected from the garden outside on the blade. When the lady known as Spectre opened the door, he held up the rose.

"Good morning," he drawled, grinning broadly.

She blinked at the rose, then down at the impudently grinning man standing there. "Be damned. Raven?" Mystification turned to delight, and she plucked the rose from his blade. "Is this a personal call, or professional?"

"A bit of both," he confessed, "but it probably won't cost you much more than an afternoon's delight—if you're of a mind."

"The price has come down then," she purred, stroking the blushing pink petals along one equally silken, pale cheek. "Selling yourself cheaply these days, now that you're on the right side of the law?"

"Which side?" he chuckled. "I had no idea there was so much delightful information to be had in a cop shop." Raven paused, then gave her a sidelong look. "So, are you going to keep me down here on your doorstep, or invite me in?"

107

Her large, dark-eyed gaze deepened for a moment. Then she shrugged. "What the hell. I'm ready for a break, and you always were an entertaining sort. Come on up." Spectre disappeared from sight, but a rope ladder seemed to oblige him by rolling itself down for his use.

Spectre's flat was really just that: flat. She'd claimed the entire top floor of this building for her use, then renovated it as one large, breezy, well-lit room. Her work studio was set up in a northern corner and was liberally littered with easels and canvas and drop sheets and screens and props; and the smell of oils, solvents, chalks, and likely some other things, which only another paint artist could discern, permeated the space from wall to wall. A male model was ensconced on what looked like a set of boxes covered by a large canvas. He appeared to be emulating someone who had been crucified. At Spectre's word, he broke his pose, nodded to Raven easily, and disappeared behind a screen, completely at ease with his unclad state.

The dark-haired lady didn't lead her guest over to the easel for a closer look. Instead, she flopped onto a rather large pile of pillows and stretched luxuriously. She was dressed, if that was the term, solely in a man's linen shirt, which appeared to have been manically streaked with all the colors of her palette. Its brevity didn't do much to hide the lovely midnight glory of her mons.

"Pour us a drink before you find a seat, would you, Raven? I'm thrashed." She motioned vaguely toward a wood and glass cabinet, then blinked a bit. "Cops are still allowed to drink, aren't they?"

"Who knows," Raven shrugged, heading for the sideboard. "I'm not playing cop today, anyway. So what have you been up to, Linda? Other than this *Mâgun-Zak* business, life in art town has been quiet. Have you evolved into an honest artist?"

She snorted. "I *am* an honest artist, you low-brow cretin. Not that you'd know. I'm even an honest whore, though the difference is minimal. I sell myself, either way." Another of those grand gestures indicated the canvas-covered easels along one wall. "So if you're not playing cop, why are you here? The other answer is the same as last time: I think you're still probably just a little too expensive to keep as a pet, Raven."

"I'm hard to train and domesticate anyway," he shot back, grinning. "And I'm here, pretty lady, for you. So why don't you shed the garments, and let's find some real privacy." The grin faded from his face as he spoke, eyes flashing to the screen where the model was dressing. He extended a glass to her and waited.

Two well-plucked eyebrows lifted. "Indeed?" she murmured softly. "Raúl! Go down to Papa Hortensio's and bring back a meal, would you? Grab some money on the way out."

A moment later, the impeccably groomed Raúl had done so, pausing only to kiss Linda on his way. She rolled over to watch him go, giving the man still in the room with her a provocative view of her pert behind. "Gods, but he is a gorgeous muse," she sighed happily. "Half the time I can't decide whether to paint him or fuck him."

"I assume you have time to do both at your leisure," Raven drawled, enjoying the sight of her presented posterior. "Are we mixing business with pleasure, or are you still trying to decide?"

"Business. *Just* business. You're too expensive for my simple tastes, Raven," she replied, rolling back over to face him, "and you come with too many complications. Legal complications, one might say." It was her turn to grin at him. "So if you're not here to buy or commission a painting, you must be here to interview the Spectre, no?"

"Not exactly. A good fuck is never expensive. Just fun and pleasurable," he grinned back at her. Then he turned serious again. "You've heard about Cooper, I assume. It's been all over the papers."

She nodded.

"Yeah, well, as usual, that's only half the story. Cooper was set up, Linda. Blatantly. My guess is we've got a new player in town who's either ignorant, or who wants your turf bad enough to start eliminating competition."

"I'd heard about that, too. This eager opportunist apparently hasn't yet learned to play by the rules," she replied. "You don't point the finger at your playmates, after all. You think Coop's being eliminated intentionally?"

"Possibly," he admitted. "But I can't say for sure. The lady used crystal wands, the ones you like to play with, to bypass the security. And she matched Cooper's style right down to the poison in the darts. That says she's got good connections," he shrugged. "Draw your own conclusions."

"It was a woman?" she asked, suddenly very alert. "You're sure? That's real news, Raven."

"She got a touch careless," he chuckled. "You don't leave over a low-pitched roof with edging, not in this town. She left a track in the coal ash."

"Well, well," Linda mused, reclining back into her cushions. "Well, well, well." She shot a significant glance at him. "You've got bigger troubles than I thought. I don't know of any local female competition who could have pulled that caper, if the roof was the real means of flight afterwards. I know I couldn't have done it—I'm terrified of heights. None of the other female members of our rather exclusive little band have the necessary abilities, either. Or, so I've heard."

"I do," he smiled.

She rolled her eyes. "You're clearly not a woman."

"Thanks for noticing," he shot back, flashing her a swift smile, but it too faded quickly. "There are exactly two cops working on the case who believe a woman did it. The other is fresh out of the academy. They don't listen to her, either. That's why I'm probably 'suspect number one' down at headquarters."

He shook his head at this. "But, I'm not pointing fingers at you either, Linda. Even if I thought you had done it, I'm sure we could find a gull."

"Decent of you," she drawled. "If you're right about this new chum getting rid of her competition, I may be next on her list, anyway." She cocked him another glance. "Now, you didn't haul that handsome ass of yours all the way over here to update me on your case, my old. So what is it you want from me?"

He smiled. "I told you, I want you. I've wanted to fuck that body for years, or hadn't you noticed?" She snorted at him. "Seriously," he went on, "the one thing that makes me an unlikely suspect is that I don't have a clue where to get those wands. You do, and it's the only lead I've got left to this mysterious lady."

Linda blinked at him owlishly. "I see."

"Curious enough to play?" He arched an eyebrow expectantly.

"One wonders how much it's going to cost," she answered him scathingly. "You're the only con in this town who can buy information and make the other party pay through the nose for it."

He just smiled, his eyes dancing merrily. "Shall I give you my up front price?"

"Oh, why not?" she asked, expansively. "Let's do this like upright citizens this time, just for the *novelty* of it."

Raven howled with laughter, nearly spilling his drink. "You're a doll, you know that, Linda? Ah me," he finally managed. "All right. Why not? Here it is: Buy me dinner and give me a night of endless pleasure in your body. That's my price."

"That's the 'up front' price," she reminded him, not even remotely swayed. "What comes out of my behind? You know, the part I *didn't* sign for."

"*That*," he drawled, "is for you to figure out, pretty lady. I can't give away *all* my secrets, now, can I? But just think of what you'll learn if you play along. That ought to be worth something to you."

Her dark eyes regarded him rather thoughtfully for a long moment. "Just what is it you want, Raven? You want a way to touch my sources, is that it?"

"To be honest, I'm hoping your source will lead me back to the person to whom the crystals were given. That might lead to our mysterious lady, or it might not, but I've got less than two days now to pop this, or Cooper's as good as shackled." He gave her a frank look. "And I'll tell you something else. I don't know about you, sweetheart, but I don't need those kinds of players running loose in my town. I've been busted once. I don't want to go through it again, not for gig I didn't play."

"Hmmm. A persuasive argument at last," she purred, rolling easily to her feet. "I knew not even Roland could manage to take the rogue out of you completely, Sultaire. It's bred into the bone. I think your great-great-granddaddy must have been a pirate." She took the clip out of her dark hair, shook it free. It fell in long, sable waves to her waist.

Raven watched her raptly, and gave a low whistle at the beauty unveiled. "I'm impressed," he admitted. "I had no idea what I was missing."

"You're still missing it," she reminded him pointedly. "I haven't yet agreed to either of your prices." Linda padded barefoot over to where a set of exquisitely painted screens only partially obscured a large, unmade bed. "And I'm not at all certain I can help you anyway. When I need high-end muscle like that, Raven, I have to tell the wind."

"Well, I didn't figure you just walked down to the local market," he drawled. "You tell the wind and the wind eventually blows back with terms and a drop. Is that the drill?"

"Pretty much," she called out over the screen, rummaging for clothing. "Are you still interested?"

"Sounds like it leaves us lots of time to fuck. Of course I'm interested."

Linda chuckled, almost in spite of herself, it seemed. "You never quit, do you?" She emerged from her seclusion, in the act of binding a ribbon into her hair, and dressed in the kind of flowing, artsy-type dress that was feminine, and yet practical, too. "We'll go speak to the wind, and see what it says. And I'm not paying either of your prices, but here's mine."

The woman who was known in elite crime circles as the Spectre flowed silently to him, then stood with her palms open upon his chest. "If I'm the next one to go down, you get me sprung, Raven. Or get me the hell out of Fernwall. I don't want to wear a collar."

Raven drank in her sultry beauty for several heartbeats, then looked into her dark eyes. "I'll meet your price if you'll meet mine," he countered.

"You buy me dinner, and we'll negotiate the rest from there," she grinned, not going down without a fight.

"Ah, no," he smiled, taking her hands. "We settle first, and you'll have to do better than that if you want me to put my neck on the line to save yours. I don't care *how* pretty it is." He ran a long finger over her smooth cheek. "You start sharing that lovely body with me, sweetheart, and I'll find a way to save it if it comes to it. It'll be worth it just for the personal pleasure," he chuckled roguishly. "And I'll even throw in dinner 'cause I'm nice. But that's about as low as I'll go."

"I'm putting my own neck on the line for you right now, you know," she reminded him seriously. "And for this, it may just be that when the Man comes to take me down, he won't be wearing a blue jacket, Raven. I don't know where these connections lead, but it's bigger and probably a lot uglier than I want to think about."

"That goes with the territory," he reminded her. "You're not already in a collar trying to play both sides of the law. *You* fuck up, you've got even money odds on a chance to fight back. I fuck up, the outcome is pretty much guaranteed. I'd rather not spend half of the rest of my adult life in a collar."

Linda's dark eyes searched his carefully, then she sighed and nodded. "Done, then. As I told you before, I'm an honest whore. And selling my body as a bit of insurance against the auction block is a fair exchange, I think."

"After you then," Raven gestured grandly, pulling the trap door closed on his way down.

It was a real yawner, but then stake-outs, for legal or illegal purposes, usually were. Typical of mid-summer nights, the cool street below his attic hide-out was half-veiled in fog. A golden halo radiated around a distant street lamp, calling to mind one popular Valïan image of the Holy Lady of

Paladins, depicted with such a halo around her head and the Divine Babe Valïa in her arms.

Religion... Angelique... naked beauty riding atop him, lovely face contorted in orgasm, the nipples of her pert breasts hard as agates, calling out his name...

It was predictable, how his mind always seemed to track from divinity to sexual ecstasy. Estranged from the love of his god, and therefore his church, he had at last embraced the love of a woman and found his religion there, too. It had been Angelique who had taught him how to love, not the Lady of Paladins, nor the gorgeous and sensual Spectre, whose bed he'd left only a few hours before and whose passion was, in comparison, deliciously profane.

Vincent, your mind is headed in a very bad direction. Very bad. Stop it. Salvation came from below.

A lone man dressed in dark clothing came walking up the sidewalk on the far side of the street. His boots clomped loudly on the cobblestones in the foggy silence of the night. The rhythm of his stride broke for only a few steps at the drop point Spectre had been given, then he continued on his way.

Quickly, Raven removed the grate that concealed him, clicked open a tiny grapnel attached to a thin, silken line, and hooked it to an eye-bolt near the roof.

He hung there long enough to replace the grate using a "line plier," a smaller device he'd had manufactured to complement the much larger and more powerful ones he'd found in his grandfather's trunk with the Raven Wing years ago. It looked something like a stirrup, but the top consisted of a complicated maze of tiny gears, pulleys, and spools, all hidden beneath a metal cover. In the stirrup itself was a trigger, on top was a thumb button, and there were two switches on the outer cover, exactly the same arrangement as on the larger versions Roland had confiscated. Once the grate to the attic was in place, he flicked one of the switches, then gently squeezed the trigger. The line plier lowered him to the ground with a soft hiss, the pressure on the trigger controlling the rate of descent.

Once on the ground, he released the grapnel. One squeeze of the trigger reeled in his line. His quarry had turned the corner and was now almost a hundred meters ahead. Raven didn't want to crowd him. He angled across the vacant street and kept his distance, moving quietly and quickly from one pocket of deep shadow to the next.

The man turned again at the next intersection. The clicking of his footsteps shuffled and stopped. *He's doubling back,* Raven thought, and froze in place. He'd just taken a step, but smoothly changed momentum, huddling down slowly in the shadows, allowing his cloak to fan out and further blur his shape. From his concealed spot, he saw the man's head appear back around the corner and scan the street slowly.

It was always a worrisome moment. Had the man discovered him? If he had, there was the chance he'd lead him to a designated location where tails would be cut off by his buddies, or worse, his employer's thugs. That was a given. At length, the man's head disappeared, and the sound of his boot-falls resumed a normal walking pace, fading down the lane.

Shadowing someone, especially someone who as a matter of philosophy simply assumed he was being followed, was a complicated game of hide and seek, liberally smeared with the need for patience. This time was no different. The man ran Raven around half of lower Merchants', just for drill. He doubled back twice in attempts to catch any tails. He stopped at not one, but two bars, and then disappeared into an apartment building.

That one might have worked, had Raven not used it himself a few times. The inexperienced tail will either wait for the mark to come back out, or rush around to the back door. Or, if they were *really* dumb, they'll assume that this is the final destination.

Raven, however, knew this wasn't it. The man had surreptitiously looked around, then expertly picked the lock to get into the building. Raven found himself admiring his quarry, if only briefly. The man was good at this.

Raven withdrew his line plier, flipped a switch, pointed it, and punched the button. The lead weight on the end of the line shot upward with a hiss as the line unwound from its spool. He released the button as weight headed over the edge of the roof to pop he grapnel open. A flip and a click later, he squeezed the trigger once more, and the line plier neatly hauled him up. In less than one minute he was on the roof, able to see his mark no matter which exit he chose.

That proved to be the service exit. It probably would have been imperceptible to the untrained eye, but Raven noticed that his pace quickened as he headed down the street. *Now the bird heads for the nest,* Raven mused. He lowered himself back to the ground with the line pliers, then resumed his tactic of moving from shadow to shadow.

Thirty minutes later, they were entering Fernwall's industrial area on the city's east side. Row after row of warehouses separated the industrial parks that produced everything from the city's bread to its red brick roofing tiles. Raven's mark vanished into one, right in front of his eyes.

"Fascinating part of town, isn't it?" he whispered to Spectre two hours later.

Having found the warehouse, he'd taken a trap back to her flat to fetch her, silently grumping about the loss of time. If Roland hadn't taken his Raven Wing, he could have flown, which would have taken minutes, rather than nearly an hour—not that it mattered, he supposed.

Now the couple stood hidden in a narrow alleyway across the street from the warehouse into which the man had disappeared.

Her body felt much more relaxed against his, after the mutually pleasurable way they'd spent the afternoon. Rather than the artsy-feminine garb she'd worn before, now she was dressed in the mottled gray bodysuit which had earned her an epithet from Fernwall's underworld. She was taking in the surroundings professionally, but it was obvious that she'd never spent any time in this end of town, even though she'd lived here all her life.

"It's more fascinating to think about what's in all those warehouses," she breathed in answer, "and why it would be stockpiled like that."

"That's why we're here, darling," Raven drawled. "My fingers have been itching ever since the mark entered this part of town." He looked the building over carefully. The lock on the human-sized door would undoubtedly be guarded with all kinds of nasties. But, typical of most warehouses in Fernwall, a beam extended out from the roof so that heavy objects could be easily lifted to the upper floor. Where one could get to the roof, there were usually good-sized vents. "You're afraid of heights?" he asked the beauty he was snuggling from behind.

"More than three stories and I'm paralyzed," she agreed, looking it over. "Two gives me fits, but I can get past it, if I have to. You're going in by the vent shafts of the roof?"

"Thinking about it," he admitted. "If the lock on the ground floor isn't loaded with fun stuff, I'll do your boy-toy 'til he screams."

"You might consider it anyway, just for fun," she replied, distractedly. "I can get up to the roof, no problem. But you're probably going to have to help me get back down if we can't find some nice, safe stairs."

"Not a problem, doll baby." He paused to nibble on her ear. "Two will get you five there's a vent grate on the far side, but I guess we'll never know if we don't get started."

Spectre elbowed him in the ribs, gently. "Then quit distracting me, and lead the way, Raven."

It took but a moment to ready his line plier. He gave a quick look around, then silently slipped across the street. Moments later, she ghosted up to him, the mottling of her bodysuit blending perfectly with the ground-fog.

"You first," he whispered into her ear, not missing the opportunity to stick his tongue in it afterwards. She elbowed him again, but neither of them failed to notice her responsive shudder. He flicked a switch on his line plier, squeezed the trigger, and almost flew to the roof.

Spectre had to crawl to the rooftop, and that was a more painstaking process. By the time she arrived at his side, Raven had already stowed his gear. She crouched there with her eyes closed, breathing deeply. "Gods, but I hate that," she breathed.

"Rather limits your methods," he murmured, closing the flap on the belt case that held the line handles.

"Why do you think they call me 'Spectre'?" she shot back. "It wasn't all just a fashion statement, you know."

The roof was sloped, but not steeply so. Large vents lined the roof near the peak to let out trapped heat, and vapors from the charcoal smudge pots that were commonly used to keep the buildings somewhere above freezing in winter. Raven led the way to the far side, where he lay down to peer over the edge.

"Bingo," he grinned at her afterwards. "One each: large wooden grate, doll baby. Let's see how secure it is." He reached for his pouch.

"Fine, you do that," Spectre shuddered, crouching a generous distance away from that precipitous edge.

Raven quickly secured one end of his line to the nearest vent shaft then disappeared over the edge. The grate had been snugly fitted, but was neither locked nor barred, probably because the only access was from the outside, by ladder or rope. It took a bit of careful prying to pop the grate out of its casing. He placed it on the roof and looked into the inky blackness. Barely discernible were the outlines of large boxes, tuns, pallets, and other shapes he couldn't make out clearly. Presumably, there was a floor somewhere in the black, but he didn't want to risk a light just then.

He rejoined Spectre. "Okay," he whispered to her. "The grate's out of the way, and there's a floor somewhere in there, but with your fear of heights...?" His look was both sympathetic and concerned.

She ground her teeth. "Honey, you're going to have to go in first and find it, then come back for me. I'll freeze on the rope if I try to go in there cold, but I might be able to keep a grip on myself if I know you know where the floor is."

He kissed her then turned his attention to re-arranging his gear. Aiming carefully, he shot a line to one of the rafters inside and sunk the claws of the grapnel deeply into the wood. Then, leaving her a wink and blown kiss to keep her company, he disappeared off the edge and swung smoothly into the building. The line plier hissed once more as he descended, until he landed at last below the grate, his feet against the wall.

No lights, he thought. *No tobacco smells, no sounds. Anybody guarding this place, they're a ghost.* He reached into another pouch, retrieved a slender tube, and carefully pulled the cap off one end. A beam of blinding light pierced the darkness cleanly, revealing more clearly the boxes, tuns, pallets, and just plain piles of stuff, all neatly arranged. The upper floor was still some two meters below him. Sixty or seventy centimeters from his feet was a huge wooden crate. The center of the floor was open, allowing workmen to move the stored items around easily using hand-trucks, pallet jacks, and the overhead hoist. *All very neatly arranged, and somebody is using up a lot of money on this.*

A flip and a click later, he sailed back up and rejoined Spectre on the roof once again. "Okay, doll baby. I'm not sure I like what I'm beginning to suspect here, but somebody was even obliging enough to leave us a convenient landing just below the vent grate."

Her dark eyebrows lifted in the gloom. "It's not a trap, is it?"

"Not exactly what I meant. You'll see once we're inside." He handed her a pair of rubber line grips. "I'll go back down. It'll only take me a few seconds. Then you follow, using those to grab the line."

The brows knitted. "How far down is that floor, again? Exactly?"

"Maybe three meters," he shrugged. "The top of the crate is about a meter and a half from the bottom of the grate."

She closed her eyes, visualizing it. "Then the only real trick is making myself jump off the edge of the roof. Right." Her lovely jaw clenched again, and she nodded. "Gods, I hate this."

"Pretty much," he agreed. "Would you like me to set up another line you can use to get over the edge? I can come back up and take it down once you're in."

"You're probably going to have to," she muttered, rubbing her face with her hands as if in irritation. "I'm just making this harder for you. I still don't know why you wanted me to come along."

"So I could enjoy the view," he drawled, grinning. It took only moments for him to hook another line plier up to the vent pipe, as he had before. He peeled off a couple of meters of line and dropped the handle over the edge. "There. Don't think you should use the line handle, doll. Takes a bit of practice to figure all the controls out. You'll have to switch to my double line to get in."

"Right." She took a very deep breath, and the mottling on her suit seemed to swirl with the fog. "Go. I'll be along as soon as I can." Her hands twitched her gloves on a bit more snugly, and her eyes were already a bit defocused from the inner control she tried to bring to bear.

Again Raven flew easily over the edge of the roof and swung through the rectangular hole for the grate. This time, he paid out line more rapidly to glide easily to the top of the crate. *Okay, doll. Your turn.* He fervently hoped her fear wouldn't incapacitate her. The minutes crawled by with no motion on either line, while the old building creaked and settled in the silence of the night. He sat motionless, the tension inside his head seeming to build with each heartbeat. She'd frozen—or ran. *No, can't do that. Two stories of empty air all around the building.* He sighed, then, resigning himself to having to fetch her, and had no sooner secured his grip on his line plier than Spectre slid in beside him on the crate, shaking so hard their entire impromptu platform trembled.

"Easy, darling," he whispered into her ear as he wrapped his arms around her. "You're down now."

"Uh-huh, sure," she agreed, notes of hysteria lacing through her normally clear, sultry voice. Her gloved hands were still clenched tightly around the line. "I hate that. Gods, I just fucking *hate* that."

"Ssshhh..." He pried her hands from the line, removed the grippers, put her arms around him, and held her until the trembling stilled. Now that they were inside, they were safe—so safe in fact, they could probably have made love without being discovered or disturbed. Eventually, her breathing returned to normal, and she loosened her grip. Raven patted her reassuringly, then uncapped his light and shined it around the room.

"Intriguing, isn't it?" he whispered into her ear, taking the opportunity to kiss it.

"Ye Gods," she assented softly, curiosity pulling her away from the last remnants of her personal terror. "Were you going to retrieve that other line before we go on down?"

"Let's get you on the floor first." He put his arm around her slender waist. "Hang on."

She complied. He stepped them off the edge of the crate and they glided to the floor, the line plier hissing in his hand. Spectre shuddered hard, again, but managed a rueful smile. "That was much better than getting in from the roof," she murmured.

"Glad you approve. I'll be right back." He flicked a switch, squeezed the trigger, and rose into the air, the line plier purring softly. Spectre had barely started to look around when a black shape flew over her head, then settled to the floor behind her.

"Done," Raven whispered. He adjusted the length of his line and quietly placed the line plier next to the large crate under the grate. "Insurance," he said then, gesturing to it. "We may need to get out that way."

"Gods, I hope not," she croaked. In his absence, she'd donned a tight-fitting leather headband with a fixture in the center that held another of the magitech light crystals which Raven himself used. Her arrangement left her hands free, however.

The inventory was wide ranging and chillingly surprising. Weapons, armor, dry food goods such as legumes, flour, cake yeast, and oats. Other items of interest included bolts of sail cloth, rope and cabling of various sizes, chain, and other marine hardware. They descended a wide stair to the ground floor. Stacks of spring steel coils, banded together for shipment, stood next to heavy wooden frames and other odd-looking components.

"These are disassembled marine ballista," Raven whispered to Spectre. "Dwarven spring steel," he pointed to the two meter stack of coil springs. "Nobody else has figured out how to make spring steel hold that kind of tension. It won't rust, either. Weird stuff. And look at that!"

Behind the disassembled ballista were stacks of bins filled with ceramic balls about twenty centimeters in diameter.

"Raven—what are those? They look innocent enough."

"Fire bombs for the ballista," Raven explained. "This is a fucking pirate supply warehouse."

Spectre's eyes narrowed. She nodded wordlessly. They moved on.

Around the edges of the military hardware were other crates labeled inanely and probably inaccurately. Tuns of 'wine' and 'cider' and boxes of 'linens.' Fernwall imported the fine, dry wines of Vin-Nôrë, but it didn't export them. Nor was there any export of cider, even the various fermented, spiced ciders that were popular around the City State. Matching the bill of lading number to the inventory sheet would probably reveal the true contents of the containers, but that would have required breaking into the shipping office, amongst other things.

They worked their way around to the front door, and found a small office room partially hidden by stores. On the outside hung a clipboard with several pages of lined paper clipped to it. A pencil hung near it, dangling from a string.

"Well, now," Raven murmured, examining the entries. There were several columns, one for the date, another for time, a third held a number, the fourth, yet another date, and the fifth, initials. The second date was often over-written with a check, he noticed, and those not checked had not been returned, presumably. "A check-out sheet. The boxes these numbers correspond to can't be too far away."

"Convenient of them to leave it out for us," she drawled. "How far back do those dates go?"

He riffled through the stack. "Nearly a year," he finally replied. "I'd guess they don't consider this very valuable information. Only the owner of these initials would know the particulars of that transaction."

She stared at the top sheet, brows furrowed. "The last time I 'leased' anything unusual was this past WinterFest. Actually Vilmath, a few days before the city closed down for the holiday. Do you suppose that might be useful?"

"The date would have been... sixteen twenty-five or thereabouts?" he asked, looking at the month-day designations as he flipped through the pages. "Okay. Got it. Can you get more specific?"

"Ah, the twenty-eighth," she said, a few deep, thoughtful breaths later, "and I was hurrying to get the transaction completed." Her grin was enigmatic under the brightness of her head-light. "You'll likely recall the theft— from the other side, of course."

The Dahlrami Maiden. Intricately carved out of Sudaani jade, the antique sculpture was worth a small fortune. It had disappeared from the well-guarded home of one of the wealthiest Urilian bankers in the city. The ensuing uproar, though modest compared to this most recent theft, had been assigned a team of investigators, who worked double shifts for weeks until the item was recovered.

Their information had led them to an outbound barque named *Sea Witch*. The port authority impounded the vessel and authorized local law enforcement to board. They not only recovered the exquisite statuette, but a cargo of slaves, drugs, and other illicit items outbound—for Sudaan.

Interesting that despite the publicity of this case, Roland wasn't using the same tactics, successful as they'd been. *Apparently one noble brat is worth as much, or more, than a team of investigators? Another line of thought you'd better not pursue too far,* he mused.

"I hope you got paid," he said to Spectre instead. "Ah. Twenty-eight Vilmath. When did you bring it back?"

"Of course I got paid," she snorted. "The item was returned to the drop point the day after the theft, which would have made it the sixth day of WinterFest."

"Good. We've a match. Now then..." He returned to the top page and began scanning backward through the list. "Right here," he said almost immediately. "They must not get much business. Third from the bottom. Same number. Looks like they were turned back in yesterday. Makes sense. You know what that means?" He returned the clipboard to its hanger and lit up the ballista parts across the room.

She nodded, and sighed. "Especially when you know that I dropped the thing I stole, *and* the crystals I used to do it, at the same drop point." Her mouth twisted into an unattractive grimace. "It means I hired out to do that job for fucking pirates. Great."

"Don't know that I'd go *that* far. I don't know of anyone who understands the complex connections between land-based organized crime and the pirate lords. The MARCUS Agency, maybe," he shrugged. It occurred to him only then, to wonder if that crew of international spies knew about the true purpose of this stockpile, and, if they did, were they having the place watched?

"I expect we'd best not wear out our welcome," he whispered. "Check the door, doll baby. If it's straight forward enough from the inside, you can go out that way. Just let me make sure the coast is clear on the outside."

"Right." Bypassing security measures was, of course, a trademark of Spectre's reputation; as such, she did not touch any part of the door until her eyes, following the light, had covered every visible inch of it. In particular, she studied that doorknob—and Raven knew he could have bet his family's holdings that she was studying what they used to ward these doors *closely.*

"Looks like several rather painful contingencies are all set to foil anyone tinkering from the outside... but the inside appears clean, Raven. The traps will reset themselves after the door latches from the outside."

He nodded. "All right. I'll go out the way we came in. Three knocks and three means it's clear for you to get out. Right?"

"I wouldn't touch the door at all, Raven. Just to be safe. One of those traps looks pressure-sensitive." Spectre frowned again. "But tapping on the wall about a meter or so away should be okay."

"Works for me," he grinned. "See you in a few."

*   *   *

Far in the distance, the Clocktower bonged out the watch, its deep, resonant notes a melancholy counterpoint to the rhythmic clopping of the steel-shod hooves of his horse. It was three-thirty in the morning. Raven was still awake, and after twenty-one hours his mind felt as blurry as the fog which shrouded the city around him.

The solid clopping of the horses' hooves turned hollow as they made their way over a bridge. Angel's house was not too far away. He'd promised to come back tonight. The fact that he actually was going back to her almost surprised him. *Almost*, but not quite. In point of fact, it hadn't even been a question. He'd left Linda outside her apartment building. She hadn't asked him to come in; he hadn't suggested it. They both knew why. She had her own life, which included Raúl. He had his, which included Angelique. They would meet from time to time, ravage each other's bodies delightfully, exchange information, then she would return to Raúl, and he to Angel.

He caught it that time. He would return to Angel. The refrain was now a familiar one: "He and Angelique." It was no longer just "he." Barbara Cole was cute and delightful, Spectre sultry and gorgeous, but they were temporal, unable to be any more than satellites in his world; at the center of it was the ash-blond beauty of Angelique Blakesly.

Face it, Vince. She's snared you. Either that or you've snared yourself, and it's high time you figured out which and why. The wonderfully sweet, yeasty smell of a nearby bakery wafted into the compartment. It was supposed to be a scent reminiscent of home, of comfort and security. For Vincent, however, it evoked a yearning for long evenings, with Angelique's lovely face framed in candlelight.

When love snares the heart, does anything else compare? *Dumb question, Vince. Would you know real love if it came up and spat in your eye?* Perhaps. Perhaps not. Perhaps that's what makes Angel so troubling. *Right. You can't define it, you can't touch it. All you can do is feel it. And that's supposed to make me feel better?*

He had choices; he knew that. He could accept what was happening and enjoy it, or be miserable, continuing to attempt to dissect it. Analysis and negotiation were poisonous to the heart, an anathema to emotion. *Sit down, shut up, and enjoy it. Right. Got it. Do I feel better yet?*

And yet, there were no real good reasons not to feel all right with this, save one: Simple fear. Cops and gangs and crime bosses and the heights of five story buildings he could face without turning a hair. But to look into the depths of his own soul. . . ?

Okay, okay. I get it. Don't be a chicken, Vince. If you love her, you love her. If you love her so much you want to marry her, then marry her. And don't ask what comes next.

The carriage lurched to a halt. He got out, paid his fare, and headed down the street toward Angel's townhouse. The dumb thing was, he'd have to be gone before the household staff arrived for the day, which gave them less than three hours.

It's in your heart, Vince. Don't argue. Don't analyze. Just love her. That's all that's required. Right? Right.

It was a beginning. . .

Chapter 8

Hours later, Raven looked glumly out at the assembled off-duty troopers and investigators milling around the tavern, and took another drink of ale. All in all, the department's morale seemed pretty high. The last two big-money heists had been successfully cracked, the latest today. The hearing had gone as he knew it must: Spider was now awaiting a formal trial, and the outcome of that was easily as predictable as the hearing. And it looked as though there was as little he could do to change *that* as there had been the outcome of the hearing.

Even worse, Angelique had scheduled a dinner party in honor of his "victory." Ostensibly offered by the Paladin ladies in gratitude for saving their collective ass, in reality, the affair was her way of helping him make his way back into society.

"I know you aren't happy about the way the case turned out, my love," she'd said, arms and legs tangled up with his in the pre-dawn gloom. *"But this the best way to begin to force those hypocrites in the church and government to live by their own rules, rather than using them to control everyone else."*

Question: *Do you care, Vince?* For reasons of his own, he knew the answer. Yes, he cared. *But what a price.*

"An innocent man, a nominal friend, is about to be collared for life, and you want me to use that as a lever back into society?" He'd demanded incredulously. Politics: He'd never liked them, and this was why.

She'd gone quiet at that. *"I didn't realize he was a friend of yours, Raven,"* she'd whispered, moments later. *"I'm sorry. I'll forget all about it if you wish, but I would ask you to keep in mind that this isn't about your friend. The ladies of the Auxiliary owe thanks to someone for saving their reputations. This you have done, in true knightly fashion. They and their husbands must have a place from which to begin looking at you and your service to the City State as honorable; Lady Emilia and I think that this dinner party is one good way to bring them to that place. Perhaps you can think of another?"*

A true knight. One who strictly follows the knightly code, and because of

121

it, lives a saintly, virtuous life, free from all the moral struggles "lesser men" faced every day. *Like me,* he thought cynically. The knightly code, while a pretty piece of idealism, rarely provided answers to the complex questions posed by modern life. Except for battle—and then only when facing another honorable enemy—the code was pretty useless, as the tragedy now known as The Great War amply demonstrated.

Of course, the church, given a century for its paralogists to address the issue, had volumes of theological teachings disputing that conclusion.

None of which make the suppositions about me being a "true knight" any less laughable or ironic. Would a true knight let a comrade-in-arms be falsely tried and convicted?

He knew the answer. *No.*

"I can't think of one," he'd finally admitted, *"but isn't it ironic that my supposed 'true knightly virtues' are to be held up for everyone to see, when any true knight would be doing battle for his falsely accused comrade, and accept no less than justice?"*

Angel had disengaged herself from him at that, and rolled to a sitting position, dangling her shapely legs over the edge of the bed. It put her back toward him. *"It is,"* she answered, voice so low it was almost inaudible. *"But then, much of life is that ironic. And more."* A light shiver took her, and she reached for her robe. *"Mar'leven, my love, I wish I had a neat, tidy answer for you. I don't. The ladies of the Auxiliary will wish to thank you for taking prompt action on their behalf, which you have done. But, because you are who you are, and more a true knight than you will let yourself believe, you won't let yourself close this case."* Her shoulders slumped once, but she stood up right away, and wrapped the garment around herself, as if for comfort. *"You won't let your friend down, regardless of the costs."*

To that, he'd had no rebuttal, just like he still had no idea how to find the real thief. It would take more than one lonely cop to tackle organized crime successfully. Crime bosses had engaged and defeated the entire department more than once. It was not a suggestion Roland would easily entertain, never mind act on. Politically, this was just one more successful case to which the politicians could point, justifying the money they asked the tax-paying middle class and nobility to cough up for their government. Politically, no single man was worth jeopardizing that funding, innocent or no.

Yet again, this was why he never liked politics.

There was a rousing stir at the door as Roland himself blew in with a gust of windy rain, shaking the droplets from his worn great-coat in the practiced movements of a man who'd done this very thing, in this very place, for more years than he could easily recall. He returned the cat-calls, jeers, and a few less derisive greetings with the same vague wave of his hand and made his way back to the bar. Raven wasn't the only one who noticed the old cop's eyes were constantly moving to take in his changing surroundings. He doubted Roland was even aware that he did so.

Commissioner Hal Roland, Raven knew, had served honorably in what was then the combined infantry of the International Merchant Marines, during The Great War. The kingdom of Cascadia had effectively become the City State of Fernwall in those years, when the nobility executed what had since come to be known as "the Lords' Rebellion," a limited insurrection to control the populist uprising that eventually deposed mad, debauched King Charles VII from the throne. Staff Sergeant Hal Roland came back on a hospital ship, his body torn open from right shoulder to left hip from a sword gash. After recovering, he'd become a cop, working his way up from blue-jacket to detective sergeant to chief inspector in record time. Now he was the city's "top cop," a position from which, with only a little bit of luck, he'd likely retire. Roland's close-cropped hair was all gray now, and his face was a study in textures: scarred, wrinkled, pock-marked, leavened with moles. He'd not been a handsome man, even when young. Now, his face was ripe with the kind of character that made it unforgettable, rather than distinguished.

He sat down next to Raven with an audible grunt and ordered a liter of Danvers from the barman. "You did a pretty good job today, Sultaire," he allowed by way of greeting.

That could be taken in any number of ways, Vincent noted. "Not that it mattered much," he snorted. "It would have taken quite a few bells and whistles to slow down the political machinery. Politics and law enforcement," he groused, taking the opportunity to vent his frustrations a bit. "Like politics and warfare, they always seem to be in bed together, but the fucking each receives is usually far more painful than pleasurable." He raised his mug for another drink. *Should really eat something rather than sitting here getting drunk on Danvers,* he observed.

Roland barely sipped his when it arrived. No one had seen the man drunk since the day they buried his wife, over ten years ago, though he appeared to drink fairly regularly. "You did what you could," he allowed, unruffled by his junior's self-pitying air. "And you gave the magistrate enough reasons to exonerate Cooper, or at least order a further investigation. You did the cop's job. Now, you let it go, and let the courts do theirs."

The courts. After the Lords' Rebellion, the Countess of Remington had rammed a new constitution down the equally new parliament's throat. The constitution, adopted by the delegates to the City State's new parliament, joined Vin-Llamáz in separating the judicial body from the legislative body by turning it over to priestesses of the highly acclaimed judicial branch of the Urilian Church. Appointed to life terms by vote of the House of Lords, they in turn appointed the magistrates. The system supposedly removed all political motivation from the courtroom, guaranteeing the City State a higher level of justice.

That didn't prevent the politicians from trying to do all they could to get around it. "Really think they'll do it?" he asked. "From where I sit, the trial doesn't seem any less a formality than the hearing, judge or no judge."

Roland's heavy shoulders shrugged, an eloquent gesture, considering. "Depends on how good his attorney is. You gave a competent defender some big holes in the testimony you presented today. Big enough to pitch a war orc through." After another, longer pull on his mug, he leaned his elbows on the worn wood thoughtfully. "If his attorney stinks, then Spider's likely to wear a collar, at least for a while. Ten years, maybe fifteen, max."

So Coop had a chance. He lived like a slob, but he wasn't really poor. In fact, he had at least as much money, and probably more, than Linda. He worked more, and spent a hell of a lot less. "That's something, anyway," he sighed. "So now I get to go be thanked for all this true knightly stuff at a dinner party Lady Blakesly is throwing for me. We're quietly engaged, by the way. Don't know when we'll decide to make it public knowledge—for obvious reasons."

That clearly surprised the older man, though he took some pains to cover it. "Er, congratulations, then," he grunted. "The two of you are closer than either of you let on."

"Yeah. I suppose we are. She probably deserves a hell of a lot better. I think I'm getting the better end of the deal."

"I'd have to agree with you," he replied, straight-faced, but there was a twinkle in his faded blue eyes when he lifted his mug. "To the future Baron of Carlisle," Roland murmured quietly. "If you can stay out of trouble that long, anyway."

"Unlikely," the younger man chuckled. Despite his gruff manner, the old cop was calming him down, making him think again. "Can I get your advice on something, off the record?" he asked, changing tracks.

"Sure." Roland barely changed expression. "I can probably shake some of the dust and cobwebs off for you, even."

"Don't strain anything," Vincent drawled, grinning. "I left my badge at home for a while last night and did a little unofficial snooping into the source of the crystals that bypassed the security on that jewel."

Roland grunted again, amused, but not surprised.

"The tracks had all been carefully laid through the front door. I thought maybe the back door would lead somewhere," Raven shrugged. "Anyway, the trail led right to organized crime—again. Second big heist this year they've had their nose in, and this time they're trying to remove some independent competition. I don't need to tell you what that could mean. I'm not sure what to do, boss. I'm only one cop, but I can't just let an innocent man go down without *trying* to crack this for real."

The older man went quiet at that, delving deep into memories and thoughts that he didn't bother to share. When he finally did speak, his hoarse voice was oddly reflective.

"Organized crime's been a problem for this city for almost as long as it's been a city," he admitted, eying Raven's now-empty mug. He motioned the barman over. "Get this kid something to eat before he drowns himself."

The barman glanced at the younger cop, nodded, then left to fetch something without noticeably interrupting the Top Cop's flow. "And since we can't seem to do anything about it, we fight a rearguard action, little more than cleaning up the mess after it's already been made, actually.

"We're not giving up, but I have to think up a better approach. And that fucking 'blue ribbon commission' to study the problem is about fucking useless." He looked as if he wanted to spit. "Prob'ly riddled with plants from the crime bosses." Roland seemed to shake himself back into his present surroundings, and managed to look faintly chagrined when he turned back to Raven. "Sorry. None of that helps you. You got any new leads on this?"

Vincent flagged the barman again. "How about a cider? Getting drunk won't help anyway." Then he turned back to the man who was ostensibly his 'master.' "No, the trail ended there. The rest of what I know, you heard in court today."

Roland nodded, then leaned forward onto the bar again. "Investigation's a funny business. It gets into your blood and bone, and after a while you can't get away from it anymore. It's how you look at everything in your life." One thick, stubby finger swirled the puddle of condensation left by his still-sweating mug. "And it's not just cops. I've heard independents say that, too. One day something happens, and before you know it you start looking at everyone and everything with suspicion. Because," he said, forestalling Raven's interruption by pointing that finger at his face, "it usually turns out that the people you least expect are always involved in it somehow."

A dark eyebrow winged upward; something in the old cop's voice made Vincent's unvoiced protest seem callow. The barman came by again to shove a plate full of smoking hot, spicy beef strips and greens in front of him. Another quick pass planted a frosty mug of cider next to the plate.

"I have a hard enough time trying to get past all the details everyone else seems to ignore. I really don't need to add a chronically suspicious mind to it," he chuckled, reaching for a fork.

Those big shoulders lifted again. "Your choice, kid. I wouldn't get into the habit of ignoring details either. Not if you want to stay alive. It's the little things that speak the loudest, if you know how to listen to 'em."

"That being the problem," Vincent said around a mouth full of beef. "Damned good, boss. You hungry? Just knowing what to do with all that information. Half the time, my choices pay well; the other half, they get me into trouble. Right now I feel like it's a little of both."

Roland chuckled, a low, grumbly sound, and gestured to the barman for another plate. "It's like that. Experience teaches you how to sort through it, but the choices don't get any easier." He sobered abruptly. "Cops can get a little possessive about their turf, just like crooks do. And whoever's at the top of each heap is *really* possessive about it. Sitting here, on the top of my heap, I'm telling you I don't give a fat rat's ass about a politician's easy answers, Raven. This is *my* town. I want whoever did the crime to do the time for it. Do we understand each other?"

That stopped the younger man in mid-bite. Roland rarely used his street name, and he couldn't ever remember hearing the old man sound like a crime boss himself. In a way, it was comfortingly ironic. Was there really any difference between the criminals and the cops? Or was this just a big game, each side winning a few scrimmages now and then?

The answer actually made the badge in his breast pocket feel quite a bit lighter, and no tiny bit more comfortable. "Oh, I think we do, boss man. I think we do."

*   *   *

His boots clicked loudly on the marble floor of the foyer as he made his way to his office in Police Headquarters at City Hall. *Roland as a street boss.* Vincent had never thought of it that way. To him, the police had always seemed to be the social extension of the noble power structure. By accident or design, the parliamentary structure of the City State vested more power in a single member of the House of Lords than the entire House of Commons combined. And *that*, proponents labeled "representative democracy."

He made his way up the staircase to the floor of the great building that belonged to the Fernwall City Police Department. It housed the administrative and investigative offices for the entire department. The "uniformed officers precinct headquarters," or UOPs, as they were also known, were scattered around the city, each commanded by a captain.

Roland obviously did not see himself as anybody's puppet. His aim was justice, as he defined it. The politicians—the nobility numbered among them—could be damned. *Little man with overgrown notions of how important he was?* Vincent rather doubted it. Delusions of grandeur were not part of Commissioner Roland's character. He knew exactly where he sat in the City State's power structure, and had become more than adept at winning his fair share of political battles and making the winners pay dearly for his losses.

A "boss" indeed.

Vincent's keys rattled loudly as he unlocked the door to his small office. He opened the lamp shade and sat down at his desk, piled high with paperwork he had yet to organize and collate for Spider's forthcoming trial. He had avoided working on it. The idea of collaring an innocent man out of political expediency made the whole process feel so distasteful that he'd come to avoid his office altogether. Roland's comment tonight had changed that; he obviously felt the same way, which freed Vincent to now work *for* Cooper, no matter what the political costs, and to find the real thief—even if he had to do it unofficially.

126

```
Report on Security Arrangements for the
Forthcoming Presentation of the Lady's
Auxiliary; Cole.  Name:  Angelique Blakesly,
Baroness of Carlisle.


Report on Bookkeeping and Accounting; Cole.
Name:  Angelique Blakesly, Baroness of Carlisle.


Points of Contact Between the Lady's Auxil-
iary and Bishop Florian Hall; Gaust.  Name:
Angelique Blakesly, Baroness of Carlisle.


Presentation Work Group; Cole.  Name:  Angelique
Blakesly, Baroness of Carlisle.


Advertising and Outreach; Cole.  Name:
Angelique Blakesly, Baroness of Carlisle.


Law Enforcement Liaison and Advisory Committee;
Gaust.  Name:  Angelique Blakesly, Baroness of
Carlisle.
```

"*. . . it usually turns out that the people you least expect are always involved in it somehow.*" Vincent heard Roland's gravelly voice again.

There were other names on the various committees and work groups, of course, but only one name appeared on all of them. Angel's. He pushed Gaust's report away from him and sat back. *You're getting overly suspicious, Vince. That old bastard has got you jumping at shadows. She's Lady Emila's protégé. Of course she's going to be deeply involved.*

"*. . . it usually turns out that the people you least expect are always involved in it somehow.*"

He tried to make himself consider that somehow, Roland was right. *Right about what? Angel's no thief. She wouldn't even know what was involved. Which says nothing about whether she was a willing collaborator or not,* he sighed, already tired of the silly argument. It was true that, from the very beginning, he'd suspected an inside informant at the very least. Someone had to copy the keys needed to get in through the ground floor. Someone had to know exactly where the guards would be, and when. Someone had to have told the thief precisely where the *Mâgun-Zak* was going to be, and what security measures were going to be in place. The logistics involved in stealing something from such a secure area were dizzying, and so were the odds that one person had put the entire operation together. The insider, whoever it had been, would have had their fingers in virtually every aspect of the show.

"*. . . it usually turns out that the people you least expect are always involved in it somehow.*"

Angel *was* involved in every aspect of the show. *Right. And she's the kind to climb up thin silk ropes to the roof, too. Be serious, Vincent.*

But the thief *had* been a woman, not a man; that, or he really didn't believe the testimony he'd presented in court. *Which you do, and you know it. Right. What's that leave?*

An unfortunate coincidence? He didn't really believe that, either.

The one thing he had overlooked, perhaps, was Angel's own naïveté. She could have been involved right up to her pretty blond eyebrows, and not even have known it. *Now we're getting somewhere. She's the junior, so she gets all the shit details and reports. . .* To whom?

Magic question.

He reached out, flipped Gaust's report closed, and stood up. He felt better now than he had in days. This was all working out grandly. There were worse things than having been played, and he could fix that at his leisure, after the case was closed. He had found the lead for which he'd been searching. *I might just crack this, yet.*

*   *   *

Blakesly House
22 Amerian 580, 0915 hours

So this is what it looks like when one takes control of one's life, Angelique mused, staring with no small amount of trepidation at the piles of folders, books, and maps that had been mounded upon the new desk she'd purchased for her equally new study. The documents she'd requested from various agencies had completely hidden the varnished top, and then did a fair job of claiming the tea table as well.

Her accountancy had sent the ledgers containing the last five years of debits, credits, taxes, fees, expenditures, and even a copy of the latest population census (with the warning that the accuracy could vary by as much as 20% in either direction; mountain folk were sometimes difficult to find). The bailiff, Sir Angus Cliffton, appointed by her liege, the Earl of Camrose, had dutifully turned over copies of the rosters of the knights under oath, and soldiers currently kept under her direct employ, listed by fortification. She'd taken the family's personal records with her when she'd departed from her first, and only, visit to her alleged ancestral holdings; it had been the book on her lap when Raven had come to reclaim her that night. . .

Angel shivered, pushing away her internal revulsion at her previous weakness with the memories of her lover's hands and mouth; the precious hours spent reveling in his embrace. He'd been working with quiet intensity, still searching for leads in a private attempt to exonerate his friend.

Angel fretted about that. She'd had no way of knowing that the Spider was Raven's friend when she'd framed him for the crime, of course. She had intended the theft to be the Iris's introduction to Fernwall by leaving a single wild blossom in place of the thing she'd stolen. It was Louis who had insisted she leave the double trail that incriminated the Spider, though of course he would not explain why he'd wanted it done. In point of fact, he'd stopped explaining a lot of things, since they'd come to Fernwall.

She frowned, and glanced out her window. Then she drew a deep breath, and tried to dismiss her worries about Louis from her mind. Done was done, and the only thing she'd been able to do to relieve her personal sense of guilt was to hire Sir Jonathan Royles on Cooper's behalf, with the stipulation that her contribution remain strictly anonymous. Angel could easily afford his retainer now, and found a rather gratifying irony in using wealth she'd gotten from a theft to give the man she framed for it the best defense attorney in the city.

Back to work, Angel. This isn't getting any easier for you ignoring it.

It was an intimidating pile, certainly, but Angel had learned a valuable lesson in problem-solving back when she'd first arrived in Püran-Khir, what seemed a lifetime ago: *When faced with an overwhelming task, do any part of it that you already understand, and which may be quickly done. The rest seems to follow along naturally.*

So saying, she went first to the maps of her desmesne, painstakingly rendered in fine pigments and bold lines. She adored maps. Careless of her wallpaper, Angel tacked the maps on one wall to get an overall sense of the lands and distances involved. The baron's castle, Carlisle itself, was strategically placed at what seemed to be the convergence of three narrow valleys, but was in fact easily accessible only by the northernmost. The villa, which had only recently been constructed, was in that valley, at the foot of the mountains, with a breathtakingly lovely view of its entirety. The three valleys were sparsely settled still, even a decade after The Great War's end, but this was not unusual. War and its consequences had depleted the world's overall human population by at least a third, the experts thought, and perhaps by as much as half. There were many baronies, earldoms, and even one dukedom in what once had been Cascadia that had been abandoned completely, their populations pulled back to within borders the depleted numbers of knights and their men-at-arms could more easily maintain.

Carlisle and Camrose had once been part of the duchy of Enselford, but the duke and his entire family had died either in the Great War, or in the Lords' Rebellion that had deposed the king thirty-three years ago. The Earl of Camrose held the dukedom in regency and it, or what was left of it, was managed by him. To the north of Carlisle was the barony of Boxley, also frontier territory and as hungry for settlers as Carlisle itself. Carlisle's western border nestled up against the Earl of Camrose's own lands, while to the southwest were the borders of the barony of Holgate, which was sub-infeudated to the earldom of Glenmont. Carlisle's entire eastern border was the real frontier. Her knights and soldiers fought back the disorganized, erratic bands of feral sub-humans that raided with dismaying regularity.

There was one village or small town in each of her valleys besides the settlements that had grown up around the fortified positions. Port-Hill, Fenton, and Tiverton were trading posts and small pockets of civilization that contained a hearty, independent breed of humanity, accustomed to getting by on their own. Carlisle, Fort Horn, Fort Grindleford, Fort Littleton, and Fort Isley were more-or-less walled towns, their garrisons holding the border between civilization and savagery.

Angel's slender fingers traced the sinuous mountain ranges that separated the three valleys of her barony (*yes, Angel, get used to thinking of it that way*), and then the narrow dirt road which led northwest and eventually to the Caspian Valley, though this map did not extend so far. Her barony was many weeks' journey away, even with good horses. She was going to have to go back there in person, and soon.

A soft smile lit her face at that. *Going back with my husband. Their baron. My God, it seems unreal even now.*

With the maps pinned up on the walls, she looked at the mountainous piles of material and decided to continue with the census results as the next logical step. Taxes and revenues could follow. She was happily comparing the long columns of information to what the maps showed when Clarice entered after a terribly brief knock. She was breathless from haste, and her cheeks were bright pink.

"My apologies, my lady, but Sir Vincent Sultaire is here to see you. Mrs. Reynolds tried to explain to him that you were quite occupied, but—"

"But he would not listen." Angelique finished the sentence with a helpless little smile. "Please escort him up, Clarice, then you may return to your preparations for our dinner party."

The girl's eyes widened. "My lady, you cannot stay here unchap—"

"Clarice." It was spoken quite softly, and yet so firmly it stopped the girl in mid-sentence again. "I am no virgin maid, my dear, but have already been married once, and will be so again. You will keep this as dearly as your own soul for now, but Sir Vincent and I have agreed to be married, when his sentence is done."

The flushed pleasure in those pink cheeks could not have been feigned. "Oh, my lady Angelique! That's wonderful! But what will the other Paladins say?"

She chuckled easily. "They will be quite happy for both of us, publicly. I should suppose there will be some scandalized whispering in the background, but with my lady the Countess of Remington's overt approval, the rest will keep any nay-saying to themselves, I should suppose."

The girl rushed forward to embrace her mistress, and Angelique surprised herself with the depth of affection she felt as she returned it. "I'm so happy for you, my lady," the maid said.

"Thank you. But mind, you must not tell Mrs. Reynolds or Hannah, just yet. They're both quite busy with the party preparations. I'll tell them afterwards. Now," she disengaged herself from Clarice's arms with a smile, "show Sir Vincent in, then return to your duties, yes?"

"Yes, my lady." She bobbed a polite curtsy, then moved with some alacrity back to the stairs. Angel used the time to smooth the loose hairs back into the clip at the back of her head. She'd barely turned from the mirror when she heard her maid's nervous, almost helpless laughter returning to the second floor. She was still blushing furiously when she curtsied Sir Vincent into the room.

Vincent spared the girl a rakishly bold look, before taking in Angel and the cluttered room in a single glance. "Carlisle," he murmured, coming over to sweep her into his arms. "You've been busy, burning bright. What's all this about?"

The answer to that had to wait for an exuberant, breathless kiss. How had he managed to grow even more handsome in the few hours they'd been apart? Angel barely heard the door close behind Clarice before her mouth opened to his, already hungry for him despite her pre-dawn attempts at annihilation through satiation. "By all the Gods, but I have missed you," she told him, murmuring the words against his lips. "You're in my veins like a drug, *Mar'leven*."

"I should hope so," he murmured, brushing his lips across hers again, ending with another distracting kiss. "So what's all this about?" he asked again, when he was finally able to bear to part from her. "Suddenly feeling homesick?"

Angel chortled quietly, then disengaged herself just enough to turn around. "Rather difficult to think of Carlisle as my home when I've spent so little time there, to date. No, my beloved, I've been informed of some rather interesting goings-on in my barony. Monies being sent on to Camrose's coffers when that should have stopped with my investiture, that sort of thing. It occurs to me that I've let many matters slide there, and that it's more than time I did something about them."

She turned her piquantly lovely face back up to his. "Unfortunately, I was not raised a baron's daughter, and so have very little idea what I should do. Considering our plans for the future, *Mar'leven*, I was hoping you would help me."

A complex mixture of emotions played across her lover's—no, her *betrothed's* face. "Stopping Camrose's siphoning is easy enough," he said carefully, leading her over to a chair. "Just tell the bailiff that he works for you now, and if any more money disappears, you'll consider it embezzlement and have him executed." He sat down, then pulled her onto his lap. "Your Carlisle staff will get the point immediately. I guarantee it. What else is going on?"

It seemed a rather draconian solution, but Angel didn't stop to consider it. Instead, she sighed, and snuggled into his arms. "Most of it appears to be along those lines. Anyone in a position of authority does what he or she pleases, without consulting me. They are good enough to inform me of their decisions—after the fact—and to be fair, I have done nothing to change this, to date.

"Additionally, my knights-captains appear to be rather dilatory about the defense of the borders. They've not ignored an outright attack by the sub-human hordes that raid so often, but they seem to do little to give those feral creatures reason to stay away from Carlisle and its people, either.

"And Raven, if they all aren't lining their pockets and pouches with the tax monies for which they are responsible, I would quite frankly be surprised." A tiny frown knitted her brows together, and she drew a deep breath. "I want to put a stop to all of it. Again, I don't really know how."

For some time, Vincent looked out the window at the sun, which had finally burned through the inevitable morning fog. "My father and my old tutor, Master Slagter, would, at this juncture, no doubt point out that a prince can afford only one kind of person in his government," he said distantly, as though recalling things he'd shut away. "Loyal persons. And there is only one way a conquering prince can gain that loyalty. Subjugation."

He felt so remote from her, so distant; even sitting there in his lap he seemed miles, or perhaps years, away. Something was wrong here, deeply wrong. Angel had survived by noticing changes like this one, and reacting to them instinctively. Uneasy, she touched his fine, strong chin with her fingers, and turned his face back up to hers. "You are troubled, beloved. May I know why?"

He smiled wanly. "I've put myself in the position becoming the very thing that I despise: a member of the ruling class. Here I am, advising you to do the very things I railed against my father for doing, and that I debated the morality of with Master Slagter for hours on end. My father thought we would create a fairer, more just government by deposing King Charles. A grand idea. I had the thrill of studying 'Crazy Charlie's' rule from one end to the other. I also observed that the change to a constitutional government made my father no less a tyrant on his own land than before. How hypocritical." He chuckled then, and looked at her wryly. "And I'm rambling."

"Perhaps." She felt her lips curl upward, and knew she couldn't have stopped herself from smiling back at him, so infectious was his own self-deprecation. His dark irony, however, had disturbed her deeply. "And perhaps, you are telling me something about you that I must know, if we are truly to marry." Her fingers drifted up to smooth his dark, clean hair, glittering in the morning sun, and she did her best to conceal the worry that tried to birth itself in her heart. "Second thoughts, *Mar'leven?*"

"Not about us," he murmured, his gaze drifting to the window once more. "But about me? I have lots. I always have, I guess. I'm not sure I like whom I'm becoming..." *Do you not?* He couldn't finish the sentence. *You've betrothed yourself to your mother—a* baroness. *Land, law and lordship; the world you left for the traps, prostitutes, thieves, and cut-purses. The very world you swore you'd never return to.* Except that, even before he'd been caught and collared, he'd learned that being the glamorous, black sheep nobleman amongst the poor, uneducated folk of the traps was more

132

inglorious and frustrating than he'd ever imagined. He'd been able to help some—and still did—but he hadn't changed anything. "But, I'm not sure I like who I'm running from, either," he finished in a whisper.

It confounded her, that he who always seemed so supremely confident in himself and his abilities should share the same self-doubts which she, who had only just discovered her own power, had always harbored. It hurt, in fact it ached so badly she wanted to laugh, because not even tears could have eased this particular suffering.

Lord and Lady, Angel. This isn't the time for laughter. Reach for something, anything! "I don't want to marry your father, Raven." She caught her breath, imperceptibly. *What* in the world had prompted that?

"Then maybe you don't want to marry at all." He murmured it so softly she barely heard it. "The marriageable young nobles have all had pretty much the same education I've had. Taught to rule, to maintain their hold on power, and to increase it. Tyranny and rulership are close cousins, if they're not siblings." And yet... without the kind of power that tyrants like his father craved, he'd found himself just as helpless as those living under the tyrant's lash. It had troubled him, profoundly, but then, nothing about the situation in which he found himself sat easily with him.

Angel felt her jaw firm up at that. "I could have had any number of *them*, Raven. I fell in love with *you*. Do you know why?" Again her fingers brought his face around to meet her gaze, her own brimming with newborn certainty. "It's not simply because you'll make me eager to get to bed early every night. It's because you are *different*." She glanced at the materials piled in her sitting room, and the maps upon the wall. "Subjugation. Having offenders shot. That's not who you really are, my love. Won't you tell me what you truly think?"

She felt him tense. His jaw clenched and unclenched several times, and finally he looked away again. "I can tell you what I think," he said again finally, "but quite frankly, what I think has been laughed at by every teacher and professor I've ever had—except Master Slagter, and I have it on good authority he was crazy, so I wouldn't take it too seriously. What you need is an experienced political operative to advise you."

He sighed explosively and took a deep breath. He hated this; *hated* it! He could hear the lectures of his father's tutors in his head. Every nobleman's son from knight to duke got the same education, based on the same pompous assumptions: Keep them occupied, keep them fed, and you'll keep the peace. Only Master Slagter had dared defy convention and challenge the assumptions behind the philosophy. Vincent had run away from home before his father could fire the man—or worse.

It was, perhaps inevitable that, in the end, he decided to trust his time with Master Slagter, and the revelations of those lessons, rather than the lectures of his father's preferred tutors. "First," he nodded at the pile of folders, "I'd ship those right back where they came from and order summary reports to be delivered to you in a week. If you don't trust the agencies in charge, then hire someone else to digest the information and give you a report. You're the baroness, not the accountant, economist, military commander, and so on. There's no possible way you can keep track of all the details. You'll kill yourself trying. That's why you have experts in each field. To summarize and advise. Their job is to give you information and answer questions. Your job is to listen and decide what's to be done with the information given. Make sense so far?" He looked up at her.

She wanted to kiss him again. Pride, love, and unbearable joy surged within, all of it constricted in the tight confines of her throat. Unable to force words through that, Angel simply nodded, trusting her smile and his acute perceptions to pick up on all she couldn't say.

"Now, while your accountants and so on are grinding out those reports, you might hire a couple of advisors for a field trip to Carlisle. As control of estates has been returned to survivors of the former families, some of the better estate administrators have gone mercenary. Troubleshooting, advising, situation assessments, whatever you hire them for that's what they'll do for you, and your fee buys their allegiance.

"So, the first advisor you need to hire is a freelance estate administrator. The other one should be military. A mercenary captain, probably, who can give you a situation report on the frontier and a troop readiness assessment. Let him command a company of his troops for protection, and for muscle once they get there, and send both of them out to Carlisle with authority to look into whatever they damned well please. Between the call for reports and the unannounced arrival of hired experts, I can pretty much guarantee your entire staff will start sweating heavily. A lot of foolishness will probably come to an end immediately. Still with me?"

"I love you, yes," she agreed, smiling happily. "Will you marry me?"

He smiled, and caressed her cheek. "Still think I'm worth it, huh?" he chuckled. "Then yes, I'll still marry you."

"I think you're wonderful. Why all the upset, though? Those sound like perfectly reasonable, rational steps to take, to me—though I'd not have thought of any of them. I had no idea such persons as 'freelance estate administrators' existed."

"No, probably not. Comes with having been raised in this crazy place. Noble life in Vin-Nôrë is probably infinitely simpler."

Angel smiled, a little wistfully. "Noble life in Vin-Nôrë is more an abstract concept than a reality, you know. Vin-Nôrë itself is a ruin of what it was, still trying to resurrect itself from the ashes of its rape and destruction during The Great War." She sighed quietly, then returned her gaze to Carlisle's maps. The last thing she wanted to do was perpetuate any more lies, here. *Time to redirect the subject.*

"Lady Emilia is right, though. You're going to make a notable baron."

"High praise," he chuckled, "but it remains to be seen. According to my father and his inestimable teachers, I'm a hopeless failure. That's why my father never gave me any real authority, you know. I hated his damned tutors and fought with them constantly. Then, as if to prove his point, he'd give me some stupid job or other, but no agency with which to act.

Predictably, I'd fail, and then be told to listen next time."

That startled her into a long moment of silence, as she struggled to understand what he'd just told her. She'd never had a father, but by the time she was old enough to notice the lack, Louis had already taken over the role, in his perverted way. That a father could treat his son so, without chaos and anarchy driving him to it, was simply beyond her ability to comprehend.

"Your father is a—" Angel bit off the word and turned her face away. She had never even met the Baron of Valemont, after all, and she was relieved he was *at* Valemont, so that she needn't have invited him to the upcoming party. She shifted a bit on her betrothed's lap. "Ah, short-sighted, perhaps," she finished, somewhat lamely. It wasn't what she'd meant to say. She knew he knew it.

He huffed a chortle, then squeezed her leg. "So, why don't we pile all this stuff into your brand new carriage and get this little ball rolling today? I know of a small but damned good mercenary company that will serve us well, and I know of an agency that can help us find the right kind of administrator, too. Never been there, but I've heard them mentioned often enough."

Her gaze returned to him, and she was smiling happily. "Us," she quoted back, taking that opportunity to kiss him lingeringly. "Yes. Carlisle will become a model barony that others will look to, in order to emulate. And it will be so, even though I know nothing of these matters—but I *believe* in you, *Mar'leven*. Unquestioningly."

"Dangerous, that," he drawled, helping her back to her feet. "But I'm afraid we have no corner on the model market. The Earl of Auberon and your own Countess of Remington already lay fair claim. Dear Lady Emilia has ruled fairly for decades, and what the Earl of Auberon has been able to do in the two short years since his reappearance has been impressive. But, assuming I'm not completely insane, we might make a difference."

Angel was laughing merrily as she and Raven scampered back out of the accountancy's office like children, piling back into her carriage in the late-morning sunshine. It was a smart-looking little number, pulled by a single horse and on this day, open to the lovely summer breeze. The sunlight glinted through her betrothed's hair like silver, and the Lord and Lady help her, but she didn't care *who* might see them together this way. The entire city would know the reason for it, soon enough.

She brought to mind Goodman Belkins' face when they'd told him what they wanted, and she laughed again, even harder. "Oh, *Mar'leven*, I thought he was going to melt down on the spot!"

"Dale and Merkline Associates, the corner of Cern and Talbot streets," Vincent instructed their driver. "Plebians who are used to getting their way with clients don't like it when the rules suddenly change," he told her, settling back into his seat as the trap pulled away. "But nobles of name, and even rich merchants, are high paying accounts that they can rarely afford to lose. A useful tidbit at times like these. Of course, a nice bonus come WinterFest, with little gifts now and then helps too."

She caught at her stylish, broad-brimmed hat before it flew off her head, pins scarcely enough to hold it as the trap rolled toward its next destination. "I'll remember that," she smiled. "Are Dale and Merkline Associates the estate administrators, then?"

"Yes. Should be interesting. I think their opinion of me is about equal to my father's," he snorted indelicately, "but they do have some of the best on their contract list."

"Well, we are not interested in their opinion of you, at the moment." She felt an almost uncharacteristic firmness as she said it, and knew it was carried in her voice and manner. "If they can't divorce their opinions from their assessments of my estates, then we will simply take our business elsewhere."

"That would be difficult, at best," he sighed. "But I think I have a way around their opinions anyway. Auberon's new earl seems to spend more time out of country than in. He's been hiring a lot of administrators to carry out his agenda for the earldom. All we need to do is ask for someone who's worked for him a few times, and we'll have a good tool, regardless of what they think of me. I understand Auberon's a rather imposing individual."

"I've seen him once, from a distance, though we've not been introduced," Angelique murmured, thinking it over. "He's as remote as any king, from what I can tell. Very strangely accented speech. And does not suffer fools gladly." She nodded, and smiled again. "I like it, beloved."

Their trap clopped into the heart of the city. Dale and Merkline Associates was in the midst of the financial and business center, surrounded by some of the world's largest banking institutions, "The Merc," as the commodities exchange was known, and Fernwall's stock trading floor. The buildings here were faced in marble or expensive brick, with columns and windows; some had courtyard entrances. Angel's eyes flickered up to the rooftops by habit, noting and appreciating the dormers, faux towers, cupolas, gables, and gutters that would make running up there an enticing challenge. Her carriage rolled to a stop then, and she pulled her mind back to the matter, and the man, at hand.

Vincent assisted his bride-to-be out of the carriage. "Imposing looking pile, isn't it?" He grinned as they headed into the building. "I suppose it's to help keep the riff-raff at bay."

She glanced up at the marble edifice, and murmured, "Color me dutifully impressed." With a tight squeeze for his strong arm, she nodded graciously at the doorman and stepped into the airy and well-lit lobby. They both spotted the conservatively-dressed floor receptionist almost immediately.

"Dale and Merkline Associates?" she asked the young man, a bit gratified by his appreciative, but quickly-stifled glance. Her Vin-Nôrëan accent sounded oddly charming, but out-of-place there, as it echoed off the marble floors and tiled walls.

"Top floor, my lady. Would you like an escort?"

"Oh, thank you, but I have one," Angelique smiled sunnily, and patted Vincent's arm. "I'm sure Sir Vincent and I can find our way."

Dale and Merkline Associates proved to be a suite of offices, fronted by another receptionist. Dark wood tones, lush green potted plants, crushed velvet and leather upholstery, paintings by well-known artists. The ambience pandered to the tastes of society's elite.

"May I help you?" a middle aged woman asked from across her highly polished wood desk. She sat with a fountain pen poised in her hand, looking at them inquiringly.

"You may," Angelique replied. "I wish to speak to one of Dale and Merkline Associates' estate administrators on the possibility of sending a team out to evaluate my estates."

"And whom might you be representing, ma'am?" the woman asked, heading to her appointment book.

"The lady happens to be the Baroness of Carlisle," Vincent murmured. "She *did* say 'her estates.'"

"I see," the woman replied, nose still in her appointment book. "My apologies, milady. However, I'm afraid—"

"We'll wait," Vincent interrupted, "and while we're waiting, we'd like to see a list of those administrators who have been repeatedly employed by the Earl of Auberon."

"I'm afraid only Sir Richard Merkline would have that information," the lady replied frostily.

"Then go get it. Or I will, and he'll be sure to get the full report on just why I, a client, had to interrupt his meeting."

The lady looked livid. Angel was just barely managing to hide her astonishment, but could not stop herself from glancing between Vincent and the woman as if she expected the shouting to start at any moment.

"And you can also be sure I'll be at the next meeting of the board, asking for your professional head on a plate, too," Vincent continued, undaunted by the woman's temper. "Now get cracking. The Baroness here has a major problem that needs to be tended to today, and we have much to do."

"I'll see what I can do," the woman grated out, rising stiffly.

Angelique was about to inquire what had gotten into him when he turned to her, face full of self-loathing.

"I hate this," Vincent murmured after the woman had vanished behind an inner office door. "If I didn't know better, I'd say my name was James. Blackmail's more honest."

She stepped close to him, keeping her own voice down with an effort. "I wondered why you resorted to force, rather than your usual charm. I would rather not lose you to your father's influence, you know."

He sighed heavily. "Irritation, I suppose. I hate these places. I hate their arrogant, pompous attitude. I hate the institutions they help perpetuate."

"Vincent." Her gaze sharpened into steel for a brief moment. She so rarely used his given name. "You're no longer a boy, you know. You're a grown man. That's supposed to mean you can make your own choices about all this, now. Deal with it on *your* terms. Yes?"

"Yeah," he grumped. "I just wish I knew what they were supposed to be." There *were* examples of good governance amongst the peers. Auberon, Remington—even crusty old Trobiere was fair, if a bit firm for Vincent's tastes; but they weren't the ones who had raised him. His knowledge of their styles of governance was intellectual rather than experiential, and he knew that as well as he knew he was being difficult, and probably childish.

A similar and highly irreverent thought caused Angelique to lose her grip on whatever sternness she'd managed to present. "By the Lady, your sons are going to be adorable. *Mar'leven,* since you so loathe the way your father does things, why not start out by choosing the opposite of what you think he would do? It may not be right either, but it certainly gets you away from your own self-hatred because of it."

"My self hatred..."

The door opened and the woman returned, a file folder in hand. She seemed a bit calmer, but her manner was still frigid. "Here are the personnel files for the administrators the Earl uses on a regular basis," she said in a neutral tone, "and Sir Richard Merkline says he can offer you no more than fifteen minutes at the top of the hour. That's the space of time between this appointment and the next. I hope you know this is *highly* irregular."

Vincent cast Angelique a quick glance, then smiled at the woman, taking the folder. "Thank you." A hand flicked up beside her head and came back holding a bright red rose. "For your pains," he murmured.

The woman's eyes went wide and about half of the frost in her manner melted right before their eyes.

Angelique chuckled warmly, plainly delighted by her betrothed's choice this time. "That's quite all right, my good woman. Sir Vincent and I are highly irregular persons." She reached up and unpinned her hat, then glanced over at the chairs along one wall. "With the information you've provided us, we'll certainly take no more than fifteen minutes of your employer's time. My thanks for making this a relatively painless procedure."

"Of course," the woman said, going so far as to crack a brief smile. She indicated the chairs, then returned to her desk, leaving the young couple to scan profiles and professional records.

"If we were alone, I'd kiss you," Angel whispered, eyes scanning the list of credentials with uncanny rapidity.

Vincent put a closed hand on top of the folder she was reading and opened it, revealing a tiny, fresh, and fragrant tiger-lily blossom.

Her eyes widened, and shot to his in disbelief. "So I shall kiss you later, when I can do a thorough job of it," she grinned, heart so full she felt it would burst.

Vincent just chuckled merrily, eyes twinkling.

"So tell me something, please. Honestly," she warned him, affixing the lily he'd given her to her hat. "Do you need more time to adjust to helping me with the business end of Carlisle? I can find 'most anyone to advise me on that, but in my life I have only one you. I do not wish to lose you."

Their carriage was now clopping in almost the exact opposite direction, toward the only Balcheri enclave in the City State. It housed an ambassador and diplomatic staff, and was also the home of the only B'nachian temple in Cascadia. More pertinently, it was also the headquarters of the infamous Red Brotherhood, a small, fiercely loyal, highly effective mercenary organization which was sponsored by the B'Nachian church.

"I've had nothing but time for four years now. Obviously running away isn't helping," he drawled, voice heavy with irony. "I either need a better place to hide or a different approach." *And an opportunity to choose a different approach is exactly what you've given yourself,* he mused, watching the store fronts pass by their trap. *She's right. You're not your father, and running into poverty didn't do a damn thing to change it. Change requires power; barons have power. Simple logic, Vince. Simple logic.*

Angel sighed and wished for the thousandth time that she were a wiser woman. Even a greater amount of experience with men might help her navigate this mine field between them; as it was, she felt as if every other step she tried to take exploded something, and always unexpectedly. *Well, you wanted to be more in control of your life, didn't you?*

Surely, but does that mean I have to control Vincent, too? This is not *the man who asked us to marry him!*

Wait. "Us?"

They had nearly gotten to East Fork Bridge, the great landmark structure that spanned the north branch of the Caspian River between Angels and Merchants. Taxes in this area were considerably higher than in the rest of the city. The rich liked their well-manicured lawns, trees, and shrubs, and wanted to see their wrought iron fences remain a consistent, lusterless, stove black.

Vincent, who'd gone broodingly quiet, distracted her by patting her leg, his eyes scanning the park-like scenery that made up most of Angels.

"Darling, you're right of course. I'll get this sorted out. You don't need to brood over it, too. I navigated the underground and got to be a decent con in this city by the time I turned twenty-one, all without any help. I think I can figure out how to be the baron you want me to be. At least I've had some training, biased though it may have been."

"Dammit, Raven!" The curse was out of her mouth before she could stop it, but Angel didn't let the surprise slow her down. She'd never before had the temerity to express anger; a very private part of her marveled at what it felt like. "To the hells with what I want! Do you truly believe I'm eager to stand in your father's stead, and be the next excuse for you to go on hating yourself? And for that matter, to the deeper hells with what your father thinks!" She took a moment to struggle for control. Shouting would have been quite unseemly for a lady in public, and she was perilously close to it.

"Be the baron *you* want to be," Angel finally managed to say, in a reasonable and slightly pleading tone of voice. "Please, beloved."

Vincent seemed shocked. A dark eyebrow winged skyward, and it looked as though he wanted to say something, but he couldn't get the words to cross his lips. A moment later, he burst out laughing, and a small knot of tension within her loosened at it. Maybe they would be all right, after all. By the time he'd regained his own measure of control, she had pressed her fingers against her lips, as if to stifle her own merriment.

"I've never gotten angry with anyone before," Angel confessed in a small voice, lips flickering dangerously. "Did I do it well?"

That set him off again. It was a highly undignified position for the future Baron of Carlisle to be in, especially since people were looking at them as they passed.

"Passing well," he gasped. "Ah, dear Lord and Lady, burning bright. You're going to kill me with humor."

She laughed briefly. "Either that, or with passion. I haven't decided yet."

"Well, hurry up," he complained, quite insincerely. "The indecision is painful."

"Too bad." Her answering smile was beatific. "You've already agreed to a life's term, remember?"

"Ouch! That's not fair. Ha! Saved." He pointed to the approaching gate into the Balcheri embassy. "If I'm quick," he told her conspiratorially, "maybe they'll let me sign up."

"Do you suppose you can evade me that way, my lord?" she asked him archly. "Go on, sign up with yon priests or mercenaries. I'll be there to sign up, right behind you. Perhaps they are in need of a lethal wit?"

"Doomed!" he announced. "Forever cursed by yon beautiful lady's charms. Neither hill nor dale can separate us, so great is her devotion to my sodden estate." It was great theater—if a bit juvenile. And imprecise.

She laughed anyway.

Technically, it was the embassy, though the word vastly overstated the grandeur of the place. "Monastery" was a much more apt term, not only for its architecture, but also for the way its personnel were dressed. From the air, the building resembled a squared-off letter "U," the connecting, central wing being somewhat shorter than the other two. Angel and Raven could both recall when it had been the original teaching hospital for the Valian Healer's Hospice. When the healers had outgrown the humble facility, a new one had been constructed in the heart of Merchants', and within months a construction crew had rebuilt the place for its new tenants, from the far northwestern kingdom of Balkland.

The Balcheri ambassadorial staff and their religious contingent had settled into the renovated complex quietly enough. The problem with their presence was that they were not the official embassy of King Olaf of Balkland. They were rather an unofficial embassy for the losing clan in the Balcheri civil war. Since the Kierkken Clan was also the former ruling clan, the presence of such an unofficial embassy in Fernwall did not rest easy with either King Olaf, or Fernwall's new parliament.

Fortunately, the Kierkken representatives rarely interfered or participated in the events in the city, restricting their activities to the affairs of parliament. In fact, they kept *such* a low profile that it was quite likely most Fernwallians were ignorant of this Balcheri bastion in their midst.

The carriage halted at the outer, wrought-iron gates, and Vincent again assisted his beloved down from the trap, where they were greeted by a tall, bearded, robust man in long, rust-colored robes. He bowed formally. "My lady, my lord. How may I serve you?"

"This is Lady Angelique Blakesly, Baroness of Carlisle," Vincent replied, returning the bow with one of his courtly best. "I am Sir Vincent Sultaire, the lady's intended husband. The baroness finds herself in need of a veteran officer of the Brotherhood, and perhaps a platoon as well."

"Indeed. Be welcome, then." With slow, deliberate formality that smacked of ritual, the man bowed again, and brought forth a ring of keys to unlock the gate. The young couple stepped through, and into the garden walkways beyond it. Rather than leading them to the center of the complex, he led them to a door at the end of one wing. The sign of the Red Brotherhood upon it was stark, quite plain, and unrelieved by ornament or other device. The tall, silent man opened the door for them, and ushered them through.

The interior office was as plain and unadorned as the sign on the door. There were, however, two wooden chairs against one wall, and their guide motioned them in with another bow. "The adjutant will be with you shortly. May I fetch you some refreshment?"

"Some water, yes, please," Angel replied softly, more than a little intimidated by the aura of the place.

"Indeed," Vincent smiled. "It has been a long day already. Water would be welcome."

With yet another bow, the man left, returning moments later with a pitcher of water and two glasses. He'd barely closed the door behind himself when one of the inner doors opened, and a woman, easily as tall as Vincent and completely under arms, stepped through.

If this was the adjutant, then "brother" was obviously meant as a title, rather than an indication of gender. Her red hair was tightly braided back. The grim lines of her jaw and the commanding set of her eyes marked her, to those who'd survived The Great War and its ravages, as a combat veteran. Her steel breastplate, scarred but shining, made allowances for her breasts, and the tip of her scabbarded sword almost touched the ground, even though it was slung over her back. Her greaves and link-chains were likewise polished, though worn with long use.

She half-bowed from the waist, utterly correct for one under arms. "I am Brother Träutin, serving as adjutant for Red Brotherhood," she began. Cascir was not her native language. "My military rank is what would be 'colonel' in Merchant Marine Army. I have authority to make contract for Brotherhood, or part, depending on need. How would you be served?"

Angel cleared her throat. "I am Baroness Angelique Blakesly of Carlisle. I wish to contract with some part of your Brotherhood to escort a team of evaluators to my estates, and also to evaluate the readiness and performance of my soldiers and their officers." She then glanced at Vincent. "This is Sir

Vincent Sultaire, Carlisle's future baron."

Brother Träutin bowed again, removed her sword-belt and scabbard, then seated herself behind the desk. From one drawer she pulled out several ledgers and opened the top one. "What dates?" she inquired.

"The evaluators who will be reviewing the rest of my estates will be ready to leave next week," Angelique told her. "The first day of Ilian."

"How many troops?"

Now completely out of her depth, she turned to Vincent, who was rubbing his chin. "The baroness is having some trouble convincing her estate administration that their term of stewardship on behalf of her liege is ended. I doubt pitched battles are in the offing, but the ability of the baroness's representatives to flex their muscles may be necessary. The barony is also on the frontier. Attacks by non-humans are also possible, though probably not in large numbers."

He shrugged. "You know your troops, but I can't think more than a platoon—to use an IMMC infantry term—would be necessary."

"Frontier out that way not far from ACSK borders," Träutin mused thoughtfully, gazing at the map of the old Cascadian territory. The mention allowed Angel to place the woman's accent, for many of the people on her barony spoke Cascir in just such a way. They weren't really all that far from the outer borders of the Allied City-States of Korak, relatively speaking. "Have problems with bandits, that far out, Baroness?"

"The reports I have received are not that specific, I am afraid," she apologized. "Something else I'd like to see changed, mind you."

"Hmmm." Träutin flipped through another ledger, mumbled something to herself, then opened a third one and began carefully making entries into it. "Platoon ready then, can leave Ilian one. Lieutenant Forrest, commanding. Good man, good officer. Veteran from last battles in Ameran Indi." She looked up to her prospective employers, then plunged ahead.

"Standard to estimate total amount, pay at least half up front," she informed Angelique in a business-like tone. "Platoon be gone rest of year, look like, counting travel-time. No looting or spoils—so price goes up. But light duty, so not up that much. Be £250, lady. Remainder due when Captain Forrest hand you his report."

Without a quiver of hesitation, she nodded. "Sound investment. Where do I sign?"

"If you will come with me, milord, milady." The man was their host for the evening, and his voice was as mellifluous as any Angel had ever heard. He smiled and gestured, and she and Vincent followed him into the Collingwood Arms' main dining room.

The day had ended well. Captain Forrest had met with them shortly after they'd concluded the business transactions with Brother Träutin. His questions had been pointed and probing, but by the time he was finished, he seemed satisfied that he and his command would be able to meet their mission with little difficulty.

142

From the Balcheri enclave, they had driven to the edge of the city to have dinner at the quiet, but pleasant country atmosphere offered by the Collingwood Arms. The only lighting in the dining room came from candles. Each table had one, covered with a red glass cone, and candle sconces lined the walls, and hung from great fixtures overhead. A string trio played soft music from a small, partially screened stage at one end of a second-floor balcony that surrounded the room on three sides.

"Here you are, gentles," the host said, indicating a small table slightly offset from the others. It gleamed in rich, woody tones in the candlelight. The chairs were deeply cushioned, the place settings real silver flatware and crystal goblets, and yet the young couple were in their street clothing and did not feel under-dressed or out of place. After the day's activities, the betrothed couple felt that a bit of celebration was in order—even if Angelique had just spent over £400 (a painful sum for a small, frontier barony) to implement their plan.

She accepted his help with her chair, and asked that a bottle of the chilled, sparkling wine vinted in the earldom of Crécy be brought immediately. "I feel like getting giggle-happy, *Mar'leven*. Care to join me?" She dimpled.

"Oh, why not," he replied expansively. "You spent enough today to damned near buy this place. I think you've earned the right."

"We'll make it all back within two years. Three, if the harvests are bad." It had been a long, long time since Angel could remember feeling so content and happy within, and was willing to believe that she never had. "The taxes at Carlisle seem a bit high to me, too. It will feel positively wonderful to be able to lower them, someday."

Vincent pushed his wine glass toward the host, who'd returned with their bottle of wine. "How do you plan to lower taxes after today? You just spent a small fortune, and I'll lay you odds that Captain Forrest is going to find out that there is much your troops could be doing to push back the frontier, but to do it they'll need training and equipment. Another outlay. I wouldn't be too hasty to lower taxes, darling. Not yet. Keep the money that's been going to the earl and use it to set things to right. And make sure everybody *knows* that's where that money is going." He lifted his filled glass in a toast for emphasis.

She responded by lifting hers, golden liquid sparkling in the candlelight. "To Carlisle's future baron."

Angel did not make the toast lightly, given some of his antics earlier that day. It was important to her, however, that he be able to come to grips with the demons that were troubling him. She meant in earnest what she'd said in anger: She did not wish their marriage and baronial responsibilities to be the next excuses for him to perpetuate his own self-hate.

Vincent's eyes were a mystery. "Let's hope he turns out to be a good one," he murmured. His voice was touched with that self-deprecating irony. "This is a lot of money you're gambling on me, you know," he continued, more seriously. "I would have thought Lady Emilia to be a better source of advice."

Angel smiled broadly. "I'm relieved you think so, my love. Because that's who I asked. She sent me to you."

He eyebrow shot up. "She did?" he blurted out brilliantly. "Of all the people I would have thought knew better... She's known me since I was a baby, you know."

Angelique chuckled warmly. "So she said, and rather fondly. I got the distinct impression that she's not been precisely pleased with some of your father's decisions where you are concerned, but she did say that your recent successes were no surprise to anyone who watched you grow up."

"She did?" He was obviously having trouble fitting his conceptions of the old matron around what Angelique was saying.

It was in her mouth to ask him if he thought she'd lie to him, but decided she really didn't want to touch on that, even in jest, until the lies she'd already told were untangled, and hopefully, forgiven.

"She did," Angel affirmed instead, feeling her broad grin soften into a fond smile. "I went to Lady Emilia yesterday to ask her advice on our rather unique situation, beloved. Blind she may be, but she gave me an entirely new way to look at the world, my place in it, and yours."

"You did... She did?" He let out an explosive breath. "Why am I getting the feeling I've been out of the loop here?" He leaned across the table. "You mean to tell me you told the most saintly lay member of the Church on this continent that we have been lovers?" he whispered. "And she didn't throw you out?" He looked completely baffled. "And then she told you to consult me on the management of the barony? She may have her issues with my father, but I can't believe she, of all people, approves of *my* life—or our unrighteous relationship, for that matter."

Angel reached out impulsively and laid her slim hand upon his. "You don't know her as I do," she murmured in turn, "and even I did not know her as well as I thought. I did not tell her we were lovers, Raven. She already knew."

"She *what*... How? Even old Roland didn't figure that one out. And he *owns* this town, or thinks he does."

She chortled quietly, and shook her head. "Allow me to quote her: 'But the Lady blessed me with blindness so that I might see more clearly, child.'" Unconsciously, she had mimicked the elderly lady's tone and posture even as the words recreated themselves from her near-flawless memory.

With a quick grin, she resumed the recounting in her own voice. "And then, when my heart was about to stop, she reminded me of the Lady's creed, 'Judge not.' I felt a little abashed, to have considered someone of her integrity even the least bit hypocritical. I should have reasoned it out for myself, and sought her counsel long ago."

Vincent let out another explosive breath and sat back in his chair as the server appeared with a tray of appetizers and menus. He waited until she'd finished and left before picking up where they'd been interrupted. "So, she's known all along and said nothing, is that it?"

She shrugged, and handed him a piece of the steaming hot bread she'd buttered. "Has known for some time, at least. I don't know for how long.

And in keeping with our Lady's words, she neither approves nor disapproves. She does not judge." Her eyes met his over the candlelight. "I think she is happy for us anyway, though. Are you?"

"Happy for us?" He picked a piece of fruit off of the tray and popped it into his mouth and chewed. "I don't know that I had ever thought of it that way. I know I'm happy, and I can't even say why. I'm hardly a virgin, but nobody has ever actually entered my life—touched me—like you have. You've made me wonder if I ever knew what being in love with someone was. I don't think I had."

Angelique, struck to her very heart by his words, nodded and settled back into her chair with her wine glass. "I can't ever remember being this happy, *Mar'leven*. Do you realize we have not spent this much time alone together, out of bed, in over a year? Our courtship has been either entirely secret, or much too public—and yet, I don't doubt at all that you are the man with whom I wish to spend the rest of my life."

"Put that way, our betrothal seems rather rash, doesn't it?" He chuckled. "We know each other's bodies well enough, but what do we *really* know about each other? The dirty laundry, I mean." He grinned then, and rather impishly. "Sure you want to marry the infamous 'Raven,' darling?"

"I said 'yes,' didn't I?" She snorted delicately. "The infamous Raven makes me feel very much alive, and in love. In those very important areas he has no competition at all." Her expression sobered. "A woman in my position could do much worse, believe me."

"A woman in your position?"

The candles flickered in the melodically-accented silence for several moments, while Angel debated how to answer that. At last, she knew the truth would suffice, even if it was only part of it. "There are too many men, both young and old, hungry for land and the titles that go with it," she began, knowing she was hedging even as she said the words. "Take Sir Eric Wilkinson-Foster of Liberaune, for instance. Likable enough. Handsome. Decent. Noble. Just. 'Wholesome' in a way you'll never be, my love."

Suddenly her glass was empty, and she was staring at it as the last of the cool, potent liquid slid down her throat and began to buzz in her brain. "I felt as if I were already in a coffin, every moment I spent with him."

Vincent refilled her glass thoughtfully, and then looked at her, wordlessly requesting her to continue. *Lady, don't let me say anything stupid now,* she silently prayed, then shrugged lightly to signal her own confusion.

"Let's just say," she went on, picking up food instead of wine, "that you could be smuggling slaves, embezzling monies from the police department, a brothel owner (and I have heard that you have patronized several), fronting for pirates… None of it would change how I feel about you, *Mar'leven*. Or how I feel when I'm with you."

"I see," he said softly, his face partially hidden as he sipped from his glass.

Silence reigned at their table for several minutes, broken only by the soft tinkling of silver on china, and enhanced by the murmur of quiet conversation. "I don't think I've ever had anyone consider me that non-disposable before." His soft snort was accompanied by a smile. "'Tis a rather novel place to be."

"Get used to it," she replied, meeting his smile with one of her own.

Chapter 9

Blakesly House
27 Amerian 580, 1830 hours

"Well, I do thank you for getting us together this afternoon, Lady Emilia," the Duke of Trobiere drawled to the aged countess. They, and a good portion of the rest of the House of Lords and their spouses, were standing on Angelique's garden-like back lawn. The late-afternoon sun was bright and warm. A slight breeze blew in off the bay, just enough to keep the sheltered garden from becoming uncomfortably hot for the impeccably dressed who lingered there.

It was an august company indeed. There stood many of the major policy makers in Parliament's upper house. Veritable kings in their own right, on their own land their word meant life or death to all who lived there.

"But I must say that I disagree with the stated purpose in the strongest terms," the duke continued. "Young Sultaire has been nothing but trouble for his father since infancy. Trouble that eventually got him arrested for blackmail and extortion. And now you insist we thank this rogue for doing nothing more than serving his master well." He sipped at his glass of champagne.

"Whereas blackmail and extortion in the name of the public good is perfectly honorable?" Lady Emilia chuckled. "You're inconsistent, Sir Henry. Your power and money have 'influenced' more lives than you'll ever know about, and the cost of crossing you without sufficient power and money to do political battle is a matter of public record. Yet, you're accorded to be an honorable knight, a member of the peerage, and co-ruler of this republic, while that young man, whose sins are far less heinous than your own, is held up to the public as a criminal and example of corruption in the ranks of the nobility."

The object of the discussion chuckled quietly as the Duke of Trobiere spluttered the nobility's standard reply about service and the public good, and a noble's duty and responsibility. It was a futile rearguard action, however. Matters of morality were Lady Emilia's strongest suits. Any who debated her could expect a draw, at best, and usually a resounding defeat.

Vincent himself was in high style, even though the view of most of the nobles present mirrored those of Sir Henry. Holding forth with a smile and witty commentary in the face of scorn and distaste was old ground. Conversations like the one Lady Emilia was having with Sir Henry were going on all over Angelique's back yard. All in all, he thought, it was a lovely afternoon.

There was Angel, animatedly discussing her roses with the elderly Baroness Victoria Staunton of Aguilar, the young Countess Thérése Teasdale of Wilburn, Baroness Mercía Devon of Bonsall, and several other ladies whose faces he did not immediately recognize. The Baroness of Aguilar's name had also appeared in several places throughout those tedious reports he'd collated last week after Cooper's hearing, Vincent recalled. Her positions in the Auxiliary tended to be honorary, these days, due to failing health. Her mind seemed as sharp as ever, if her pointed remarks were any indication.

Even though the ladies deferred to the age and wisdom of Aguilar, there was no doubt that eyes found themselves turning, again and again, to the inexplicably radiant loveliness of Angelique herself. She hadn't stopped smiling since the guests had started to arrive, and her low, delighted chuckling interlaced conversation and clinking crystal-ware with understated grace. Even irascible old Trobiere seemed disposed to be charmed with her, and that was no easy feat to arrange in these last few years.

In the time Vincent had known her, Angel had never once missed dressing perfectly for any affair, and this early evening dinner was no exception. These were the times when he felt he could employ his hard-won skills in observation to a most enjoyable result. Angel's muted green gown wasn't glittery enough to be true evening-wear, nor was it cut in the same way a gown for afternoon tea would have been. It was instead some engaging combination of the two, worn slightly off the shoulders, tailored impeccably in bodice and length, sashed and laced in rich, creamy ivory. A thickly woven strand of gleaming freshwater pearls at her throat, matching the earrings and the combs in her luxuriantly up-swept ash-blond tresses... Other ladies were also dressed in keeping with their station and wealth, but few of them managed her quiet, simple elegance in either apparel or demeanor.

"And what say you about the School Masters' Petition, Your Grace?" The portly William Florian, Earl of Marcelle, had interrupted Vincent's rather pleasant musings of his future bride, as well as the conversation Countess Emilia and the Duke of Trobiere were conducting. As Marcelle was a greater earldom, William's wife, Katheryn, was an influential member of the Auxiliary. Katheryn was very quiet, however, and rarely used the power and influence her station granted her.

"Huh," Trobiere grunted, "more money. All anybody in this Republic wants nowadays is money. More money for roads, more money for schools, more money for law enforcement. Why, when I was a younger man..."

"We had a king," Lady Emilia interjected smoothly, "and the king had to deal with roads and schools and law enforcement and other internal matters of state while you, Sir Henry, could whine and snivel all you wanted, because it wasn't *your* problem."

"Which still doesn't explain why the Republic should have to educate every snot-nosed brat in the City-State," Trobiere countered, undaunted.

"Some would say it is an investment in our future," Sir William grunted around a sip of wine. "Educated people are less likely to be blind sheep than uneducated oafs, after all."

"Why what a grand idea!" Trobiere exclaimed sarcastically. "So we create an entirely new bureaucracy to suck up funds like a dry sponge and use them to brainwash our children. Brilliant, Marcelle. Absolutely brilliant. Did we move to the Empire while I wasn't looking?"

Sir William flushed.

"Gentlemen," Lady Emilia interrupted. "Before we send for the master-at-arms and register you both in the lists, why don't we look at this from a more practical perspective? Clearly, we cannot hope to maintain our position in the world, or even our sense of security, without some education of our people's young. If the Great War is testament to nothing else, it clearly demonstrates the price societies pay for ignorance and isolation.

"But!" She chopped off Trobiere's imminent protest. "That does not mean our government must step in and take control of our children as is done in the Sudaani Empire..."

Vincent moved out of earshot of Lady Emilia and company and leaned against an apple tree to watch a small group of the very youth his elders were discussing. The nobly born Spring Maidens, virgins all, were dressed all in white, and their over-dressed male suitors laughed and postured and tried to be witty. The younger sons and daughters of the influential guests, born into the leadership caste. Like Vincent, few of them would be afforded an opportunity to exercise their supposed birthright. Unlike Vincent, these young people retained their innocence, an innocence his father had never allowed him. He had been pushed and prodded, folded and molded from as far back as he could remember. Sir James Blackmore-Sultaire was going to have the son he desired, and he had started on the project early.

A break in the music the tasteful string trio thoughtfully provided, and Angelique's sweet Vin-Nôrëan accent carried to him on the breeze. "How fortunate that these venerable old bushes had been so lovingly preserved," she smiled, gaze now ranging over her garden party and guests. "They, and the view, were the reasons I agreed to renovate the old family hall, when my solicitor brought it to my attention." Her eyes, as green as her gown, came to rest on him affectionately. "But there alone stands the evening's guest of honor, my ladies, and that is not at all proper."

"Indeed," Lady Victoria said, intonation making the word more a question than an affirmation. She did not refuse Angelique's subtle assistance in moving their discussion over to include him, though he noticed two of the other, younger ladies quietly excusing themselves. "I am more of old Duke Henry's mind, you know," she asserted warningly. "I fail to understand why we are making a fuss in order to thank a man for simply doing his job."

Vincent chuckled to himself. The pomposity of the nobility was pathetic. Why offer thanks to a functionary merely doing their job? His father's words trickled through his mind, closely mirroring those of too many others present: *"The only thing the common people understand is authority, my boy. Work them hard and call them lazy. When the famine strikes, you'll be glad you did! They'll give you more than even they themselves could have guessed."*

Sure. And they'll hate us every moment for it, too.

Angel's eyes flashed, but her tone, when she spoke, was sweetly reasonable. "I hardly need to mention that it was Sir Vincent's prompt actions on our behalf that spared us all weeks of uncomfortable testimony in front of our lieges in the House of Lords," she began primly, motioning one of the footmen to bring a chair for the elderly baroness. "Nor that those same actions valiantly restored our besmirched reputations with our peers. Had he treated our plight with the casual indifference which he has been treated, we would be in a much worse state, my lady."

Remarkably, even Lady Mercía nodded along with that, and the Countess of Wilburn's expression was quite thoughtful. "My lady Angelique," she inserted smoothly, "I have not had . . . the *honor* of a formal introduction to our savior. Would you be so kind?"

Lady Victoria didn't quite dare snort openly at her social superior's request, but her closed expression said all that was needful. Angelique assisted her into her seat deferentially, then turned to the countess with a sincere smile.

"It would be my pleasure. My Lady Thérése, I present Chief Inspector Sir Vincent Blackmore-Sultaire, late of Valemont, now serving our city in its law enforcement branch." She turned to Vincent himself, and only he knew her well enough to pick up the suppressed twinkle in her eyes. "Sir Vincent, this is Lady Thérése Teasdale, Countess of Wilburn. She has found reason to grace our summer season in the assistance of her sister, Perrault's Duchess, who is lately delivered of another infant daughter."

The noblewoman had smiled and extended her hand, palm down. "It is a pleasure, Sir Vincent," she said clearly.

"My lady Countess," Vincent replied, bowing floridly over the countess' hand. When he let it go, it held a closely trimmed white rose. "And congratulations on your new niece."

"Thank you, good sir," Lady Thérése replied, sniffing her rose delightedly.

He turned to the old baroness. "And this can only be the renowned Lady Victoria. Your reputation precedes you, milady." Again he bowed. His hands worked quickly to produce a blood red rose, which stood as a symbol of knightly martial virtue as much as anything else. In her youth, the Lady Victoria had been one of the Merchant Marine's most brilliant field commanders, which was part of the reason for her present frailty.

She eyed the blossom much as she might have a snake, but even she could not bring herself to be affronted by such a gesture. "Charm you have in abundance, Sir Vincent," she told him, accepting the rose, "but such an abundance cannot substitute for character."

"It *does,* however, complement it nicely." Lady Therése's mild words were a subtle barb. The older baroness' head came up sharply in response.

"I quite agree," Vincent replied with aplomb.

"Then perhaps you will develop the latter quality in your term of indenture to the constabulary," Lady Victoria said. Her glance flickered to Angelique, and she arose painfully from her seat. "I, for one, should like to see a pattern of such honorable behavior before honors are returned, but I am old and lack the strength to debate these issues overlong."

Angelique caught the attention of one of the young men dancing attendance on the Maidens, and quickly motioned him over to Lady Victoria's side.

"Or, perhaps the definition will yet again change to include more of humanity, and less of cruelty," Vincent said to no one in particular, eyes twinkling. "But as *you* say, milady," he bowed to the old woman. "Far be it from me to gainsay my elders. My honorable father would have me flogged—again."

Lady Therése's eyes narrowed at that last statement, but it didn't slow down the baroness at all. She nodded to them all in a rather vague way, then accepted her young grandson's help in returning to her husband's side.

"You must not think the Baroness of Staunton speaks for the entirety of the nobility and church, Sir Vincent," Lady Therése said quietly, her fine dark eyes searching out his. "It's true her views are shared by many, but not all."

"The Countess of Remington in particular seems to think quite highly of you," Lady Mercía agreed in a breathless rush. There was too much lace on her dress by half, but it did seem to give her something to fuss with in the quiet moments. "Her words even managed to convince my lord the baron to reconsider your state, Sir Vincent." She giggled girlishly. It wasn't an attractive pose.

"Then I shall count myself fortunate to have such supporters," Vincent smiled to the round baroness. "The Countess of Remington is a formidable woman." He half-bowed to the remaining ladies, a gallant acknowledgment of their support. "And I thank you."

"Lords and ladies, if you will attend," the voice of Sir Armand, Remington's butler, on loan from Emilia until Angelique found one of her own, boomed out across the lawn, interrupting Lady Therése's reply. "Dinner is served!"

"Ah," Angelique murmured. "If you will excuse me, gentles, my presence is required."

The footmen had set out extended tables laden with long, lidded silver pans. Underneath, many small candles burned, keeping the contents warm. The staff bustled to the tables that took up nearly a third of Angelique's yard, setting out ornately arranged platters of appetizers, and filling crystal goblets with a delicate white wine.

Angelique waited until most of the assembled nobles had found their seats, then accepted Vincent's help into her own. Seated with them was of course Lady Emilia, the Duke of Trobiere (as Vincent's father's ultimate liege), and the Patrons of Name for the burglarized exhibit, the Earl and Countess of Liberaune. The sun's long rays were not kind to the faces of the latter two, which had aged noticeably since the theft of the *Mâgun-Zak*. Angel felt a brief, guilty flush rise in her cheeks at the sight of them, and took a generous sip of the sweet, sparkling wine to cover her momentary silence.

"Well, my young lord," Lady Beatrice began, after the soup was served. "From the reports we've received of the hearing, you presented a rather ambiguous case to the magistrate on the matter of David Cooper's culpability for the theft of the *Mâgun-Zak.*"

You noticed, Vincent thought. *All right, boy. Dance.* "Quite correct," he smiled. "One of the points Commissioner Roland stresses with his investigators, especially the chief inspectors, is that we're fact-finders. No more. No less. Politics belong in Parliament, and guilt or innocence are matters for the courts, not the cops."

His reply apparently took the lady aback, and the attention Lord Craigmont had been paying to the exchange sharpened perceptibly.

"In your opinion," Lord Foster-Wilkinson said, his quiet voice barely audible over the sounds of polite dinner conversations, "is there enough evidence to convict Cooper?"

Vincent's smile was ironic. "To quote the commissioner, that depends on how good his lawyer is."

"Well, hadn't you heard?" Lady Beatrice asked. "Sir Jonathan Royles has taken Cooper's case." She shook her head primly. "Crime must pay well, if he can afford Sir Jonathan's fees. They're the highest in the city."

Craigmont looked astonished. "He works closely with the Ministry of Legal Affairs in the Upper House. His reputation is flawless, and his record nearly so."

Vincent chuckled, and reached for his wine glass. "It doesn't pay *that* well. Goodman Cooper obviously has friends in high places."

"Obviously," old Trobiere huffed. "But I'm surprised to hear you spouting Hal Roland's lines, Vincent. Are you actually learning respect for the laws and authority of this land, after all?"

"What makes you think I ever lacked them, Your Grace?" Vincent countered easily. "Respect is earned, not bestowed, and it turns out that a flogger is a pretty poor teacher. Roland, however, teaches by example. His whole life is a testament to what he firmly believes. *That,* I can respect."

It had earned him the attention of everyone at the table, as well as a tiny bit of the very respect of which he'd just been speaking. The duke held his gaze for one intense moment, then nodded his understanding of what the knight had said, and what he hadn't.

"Well stated, Vincent," Angelique murmured. "Our city is better served by Commissioner Roland than we knew."

"And this young man just may be one of our most misunderstood peers in the City-State," Lady Emilia murmured. "Your point is not only well stated, young Sir, it should be heeded. Far too many of the peerage think their title demands both respect and deference. The day that entitlement is granted I fear for our sovereignty."

Vincent arched an eyebrow, but said nothing. He knew Lady Emilia liked him. He hadn't expected such overt support.

"I would be worse than a fool to disagree with you outright, my dear Emilia," Lady Beatrice said after a moment of rather awkward silence, "but I must ask you to clarify. Even in the Writ of the Oracles, we are all exhorted to the virtues of respect and honor for those above our station. Are you truly saying this is incorrect?"

The old woman smiled. "Respect and honor 'due the care taken,' is how that verse is completed—a clause omitted rather frequently when it's quoted back, as you just did, my dear. Respect and honor are the *result* of good leadership, not the wellspring from which it flows."

Angel watched carefully as those at table with her murmured agreement with Lady Emilia's explanation, which of course needed no embellishment. As their hostess, she took in the progress of her table-mates with a single glance, then nodded to dear Armand to signal the beginning of the next course.

The rest of the dinner progressed smoothly, settling the young baroness' understandable nerves. Lady Emilia fed their guest of honor questions with answers designed to bring out the finer points of investigation and evidentiary procedures. Angelique caught on quickly, supplying quiet rejoinders or clarifying questions to that end. Vincent's replies, sometimes thoughtful, others flippant, provided no small amount of information and entertainment, and even old Duke Henry found himself chuckling wryly at one of the young knight's observations.

"Well, Vincent, I must say that if your indenture serves no other purpose, it will certainly bring a level of investigatory expertise to the peerage that we've lacked to date," the old duke concluded, pushing back his plate with a conspiratorial grin. "My thanks to you, dear baroness, for the opportunity to get reaquainted with a vassal."

"And our thanks as well," Sir Armand put in, with a quick glance to his more outgoing spouse. Angelique merely nodded her acceptance of their gratitude, and Vincent wasn't the only one who noticed how her smile seemed to illuminate her from within.

"I must confess, I was not pleased to learn you'd been assigned as the head of this investigation," Lady Beatrice told him, "but our young Vin-Nôrëan baroness has been insistently holding up the Lady's Creed to us all, in the matter of your indenture. I'm chagrined, but also relieved, to admit that she and her mentor, the inestimable Countess of Remington, may well have had the right of it all along."

The sun had set beyond the western mountains by the time the guests had risen from their tables and congregate into smaller social groups once more. It was a warm evening. The stars would soon be out, and the twin moons occupied opposite hemispheres of the sky. The larger of the two, Silvana, was just rising above the eastern horizon, and the smaller, Thorian, was westering. Footmen moved about the edges of the gathering, uncovering the magically-lit globes of the large, decorative lamps to provide better illumination for the guests who lingered to enjoy the company of their peers.

The oldest of the guests, and those with farthest to travel, had begged excuse to leave shortly after dinner, and had departed. Vincent stood off to one side, watching as Angelique said her goodbyes, when old Dr. Martin approached Vincent with a gentle smile.

"Again, good show, lad, on how you handled the investigation," the old fellow smiled, shaking the young knight's hand enthusiastically. "My dear Lady Emilia has said we underestimated you, and I believe she was right."

"Why, thank you, Doctor," Vincent replied, "and I don't think I ever had the chance to thank you for interrupting your evening at the Liberaune party to attend Angelique. Let me offer them now, in addition to thanking you for attending her party."

White, bushy eyebrows lifted in acknowledgment, for there could only be one way the young man might have felt entitled to express such a sentiment. "You and the baroness are...? Well, of course you are. That explains all those doting looks she's cast your way tonight She's an exquisitely lovely young lady, my good sir. Elfin-like in form and proportion, so delicate in health. You mind that heart of hers carefully. It's not as robust as we might think, eh?"

Vincent's eyebrow shot up. In his experience, Angel was as fit as any soldier. "Speaking metaphorically, Doctor?" he queried.

"Eh? Oh, you mean romantically." Dr. Martin chuckled good-naturedly. "Well, of course we would wish only the best for her, widowed once and all, but I was speaking a bit more pragmatically. Has she not told you of her condition?"

"I was not aware she *had* any conditions," Vincent drawled. "She's always seemed as fit as a marine, a rare quality among nobly born young women. Though perhaps I say too much," he chuckled uneasily, realizing he'd just spoken indiscreetly.

Those wild eyebrows waggled again, and the old fellow shook his head. "Well, of course, a man of my gifts sees many things in his career. And, if she's not experienced any difficulties with it to date, then it's not likely to signify much, except perhaps in pregnancy." The doctor waved a hand airily, and gave Vincent his best reassuring smile. "You needn't concern yourself. Heart murmurs sometimes go away. We don't always know why, but even if it does not, her condition is correctable for a gifted healer, certainly."

"Heart murmur...?" Vincent repeated. "Is it the kind of thing a layman could hear? Something like a stutter, or missed beat of the heart or something?"

"What? Well, if you knew what you were listening for, I suppose you could hear it. A severe one, certainly. A mild one, such as the baroness'?" He shrugged expressively. "Perhaps. Especially after exertion, or in moments of stress..."

"Hmm..." Vincent looked away thoughtfully.

"... *it usually turns out that the people you least expect are always involved in it somehow.*" Vincent heard Roland's gravelly voice reciting those words again, almost as clearly as if the Top Cop were right there.

You're being cynical, Vince. Or are you? "Well, thank you for the warning, Doctor Martin," he smiled suddenly. "I must say, it wasn't exactly the kind of thing I expected to hear this evening, but I guess it's the surprises that keep us young."

The doctor chuckled. "It's proper care of the body, and prayerful care of the heart, that keeps one young, aside from alchemical assistance, of course. Ah, here comes our gracious hostess now." He beamed at Angelique as she returned to the foyer, smiling at the both of them with impish inquisitiveness.

"Good Sir Alfred, thank you again for attending, and convey my regards to your wife, Lady Cecile. I understand she's staying with your youngest daughter? Another grandchild due?"

He bent to kiss her hand. "Indeed. Our fourteenth. The Lady's blessings extend even to my progeny, for which we are grateful." He looked at the two of them, then chuckled and placed Angelique's hand in Vincent's. "May She bless the two of you as kindly. Vincent here has indicated you two are courting, eh?"

Her delighted surprise was evident in her face, and she turned to query the younger man with clear green, sparkling eyes.

"More accurately, the doctor is observant," Vincent chuckled wryly, "but it is a bit more than that," he added, turning back to Sir Alfred. "We have not made it public yet, but we are engaged. Lady Emilia knows, of course." Angel hugged his arm tightly, surprised but delighted that he'd chosen to reveal it to the kindly old gentleman.

"Well, well, of course you are! Congratulations then. What wonderful news! When will the public announcement be made?"

"There are matters to be resolved before we may do that," Angelique replied, smiling her joy. "We have not informed his lordship of Valemont yet, and there is the matter of Vincent's indenture, of course."

"Of course," Sir Alfred agreed sympathetically. "Have you taken further legal counsel on that last matter? Your representation at your trial was perhaps not what it should have been, my young lord. My younger sister, who is a solicitor herself, said so to me only just recently. It may well be that a competent and interested attorney might find a way to help you shorten your sentence. My lady Angelique, you have an attorney in your employ, do you not?"

Her chin came up a bit, at this. Her solicitor, and the problems she had yet to resolve concerning him, were the last things she wanted to discuss that evening. "I do, certainly, though I know not how much criminal law he practices, however." At the doctor's further inquiring look, she tightened her jaw and added, "He is Louis Arnot, Esquire."

Vincent's eyebrow got cozy with his hairline. "Oh, really? I'm learning all kinds of new things this evening. I had no idea Arnot did anything *but* criminal defense. He got Baron van Trapp off on a legal technicality that made the entire police department wince. I had that overbred scoundrel dead to rights. One count of smuggling and twenty three counts of illegal slavery and drug use. Arnot beat them all."

It was Angel's turn to blink, and to look more than a little distressed. "I had no idea," she murmured, quite distracted at this. It was an effort for her to turn her attentions back to her guest. "Dr. Martin, it may well be you've given us both new hope. Thank you for expressing your concerns in this matter."

"Why, not at all," he assured her, bowing over her hand once more before clasping Vincent's. "If I can pass on some slim margin of the same happiness with which I've been blessed, then I count myself thankful. Good night, gentles." A correct half-bow, and he stepped out to hail his carriage.

Calmly, Vincent. One and one make two, not three. He turned to put Angelique on his arm, then headed toward the back lawns, where the rest of guests still congregated. "Arnot was the lawyer who helped get you here and set you up, wasn't he?"

She nodded, but spoke distractedly. "Yes... He handled most matters, in fact, the transference of my accounts, contacting the proper authorities here, satisfying the heralds that I was a missing cousin in the Blakesly line..."

"I see. So you've simply retained him. Makes sense." *And I wonder what other surprises he has up his sleeve.* "Call me suspicious, but I wonder just how much of your trouble managing Carlisle is his doing."

Her eyes had reverted to that hazel mix again, a sure sign she was troubled. "I don't know, *Mar'leven*. At our last appointment he was quite... insistent that I take control of matters at Carlisle on my own. He has never once mentioned having been before the court in criminal matters, though."

"Of course."

He opened the door and ushered her back to her party. It was a decidedly younger crowd, except for Lady Emilia, who held court as grandly as any queen in their midst. She was uniformly well-regarded, even by her political enemies. In her, the younger nobility had found one elder who would not judge or reproach them for their choices. Her sightless gaze turned to the covertly affianced couple as they returned, and her firm smile of approval told everyone present just what she thought about their possibilities together.

"Ah, well," one of the young knights sighed, seeing Angelique stroll back towards them on Sir Vincent's arm. His crestfallen expression spoke the rest of his thought eloquently.

"Don't grieve, Sir Andrew," Lady Emilia advised. "Lady Angelique is hardly the only lovely young lady in the city, and her life is probably more complex than you're ready to begin managing anyway."

"I count that as a bit unfair," Sir Andrew complained. "My education was at least as good as Sir Vincent's."

"Better, in fact," Lady Emilia agreed, "which is precisely the problem."

"I am not sure I followed that, my lady," Angelique admitted with a smile. The chorus of agreement spurred the countess into further discourse.

"We learn very little, and retain less, from a placid life. For many of the very reasons he is disliked by many, your young sir has had more real life experience at twenty-four than many ten years his senior," Lady Emilia explained.

"I hope that's not an argument for a life of adventure," Vincent drawled. "Adventures are fun, but a steady diet is beyond fatiguing." *And this one is obviously not over yet.*

"Of course, it isn't," Emilia chuckled, "but bless the adventures when they do come. They are the Lord's and Lady's way of saying 'school is now in session. Pay attention!'"

"Let us not forget the courage shown on Lady Angelique's part." The Countess of Wilburn's quiet voice had a quality that carried quite clearly in the warm night air. "I have heard some of the younger girls whispering over Sir Vincent's charm while bemoaning the unavailability of his 'status.'" Her glance flicked over the two remaining white-gowned girls, and some of the younger ladies in attendance near them. "Lady Angelique had the courage of her convictions, and did not shun Sir Vincent's company in fear of what her peers might think. My late father always said that courage would carry the day," she continued, nodding her respect to Angelique. "I see he has been once again proven correct."

Angelique blushed a little, largely unnoticeable in the lantern-light. "Aren't we quite the couple now?"

"Apparently so. I'm afraid the secret's out," he sighed in mock tragedy.

"Violins," Sir Andrew said. "We need wailing violins. Society's most notorious bachelor has been caught!"

His remark released a great deal of laughter into the conversations. Angelique squeezed Vincent's arm again, then leaned over to catch Lady Emilia's ear. "One is curious to know why you believe my life is so complex that it takes a man of Vincent's... ah, 'character and experience' to manage it," she murmured with light, dry humor.

"Time, my dear daughter," Lady Emilia murmured. "Time reveals all secrets, and clears all confusions."

Vincent, however, had noted the exchange. Was she startled by such a serious answer to a playful question? *Easy, Vince.* Astonished, perhaps? Bemused, certainly. Angel glanced up at him, and he was careful to maintain his slightly playful countenance, even though the knot in his stomach was tightening by the heartbeat. *Third point? Or am I just being suspicious?*

"Can we borrow him from time to time?" one of the white gowned virgins asked playfully. Her companion clutched her arm, and they giggled helplessly.

"How do you do that?" Sir Andrew demanded. "You've one of the loveliest creatures in Fernwall attached to your arm, and they're *still* chasing you."

"Natural talent," Vincent grinned. His betrothed rather quickly recovered her wits, however, and adjusted her tone to the broad jesting of which she was so fond.

"Only if you promise to return him in as good a condition as you got him, my ladies," she called out lightly, evoking shrieks and more tittering laughter from their young and virginal ranks. "And Sir Andrew? It is regrettably true that some women simply cannot resist 'bad boys.' A character flaw, perhaps," she smiled, glancing at Vincent again, "but one I cannot bring myself to regret."

"It's because we're so *good* at being bad," Vincent said airily, tossing the year's Spring Maidens a meaningful look.

Sir Andrew looked suddenly uncomfortable. The virgins blushed prettily, and giggled even more outrageously.

Lady Emilia, however, had attracted Angelique's attention once more, and she bent to catch her elder's softly spoken words.

"I hope you were at least partially serious, my dear."

"About what, my lady?"

"Your offer to the young ladies," the old crone chuckled, as if it were obvious.

Angelique shook herself as if waking from sleep. "And why would you hope that?" she asked, startled beyond civility by the suggestion.

"Because," Lady Emilia continued evenly, "a man like Vincent Sultaire isn't the sort to be tamed. His father couldn't, the City State obviously has not, and you won't, either. He'll love you always, but more so if you understand that about him, and act accordingly."

Her voice, full of good humor and well-meaning affection, was yet low enough that her words were covered over by the general merriment around them. Even Vincent could not have heard them, but Angel felt her face go completely blank in response.

"I see," she whispered, uncertain that she'd heard her mentor correctly. "If I understand you aright, Lady Emilia, you are advocating tolerance for my future husband's unfaithfulness. What a *novel* suggestion."

It was not the time or place for any playful conversation-turned-serious, and they were both aware of it. The countess shook her head slightly. "Perhaps we'll speak of it another time," she murmured, "and do forgive me, if I've spoken out of turn."

Angel was about to press the matter, but found herself forestalled by the subject of their discussion.

"Is this a private conversation? Or may anyone join in?" Vincent hadn't failed to notice Angel's sudden flush of hot embarrassment, nor her set, closed expression as she stood upright, next to him.

"It was," Lady Emilia said pointedly, "but I think it's concluded, and I should be going." That was the cue for Rebecca to nod, moving forward with her mistress's shawl. The chorus of farewell was nearly as deafening as the earlier laughter had been as the elderly countess headed toward the house, with Angelique at her side.

"You are ever full of surprises, my dearest lady," Angelique murmured, grateful that Rebecca had lingered a step or two behind, as they walked. "Or was I mistaken? Did I take seriously that which was meant in jest?"

Emilia patted the younger woman's arm comfortingly. "I was not jesting, but it was perhaps a poor choice of venue for such a discussion, Angelique. You must forgive me for that."

"There is nothing to forgive," she responded automatically, still quite bemused by her friend's words. "I confess that I am taken aback by your stance in this matter. The fidelity of lord and lady, of husband and wife, is sealed by a sacrament of the church, one that prevents abuses of power due to mis-spent sexual urges. Surely, in marrying Vincent, I should be helping him, ah... curb, those activities?"

Angel knew she owed her very existence to the flouting of those socially-accepted mores, a "tradition" of bastardy which had existed in the duchy of Asbury for generations. Her life as a *noble woman* there in Fernwall had taught her that Asbury was considered an extreme case, in that the powerful duke and his family did not bother to hide how they exploited and used those in service to them. In fact, they had codified the issue of those abuses by granting them a separate family line. "The Roses of Asbury" did not bespeak the fine botanical skills of its gardeners and landscapers, but rather the veritable garden of illegitimate children that had been born of that family for a long time.

What's more, she knew Emilia knew it too, though of course the lady could not have known that Angel herself was one.

"Of course, I am not; but again, this is neither the time, nor the place," she reminded Angel gently. They had come to a stop to one side of the large, double doors that let into the drawing room at Blakesly House. "The matter is never as black and white as it appears, but it requires more attention and concentration than either of us can give it at present. If you wish to speak more on this matter—and I hope that you will, for your sake as well as for Vincent's—come for tea, and we'll talk then."

Troubled now on more levels than she was comfortable trying to track, Angelique nodded in some relief. "Of course, I shall, and soon." She kissed her older friend's wrinkled cheek, then nodded to Rebecca. "Go safely into the night, my dearest lady, and the Lord watch over you and yours."

"And you, my dear. Good night."

It wasn't long after Lady Emilia's departure that the rest of the guests began to make their excuses. Some did, indeed, have long rides home, and others lived closer to the city or had houses in Fernwall itself. Vincent remained at Angelique's side until nearly all the guests had left, then arose to make his own excuses.

"It would never do for me to be the last one out your door this evening," he said, bowing over Angelique's hand. "Some might talk, and ruin my spotless reputation."

There was more laughter from the remaining young nobles, including Angel. "Far be it from me to offer such temptation," she told him, kissing his cheek fondly.

"Rumor has it that you two have been seeing quite a bit of each other," young Lady Demetria of Trent giggled. "And all over the city, too!"

"I suppose you'd like a front row seat?" Vincent inquired outrageously.

She blushed several shades of crimson at that. It was Lady Therése who rescued her. "Come along, my dear. You too, young ladies," she motioned to the other Spring Maidens. "Good night, dear Lady Angelique. I do hope we'll have time for further acquaintance soon."

"Good night, Lady Therése. I would be delighted," she agreed, with no little amount of sincerity, Vincent judged. "Sir Vincent and Sir Andrew will see you into your coach, I'm sure."

"With pleasure, Baroness," Sir Andrew replied, bowing over her hand, "and if you ever decide to simplify your life, I and the rest of the city's males will rejoice."

"No doubt," Vincent drawled, "and then where would we be? Another war, probably."

"That would be a worthy cause," Sir Andrew agreed. "There have been worse reasons for war, to win a fair maid's hand."

And he means it, too, Vincent groaned to himself. "I can think of better things to fight over," he chuckled.

"Of course," Sir Andrew replied sagely, "but you should read more history, Sir Knight. Some of the most glorious battles in history were fought for the love of a woman."

Angelique rolled her eyes dramatically. "Or the right to marry her fortune, perhaps. I think our generation has had quite enough of war, Sir Andrew. Let us instead read of reasons to make peace."

"Well said, my lady," Countess Wilburn murmured.

Vincent opened the front door, and then stood with Angelique as she said goodbye to her guests. At length, he bowed over her hand once more, and then left with the last of them, escorting the stragglers to their coaches before climbing into another, tossing off instructions for the driver to take him to his Queens Street flat.

He changed those as soon as they were out of sight and earshot. Less than fifteen minutes later, he had climbed the trellis into her bedroom. The staff had already cleared all but the tables and chairs, which would be collected the following day. By the time Angel closed the door on the last of her guests, they would have as much privacy as Blakesly House could afford them.

By prior arrangement, her window had been left open. The reading lamp burned with low, cheery light, illuminating the turned down coverlet and fresh white sheets. The oak vanity table and roomy armoire lent a rich, warm glow to what was otherwise a rather sparsely decorated chamber. Feminine, but practical, much like Angelique, herself. She wasn't there, of course. She would have still been instructing her staff on the morrow's business, the last few details before she retired, and once again became all his.

He sat down in her chair by the window to wait.

"... *it usually turns out that the people you least expect are always involved in it somehow.*" He couldn't get that line out of his head, nor could he ignore the line of reasoning that appeared, as if of its own accord, and refused to be dismissed until he'd considered it.

Dr. Martin, a paranormally gifted healer, had insisted that Angel's heart was bad.

Vincent wasn't a doctor, to be sure, but he'd spent night after night listening to that heart. To his untrained ear, it had always sounded like thunder in her slender chest, strong and regular. If the problem were so severe that she might have problems in pregnancy, how could she maintain such a high level of personal fitness?

And, for that matter... aside from our sexual interludes, until lately irregular at best, how does Angel maintain that physique, anyway?

Am I just being paranoid?

Her lawyer was Louis Arnot, a man known for his brilliant defense of criminals rich enough to be in league with organized crime. Was Angel really ignorant of that?

Unlikely. That Arnot had built his career out of defending such questionable individuals was a matter of record. That he was, himself, involved with organized crime was pure speculation. It was also nearly an article of faith among some of the police inspectors he knew.

No proof. *Which proves nothing and you know it.*

The game of information was won by playing hunches, like the inference of the thief being a woman. It had been a deduction based on the size and shape of the footprints in the ash on the roof. *Petite footprints, at that. About Angelique's size.*

His gaze drifted to her armoire. Reflexively, he got up to open it, then knelt to examine the rack of footwear. A pair of dark boots were only partially concealed in the rearmost rack. *Very similar to that...*

Ash. His heart twisted painfully in his chest as he lifted the boot, and found the gritty powder lining the edge of the boot, where the sole and uppers were sewn together. The room swam around him, and he had to concentrate to get the boot back on its holder. He picked up its companion. More ash. His skin went clammy, and his hands started to shake.

Forcing himself to focus, he reached for his pen knife and scraped a bit of the ash onto a square of note paper, then folded it carefully and tucked both away in his jacket pocket. Then he put the boot back in place and returned to his seat.

"... *it usually turns out that the people you least expect are always involved in it somehow.*"

He felt sick, as pieces he'd been unable to reconcile began falling together, unbidden, in his mind. She'd had to leave him early that night for the

161

opening of the exhibit. Why? To get ready for the theft. An upstanding citizen, she'd have to have an iron-clad alibi.

Heart. Heart, heart, heart... *She couldn't fool a gifted healer about something that. There had to be a double.*

He went back to the armoire, his mind an unruly uproar of determination and unwillingness to believe what his own actions were revealing. The dress she had worn at the Liberaune party that night was hanging there. Her perfume was still on it, wafting up to his nostrils like a plea for mercy.

She'd been sick, remember? Or had staged it to exchange places with her double. His hands angled the gown this way and that in the light, frantically searching for what he desperately hoped he would not find.

He did. Tiny, cleverly concealed closures on the front of the dress. She could have gotten into and out of that gown by herself, at need. She'd lied to him, lied by omission as he'd removed it from her trembling body, and then, oddly enough, had kicked the expensive construct into one corner of his bedroom...

Years later, he could not recall how he'd gotten back to the seat by the window. The facts clicked into place with the precision of a jig-saw puzzle. He had his thief—or she had him. Other questions whirled through his mind at a dizzying speed. Was she really the baroness? Was she really from Vin-Nôrë? Was she really who she claimed to be? She'd been lying to Lady Emilia, lying to the entire Lady's Auxiliary about her piety, conning them all about her true purpose for being there. Was there any truth to her at all?

It was too much to hold in. Too much information to process. Tears streamed down his face. He didn't even notice.

Arrest her. *No!* The very thought made the pain nearly unbearable.

So you love her then? *Why the hell do you think this hurts so badly?*

No answer.

Lady's girdle! That's the real problem, isn't it? How can you love someone you can't trust? Where does the conning end and the real person begin? and how many times had he asked himself that very question with regard to himself? He'd had to sort out the answers to those questions. Had she? Did she know where the game ended and the real person began? Could he believe her if she answered him? Could he believe that she wasn't conning herself as well as him?

For a few moments, that vicious circle spun around in his mind, making it hard to think clearly. He closed his eyes and forced himself to breath deeply, to calm, to order. Then it came to him. If *she* hadn't been forced to answer those questions, then *he* would, for himself. He deserved it, if for no other reason than what he'd given her: his heart. That, she and no other had received.

Never again, he promised himself. *Never again.* If pain was the result of an action, it stood to reason that stopping the action would prevent any repeats of the pain. He'd lived without being in love before. In point of fact, he'd never been in love before. Just then, having seen and felt this new love turn to grief so swiftly, he was sure he never wanted to attempt it again.

Logic. That was what he needed now. It was a chillingly comfortable place. No feeling. No love, no hurt, no disappointment. Just data points. Data points, and biology. It made him feel better.

It didn't hurt anymore. It was simply a fact. He loved her. Data point. She owed him the truth. Data point. He was damned well going to get it. Data point. And she would undoubtedly lie about it if he questioned her.

That point coldly infuriated him. She would lie, wouldn't she?

She's been lying to you for almost two years. What makes you think it's going to change now? Dumb idea, Vince. Very dumb.

Piece by piece, he felt himself fall back into that familiar, cynical place that had served him so well in his father's house. Play the game, observe, wait. If she could con him, he was damned well certain he could con her until it was time...

Time for the reckoning. *But you still can't bring yourself to arrest her, can you?* It was a cold truth he found deeply, comfortably, ironic.

The tiny, delicate clock on the mantel in her sitting room chimed an elegant, harmonious counterpoint to the Clocktower's deep gong. Twenty-two hundred hours. He heard the door to Angel's sitting room open. Through the door of her bedroom, he watched her enter, then place her forehead against the doorjamb after she'd closed it.

She was a lovely creature. Not so exotically beautiful as Linda, nor so country fresh as Barbara Cole. *Data point.* Long years of practice in his father's household enabled him to paint the proper smile on his face. It was perhaps the only good thing he'd ever learned there—Master Slagter's lessons excepted.

"Out of practice?" he queried.

Startled into motion, Angel pushed herself away from the door, and then smiled at him. "This poor house has never seen such august company," she sighed, gliding into the room with him. "I believe it went well, though."

"You could nearly have held a session of the upper house," he drawled, drinking her in again. There were some women that were always a pleasure to look at. Angelique Blakesly was one. "Didn't you have a quorum here this evening?"

"Ah, but the debate of the evening was you, Raven," she chortled, and the low sound of it was like music. Her hands were at her ears, carefully removing the sprays of pearls. "How do you suppose the vote would have gone?"

"Probably not well," he chuckled. "There would have been too many abstentions."

"A sure improvement over the nays that resounded only a few short weeks ago," she reminded him, placing the jewels on her vanity.

"No doubt." *And the sooner you get out of those clothes the better.* It was amazing. She was lying to him, had been deceiving him since the day she

163

met him, probably, and what did he want to do? Fuck the lies right out of her.

Primal thoughts. *Data point.* No conflict.

He flowed up out of the chair to embrace her, caressing her through her dress, from slender waist to small, perfect breasts. "Stalling for time, darling?"

Pale brows flickered in mild bemusement, but she melted into his embrace. "With you? Never," she told him, palms pressed against his jacket.

"Then pray, milady, why are you still clothed?" His hands sought out the buttons on the back of her dress, wondering more than idly whether this one had the extra set of fastenings, too.

"Should I have scandalized poor Clarice by requiring her to help me undress for you?" Angel laughed softly, her hands going to the clasp of her necklace. "She's having enough trouble with this as it is."

"Umm... That could have been fun. I don't think I've ever been party to that sort of thing. Want to try?" His eyes were dancing with suppressed mirth.

Hers were rather mystified. "Try what, *Mar'leven?*"

"Having Clarice undress you in front of me," he chuckled. "Sounds like fun."

She looked away at that, but her necklace came unfastened, and she placed it on the vanity with a loud clatter.

"I hardly think scandalizing an innocent is 'fun,'" she replied softly, "but perhaps I lack the proper perspective for such things. You and dear Lady Emilia seem to have the gift for shocking me this evening."

"Lady Emilia? And here I thought I was being original. Well, original for a Paladin-type person. I doubt there's much in the world of sex the Urilians haven't tried."

"I don't suppose," Angel agreed, "but it was Lady Emilia who suggested I not request an oath of fidelity from you. I still don't know quite what to think of that."

"Ah... And you have been true to me since the beginning?" he asked playfully. *Not that I'm going to believe the answer.*

She snorted. "I've had all these opportunities, obviously. Paladin ladies are just overwhelmed with them."

"Of course." His eyes glittered, in ironic appreciation more than amusement. "So have you taken any of them?"

"Every one I've been offered, darling," Angel drawled sarcastically.

"Good." Her arms came free at last, and before the dress puddled upon the floor, his hands were at the fastenings of her undergarments.

"Well, I should hope you would think so, since you've been both agent and beneficiary of them all." She went quiet for a moment, humor draining away from her. "I have... given myself to no other since I arrived here, Raven. Though I suppose I can see why you would doubt that."

And you can take that in any way you like. He shrugged. "To be honest, it hasn't exactly been at the top of my list of concerns." He worked the

164

foundation garment loose, and she took her usual deep, quivering breath as it dropped to the floor. Clad now only in garters, hose, and heels, she stepped clear of the expensive pile of cloth and turned to face him, hair still upswept in the coiffure she'd worn, and looked him over.

"Stalling for time, darling?" She tossed his question back at him, lips flickering in a secret smile.

He chuckled roguishly, then bent to kiss and nibble a bare nipple, then took her into his arms to kiss her thoroughly. "Never," he breathed into her open mouth, robbing her of any ability to reply. Instead, she kissed him again, tangling her fingers in his soft, dark hair, and writhed against him in that way that stirred his manhood to hardness even through the layers of clothing he wore.

He picked her up and carried her to the bed, garters, hose, heels, and all, spreading her out before him like a banquet to consider what was before him with some anticipation. There was nothing quite so arousing or primal as having a lover writhe in ecstasy at one's hand. It was enormously empowering, doubly so when that lover was as in touch with her body as Angelique.

He brushed her pale bush with the backs of his fingers, smoothing and parting the hairs that grew there with deliberate, exacting care. Angel felt herself quiver from thighs to shoulders at his touch, fingers and toes curling reflexively. *This* was what she knew she lived for, these moments alone with him, when each could explore and satiate the other's body, enjoying pleasure without limit. It was worth all the preparations for a dinner party, all the measured cadence and drill of a semi-formal Paladin affair, all the cold rudeness of Victoria Staunton and the mindless babbling of Mercía Devon to have him with her like this, just the two of them, sharing intimacies neither of them had known before.

Worth all that and more. Even as his lips touched her there, thrilling her, taking command of her, she knew there was really nothing in this life she wouldn't sacrifice if he asked it of her. Even her own life, for what little that was worth, and gladly.

"Oh, *Mar'leven,* she breathed, writhing upon his tongue probing deeply into her cleft. "I love you, by the Gods I love you so..."

Data point. He let the obvious response flow through his mind, and nestled his mouth deeper into her cleft. Her entire body shifted toward him, her arms lifting up and over her head in the universal gesture of unconditional surrender. He flicked his tongue in and out of her musky sweetness,r and her response was stunning, torso arcing as if she'd been struck by lightning, lifting away the bed even as it thrust her hips into the lush delight his mouth offered.

It ripped though him and sparked the end of his throbbing shaft as palpably as though she'd scraped a fingernail across the tip. Once again, he was reminded of just why he kept coming back to her, to her bed, and her body, over and over again. She was unrepentantly immersed in her sexuality. The righteousness of her Paladin facade was gone, replaced by the simple, carnal truth of the utter slut she really was.

On and on he drove her, body arching, crying, screaming, pleading, convulsing again and again until there was nothing but weak screams as exhausted muscles tried vainly to convulse one more time. By the time he stood over her once again, sweat ran in a small stream from between her heaving breasts, and down her temples, and there was a generous pool of feminine ejaculate on the coverlet beneath. Her eyes were glazed, and her whole body quivered as exhausted muscles fought their way back to life.

It was a beautiful sight, he thought, and began removing his clothing. What he wanted more than anything just then was to fuck her—hard! The very thought of her, caught yet again in that hypnotic, orgasmic state nearly made him swoon in desire.

Angel struggled partially upright, the room swimming around her dizzily, hair tumbling free of its combs and down her shoulders, trying valiantly to bring herself to some level of control that would allow her to return him at least some measure of the erotic delights he'd given her. The sight of his body, emerging from its societal constraints, was a joy to behold in any case, as lithe and graceful as a hunting cat's. And his manhood, when finally revealed, pulsed upright, purple with its need of her. She gave a visceral, ecstatic shudder. That magnificent piece of manhood was about to impale her, and there was no part of her that didn't at that moment ache for it passionately.

Naked and painfully erect, he stood there stroking himself, and the moment dragged on deliciously. She watched him like an animal in heat. Drenched in her own sweat and carnal fluid, the nipples of her pert breasts hard as agates, legs spread, glistening cleft bright red and swollen in anticipation. She was an insatiable slut who belonged in a whorehouse more than a church.

It was refreshing to see—to feel. The naked, unabashed truth of her, exposed and raw. The hunger and lust in her eyes, the simple, primal *need* radiating from every pore in her body were beautiful counterpoints to the string of lies she'd told and retold. How sad that, with all the complexities of this world, it took something so base as the urge to couple to reveal the truth of her.

Angel coughed, clearing her throat. "Stalling for time, darling?" she asked again, voice husky and low. The sound of it entered his ears, then wound around his spine, sizzling in his groin expectantly.

"Impatient?" he queried. Stepping between her legs again, he massaged her cleft with the end of his shaft, rubbing her swollen clitoris, and dipping lightly into her sex.

"You know I am," she groaned, reaching for him, "and you taught me to be. Have I learned my lessons well?"

"All but one," he murmured, batting her hands away, then grasping her ankles to push her legs up over her head. He resumed toying with her cleft, thrilling to the desire that scorched him, and her, each time he pulled away. "You have yet to learn to properly beg."

166

LOUIS!

Angel gasped. The eroticism that had enlivened her instantly evaporated, leaving her terrified and confused in the aftermath. There were few things in her life that made her want to run screaming, but the memories of what Louis had done to her, to make her beg, were among them. Though she knew, on one level, that this was Raven, and that she was safe, the emotional tumult had dragged her under before she knew what triggered it, and she struggled, in earnest, to get away from him.

"No," she choked, terrified. "No!"

Vincent's eyebrow arched questioningly. That wasn't exactly the response he expected. *Data point.* "Easy, darling," he murmured, sliding into her completely. "There, that better?"

Panic. Flight. Lancing fear, turned to incandescent rage. *Fight! No, fight Louis! Not Raven!* Her breath was still coming in great, heaving gasps, and though she still struggled against the way he held her legs (the way Louis had held her legs) to pin her down, and there was a veritable chorus of voices crying out inside her.

Stop it! Stop fighting! This isn't Louis, it's Raven!

He wanted us to beg!

Raven in her bed, in her body. Beg to be hurt? For pain, humiliation, degradation?

KILL HIM.

No! *Raven loves me, he would never want t' hurt me.* Not like Louis, who only used, demeaned, and beslimed everything he touched. . .

"Not for you. Not for anyone," she swore, near to tears she refused to shed. "Never again, Raven. *Never!*"

"Never. . . *again?*" he repeated, releasing her legs to slide his hands up the length of her slender frame. He slid in and out of her sheath in an easy, automatic rhythm, as if trying to calm her. With the weight of her own legs off her, breath came more easily, and so did rationality. The other voices faded away, leaving only those that calmed and soothed.

This was Raven. *Raven.* Not Louis, never again Louis. She was going to make sure of that.

"Never again," she agreed, somewhat less vehemently, forcing her fingers to release their death-grip on the coverlet, and her body to still its trembling. "I. . . I can't explain, not now."

He continued his leisurely pace and considered. The encounter had taken the edge off. Orgasm was no longer imminent. *She couldn't explain.* "Secrets," he murmured, as much to himself as to her.

Still, her reaction was useful. The word had caused her to burst into tears. "Raven. . . you know I love you, more than anything, more than you know. . . ."

More than useful. *She wasn't about to explain. Data point. The rest would come out soon enough.*

"Later," he agreed, caressing her breasts.

167

She sobbed even harder, but in that odd alchemical metamorphosis of emotion, fear and sorrow channeled themselves into aching lust, a driving, almost animal need for physical closeness, and a demand for a reiteration of their love, which he'd yet to give her in words. Her torso lifted itself, pressing into his hands, legs reaching up to entwine him, to pull him down to her, skin to skin. He went down easily, scooped her up in his arms, then rolled them over, putting her atop him.

Even as they moved together anew, Angel couldn't allow her eyes to leave his face, not even for a moment. So long as she kept it there before her, and stroked his lightly-stubbled cheek with the tips of her trembling fingers, she could *know* this was Raven, and no other. Raven's handsome face, strong jaw, satin-dark hair; Raven's arms, hands, chest, and Raven's erection that thrust so deeply inside her. Raven, Raven, Raven, a veritable chorus of the beloved resounding within her, chasing back tears and regrets. He loved her enough not to press her, and in that love she knew she could do *anything*.

The fires he so painstakingly stoked caught at last, and spread slowly within her, igniting her heart and body to burn with need and love of him. It flamed out of control and raced like wildfire in her veins, searing away her own impurities, and consuming irrelevancies. What was left of her rebirthed itself from the very flames.

It was a visible thing, a transformation, breath by breath, tears and sadness, to adoration, to reborn lust, seething into an orgasm that arced her over backwards in its power. Heedless of the open window, of her household staff on the premises, Angelique shrieked out her release in larynx-punishing volume, exulting in the balefire that consumed her.

Raven watched her, heard her, *felt* her climax rage through her with punishing intensity. It cascaded through him with savage force. She rocked forcefully atop him, and he too cried out. The second time her hips slammed down, he thrust up to meet her, and pain turned to white-hot, searing release.

Angel's tears fell upon him again, just before she collapsed, shaking, blond hair spread over them both like a tangled silken coverlet. She'd told him once that tears of joy tasted differently than those born of sorrow. What she hadn't been able to tell him was that until she knew she loved him, she'd never tasted the former, and thus had never known the difference. That night, Angel thought she might get drunk on them, and wondered whimsically if Raven might be inclined to join her.

No, perhaps not. Too close to revelations, still. Too close to truths she couldn't tell him yet. But soon, she promised herself. *Soon. After I've taken care of Louis.*

She remained quiet instead, enjoying the wordless afterglow, allowing herself to anticipate, for once, a lifetime of nights spent, just like this one.

He remained quiet too, reveling in the aftermath, and unable to stop the thoughts that lashed him in the aftermath. Revelations. Truth. Lies. Her passion spoke of all that, and more. How many of her secrets revolved around the *Mâgun-Zak*, or Louis Arnot, or both? Beyond her insatiable lust, how much of this beautiful woman was real, and how much was false?

Questions. Nothing but questions, and damned few answers.

Hours later, as he slipped quietly through her bedroom window, he still had none. But he did have a plan of action. . .

Chapter 10

Blakesly House,Lower Angels
28 Amerian 580, 0930 hours

When Angel had awakened, Raven was gone. For him to have left without waking her was unprecedented, and the sight of his empty pillow the first thing that morning had brought with it a visceral tremor of dread. What could possibly have taken him from her side?

Clarice's questioning, half-embarrassed glances told Angelique quite clearly that her maid had overheard the louder fragments, at least, of their lovemaking the night before. She forbore noticing the younger woman's bemused state, however, and merely directed her to bring in some mead-owsweet tea for a headache. In fact, it was her throat that hurt, but the tea was analgesic, and with lemon and honey would soothe what little damage her shrieks had done.

Angelique tried not to be overly concerned with Raven's absence, noting prosaically that he'd been acting a bit erratically ever since he'd asked her to marry him. "Commitment nerves." She'd heard of that before—tales of the nervous bridegroom were legion in their culture, and with good reason: There was no divorce for their kind. All marriages in the Guardian Paladin Church were lifetime commitments. Divorce was not completely unheard of, but it was exceedingly rare, and took a direct decree from the *Imprimae* Herself.

There was something else, some fact or point that niggled at her just beyond her conscious awareness, some knowledge that she was not yet seeing clearly. Instinctively, she could *feel* it, but as had happened to her in the past, struggling to bring it forth for examination only further obscured it. With a strangled sigh, she firmly pushed her frustrations with Raven aside in favor of the priceless gift of information he'd given her the night before.

"*...I had no idea Arnot did anything* but *criminal defense. He got Baron van Trapp off on a legal technicality that made the entire police department wince....*"

One count of smuggling. Twenty-three counts of illegal slavery, and then, of course, drug use. Louis had gotten his guilty client clear of all of

171

them. Angelique had not been in the least surprised to hear it. Her only astonishment had come from her own inability to understand something so obvious about her "solicitor" sooner. He'd been quite busy after they arrived here two years ago, having sent her out to Carlisle with an armed escort before turning himself toward establishing a client list within the city. By the time she returned, some six months later, he was already practicing his "official" profession with a laudable degree of success.

And that was all Angel had known of it. It was all she had cared to know. Her new life filled up around her, taking her further and further out of Louis' orbit. Their meetings became mostly business, both legal and extra-legal, punctuated firmly with his ever-more distasteful use of her body afterward.

Of course, Louis is up to his ears in organized crime, or at least well-connected to it. She'd always understood that, though since their return to Cascadia, it was out of her direct experience. Louis had been a comfortable buffer between her and the things she had not cared to face. It had been so in Püran-Khir, too, with Angel committing the thefts for which Louis provided the information and equipment. Back then, she was stealing information as often as valuables, and had guessed that some of her stolen information was eventually used to install her as the Baroness of Carlisle.

Angel remembered how to lift information without having it noticed. Louis had also coached her thoroughly on document forgery and in replacing papers, at least in bulk, until copies could be made. He trained her in how to break into a site a second time, safely, to replace what had been "borrowed." It was always the more dangerous part of the caper—had the victims noticed, and set up a trap? Then, there had been the things Louis *didn't* know she'd learned, about how to use that information once it had been obtained. She and Louis had lived in much closer quarters then, and he hadn't been able to hide everything from her. She'd also enjoyed her role in his bed, too, though she wished she could forget that part.

In fact, she'd tried hard to forget most of what had happened to her in Püran-Khir, ruined capital of what had once been a lovely land. The Confederation had done a thorough job of destroying it, long before she'd been stranded on its shores. Most of its inhabitants at that time were only just surviving at subsistence levels, just four years after the war's "official" end. Louis had shown her how to abandon what pitiful remnants were left of her morals and ethics. They'd managed to live very well in the midst of so much barbarism, cruelty, and squalor. It was painful for her to recall how she'd ever ended up in such a place...

With determination, Angel shook her mind clear of those things. Her restoration to her homeland and elevation to its noble class had reminded her of the very morals and ethics with which she'd been raised, and which Louis had tried to erase. Lying had become intolerable to her, and was the first of her offenses that needed rectification. If she was successful, she hoped, the consequences for those past actions would be minimal.

First things first: Where would Louis keep the evidence for Baron van Trapp's case? The courts would have copies, of course, but those were some of the most heavily safeguarded records-storage vaults on the planet. Without Louis' connections, successful retrieval was unlikely, and for obvious reasons, Louis' help was out of the question.

That left Louis' own copies, and from earlier association with him, she felt she knew where they must be kept. The man was brilliant, but he tended to form habits, especially when those habits proved beneficial. He'd kept everything in Püran-Khir in a small cellar room under their house, once they'd settled in it, and the entrance to that secret room was concealed. It also doubled as a bolt-hole. If any of his enemies came looking for him, the secret room had a back door leading to a tunnel, that in turn let out in an alley several blocks away.

That must be it. Risky, but there are no other options. If I'm going to get clear, and stay clear of Louis, I'm going to have to out-think him, and out-manipulate him. That means I have to find his secret room and his files. I'll have to make sure I've got the correct evidence, too. I know little enough of criminal law, but from what Raven told us all last night at dinner, I think I can guess what Louis did to get Van Trapp exonerated. A legal loop-hole wouldn't have been sufficient on its own, not with overwhelming evidence. He had to have tampered with the evidence, or rather, hired someone to do it.

She chuckled softly, ruthlessly. *And then, to keep the baron firmly under his thumb, he'll have kept real copies of the evidence in his files. Van Trapp's a lecherous fool by all accounts, and wouldn't have had the wit to extricate himself from Louis' grip, especially if Louis himself were then to help Van Trapp keep well-supplied for his particular vices.*

Her nose wrinkled at that. The charges had been over illegal slavery and drug use. She could deduce what Van Trapp's weakness was. *Abject slaves, in heat all the time from the "slave milk" in their veins... who die within months after that drug has burned them out from the inside. Gods, I'm tempted to turn the evidence back over to get him collared for good.*

Angel hesitated then, and it was a dainty, coldly pragmatic pause. *That also gets Louis out of your life for good... except that he'd probably turn around and implicate you in every crime he's ever arranged here, whether you actually committed it or not. First things first. Get Louis muzzled and walking on a short leash. Time to give the marching orders.*

"Clarice?" Angelique called, voice sounding impossibly light-hearted in the face of the tasks before her. She smiled warmly at the girl when she stepped into the room. She was still only fifteen years of age, and was a younger daughter of one of her own knights at Carlisle. Clarice was lovely with the first blush of her youth, and as loyal as anyone could wish. Angel hadn't stopped to think of children often, but mused briefly that if she ever were blessed with a daughter, she supposed that one like Clarice would be most agreeable.

"I didn't mention it before, but you are glowing today. Did young Armand Pettiforth completely steal your heart at our party last night?"

The girl blushed rosily, but to her credit, answered honestly. "I like him very much, my lady. And he has invited me to watch the yacht races in the harbor tomorrow afternoon. I told him I was not sure..." she rushed on to add, anxious for her lady to know she had behaved correctly in this matter.

Angel chuckled. "Well, you must compose a note to him accepting his kind invitation, if you wish to attend. Afterward, if he wishes to escort you, with a group of other young persons to a shop for ice cream, that would also be acceptable. I will be most busy tomorrow, and have no need of your personal services so long as your duties are current."

"Oh, they are, my lady!" Clarice assured her, smiling happily. "Thank you!"

"It is my pleasure, Clarice. You should see more young persons of your age and station. I have been remiss in not seeing to it personally. Now," she said, bringing the girl's mind back to her duties, "I have errands for you today in addition to your other responsibilities. Here is some of my personal correspondence to go down to the courier's post near the entrance to the Merchant Marine base. And I believe Hannah has some purchases waiting at the grocer's. It would be a kindness for you to pick them up while you're out. Last, there is this," she handed a card envelope over to her. "Delivered by you personally to Baron Lansdowne's house here in the city. My regrets to the Baroness, but I am unable to attend the meeting of the Auxiliary tomorrow, due to conflicting appointments."

"Yes, my lady. I'll leave just after I've composed my acceptance for Squire Pettiforth." Clarice curtsied, and then withdrew.

Angelique's eyes turned back to the window, and the sunlight dancing on the wind-swept waters of the harbor. One of those letters would arrange an appointment for the following day with an attorney who was *not* Louis Arnot. If all went well, she would be handing him a generous retainer, a packet of information, and some finely detailed instructions on its storage and eventual use should Louis ever find a way to double-cross her. "Dead man triggers," Louis had called them, and had shown her how to arrange them even though he was not aware he'd done so. It meant that, at regular intervals, for so long as Angel was alive, she must send a coded message to this attorney, a dummy message, actually. The simple receipt of it at regular intervals kept the trap armed and ready to spring.

If any harm ever befell her, the message would not be sent. The attorney's instructions upon *failure* of receipt were to take that packet of information straight to the nearest police precinct headquarters, and without any delay whatsoever. *And, if he's smart, he'll find a way to disappear afterwards, but I probably won't be around to know whether he manages it.*

There were back-ups and redundancies to arrange, of course. Something this critical could not be left to chance where chance could be eliminated. Again, Louis' own tutelage would be served against him. She knew, or could guess, how those redundancies should be managed. Simple code books could be purchased in Docktown near the Merchant Marine base, and would provide ample security for a task so minimal.

This day would be spent arranging discreet queries into Louis' schedule, and would require at least one disguise, for many of his household slaves knew her by sight. She needed a long-ish interlude where he would out of the house completely. His slaves would be more lax in their diligence with their master gone.

And once I've got him by the balls, I'll have to face him with them, clenched in my fist. The trembling that took her in response to that metaphorical thought was very like a sexual thrill. *I'm buying back the mortgage on my future. My life. With Raven.*

A frown rippled across her brow. *But why. . . ? Why did he leave like that?*

*   *   *

492-B Queen's Street
Raven's Flat
28 Amerian 580, 1500 hours

The Clocktower bonged, then bonged again, pulling Raven back towards the waking world. With consciousness came a sick feeling in his stomach that, at first, he ignored. The Clocktower sounded again. Memories of Angelique, writhing in ecstasy, swirled back into focus, and with them came an almost uncontrollable urge to vomit.

The Clocktower bonged a fourth time, a fifth, and a sixth. Six bells, fifteen hundred in the afternoon. He ruthlessly suppressed the nausea and reached for the bell pull, then staggered into his sitting room, pulling on a robe as he went. Moments later, one of the cook's servants appeared with a tray of cold meat, cheese, some warm bread, and coffee.

She did it. She stole the Mâgun-Zak. *She's conned the entire Lady's Auxiliary, the security people, me. . .*

The nausea wafted over him again, and again he forced the urge to vomit back down. He made himself take a bite of cheese, then poured a cup of steaming coffee. *Vince, this isn't getting you anywhere. Where is your iron resolve, your precious logic? Does she mean so much to you?* He didn't want to think about that, but another wave of nausea forced the question.

She had really done it. She *had* stolen the Mâgun-Zak.

He picked up a bit of bread, took a bite, and chased it with coffee.

You let yourself fall in love. Try though he might to stop them, tears began to stream down his cheeks. *With Angelique.* Her name alone nearly doubled him over with grief. He could feel the heat of her body against his, as it had been last night. He could hear her cries of ecstasy, feel her moving around him like a moon orbiting a planet. Her voice was in his head, a song that wouldn't fade. She was so alive, so *real*—and yet so false!

Angelique.

He tossed what remained of his breakfast back onto the tray. He couldn't eat. The nausea was nearly gone, but so was any desire to do anything. Had he lost her? No. She wouldn't even suspect the true reasons for his departure, though it might puzzle her that she awakened to find him gone.

175

He hadn't lost her. This wasn't about a break up, or a fight. *No. It's about lying. It's about falling in love with someone who isn't even real. She's just a pack of lies hammered together to set up jobs. That's what this is about. How do you love someone you can't trust?* It was a damned good question, but it wasn't exactly the whole truth, either.

He suddenly felt lonely. *Very* lonely. As though that sense of family, of belonging, that had taken root inside him was now gone. He was back to where he'd been before... *before Angelique.*

It wasn't new. He'd been alone for most of his life. His elder brother had joined their father in rejecting and rebuking him. Prior to Master Slagter, his tutors had all treated him like he was a dunce. In defense, he'd learned how to con information out of other people, useful information, the kind that gave him at least some power over his own affairs in the face of the near-constant rain of abuse from his father and eldest brother.

About a year after Master Slagter's arrival, he had discovered his grandfather's Raven Wing, and then had learned to fly it. That had increased his range enormously. He had discovered girls shortly thereafter and, of course, sex. Soon, he was on intimate terms with many of the girls on the estate and, thanks to the increased range the Raven Wing afforded, no small number from the surrounding earldom. An hour or so spent rolling in the hay, or on a forest floor, usually included not only exchanging mutual sexual pleasure, but useful tidbits of information, as well.

But true friends and dear loves? Those he'd never had. Everybody seemed to *like* him well enough, but no one had ever trusted Vincent Sultaire—until Angelique Blakesly.

The tears fell more softly, and were more cleansing than hurtful, more regretful than angry. It was as it ever had been: In having never been trusted, he had learned not to trust. It had taken this to remind him.

He returned to the food he'd abandoned earlier, and by the time he'd finished it and turned to his daily toilet, the nausea was gone, as were most of the emotional recriminations. All that remained was numbness, and an iron-clad resolve to find the truth. Boiling water from the lunch tray steamed up his shaving mirror. He cooled it slightly with cold before putting a steaming cloth on his face. It felt wonderful, like a tonic.

The matter of Angel's physical heart was easy enough to answer. He knew her physician, and her physician kept her records in her office. The woman was a gifted healer, just like Doctor Martin. If Angelique really did have a heart problem, Doctor Lagrange would know about it.

That made him feel better. *Work, Vince. The best therapy is to keep busy. Less time to brood.* He lathered up his day-old beard and considered further. If he was correct, the woman Doctor Martin examined on the night of the party *wasn't* Angelique Blakesly. It had to have been a double, a near look-alike whose face would have fooled anyone who didn't know her closely. There was never a shortage of slender, fair-skinned blondes in Fernwall; he could recall a half-dozen who might have qualified, especially when seen only in the sick-room's shaded light.

If his suppositions about the double were true, a *second* dress had to have been ordered. Angel's dress would have been specially designed with the extra set of fastenings that allowed her to get into and out of the intricately constructed garment on her own. The double's dress would not have needed the additional clasps, but orders for both dresses should have been placed at nearly the same time.

Finding Angel's double, at this late date, would have been difficult, if not impossible. However, finding the paper trail for the gowns? That should be child's play, in comparison.

It wasn't sufficient to satisfy a court of law, but Raven wasn't looking for that kind of evidence. He was looking for personal evidence, for facts to support or disprove his suppositions. He made the last stroke with his straight razor, then wiped the remaining shaving soap from his face and dropped a towel for a sponge bath. Not as thorough as soaking in a tub, but he hadn't the time just then to visit the baths.

Assuming the first two postulates were true, he was left with the problem of just who "Angelique Blakesly" really was. Her legal brain had been with her since Raven had met her, which meant Louis Arnot was no doubt involved up to his crooked eyebrows. Arnot's files would undoubtedly be well-protected, and he didn't have time to go through the rather arduous process of learning how to defeat those defenses. But again, financial records could also tell a lot, and those would be kept by Arnot's accountant, not by Arnot himself. It just so happened that Angel's accountant and Arnot's were the same.

Coincidence? *Not likely.*

The Records Office of the Guild of International Heralds could help him, too. They maintained the heraldic and genealogical records for every noble family in the Old Kingdom of Cascadia, and had access to the records of every noble on the planet, if there was need. It was that august body which had legitimized Angel's claim of ancestral patent before the peers would agree to acknowledge it in general assembly. A patent certified as legitimate, and forwarded to the House of Lords by the Guild, was almost certain to be approved.

Raven felt much better by the time he'd toweled himself dry and dressed. Action. Action always drove away the blues.

Twenty minutes later, he was clopping across town to the offices of Doctor Martha Lagrange.

The Lagrange Office, Three Quarters
28 Amerian 580, 2015 hours

The interesting thing about doctors is that they're so honest, it hurts. Which means you can expect their offices to have simple security, at best.

Vincent stood across the street from Doctor Lagrange's office in Three Quarters, an odd part of the greater metropolis where the districts of Docktown, Angels, and Merchants' all met. Three Quarters was famous for its festive atmosphere, and for its plethora of shops and booths that offered unique crafts, or regular crafts with a unique twist. One of the city's best puppet-makers were in Three Quarters, as was the most famous clocksmith in the City-State.

Doctor Lagrange's office was several hundred meters northeast of Three Quarters' shopping district. It was just getting dark. The building was an older home on a corner. The upstairs residence was lit; the downstairs rooms that made up her professional offices were dark. Martha Lagrange was a younger woman, Vincent knew. Career oriented, she'd never married, and did not seem interested in changing that status. She was known to attend Urilian temple on occasion, and most of her patients came from Fernwall's moneyed aristocracy, also largely Urilian.

Translation: There's better than even odds Doctor Martha is not alone tonight. There were also better than even odds that she'd be paying little to no attention to her offices downstairs.

He crossed the street and made his way along the side-street to the back gate. There were no signs of dogs or guards. *Not surprising.* After a quick look around, he vaulted the wrought iron gate, and then walked quickly to the back door. His hand flash revealed a lock of standard local manufacture, and a cautious insertion of a probe provided no hint of modification. The pins all thrummed smoothly, and there were no buttons at the back of the key-way.

He quickly tucked the light tube under his wristband and set to picking the lock in earnest. In moments, the barrel turned. He opened the door and slipped inside, finding himself in the waiting room, which had once been a parlor. A fireplace occupied one end. All the major daily papers were stacked neatly on a table in the center of the room, and chairs lined two of the walls. Opposite the fireplace was a half-wall, and behind it the clerk's office. Carefully, he pulled the door closed, and relocked it.

A single door led out of the waiting room. Immediately to the right was a split door, with a shelf attached just below the split. That one led into the office. In the long room just beyond, two walls were lined with cabinets full of patients' files.

'B' for Blakesly, and it was right near the door. The file wasn't very thick. *To be expected. She hasn't been here very long.* He opened the file and riffled quickly through the papers clipped to it.

Doctor Lagrange had given Angelique a thorough examination when she'd first taken Carlisle's new baroness under her care. According to the records in his hands, Angel was suffering from trauma-induced childhood amnesia. She couldn't remember anything from her girlhood prior to about age ten, when she claimed to have been taken in with the Sisters of the Lady's Mercy in Vin-Nôrë.

Raven found that tidbit somewhat fascinating, though it agreed with what little Angel had said of her past. As he read on, he discovered that Doctor Lagrange had needed visits over several weeks to treat her new patient for some internal injuries that he couldn't make out, from the terminology used. Further on, he discovered that Angel had arrived with a number of ugly scars in several places on her body, some from lacerations, some from burns, as well as a number of broken bones that hadn't healed properly. *Very odd for someone of supposedly noble birth.*

More entries showed where the doctor had dealt with these old wounds, correcting tissue damage and so forth, but nothing indicated any heart or vascular problems at all. In fact she was, and remained, in remarkable health and physical condition.

Supposition one proven true. Angel has no heart problems. He carefully returned the file to its proper place on the shelf and made his way out.

*   *   *

2313 Compton Place, Upper Merchants
28 Amerian 580, 2130 hours

In the cover of darkness, Angel watched an impeccably-dressed Louis Arnot leave his posh Merchants' townhouse and enter a spacious coach, on his way at last to an evening at the theater. Her eyes narrowed briefly as she checked her watch, then added the time needed to travel to and from the theater to the performance time, and then the late supper he'd likely reserved at The Greens, afterward.

She nodded slowly. It would be four hours, at least. She doubted she'd need so much as one.

From her vantage point, there in the hedges of the adjoining property, Angel shifted the pack she'd brought, trusting her dark-colored body suit and the deep shadows to conceal her presence. She watched the slaves bustling in and out of Louis' house, studying their movements through the unshaded windows. Her keen ears picked up strains of laughter, something one never heard when Louis was resident. His slaves didn't dare draw that much attention to themselves.

A half-hour, she judged clinically. *Give them a half-hour to settle into their routines, and to get used to the fact that he's gone. Then it will be time.*

She used the interval as well as she could, parceling out in her mind the probable locations for the concealed door, monitoring the routine movements of house slaves and guard slaves, watching the windows where Louis' bedroom was located, noting the complete lack of lights. *Figures. The bed slaves won't go in there to get ready for him until much later, and his valet is officially off-duty now.*

While most of Angel's mind was occupied gathering information about her target, another quiet corner was amazed at just how easy all this had become, at how good it was to slip back into these clothes, this role, and at how powerful and alive she'd felt, coursing at a dead run across the treacherous skylines of Fernwall, her life on the line with every move she made. There was a sense of exhilaration in these things that rivaled some of the most intense lovemaking sessions she had ever shared with Raven.

179

And yet, if the night's efforts were successful, it might well be needful to put these things behind her.

Could she give this up, this keen sense of excitement and adventure? Did the promise of becoming Angelique Blakesly-Sultaire, forever and for always, compensate for all she was setting aside?

Was it really going to be possible to live happily ever after with Raven?

Far distant, the Clocktower's enormous bells signaled the hour. Angel, firmly back into what she thought of as her "Iris mindset," dismissed such notions as she gathered herself, then dashed across the open ground between her current position and the next, an artfully landscaped willow grove near a small pond. She'd always hated questions like those, and focus was critical at this juncture. *The next moves here are mine. Stakes on the table are pretty high: A wrong move means capture and exposure, if not death.*

A small smile curled tightly in the corners of her mouth. *Game on, Louis.*

The only two guard slaves that concerned her this particular evening were malingering in back of the house, smoking their tobacco cigars and talking in bored, resigned tones. She could hear them clearly as she made her approach to the window she'd selected, though she would be out of their direct line of sight. *Louis would have had them beaten, if he'd known. After he'd taken their balls as trophies, of course.*

Working swiftly, Angel disabled two traps (one lethal and highly illegal), then eased the catch with a thin blade. It *snicked* open almost silently; after a pause to ensure the guard slaves hadn't gotten lucky, she exhaled softly, then pushed open the window. The room was empty and dark. No alarms, no signs of alert. She rolled in over the sill like smoke, then knelt for a moment to breathe, and steady her hammering heart. Her first objective was complete.

Reset the traps. You won't be going out that way. She did so, then drew the heavy drapes to conceal her movements and the flashes of the light tube she'd brought along. Set in a metal cylinder, the enchanted crystal focused a very narrow beam of light, directionally rather than radially. "Thieves' flashes," they were commonly called. Louis had given her the first one, years ago.

Eerie, how different the room looks like this. Angel pushed away the ugly memories of what had happened to her the last time she was here. A forlorn voice inside her let out a long, despairing wail. *No time for that. Ignore it. You have to find that concealed door.*

It wasn't behind the wardrobe. Nor his vanity. Nor was it in his dressing room, behind the racks and racks of stylish suits and coats. That left a floor entrance as the only remaining option. Of course, it was going to be difficult to find. Pounding on the floor, although the most expeditious way to test, would have alerted most of the house. Angel steeled herself for a painstaking, fingertip search of the floorboards, ears tuned to any motion in the hall outside the door.

She experienced an odd moment of vacillation, followed by paralyzing indecision, as she glanced around, and tried to consider where to begin. And then, impatient with herself, she forced herself to go quiet, and to think. It was harder, but it took up much less energy. *The most logical place to start would be... the bed.* She directed her flash there in response. *A quick retreat, in case trouble arrived unannounced.*

She found her clue on her second pass, an irregular crack, slightly out of pattern. It was unlikely to be trapped, for Louis planned these things to be accessed in a hurry. The irregularity turned out to be a handle that lifted out easily. The trap door must have been counterbalanced, as it arose soundlessly and effortlessly with the gentlest tug.

Steps. A concrete floor, perhaps two and a half meters below.

Second objective complete. Hands shaking in triumph, Angel descended the stairs and pulled the door down behind her. A small latch on the interior allowed her to lower the top-side handle back to near-invisibility on the other side. She took the narrow, steep steps carefully, then trained the flash along each of the walls. Cabinet after cabinet of file drawers lined two of them, floor to ceiling.

Just like Püran-Khir, right down to the arrangement of the cabinets. Oh, Louis, you obsessive little weasel. You never change, and I'm going to make you pay through the nose for it. It had been one of Louis' oddities for as long as she'd known him: He had a compulsive need to document everything he did. Angel had once asked him why, for it seemed dangerous, to her, to leave so much evidence in writing, and all collected in one place, to boot. He'd just smiled that oily smile of his, patted her on the head, and said, "*...sometimes the best audience is paper and ink, Angel-baby. Don't you worry your little head about it.*"

She'd shrugged, and life had gone on. Years later, here she was again, looking around in amazement at the size of Louis' accumulated "audience."

Gods. Can they all be full already? We haven't been here that long!

In truth, Louis had lived in Fernwall for many years before he'd ended up in Püran-Khir. He'd never said what caused him to leave Fernwall, but Angel wasn't stupid. *He could have had these records in storage for all the years he was in Püran-Khir. Information is one of the few shelf-items that doesn't need to spoil,* she reminded herself.

Oh, what an utter wealth of it he's collected, here, she mused, moving closer to look at the legends on the doors. She did not touch them, however. Attached to each drawer was a lock, and she wouldn't have put it past him to have them all intricately trapped.

Or would he? His protections in Püran-Khir weren't so elaborate. Has anything occurred to cause him to change his patterns? She paused, and exhaled nasally. *No way to know. I just need to assume that they're all trapped, for now. Let's pick a likely candidate and look at it.*

There were no traps that she could detect. *None at all? Is that suspicious, or am I becoming paranoid?* Angel snorted, and shook her head. *Whatever it is, it can't be lethal or disabling, they're too difficult to set up without traces. I'm sure I'd find them. And, after tomorrow, it won't matter whether he discovers something's been stolen. By then, he'll know.*

She pulled a slender straight pick and a hooked one from the case on her belt. *In combination, on the lock, twist just so...* A soft, agreeable *snick* told her the tumbler had fallen, but oddly, the drawer did not open. Angel frowned, caught her breath, and turned the combination again. There was another, more muted click, and the entire drawer gently sprung free, rolling itself out obligingly for inspection.

Angel let out her breath slowly, and made her muscles relax. A double lock, perhaps? It would have been enough to foil a less experienced thief certainly, but no extra trouble for the man who knew the set-up, and who had the right key. Again, it was largely irrelevant, so long as she got out of this alive and with her information intact.

She began riffling through the files quickly. *Damn, Louis, you are tpo predictable. The information is stored by date...* It took her less than a quarter hour to find the file, dated just two months after their arrival in Fernwall. Baron van Trapp's case was listed by number, and it was a sheaf of three thick file folders, one marked CONFIDENTIAL.

The first file contained official court documents and testimony. There were purchase invoices for the slaves in question, and physician's reports on the state of health for all the slaves in the Van Trapp household. It all looked very tidy, indeed.

Second file held the court transcripts. Evidentiary listings. Findings from independent agencies contracted to the courts... Ah, yes! Buried under an anonymous heading was the baron's testimony as given before a Valïan Seer, under the influence of a truth serum. *Now, how had Louis managed to counter a Seer's testimony? That's not supposed to be possible!*

Chicanery, of course, consisting of an entire tapestry of misdirection, planted evidence, and bribed witnesses. First, Louis had "brought forth an irregularity" in the administration of the drug. It was enough to call into question the information gained while under its influence. The technician had proven susceptible to bribery, though Louis had been smarter than to bribe him directly. He simply had discovered the man's weakness (character evidence supplied by the prosecuting attorney's staff no less!), and then had exploited it in his client's behalf.

Van Trapp had incriminated himself over and over again, according to the Seer's testimony. Angelique could hardly believe it even as she read it, but Louis had even managed to discredit the testimony of the Seer! More planted evidence, suggesting and proving outright at least once that the man had, in the past, misremembered the facts in the performance of his duties.

Sick to her stomach, she turned to the end of the court transcript and read the testimony of the physician Louis had most certainly planted on Van Trapp's estates, who claimed those slaves had been on the property because he'd been using them to develop a cure or antidote for that most notorious, extremely illegal, and lethally addictive drug.

Angel clenched her jaw and deliberately closed the folder, knowing she'd found that for which she'd been searching, resisting again the temptation to turn this whole matter over to the police. In the CONFIDENTIAL folder were the *real* accountancy registers, invoices, the truth of the "physician's" origins, and the unofficial, secret testimony Van Trapp had given to his attorney. Angel could do no more than glance over it before she felt her blood begin to boil. *This* was what Louis was holding over Van Trapp now, using the baron and his noble resources to further whatever other slimy skull-duggery he was concocting, no doubt.

Angel placed the folders on the sole table in the chamber, then withdrew from her pack a similar bulk of papers. *Almost not enough.* She chuckled softly, and placed them carefully in the drawer. *Who would have guessed one court case would generate so much paperwork?* She slid the door closed, heard the lock set... and only then did she realize the subtlety of Louis' secret file room. The lock clicked once, followed by the almost imperceptible sound of gears turning back and forth. And then the lock clicked again, apparently satisfied. Set to lock by weight, perhaps? What would have happened if the weights didn't match?

Again, she chuckled quietly. Right then, it simply didn't matter. The door to the secret exit was exactly where it's counterpart in Püran-Khir had been, and also untrapped. The tunnel just beyond was narrow and damp—they were near the north branch of the Caspian, after all—but led more or less directly to a delivery alley behind a bookstore three blocks away.

Predictable, predictable Louis! Angel didn't laugh aloud, but it was difficult; their bolt-hole in Püran-Khir had also let out behind a bookseller's shop. She eased out into the darkness above, rearranged the crates which concealed the low door, then slipped out into more public, better-lit streets, humming happily under her breath.

Twenty-two forty-five. Angel grinned widely and hailed a taxi, flashing the driver a glimpse of taut fabric over her pert posterior, a sight he'd never have gotten to see were she in the voluminous skirts Lady Blakesly customarily wore. She then had the better part of an hour, while the horse clopped smartly toward her house, to wonder if Raven had sent a message explaining his absence that morning. *Or will he already be there, waiting?*

The thought subdued her as the trap wound westward along the river. This was going to be difficult to explain... but then, it was never going to get any easier, either. If he wasn't there tonight, then she would go see him for herself tomorrow night—*after* she'd dealt with Louis. It was time and beyond time for the truth. If anyone in this city would understand what she'd done, it would be Raven. Angel felt serenely certain of that.

But again... Why did he leave last night without saying goodbye?

* * *

Central Merchants
28 Amerian 580, 2230 hours

"Covente Lampbert & Bertram," a copper plate fastened to the building said.

Raven stood atop a roof in the middle of Merchants, surrounded by the buildings that represented the wealth of the City-State of Fernwall. He was, in fact, less than a block away from the offices of Dale and Merkline Associates. *Where you took Angelique with your heart full of the foolish idea that you were going to be her husband, and the Baron of Carlisle.*

It was his gut that twisted at that thought, not his heart. He nodded to himself, gratified, if not satisfied, that he had his emotions so tightly under control. The building on which he stood happened to be one of the tallest buildings in the district. The roof sloped steeply away from the peak to prevent the build-up of snow, and there was little cover along the peaks to disguise a human silhouette.

Below and around his lofty perch, beat cops and private security goons were everywhere. The financial heart of the city was patrolled as thoroughly as a fort. Walking along the peaks would eventually have gotten him noticed. Fortunately, that wasn't what he had in mind. The answer wasn't elegant or stylish, but ... *hey, who said you always had to go with style?* He'd had to do worse in his time. He attached one of his line pliers to the main chimney spire, then doffed his cloak and the bulk of his equipment. Next, he put on a thin, black jumpsuit, complete with hood and face covering, then climbed the chimney.

Oddly enough, getting in and out of the chimney was the most dangerous part of the whole job. For that one moment, it was going to be easy to be spotted. *It's all or nothing, kid. You've got to know the truth.* The best one could hope for was a quick acrobatic roll over the top and down into the flue, but by the Gods, don't miss!

The truth. Was she worth that much, he wondered? *Don't go there, Vince. It's not healthy, just now.*

Once inside, it took a few seconds to get everything adjusted for an easy descent. Then, his line plier purring, he descended the five stories fairly quickly. The smoke wasn't thick this time of night, but the fumes from all the banked fires on this end of the building made breathing difficult until he got below all the smaller draw flues. He knew there would be no exit until he reached the basement, anyway, so there was no point in wasting time.

With a puff of ash, Raven came to the bottom of the flue. Down here, nearly six meters below the first of the smaller flues, the air was clean and cool. There was a strong draw through the clean-out grill down at his knees. The grill also served as an entrance for the chimney sweeps. All he had to do was bend down slightly (not an easy feat in a chimney that wasn't much bigger around than he was) and, using his pocket knife, flick open the latch, kick the cover open with his feet, and slide out, leaving the line plier in place for egress, later.

There wasn't a living soul in the basement storeroom, nor had he expected one. The place smelled of burnt coal ash, cleaners, and polishing compounds. He peeled out of his soot-covered jump suit, folded it carefully, and placed it back into the chimney flue. A few more minutes were spent cleaning shoes and anything else that might have gotten soot or ash on them, and he was on his way, with nobody the wiser. *You hope. No job's done till you've tidied up, and we're a long way from the tidying up part.*

The basement level was vast. Dim, unpainted and unadorned, but vast. The main stairwell didn't go down this far, of course; the snooty-nosed occupants who paid a lot of money to lease those offices weren't interested in being reminded that there even *was* an unadorned, unpainted basement just meters below their impeccably polished shoes.

Some minutes later, he was on the stairwell side of the service door to the fourth floor, where the offices of Covente Lampbert & Bertram were located. *Guards or no guards? That is the question.* He could detect no glimmer of light from around the door. Either it fit into its casing extremely well, or the hallway beyond was dark. Carefully, he turned the knob and peered beyond. The hallway was black. The only light entering came from windows at either end of the hallway, where the doors let out into proper stairwells for the clients to use. Security personnel, he knew, patrolled those stairs.

And she's worth all this trouble, right? *Right. Got to get to the truth.*

He checked a couple of the doors to determine the direction of the suite, letting the light peek out from between his gloved fingers, then ghosted down the hall.

He found the right suite by the name on the polished brass placard on the equally polished doors. The button on the inside knob sounded incredibly loud as it popped under pressure from his spring. A few seconds later, and the barrel of the deadbolt turned; after some quick work with a blank lever key, he was safely inside.

Clerk's room on the right. The flash in his hand followed his thought. The door wasn't locked. He cracked it open, and looked inside. The number of ledgers lining the walls was staggering. *And I can't even use my light to make this easier. Logic, my boy. All things give way under force of logic.*

Including Angel?

No time. Shut up and focus! He checked the spines of several rows of ledgers near the floor, careful not to let the light spill out from around his glove. *Alpha-numeric by year. Five fifty? Gods! Do they ever throw these things away?* The great, hardbound leather volumes looked older than their thirty years of age.

The order went down and right. It took less than five minutes to find the books he needed. Helping himself to a clerk's table out of the way of the row of windows on the street side, he began searching the recent ledger entries of the Carlisle Barony's privy purse. *Damned good thing I don't need the entries for the barony proper.* Those were still in the hands of the accountants, producing the reports Angel had ordered at his behest.

Don't need to follow that line of thought, either.

The entry he sought was dated back to three months ago. Purchase of a dress with extra fabric. On the same day, a purchase order for another dress, minus fabric, sent to a different dressmaker.

Second postulate confirmed. There were two dresses. She had even been smart enough to have them made by different seamstresses, but from the same bolt of fabric to prevent any possible dye and pattern differences. Smooth. Reluctantly, he found himself admiring her ingenuity. *Under other circumstances we could have made one hell of a team.*

But now, for Louis Arnot, Esquire.

Finding the ledgers was easy. It took nearly an hour to find and piece together the information he was after. By the time he'd formed a mental picture of what had transpired, he was feeling sick again. Two first class tickets had been purchased for passage from Püran-Khir to Fernwall. One cabin, large bed. Meals, baths, drinks, everything had been purchased for two. Laundry expenditures included "fine washing; lingerie & feminine apparel" along with the meticulous requirements needed for virgin wool suits. And here: an entry for Angelique's dressmaker, shortly after arrival. "Clothing purchase; evening gown." No size, of course.

But the dates listed matched those Angel had told him she left Püran-Khir and arrived in Fernwall; and there were only two passengers. She either booked passage on her own, or she was playing the part of his mistress.

He felt sick again. *And just why would Angel travel separately from her lawyer, stupid?* He couldn't answer that one. *Right. That's what I thought.* Glumly, he closed the ledgers and returned them to their shelves.

*   *   *

Records Office, International Heralds' Guildhall, Angel Heights
29 Amerian 580, 1400 hours

The venerable old building had been standing just below what had once been the Royal Palace for nearly as long as the palace itself. The granite was that same, weathered gray, and on the battlements were the same pennants and banners that flew from the government buildings just up the hill. The lawns and flowerbeds were manicured with the same exacting care, functionaries moved about with the same sense of quiet purpose. Some termed it "self-importance." In its way, it stood for all the congenital arrogance and intransigence of his social class, and looked about as open to change.

Once known simply as "the Heralds' college," it had expanded beyond its original capacity with the civilized world's call for a united front against Confederation barbarism during The Great War. The heralds from all nations banded together to form the International Guild of Heralds. In addition to their functions as genealogists, they found themselves becoming the first truly impartial diplomatic corps on the planet of Menelon. The Heralds were now a path to gentility for the common-born, if not outright nobility, for the Heralds were nearly always recruiting for likely additions to their ranks from most classes and social strata.

What was left of the "college" was situated to the rear of the grounds and consisted solely of trainees and their instructors. The education provided by the Heralds was one of the most thorough in the modern world in matters of geography, diplomacy, government, etiquette, and political science, not to mention requiring the memorization of hundreds upon hundreds of heraldic devices as well as the rather exacting art of heraldic blazonry.

Raven's business that day was with the genealogists themselves, and with that portion of the Heralds' Guild that kept the familial records for the nobility. Was the woman with whom he'd fallen in love *really* Angelique Blakesly, Baroness of Carlisle? His quest for the truth of her had become something akin to obsession, and it drove him onward, hoping the records kept here might provide the answers he sought.

He paid his taxi fare, and climbed the steps up to the entrance, noting the almost cathedral-like aura of the place. Within, the inner rotunda contained a fair amount of persons, all sporting heraldic devices of some kind. The Heralds themselves wore distinctive, uniform tunics and were easy to spot. Staff members of noble households wore the badges of the house with which they affiliated, and the few nobles present had donned their own family pins or sigils, including Raven himself.

Placed equidistantly between the two curving staircases on either side was a circular area offset by marble rails, and three Heralds' trainees (so designated by their blue tunics) had the duty to greet and direct newcomers. One, a plump blond girl with a pleasant smile, caught his eye.

"Good morning, Sir Vincent," she greeted him, sharp eyes having spotted the Valemont pin, complete with its mark of cadency, on his lapel. "May I help you?"

"I need to see the records for the Carlisle Barony," he replied, putting on his best winning smile.

"Carlisle?" she asked, smiling back. "Strange request from Valemont, isn't it?" Despite her question, which he was sure was only meant to be friendly, she *was* letting herself out of the little Heralds' corral, as it was informally known, to accompany him to the vaults.

"Perhaps not so strange as it may first appear. I've been assisting the Baroness on several administrative matters these last few weeks." *And you have no idea how hard it is for me to say that in a perfectly neutral tone, young miss.*

"That's kind of you." She directed him through the heavy oaken doors, the locks on which would have defeated the skills of most thieves in the city. Within was a large, low-ceilinged room with several long tables. Heralds' trainees of lower rank sat at the tables, carefully inscribing records. Other trainees pushed around carts full of scrolls, boxes, papers, folders, and even bound books, moving tremendous amounts of information from site to site.

"As you probably know, the archives are arranged in order of alphabetical sub-infeudation," the young woman explained. "That means we'll have to go to the Duchy of Enselford's hall, and then work our way back."

What the young lady did not say was that, because lands in the City-State were held at the pleasure of the liege, the Office of Records also doubled as land office and title bureau. Questions of land grants could not be resolved without consulting the heraldic records anyway, so the doubling of duties was a natural evolution and, for once, reduced the number of bureaucracies solicitors had to deal with, rather than increasing them.

Vincent, who'd been here many times before, knew more or less what he was looking for and where it would be. Carlisle's direct liege was the Earl of Camrose who, in turn, held from the Duke of Enselford. That the Earl was the acting bailiff of the Duchy made no difference to the Heralds.

He located the books pertaining to Carlisle even before the apprentice. "Here they are." He stooped down and pulled out the two most recent books.

"Good eye, my lord," she smiled again, lingering at his side. "Was there something specific I might help you find?"

She was being a bit obvious, but then, at her age he'd been *more* than obvious about it, when nearly alone with an attractive girl. "I'll need some time, darling. Is there a place where I can study these in relative privacy?"

His words deflated her a bit. "I suppose so," she sighed, tossing her pale, buttery hair over her shoulder. She led him back to the door, then preceded him into a room they'd passed on their way, just inside "Enselford's Hall." There, chairs and long tables were set out for use, though none were currently occupied.

The girl's smile had turned into something of a rueful grin when they entered. "Is this privacy relative enough for you?"

"Depends on what you had in mind," he grinned, rather enjoying the flirtation, in spite of himself. "Oh, you mean for me? Yes, I think it will do. And where will I find you when I'm finished? I'm sure I'll need help putting these back." In point of fact, only the Heralds—or Heralds' trainees, to be more precise—were allowed to re-shelve volumes. She knew that even better than he did.

"I'm supposed to return to the reception area," she told him, eyes twinkling. "But I can arrange to be in the scribe's hall, if you need me to be."

"Well, I think it would be in the best interests of Carlisle, don't you?"

She glanced at the volumes in his arms. "And the Heralds, certainly, my lord." With a quiet little wink, the girl turned on her heel and withdrew, leaving him alone with his task.

Vincent found that the records for Carlisle went back at least five hundred years, not that he was the least interested in its ancient history. He'd grabbed the older book simply to add complexity to what the girl saw. What he wanted would be newly bound into the most recent volume.

As expected, Angelique had been discovered by a journeyman herald on post-war field duty. The smoke had barely cleared from the battlefields before the Guild had begun sending young heralds into the field to find lost heirs to the noble families whose entire lines seemed to have been killed. All over the modern world, governments had been forced to pull back their borders to those which were more easily defended by the populace that remained, after war and disease had had their way, letting the land return to the wild. Inside the shrinking boundaries of civilization, the numbers of estates under the management of bailiffs was painfully large.

Until Angelique surfaced, Carlisle had been one such barony. According to the records, the last lord of the barony had been an infantry officer killed in action shortly after a term of leave. His young wife and baby son had joined him in the kingdom of Vin-Llamáz, the far southern neighbor to Vin-Nôrë, then he had returned to his company, stationed in the north. He was killed days later in an assault on a fortified position. His wife and child disappeared afterward, and were never found.

That had been seventy years ago. There was a generational gap between that Lord Blakesly and the man who might have been Angelique's father.

No birth record existed for Angel. Considering the chaos, that wasn't surprising; but there was one for her late husband, and one for her father, and another for her mother. There were also death certificates from the coroner's office in Püran-Khir for all of them. They were recent additions to the volume, and had been certified and imprinted by the Guildhall in Vin-Nôrë.

And if you believe that...   He took out his penknife, a carefully folded piece of waxed paper, and a small vial of clear liquid, numbered "1." Starting with the death certificate of her late husband (dated some three years previous), he scraped around the margins of the page with the edge of his knife, brushing the fibers onto the waxed paper, being careful not to miss, thereby damaging the inked part of the page.

When he had enough, he took the lid off the vial, folded the waxed paper, poured the fibers into the liquid, recapped and shook, labeled it, then returned it to his pocket. Taking out another vial, he repeated the process with her husband's birth record, then again with the records for mother and father, and once more for her certificate of marriage. When he was finished, he had seven numbered vials, and the parchment looked no worse for the experience. Satisfied, he closed the book and took out the first vial.

No change. The second vial. Dark. The third vial. No change. One by one, he looked at them all. Only one out of the seven had darkened. *Ridiculous!* Her father's birth certificate was supposed to be over forty years old. The paper fibers should have turned a dark brown, very nearly black, in the solution. For there to be no change meant the paper the birth record was written on was less than five years old. Specifying how much less would require a more sophisticated test than Vinent had at hand. In any event, it certainly hadn't been imprinted by the International Guild of Heralds in five thirty-eight like it said!

The conclusion was inescapable. Not only was Angelique's claim to Carlisle a fraud, so was her entire ancestry. Even her marriage was suspect. Her supposed husband's birth record appeared to be genuine, but about the certificate of marriage he was uncertain. Dated only five years ago, it was at the edge of his rather crude test's abilities. Still, there should have been *some* change in the color of the fibers, and there hadn't been. Possibilities:

Nuptial papers could have been forged, marrying her to a deceased Vin-Nôrëan knight.

The marriage could have been real, and the death real.

Or the ceremony could have been performed, the date could have been bleached out and modified, and her husband, having served his purpose, might then have been "eliminated."

Mix and match as necessary.

He collected his row of little bottles, tucked them back into his pocket, and stood up. This had taken some doing: connections in two countries, pre-planted information and informants, and the ability to forge documents at a very high level. Had the paper been aged properly, it would have been the perfect forgery.

Data points: Louis Arnot was into organized crime up to his plucked blond eyebrows, and he most *certainly* wasn't above eliminating people when they became inconvenient.

Next question: Was Angel that capable?

Data points: She took out six trained guards to commit that crime, then climbed two stories up a thin silk rope to make her escape. On the other hand, she didn't kill, or even seriously injure, any of them.

Raven found his teenaged suitor in the scribes' hall, just as she said she'd be. "Ah, I see you're waiting for me with fluttering heart and blushing cheek," he bowed floridly. "I'm through with the books."

"Well, then," she turned, stepping over to him pertly. "Why don't we see about getting them back to their proper places?"

"Certainly." He held out an arm indicating she should lead, and pausing only to retrieve the volumes he'd removed, she took them both back into the stacks of archives. Another flip of that buttery hair, and they were back in their proper slots.

"There," she said, smiling a little breathily.

His eyes smoldering, he put a hand on each of her cheeks, and slowly drew them back. By the time they got within her range of vision, they held a lovely, pale pink rose. "There you are. Something to remember me by." It wasn't exactly the right color for a young virgin, but it was the best he could come up with on the spot.

Then again, perhaps she wasn't a virgin. Her eyes flickered from the blossom to his face, almost as if she were accessing her school lessons for the proper response. "Thank you, my lord," she finally returned, wetting her lips. "You're quite as charming as it's said you are. But not nearly so bold, it would seem."

"You're on duty, young lady, and so am I. Were that not the case, we just might see what parts of your loveliness matched the color of this rose—at length."

"Spoilsport," the luscious blonde returned sweetly. Regardless, she stretched up on tiptoe to kiss his cheek, missed, but caught his quickly presented lips. Quick-witted, she pressed into them rather than starting back. When she withdrew, a devilish sparkle lingered in her eyes.

"Stop back by when you're off-duty sometime, my lord Sultaire," she whispered. "We can take care of any color comparisons you might wish to do then."

"Deal," he whispered back, eyes twinkling mischievously. Education of the young *was* a noble's duty, after all...

Lady Angelique Blakesly pulled up the hood of her light cloak and left the offices of Warren Andrews, Esquire, stepping quickly into the waiting taxi.

Hiring it, and the string of similar conveyances she'd used that day, had been a necessary security precaution. Money wasn't really an obstacle for her any longer, and Louis had inferred that he was having her watched. In an attempt to capture those eyes, she'd sent her brand new carriage back to the wainwrights' with spurious complaint about the interior, with orders to the driver to take the most circuitous route around Docktown that he could find. Most of her afternoon had been spent in shops and offices today, under the most innocent of auspices of course, and always leaving by a different exit. New taxis, new drivers, circuitous routes—a giddy young noblewoman, enjoying an afternoon out on the town.

She'd paid the last taxi to head directly to the Lansdowne's townhouse, as if she were going to attend the meeting of the Ladies' Auxiliary. In fact, she had ducked out the back door, hailed another cab, and kept her appointment with Goodman Andrews.

"Prevention costs less than repair, as you know." Even the memory of Louis' unctuous tone irritated her, but it was yet another lesson she'd taken pains to learn.

As he was about to discover for himself.

Chapter 11

2313 Compton Place, Upper Merchants
1 Ilian 580, 2200 hours

Louis Arnot was hurled into the wall next to his own bed. He heard the door-bolt slam home before his body bounced off it, and the sound of muffled sobs from somewhere nearby. The room was dark; the drapes pulled. His eyes were still dazzled from the lighted hall just outside and from a blow to his head. Something moved in the darkness, some darker shape against the black. He struck out at it with a half-strangled, terrified scream.

A booted foot planted itself forcefully in his crotch. The gorge rose in his throat. The chop to the back of the neck sent him sprawling across the floor.

He tried to rise, but a foot planted itself in his belly, forcing him back to the floor. The air in his lungs vanished, and he flopped like a caught fish.

Light, flaring in the darkness, blinded him again. Louis coughed, and struggled to heave something into his lungs that felt less dense than wood. He tried to scramble to his feet, and made it up to one knee, and pulled the knife he'd hidden in his boot. His attacker rasped out some sound between amusement and malevolence, and flicked one wrist.

The knife thudded to the floor from his benumbed hand. As one, their eyes moved back to the blood that poured down Louis' right arm, and then to the blade that had embedded itself into the floor just beyond him. His knee buckled, and he collapsed again to the floor, left hand clutching at the fresh wound. "Wh—who are you?" His voice was shrill. "What do you want?"

The same wrist that had flickered so lethally reached up to remove a tight fitting, full-face hood in dark-colored silk. Angelique shook her hair clear of it, smiling without humor at his stunned reaction.

Louis, she knew, only respected power. She knew that force, and its intelligent application, from a source he had not suspected, would command his respect, where pleas for mercy and compassion had not, and never would. She kicked the knife he'd dropped, and it skittered to a stop near the two bound and gagged bed-slaves. Arms crossed, the black-garbed woman looked down at him from where she leaned against one of the polished bedposts, in a deceptively lazy stance.

"Tell me I have your full and undivided attention, Louis."

"Wha...?" he croaked, never so toad-like as when he was in distress. "Angela? What is the meaning of this?"

She clicked her tongue in mock dismay. "Predictable, Louis. I should think the meaning is perfectly clear." All signs of humor abruptly left her expression. "I am taking my life back."

Incomprehension crossed his face. "Your li—? What are you talking about? Have you gone mad?"

"I sometimes do wonder," she agreed, watching him much more closely than she'd ever let him know. "Perhaps for clarity, I might rephrase: You and I are through, Louis."

He looked stunned, for just a moment. Angel thought it might have been the only honest expression she'd ever seen there, and it was gone too quickly. "What more could you want than what I've given you? A barony, and all the wealth and comfort that goes with it! Is this how you reward your benefactors?"

"Oh, if you can't do any better than that, shut up," she snapped. "Guilt won't work. You've been using me, my talents, my gifts, my abilities, to your own ends here in this city, and now we both know it. To our mutual benefit? Certainly—but you had your own reasons for saddling me with a fucking barony. Try hard not to pretend otherwise."

"Do you have any idea what you're talking about, Angela?" he snapped, struggling upright just enough to sit upon the bed. "Do you have any idea what kind of resources it takes to make life so simple for you? Ensconcing you as Baroness of Carlisle cost me thousands of pounds. *Thousands!* Your theft of the *Mâgun-Zak* involved dozens of persons you don't know, and have never met."

He paused to catch his breath, laboring to force air into lungs that didn't want to expand. "Just how easy do you think it is, to hide all that money you've made, right in front of the entire banking industry? I suggest you *think*, Miss Angela Rose Corwin, before you do something you'll later live to regret."

Her laughter pealed right across the end of his words. "Too late! I've already got a stack of them! But, heed me well, Louis: Another lie like any in the string you just told might cost you your tongue." Her tone remained light, but the threat was not. "You have evidently forgotten how close the quarters were, there in Püran-Khir. I was a *very* apt pupil. I *know* how you do business. Any money you expended to set *us* up here—you *and* me—you've made back from the profits of the *Mâgun-Zak* alone. Monies, I might add, you got primarily from selling *my* body, or risking *my* neck."

"Well, of course I have," he snorted indignantly. "Why *else* would I have spent such a vast sum of money on you? If you must know, the *Mâgun-Zak* sold for nearly a million. Of which I saw less than half, and netted between a quarter and a third. Usual, for such an operation. If you're as apt a pupil as you think you are, those numbers should tell you quite a bit about just how little you really do know."

He sat on the edge of the bed and crossed his arms, a clear bid to take control of the encounter. The bleeding from the cut had nearly stopped; still, he kept pressure on the wound. "But, you're *obviously* not going to believe anything I might say, and I'm *certain* you didn't break into my home and assault my person simply for the pleasure of a lesson in the economics of high level crime."

Angelique's derisive snort interrupted his efforts, but he only stumbled for a moment. "So, why don't you tell me what you *really* want so I can repair this mess and get on with my evening?"

She found herself begrudgingly admiring how fast the man could attempt to regain control of a situation. Little Angela would have collapsed in tears, in the face of his anger and harsh words. If this new Angel's strength concerned him, he was doing a good job of hiding it, though not the effort it cost him.

"Now that you've stopped all that petty carping about money, it would be a pleasure," she replied, keeping ample space between them. "You think this is just a temper tantrum, don't you. You think that if you just play me long enough, and well enough, you'll weather this storm, too. You go quiet, and you watch, and you wait. And, if I didn't come crawling back in what you consider to be a suitable amount of time, you'd send your hired assassins after me to have me quietly killed. You're such a gray little weasel, Louis.

"Tell me," she urged him playfully, mockingly, delivering a brutal verbal blow gloved in velvet, "on which end of that scale does your relationship with Baron van Trapp fall? Black? Or white?"

There was a tell-tale hesitation, an ephemerally brief moment in which Angel could almost *see* Louis Arnot in the act of mentally backtracking.

"Just *what* does Baron van Trapp have to do with this?" he demanded.

"Oh, I'm sure he's nothing, in and of himself," Angel told him in her *most* reassuring "Paladin noblewoman's" voice. "But the court case? Tampered evidence, false testimony, phony physician. . . " She ticked off each item on gloved fingers, musingly. "That's a very different matter, of course."

"I see." To his credit, Louis didn't so much as flinch. "What do you want?"

"As I told you," she explained, all humor draining from her, "I want my life back. Control of it, to put it a bit more precisely. I discovered the last time I was here—ah, the last time you *guested* me here," Angel amended, the memories of that night coating her words in bitter gall, "that I did not care for your threats, neither the veiled ones, nor those more direct." Anger and hostility sizzled in her voice, lending it a quiet kind of menace that neatly silenced the two blindfolded slaves, and even held Louis momentarily silent.

"Specifically, we're going to arrange things so that all of Carlisle is transferred out of your care, and into mine or agents of my choice. You're going to tell your hirelings to cease monitoring my affairs and movements. I have already begun the processes which will separate the barony's accounts from yours, but this won't be complete until the last of the money from the *Mâgun-Zak* has been deposited in them.

"You wanted me to 'assume my role,' and 'take control of my barony,'" she laughed, knowing she'd scored by the souring of his already petulant expression. "And so? You're getting what you wished! In return, *I* get a life I no longer have to lie about. Is there anything else unclear for you, here?"

"For that, you break into my house, assault my staff, attack me, and lay waste to my bedroom?" he asked, striving for an incredulity in manner that he couldn't quite muster.

"Consider it my way of getting your attention," she told him coolly. "I won't even charge you for the privilege, though if I find I have to do this again, you can expect a fat bill for my services."

"So you don't intend to leave your life of crime behind completely— *Baroness?*"

"Oh, *nice*," Angel complimented him. "I see no reason to give up activities that I enjoy simply because I finally got smart enough to rid myself of the part I don't enjoy: You." Her gaze never wavered. "The Iris may not pull many crimes, but those she does will be memorable. Just keep your people out of my way and off my tail, Louis. My rates for educating the idiots you traditionally employ are only going to go straight up, from here."

"Of course," he drawled, striving for a casual, almost-bored tone, "but, I'm sure you're not through making threats. So indulge yourself, Angela. Tell me what happens if I don't cooperate with these… terms."

"I might do that," she agreed, "but you're just trying to make me reveal more of myself than I intended." Her eyebrows flickered. "I was a *very* apt pupil, and you were an exquisitely thorough teacher. Let's see if I can drop you a bigger hint."

Angel rolled her eyes up toward the ceiling, as though in thought. "I'm sure you remember Althas Duronin?"

She'd scored again. She could tell from the way his gaze tried to slide away from hers. Duronin had been a powerfully positioned crime lord in post-war Püran-Khir, a cold, heartless savage with a rumored history as a Confederation collaborator. He'd had eyes and ears in critical places, and muscle everywhere. Duronin demanded, and got, quite a cut of every theft or transaction done in that particular "emergency management district" of the city. Within six months of their ascent in that lawless underworld, Louis had sent her out after information that implicated Duronin in the sell-out of six of his closest lieutenants to the military police. They had later been tried, and hanged, for racketeering and trading in black market slaves.

That was the first time Angel had ever heard the term "dead man's trigger" used. The threat of the release of that information kept Duronin off their backs until the thug died under "mysterious circumstances." She was privately convinced that Louis had had him murdered, once he'd outlived any possible usefulness.

"Predictable," Louis mused. He'd begun playing his cards very close to his chest. Louis had always gotten quiet and circumspect when negotiating, especially when he knew himself to be in the weaker position.

"Then why didn't you anticipate it?" his former apprentice asked sweetly, then waved away her own question by withdrawing her throwing blade from the wall. "The details, of course, are known to no one but me, so now you have plenty of incentive to look after my continued health. Not that you didn't keep me in your prayers anyway," she conceded disingenuously, "but this does provide a bit of extra motivation, doesn't it."

A long, uncomfortable silence followed those words. Louis refused to meet her eyes, but she knew he was scrambling, inside. She'd just dealt him one blow he apparently had never anticipated. Guilt and remorse flashed through her then, for it had, after all, been Louis who'd taken her in, in Püran-Khir.

That only lasted until he opened his mouth. "Well," he sighed at last, "I suppose you deserve what this is going to cost you. Now, if you're through, you'll find the front door a much more convenient exit than crawling through windows."

"Convenient for you, perhaps," Angel snorted, her moment of nostalgia passing in an instant. "I'm not so sure about that, personally. Oh, and you'll find your guard slaves trussed up much like these two, and in your tool shed," she added off-handedly, flicking open the drapes. "Have you ever noticed that big men are horribly *slow* to react in a fight?"

Angel knew, as she slipped into the darkness outside, that she was going to treasure that last look on Louis' face for a long, long time. Shaking with triumph, disbelief, and an almost unbearable need to crow, she sped off on foot, toward Raven's flat, deep in the heart of Merchants'.

It's done. I'm free. It's done. I'm free! Free of Louis, and now almost free of the lies... Her thoughts pounded out the same rhythm as her feet, smiling and laughing at the passers-by she dodged, seeming little more than an exuberant youngster out on a night-time lark. Joy propelled her even when her legs and lungs wanted to give out, and she'd run halfway to her destination before her breath shortened, prompting her to hail a cab that was just disgorging its occupants in front of a residence. Angel rushed in behind them, thanked them laughingly, shouted the address to the driver, and sat back to catch her breath.

It wouldn't hold forever. She knew that with the same kind of distant inevitability, she'd die one day. Louis would discover how to outwit the trap, and the game of wits might begin all over again. Or she might find a way to neutralize him permanently. Or he might just do her an exquisite favor by dying in his sleep!

Angel laughed again. *Or he might just decide to kill me. But by the Gods! It will all be worth it, all of it. If it's even a year, it will be a year free of lying, to Raven at least.*

The last thought sobered her, and turned her mind toward what she was going to say to her betrothed. She'd not seen him since the night of the dinner party. No letter, no card, no flowers, nothing but unexplained silence. The niggling memory that had been evading her for days revealed itself to her then, as the cab was taking the last turn to the apartment house in which he stayed.

He hadn't told her he loved her at all that night.

"Secrets," he'd said, in that quiet, distant voice. She'd come so close to spilling everything then, and perhaps she should have. Perhaps the damage could still have been contained.

Oh, well. That's done, and this is now. The trap creaked to a smart stop at the stoop. She tossed the driver his fare with a jaunty little salute, and waited only until he'd pulled away to pick the lock on downstairs door. Her rush up the stairs would have done justice to any of Raven's, and she ended up at his door, laughing breathlessly.

He didn't answer her first knock. Nor the second. Nor the third, in which she pounded so loudly it drew the complaining attention of his neighbor. Angel apologized profusely for disturbing him (an older man, definitely grumpy at being awakened by a young beauty pounding not on his door, but his neighbor's), then rather quietly retraced her path back downstairs.

In all her plans for today and tonight, in all the keyed up excitement of preparation, she hadn't really counted on Raven's *not* being home. It was like a dash of cold water, bringing her back to her senses. Where could he have been? Was it work? Or another woman?

Dammit, Raven. Damn, damn, damn. Did you have to be out screwing around on me, this night of all nights?

She could go look for him. Sure, she could do that. But eventually, all this racing around in the middle of the night was bound to get her noticed, and notice was really one thing Angel still could not afford to draw to herself. As badly as she wanted, *needed* to talk to Raven, chasing around kilometers of city streets to find him was out of the question.

Not that I'd have a chance in any hell of finding him, anyway, she thought glumly. He knew this city much better than she, and wouldn't be found if he didn't wish it.

Another cab, and another, more thoughtful trip back to the drop address near her own townhouse. Was he avoiding her now? It was a question she couldn't dismiss lightly, and she certainly got to dwell on it for the hour or so it took the cab to return her to her neighborhood. By the time she was climbing the trellis that led up to her bedroom window, she'd decided the most she could do was send notes to police headquarters and to his flat, the next day.

She was mentally composing them as she slid through the open casement, into her room.

*   *   *

Blakesly House, Lower Angels
1 Ilian 580, 2330 hours

The clock ticked softly in the darkened room, and the air around was him thick with Angelique's sweet, familiar scent. His stomach tightened again, involuntarily. For all his resolve, tears threatened to fall. There was a surreal feeling to being here in this ever-so-familiar room, waiting to corner

198

Angel rather than make love to her. He was wearing the paraphernalia of the Raven, the thief and con man, a far cry from the young nobleman who, on uncounted nights, had stolen into this room to share hours of sweet pleasure with its owner.

So many things reeked of the caste from which he'd struggled so hard to free himself. A beautifully sculpted depiction of the Lady, surrounded by a golden oval aura, looked down at him from over Angel's vanity. On a jewelry tree hung a tiny heraldic diamond on a golden chain. The arms of Carlisle were dimly visible in the faint glow from the shuttered lamp on her bedside table; and of course, nothing was out of order. Everything had a specific place, and her maidservant made sure they stayed there. Hairbrush, comb, jewelry box just so...

Jewelry box. He picked it up and carried it over to the window, uncertain why he did so. The inside was a jumble of rings, pins, necklaces, and earrings. Carefully, quietly, he dumped the contents out onto the small table and began sorting through it all with a gloved finger. It was quite a collection. Despite the state of her barony, Angelique was obviously wealthy enough to afford diamonds and pearls and rubies and... *What's this?*

No. Glinting in the light as though to attract his attention was a tiny, ornate sword. The top of the pommel had a loop for a chain. It could have belonged to only one person: her late husband; and had she really been married, it would have been buried with him. That was a tradition so old it was very nearly inviolate. That the tiny jewel was here, in the bottom of her jewelry box, could mean only one thing: Her "marriage," like everything else, had been a sham to help sell her story of noble suffering to Paladin society. The teary-eyed members of the Lady's Auxiliary undoubtedly swallowed the lie whole, immediately took Angel into their fold, and clucked over the young widow like mother hens. It was a beautiful ploy.

Yet another lie. Tears fought to hold their place against growing anger as he tucked the sword into his jacket pocket, then scooped the rest of the contents back into the box. *The last question is answered.* He carefully placed the jewelry box in its proper spot and stepped into the blackness of her wardrobe. *Now, all you have to do is wait.* Absently, he drew his sword.

It didn't take long. Angel made her way into her bedroom the same way Vincent had: through the open window. *Out on another job,* he snarled internally; and yet... and yet she was even more beautiful in her dark body suit—glamorous, seductive. Her body moved like ink in water, flowing in over the sill, and then to her feet, as if she had no bones until she needed them.

He hated this. Gods, he hated it! *Why could she not have just been who she said she was! Why?* he railed silently as he watched her lithe, slender frame straighten. She stooped to push the window partly closed, cutting off the chill of the night air, then stalked right past him, a sleek hunting cat who thought herself safe in her den. She went to her vanity and unbuckled the belt at her waist, dropping it into the chair along with the two sheathed knives attached to it, then stepped back and half-turned, as if to face him.

Without warning, he slashed at her with his sword from his hiding place, deliberately connecting with no more than the air that rushed in to fill the place where she'd been. Instincts primed by her activities that night, Angel dodged, twisted, and dove to put the bed between them, rolling up to one knee with yet a third knife glittering in her hand.

Another question answered, he groaned silently.

She flung it at the threat in the darkness with all her strength.

"Dammit!" she shrieked, all traces of Vin-Nôrean accent gone. "Could you not even give me one night's reprieve—!"

The knife clashed against the blade of a sword, a bare glint in the shadows, and he stepped out of the closet. His cloak flowed out behind him, revealing the equipment and weaponry of the Raven, things she'd never seen on his person before.

"Well, well, well," he began in a low growl, grief and rage battling for control. "Perfect local dialect, *Angie.* Or is it Angela? I assume 'Angelique' is as much a fraud as your *marriage!*" He threw both the word and the little sword at her. Reflexively, her hand came up to pluck the latter out of the air before it buried itself in her breast.

"Fake! Like your Vin-Nôrëan heritage," he spat as anger threatened to gain the upper hand, "and your ties to the late Lord Blakesly and his family, but I *doubt* Louis Arnot had the imagination to change his little whore's name completely."

The impassioned words rolled over her like an avalanche, knocking her senseless as surely as she'd done to Louis, earlier. The shock of it, of him, *here,* was a like scene out of every nightmare she'd had for the past two months. It was surreal, and she wanted nothing more than to wake up from it. He seemed to be unaware of the tears which streamed down his cheeks, focusing only on her, and on the hateful, angry words which streamed from of his mouth.

"Raven," she breathed, feeling color and life leech out of the pores of her face.

Too late!

TOO LATE!

Too late!

Too late.

The chorus of voices went on shrieking inside her head, some in terror and grief, others in glee. Angel shook her head, trying to silence them so she could think, *dammit, think!*

"Y–You're here," she stammered, fighting off panic and despair. "Why—?"

For a moment, it looked like he wanted to smash her vanity mirror in a fit of rage. "Why?" he snarled from between clenched teeth.

"Raven. . ." In her panic, the name had no more substance than smoke. "I have to—you must—"

"Must what?" he demanded, the words every bit as pointed as the tip of the sword he leveled at her chest.

"Just let me explain," she pleaded, holding her empty hand up in supplication. "Please, just let me—"

"Explain?" he spat. "You want to tell me another story? I'm done with your stories, you false, faithless bitch! Why don't *you* let *me* tell *you* a little story, *Miss* Angie, about a young woman who moves to Fernwall from Vin-Nôrë with a sob story about being widowed at such a young age; about how that young woman used that story to weasel her way into Fernwall's rather insular high society, even into the core of the Church. And then, how that young woman used those connections to stage one of the biggest jewel heists in history, wreaking havoc on the very society that had sheltered and protected her!"

Inwardly, Vincent cringed. His every inflection and gesture was familiar to him, but they weren't his own. Mute, terrified, Angel took a shocked step back. Abruptly enraged again, he followed her, *pressing* her with the point of his sword, and with words that were even sharper.

"Shall I go on? How about the double," he bored in, unable to stop himself, "complete with a dress made out of the very same material as the one you wore to the party? Except for the clever little closures at the front, of course. How about the wands used to disable the magical protections around the *Mâgun-Zak*?"

Stop it, Vincent! Stop it! This was wrong; it was all wrong. Every word was a nail hammered into her heart. He was not his father; *he was not his father;* but it was as if some sickness drove him. His sword pressed into her chest, and she sobbed, and stumbled back.

"Oh, no," Angel gasped, bumping against her nightstand. Light from the lamp flashed once, burning the sight of him and the sword and the room into her guilty conscience like a brand. "Raven. No. Please, you've got to listen to m—"

"Oh, yes, burning bright," he sneered, ruthlessly, stabbing at her with what had once been an endearment, "I finally ferreted it all out. Lies. All lies. From the very first day we met to the night before last, you've been playing this little charade, even with *me!*" he shouted.

Angel choked, fist clenching around the slender, slippery piece of metal in her hand. He'd found her out, he'd uncovered her lies, and it was the old night-terror, come to life. With a sinking heart, she knew at last that what she'd done to free herself had come much, much too late. His sword stayed leveled at her chest and pushed her back to the wall, a length of iron-hard distrust between them. That thought choked her again; the sword itself seemed to choke her, and she could not stop her own tears.

It's true. It's all true. Hear how he hates you, now? Look at the hurt, there on his face, a face that you claimed was dearer to you than your own breath. You've lost him.

LOST.

It's over.

"It would be a kindness," Angel sobbed at last, knowing that a quick death at his hand was more mercy than she deserved, "if you'd simply kill me now."

"Only if you'll do me the same favor," he grated from between clenched teeth. *Because you hate her, or because you hate yourself?* The sword finally wavered, and he dropped it to the floor, staggered over to her bed, sat down, and buried his head in his hands, heartache and misery radiating from him in waves.

The sight tore at her, and though she knew remorse was inadequate, she had to say something. "I'm sorry," she whispered, forcing the words past the acrid lump in her throat. "Raven. I'm so, so sorry. You're right, about the part you know. What you said. I tried..."

Those words died on her lips as her own acute memory nudged her conscience. She hadn't tried hard enough.

"I wish I'd cut out my own heart before you were hurt like this."

"Do you?" he snapped, looking up suddenly. "Do you really? What a lovely thing to say, Lady Blakesly. Is this sudden confession the same as the ones you use in church? Is this like the professions of piety you parade before Lady Emilia?"

It was too much. A part of him desperately wanted to believe her, to believe something, *anything* about her that would ease the pain; but he didn't know how. "How am I supposed to believe you?" he whispered. "*How?* You've conned the entirety of Guardian Paladin society, all the way to the lords and ladies of Parliament. You conned *me*, Angel!" *That* was what hurt most of all, and the agony it seethed in his aspirated words. "Yet you want me to believe you? Based on what, pray do tell?"

Based on what, indeed, Angel? The chorus erupted again, and voices raged or wept inside her, while others fought the old numbness that threatened, once again, to invade in the face of overwhelming sorrow. Everything she'd ever said to him, or been to him had become...

"Nothing," she whispered. It had all been for nothing, and she had nothing left in her at all, nothing that might convince him to believe her, and yet she could not stop herself from trying. "I love you. You ought to believe that. Remember the oath? Or have I even forfeited that with you?"

"*...by the Paladin Himself,*" she had cried out that night, writhing atop him in a sensual frenzy. She'd reared back to capture his eyes with her own, and said, "*and by the Lady who embodies Him do I love you! In that name I swear it*, Mar'leven... Raven... Vincent! *I swear it!* I love you!"

He snorted, warding off the tenderness of the memory with another, more recent, and much more bitter. "You signed a marriage certificate, and a certificate of patent, both *sworn* to be true. Are they?"

"No." Her sigh was soft, very like despair even in her own ears, and with the admission, she collapsed into her chair, where she'd been that night when he called her forth from living death. This time, he was breaking her heart, and she could not lift a hand to stop him.

"And so, the only true thing in my life, the only thing that made living the lies bearable, is now a lie by association. How... fitting." She nearly strangled on the last word, throat clogged with acrid self-hate and loathing.

Her left hand fell open in her lap. The tiny sword, bright blade now dulled by her brighter blood, protruded upright from the gathering red pool in her palm.

Raven stared at her numbly.

Where, oh, where now is your precious truth now, Raven? You set out to find it, turning your back on your religion and your caste. Have you? Have exposition and confrontation made you any happier? Or, like your father, have you crushed the spirit of another precious life in the name of duty, truth, and honor? Look there. Yes, over there in the chair, at the woman you promised to marry. Is the truth of her actions more valid than the truth of her emotions? Have you expunged from the human race a vile villain, a threat to society? Or reduced to nothing a rare and precious jewel?

Oh, what a nasty web we weave when we presume upon ourselves such holiness that vengeance becomes a right and proper action. That you, meanest of all noble persons, could take it upon yourself to judge another—and for what?—no more than what you yourself have done! And then, to condemn her to your own living death for no more than your unwillingness to see your own reflection in the mirror of her life.

Oh, burning bright, what have you wrought? A flame so bright, it kills or maims us both.

Silenced by his own conscience, unable to face what he'd done, the bird flew the way he had come, through a half-open casement window of a manor house in lower Angels. Unwilling to call out the words to stop him, unable to do anything but weep, the woman who loved him more than he could allow himself to believe watched him go.

Appendix

On the following page, you'll find the common calendar to which we make repeated reference throughout this book. The common calendar is unique in a several of respects: First, readers will immediately note that the calendar is broken up into festivals which occur between three month periods. The second difference that's immediately noticeable is that Winterfest splits the old year and the new; the new year starts on the fifth day of Winterfest; literally, on midnight of the fourth day of the festival, the exact middle. Third, each of the quarterly festivals occur after the first month of the season. So winter officially starts in Vilmath; Tuela is the second month of the winter season. Spring starts in Pælana, summer in Urliana, and so on. Finally, it should be noted that for record keeping purposes the festivals are counted as months, giving the common calendar sixteen months, rather than twelve. A child born on 1/5/580 (to use the month/day/year style of notation) would be born on the fifth day of Winterfest, 580; a child born on 5/2/580 would be born on the second day of Springfest, and so on.

For more information on the calendar we encourage readers to visit our website, *metaphorpublications.com,* where you can find more information on the world of Vincent and Angelique, including a map of the City of Fernwall, the former Kingdom of Cascadia, The Great War, and much, much, more! No registration is required. Simply visit *metaphorpublications.com* and click the link to the wiki.

Enjoy!

Michael and Alesia

The Menelon Calendar

Winterfest

5	6	7	8

Tuela							**Celestiath**							**Pælana**						
1	2	3	4	5	6	7	1	2	3	4	5	6	7	1	2	3	4	5	6	7
8	9	10	11	12	13	14	8	9	10	11	12	13	14	8	9	10	11	12	13	14
15	16	17	18	19	20	21	15	16	17	18	19	20	21	15	16	17	18	19	20	21
22	23	24	25	26	27	28	22	23	24	25	26	27	28	22	23	24	25	26	27	28

Springfest

1	2	3	4	5	6	7

Læmath							**Eldor**							**Uriliana**						
1	2	3	4	5	6	7	1	2	3	4	5	6	7	1	2	3	4	5	6	7
8	9	10	11	12	13	14	8	9	10	11	12	13	14	8	9	10	11	12	13	14
15	16	17	18	19	20	21	15	16	17	18	19	20	21	15	16	17	18	19	20	21
22	23	24	25	26	27	28	22	23	24	25	26	27	28	22	23	24	25	26	27	28

Summerfest

1	2	3	4	5	6	7

Amerian							**Ilian**							**Chadane**						
1	2	3	4	5	6	7	1	2	3	4	5	6	7	1	2	3	4	5	6	7
8	9	10	11	12	13	14	8	9	10	11	12	13	14	8	9	10	11	12	13	14
15	16	17	18	19	20	21	15	16	17	18	19	20	21	15	16	17	18	19	20	21
22	23	24	25	26	27	28	22	23	24	25	26	27	28	22	23	24	25	26	27	28

Harvestfest

1	2	3	4	5	6	7

Clamath							**B'nath**							**Vilmath**						
1	2	3	4	5	6	7	1	2	3	4	5	6	7	1	2	3	4	5	6	7
8	9	10	11	12	13	14	8	9	10	11	12	13	14	8	9	10	11	12	13	14
15	16	17	18	19	20	21	15	16	17	18	19	20	21	15	16	17	18	19	20	21
22	23	24	25	26	27	28	22	23	24	25	26	27	28	22	23	24	25	26	27	28

Winterfest

1	2	3	4